From "White Bed", her first published story, which appeared in a feminist horror anthology in 1993, Kaaron Warren has produced powerful, disturbing fiction.

With four novels and six short story collections in print, and close to two hundred short fiction sales, Warren's award-winning fiction tackles the themes of obsession, murder, grief, despair, revenge, manipulation, death and sex.

Kaaron has won many awards such as the Shirley Jackson, Aurealis, Ditmar, Australian Shadows and ACT Writers and Publishers Awards for her novels and short fiction, including *Slights*, *The Grinding House*, *Through Splintered Walls* and the novella "Sky". She's lived in Melbourne, Sydney and Fiji and now in Canberra with her family.

IFWG Publishing Australia's
Dark Phases
Masterpiece Title Series

Peripheral Visions: The Collected Ghost Stories by Robert Hood (illustrations by Nick Stathopoulos) 2015

The Grief Hole by Kaaron Warren (illustrations by Keely Van Order) 2016

Praise for The Grief Hole

"The Grief Hole is a tour-de-force of personal despair and abject horror. Restrained yet horrific, and brushing up against the kind of themes polite society rarely wants to discuss. But at its heart there is a small, bright spark of hope."
> — **Gary McMahon**, author of the Thomas Usher novels and the Concrete Grove novels

"The Grief Hole, like all Kaaron Warren's horror fiction, has a particular nightmare flavour. On one level it's a pure, anguished howl against the exploitation and abuse of the powerless. On another it's like The Slap with added bamboo under the fingernails. Ghosts weep and grotesques loom against a cruelly barren, detritus-littered suburban background. You wouldn't trust half these characters as far as you could throw them, and the other half you wouldn't want to be. But beneath their machinations runs a continuous trickle of laughter so faint it might be pity, it might be inky tears. You can't help but follow them, full of dread, into the darkness."
> — **Margo Lanagan**, Word Fantasy Award winner

"It takes a writer of Kaaron Warren's talent and imagination to unflinchingly convey the horrors of the real world. The Grief Hole is one of the most effective and affecting ghost stories I've ever read."
> — **Jeffrey Ford**, multiple international award-winning fantasy author

"The Grief Hole is a gripping journey to a very dark place indeed. Psychologically devastating, resonant with references to art and mythology, tightly plotted and with a climax that will haunt you for a long, long time, this is Warren at her finest. Few people have thought so subtly about the true nature of despair and the precise contours of evil. An unforgettable read."
> — **Melinda Smith**, Prime Minister's Prize for Poetry Award Winner

"Kaaron Warren's The Grief Hole is a powerhouse of a novel; creepy, disturbing, and genuinely moving. Theresa's interventions and, of course, the devastating aftermaths will haunt you long after you finish this book."

— **Paul Tremblay**, author of A Head Full of Ghosts and Disappearance at Devil's Rock

"Kaaron Warren's writing is always simple, elegant and deadly. It's like quicksand - a few steps in and you are waist-deep and never, ever getting out. She writes with the logic of a madwoman - which is to say that her words are irrefutable and have the terrifying ring of truth. The Grief Hole may be my favorite of all her books - sentence for sentence, as always, she makes me feel like a fraud for calling myself a writer. The Grief Hole put me immediately into a world I wish I'd never seen and never wanted to leave."

— **Leslie Bohem**, Emmy Award winner

THE GRIEF HOLE

HOLE

by

Kaaron Warren

The Grief Hole
All Rights Reserved
ISBN-13: 978-1-925496-49-9
Copyright © 2016 Kaaron Warren
Internal and cover illustrations and layout by Keely Van Order
V1.0 US

IFWG Publishing International
Melbourne, Australia
www.ifwgpublishing.com

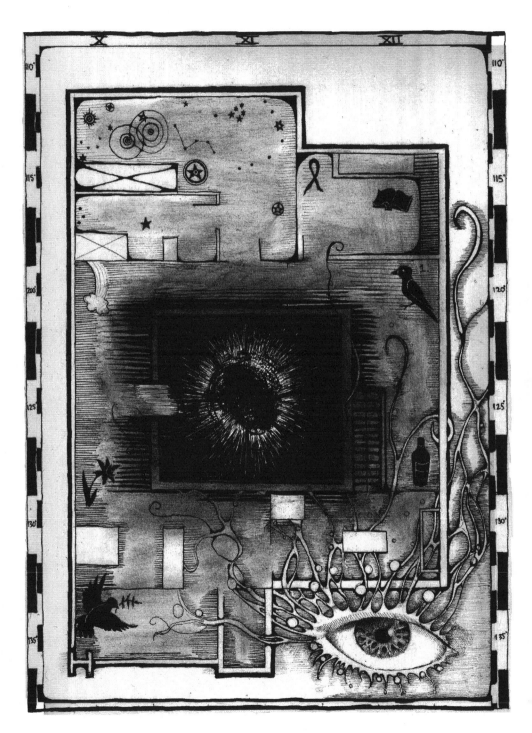

For my sister and her godson.

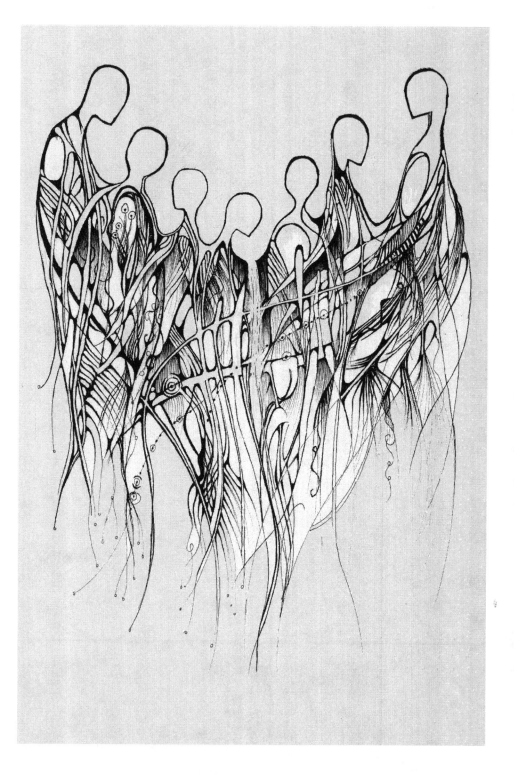

For every intervention there was aftermath. A blank space in her memory, a slowing of movement. Theresa knew this, but some monsters had to be dealt with.

Many times she didn't intervene, if the ghosts were quiet or their message unclear. She never acted unless she was sure.

It was the rise of the ghosts that pushed her.

When the ghosts flew so thick she could barely breathe, she had to act.

The First Intervention

Client A sat in the kitchen of the rented apartment Theresa had found for her. Her oldest child cooked the dinner; it smelt so good Theresa hoped they'd invite her to stay, although she'd say no, to maintain the boundaries. One child was at the table doing homework; the other two, watching cartoons.

"My husband used to manage all the finances. The rent, all that," the woman told her. "I looked after the people, he looked after the things. We always did it that way."

Theresa said, "I lost my man, too. That's an emptiness that can't be filled. We can only try."

"We were saving for a home," the woman said. Most of that went to medical and funeral expenses. "He was going to do all the cabinet making. It would have been beautiful. He wasn't a clumsy man. How could they say it was his fault?"

The woman spoke quietly. Her children had not seen their father's body; that was an image none of them needed.

The phone rang. "Mum, it's the man from the real estate."

Client A sighed, and Theresa thought she caught a glimmer of something shifting near the fridge.

"He wants to do another inspection."

"Do you want me to be here?" Theresa asked.

"No. I need to be independent. I can do it."

As Client A talked, Theresa could see the ghosts coming for her. Crawling hand over hand, broken legs trailing behind them, the more she talked the closer they got. And around the 15 year old were what appeared to be teenage girls, pregnant, blood pouring down their thighs.

Curiosity sparked by the ghosts, Theresa waited in her car until the real estate agent arrived. Faces from every window watched as he walked up the path. Searching for information on her handheld, she found nothing but praise for his work and his dedication, but as he walked, ghosts scooted around. They knew an ally, *hurry up*, pushing him forward, *get it done*.

Theresa followed him for three days as he visited clients. She asked discreet questions, took the occasional photo. When even a forty-eight year old bikie's widow was surrounded by beaten ghosts after he visited her, she knew this man was a destroyer; perhaps one who preyed on widows.

"Can I help you, love?" she heard. A gentle, masculine voice.

A man dressed in leathers, long beard, tattoos. He held a cigarette between two yellowed fingers and, incongruously, balloons tied to the handles of his motorbike.

"Oh," she said.

"It's just that you're staring in at my mate's wife. And my mate's dead, so we're watching out for her. And she's not keen on being stared in at."

Theresa thought, *Am I going to do this?* The real estate agent left the house, wiping his mouth. The woman's ghosts leaped up and down, broken legs buckling, trampolining their excitement and she knew she had to intervene.

"It's that man. I've been following him. I've seen some terrible things."

The real estate agent fought back; he was strong and wiry. But he was never going to win. Theresa was there to watch; if they expected her to call a halt they were surprised.

She didn't regret the intervention, but she physically reacted to it, coming out in boils. She considered it worth the aftermath because of the solace it brought her, and because when next she visited Client A, there were no ghosts to be seen.

Even after five years working at the refuge, barely a morning dawned when Theresa didn't wake thinking of who she would help that day. When asked why she did it, why she made such sacrifices for others, she said, "I just want to help," but truthfully, helping others helped her to forget, distracted her from her empty life. It made her feel good.

She listened well, mostly because she didn't want to talk about herself. She had an extra skill; she could see the ghosts of beaten women around those clients who would die that way.

Some surprised her. A bossy woman in an office, a famous athlete, a respected dancer; they all had ghosts.

It wasn't only the women. Men, too, had ghosts. Some of them beaten, many of them ill, many of them murdered. *Join us, join us*, she sometimes heard. And the children; she saw the ghosts of molested children but what could she do? She couldn't adopt them all, keep them all safe. Her crazy aunt Prudence sent her greeting cards periodically, with instructions on them like "Let Fate Be," as if she had any control over it. These cards went straight into the recycling bin.

Theresa did what she could for her clients, and sometimes the ghosts would vanish. More often, though, they'd be replaced by others. The ones beaten with a baseball bat would replace the ones drowned in the bathtub. Or the ones kicked to death would replace the ones gutted. It was exhausting, depressing and emotionally draining. So many times she wanted to say, "Go. You don't need to be a victim. Leave. Find a new life."

But she knew that couldn't work, that it was a letter to the editor opinion, and she'd help no one by expressing it. All she could do was watch the ghosts, help house the clients and sometimes, if it was called for, intervene.

So many times she didn't intervene and most often she knew this was right. Other times, she made small choices, small changes, and hoped these were enough.

Then her inaction led to the death of a client.

The Second Intervention

The second intervention was a woman. Client B was reluctant to accept help, as many were, but had been ordered to do so. She said, "You're never so alive as when someone is beating the crap out of you and you're not sure if you're going to survive it." She didn't mind the pain, or the humiliation.

She had no ghosts, was the interesting thing, and Theresa was annoyed to have to find her a place she knew would be abandoned in weeks. So many others needed it.

She went to the woman's new home to help her settle in. There were men's shoes in the hallway; two packs of cigarettes on the table; a man's coat thrown on the floor. "It's his stuff, that's all. He's not living here or anything," Client B said.

She wasn't settled at all. Nothing unpacked, nothing clean. She drank a bottle of wine, pouring it, glug glug, into a large water glass. She slurred her words and smiled at Theresa as if she were a friend.

The kitchen was full of takeaway containers, half-eaten chicken nuggets sitting in cardboard buckets.

"That's the kids," she said. "They are fucken pigs, they are. You can't teach them a fucken thing."

"Kids?" There had been no children listed. Theresa felt her heart slow. Client B stood, staring at her.

"Fuck," she said. She hadn't told them about the kids. This was a new, one-bedroom apartment.

"How many children?"

"Two."

"Are they his?"

Client B shrugged. She stank of smoke, of sweat, of booze.

Theresa heard it then; a thin wailing noise. She'd thought it was the water taps.

"They never stop whinging," Client B whispered.

The ghosts appeared then, tiny children squatting in the hallway, their arms wrapped around their knees, their heads lolling sideways.

Client B took up her handbag. "I'll only be a minute. Can you mind them? I have to get something from the shops."

Theresa reached out her hand and grabbed the woman by the neck. Gave her a quick jab under the jaw to knock her out.

Then she checked on the children.

Both were strapped into strollers, although one was at least seven. They looked the weight of children half their age or less. There were deflated party balloons and ghost children littered around the wheels of the strollers like dried twigs.

Theresa unstrapped them and helped them lie on their mother's bed. She found stale bread and peanut butter and made them piles of toast, and then she shut the door and went back to Client B who was blinking, holding her jaw.

Theresa knew where to land the blows; the voice box. She called the police after laying the evidence on the ex-husband; she didn't want the children in his hands, either.

The children were placed in foster homes and while Theresa couldn't track them, she knew they were in a better place.

It couldn't be worse than where they'd been.

The aftermath was three days of vomiting, a blinding headache that lasted a week, and a failure to remember her mother's birthday.

The Third Intervention

Theresa intervened for the third time after three years on the job. She'd been working with this client for six months; had placed her away from her violent husband and facilitated her visits to the hospice where her mother lay dying.

They stood together in the corridor, Theresa wanting to leave. Client C dragged her into the room. "I can't stand to be alone with her. Please."

The attending nurse bent to stroke the dying woman's brow; her ghosts clustered by him, pressing up against him, three old women, crowded round the bed, heads bent, praying. Client C approached the bed and they hissed at her like witches.

Naked they were, naked as they were born; Theresa knew this was what they thought. Spines out, skin flabby, but they prayed for the mother until her spirit lifted out and they drew it along with them.

"It'll be all right," Theresa told Client C, who wept hysterically. "She's gone to a better place." Theresa had learnt the words to say from her counsellor. She knew some people found them comforting.

The attending nurse dispensed tissues. "She is lucky," he said. "She's in paradise, now. No more suffering. You can take solace in that."

Client C nodded and Theresa tried not to be offended that she'd accepted comfort from the nurse and not from her.

He had no ghosts around him, not even at a distance. He took Theresa's hand over the bed. His palm was cool to the touch.

"She's not my mother," Theresa said.

He winked at her. "All mothers belong to all children," he said. He put his hand on Client C's shoulder. "You tell me if you need anything. You ask for me: Jason."

He left the room and Theresa followed him, curious.

As he walked along the corridor, ghosts roared. Emboldened, excited. She thought, *He did it, he killed her.*

He poked his head into the room of a young girl. Recovering from a life-threatening disease if the number of stuffed toys and 'get well soon' balloons in the room were anything to go by, and the sulky ghosts, pale, skinny, scarred, who clustered in the corner as if deciding where to go next.

As the nurse, Jason, walked in, the ghosts grew. *They glowed,* Theresa thought, filled with new energy, and they ushered him forward; *Come in, come in sir.*

He winked at the girl in the bed. "I'll check ya later," he said, hands in his pockets as if it all meant nothing. The ghosts sucked in close, happy, ready, they knew him.

She followed the nurse to a bar, she drank with him, she went home with him. She'd researched him, asked around; he was an unlucky one, people said. Wonderful carer, but unlucky. So many patients lost.

She didn't have sex with him; she hadn't had sex with a man since Ben's death. Instead, she doctored his drink and watched as he tried and failed to fight sleep. She washed her hands in the bathroom, ignoring the pale, drained ghosts perched on the edge of the bath. She found enough in his home to know what sort of man he was. Boxes with a photo of a dead person in a hospital gown and an item; an earring, some fingernail clippings, a bedsock. Items he could steal without anyone noticing. It was evidence she understood, but not that the police could act upon.

Theresa sent the nurse some extra material in the mail, and she made sure he was at home before she called the police. She knew they'd find enough to lock him up. Magazines, DVDs. Evidence of an unhealthy obsession with children and death. He spent a week in remand before being released on bail. Three days later he committed suicide in his bathroom; his father was a priest, his mother a nurse in a Catholic hospital and it seemed he couldn't face the shame.

He would make no more ghosts happy.

She suffered memory loss, or more precisely, memory replacement. She remembered things that had not happened, she was sure of it. Her head ached for a week—a thin, high pain behind the eyes—and she didn't speak to her mother or her sister because they would know there was something wrong and she didn't want to field questions. She didn't want to hear 'since Ben died', words she heard too often from both of them.

The Fourth Intervention

Theresa intervened for the fourth time when she worked to find a home for a father and his two teenagers. He was a huge man, silver-haired, charismatic. Theresa had been as convinced by him as everybody else. His charm and his apparent kindness blinded people.

"We had to sell the house to pay for her defence," he said. "And the car. And cancel birthdays and Christmas." He blinked tears. "And we still failed. All that and we couldn't keep her out of jail."

Manslaughter; driving home drunk his wife had killed a father of five and badly injured his fifteen year old son.

"I told her not to drink," Client D said. "I begged her."

Theresa found them a clean, sizable house, near the shops and schools. She dropped by with her usual basket of settling-in treats; biscuits, cheese, chocolate.

The young girl who opened the door was pale. *Still grieving*, Theresa thought, but then she saw two ghosts, sitting on the bottom step, wrists slit, blood pooling at their feet.

"Is your dad home?"

The girl lifted her shoulders, not quite a shrug. "Dunno."

There were voices from the lounge room. "He said it was okay to have friends over."

Her brother appeared; he bore a stark resemblance to his father. His ghosts, green, their arms pocked with needlemarks, joined the others on the stairs.

"You're the one who got us the house," he said.

Theresa nodded.

"Thanks. Drink?" He held up a beer can and she nodded, then shook her head.

"No, I can't." She wasn't sure how it worked; the alcoholic mother was locked up, so these teenagers should be safe, yet still the ghosts sat there.

She followed him into the lounge room.

She could barely tell ghost from teenager in there.

All of them? she thought. "Is your dad at home?"

The teenagers exchanged looks; the ghosts swirled, seemed to swell and gain colour as she said his name.

She took a beer, sat down with them and let them talk. She didn't figure out what it was he'd do to them; she didn't want to know. She did ask about him, though, made her discreet enquiries.

She loved the details of other people's lives. She was good at facts. She didn't want to rely solely on the ghosts she saw; they were unreliable because the answers were her interpretation.

Theresa knew he visited his wife in jail twice a week and she let slip to a police contact what she suspected him of. Past and future. The police contact let slip to the lifers. It's always the lifers who do the dirty work. Nothing more to live for. Lifers who don't care clean up the human messes. Visiting room, one-two and it's done, and the wife left there stunned, perhaps relieved. Grieving, lost, alone, but relieved. *She must have known,* Theresa thought. And that's why she drank.

The aftermath was hard. She felt numb from the elbow of her left arm for three days, as if she had lost her hand and was suffering from the phantom presence of it. She came out in a dark purple rash. She couldn't keep anything down beyond water, and even that tasted salty.

Everything tasted salty.

And far worse than that; she got it badly wrong.

For her own pleasure, she went to the burial—to be reassured, she told herself—but she knew she wanted that glow of watching those she'd helped.

Instead; the teenagers' ghosts were far stronger. Closer, and fat with sorrow.

The children held each other and wept.

I achieved nothing? Theresa thought.

She was gutted.

She swore she would not intervene again.

The Fifth Intervention

Client E came in, three kids around her legs, the oldest boy leaning on her shoulder.

"I kept them out of school today," she said. Widening her eyes as if she had more to say but didn't want to say it with the children listening.

"Kids, I've heard rumours there are chocolate biscuits left in the playroom. Want to go look?" Theresa said.

"There's nothing to do in there," the eleven-year-old said.

"You can eat chocolate biscuits." Theresa smiled at him. "And the TV is working. Next time I'll try to organise some games for in there. Not all kids are as good as you guys so stuff gets wrecked. Next time, I promise."

The three kids trailed reluctantly away from their mother, who had her usual ghosts; tired women with slumped shoulders standing close behind her.

"How are you going?" Theresa said. She pulled out the client's file.

Theresa wished she could smell evil on all of the files she held, wished she could follow her nose and find those evil men and poke their eyes out with her paper knife.

She wanted to take a wire cutter to them. She wanted to shout at the women who came to her, "Fuck him up! Fuck that fucker up!"

Instead, she said, "How are you going?"

The client told her that her husband (ex, she called him, though no papers had gone through) was threatening harder than ever. "He said he'd take the kids for the weekend," she said.

"Take them where?"

"He said he'd take them somewhere and make sure I can never see them again. That they would never think of me again. He said he'd make it so that I never even existed. I can't think what he means. I don't want to think about it. I feel so helpless. All I dream about is him being dead. If he was dead we'd be safe, and we'd have enough to live on."

"Don't feel bad for thinking that. You'd be surprised how many women say exactly the same thing. It doesn't hurt to dream, although sometimes it can be hard to wake up again. Harder to face reality."

"But what am I going to do? His grandfather lived to 98. He could last forever." The woman's ghosts moved around her, spanned their hands over her body as if measuring her. Theresa thought their presence meant, *keep her safe. Keep her away from him and she'll be safe.*

Theresa nodded and picked up her phone. She arranged for the woman and her children to be placed into a safe house. If he didn't leave them alone she'd take it further but she didn't like to act until she knew she had to. She did hate the aftermath; guilt, regret, doubt.

Client E seemed relieved, and called her children, telling them they were staying the night in a hotel. She'd organise them a safe place in the meantime.

"Room service?" the eleven year old said. "TV?" She nodded.

Theresa was pleased with herself. But as they walked away, she could see the ghosts following her client, almost pushing her along in their excitement to get her to where they wanted her to go. They were close, but Theresa thought, *I've kept her safe. They'll leave her alone, once it sinks in.* Theresa had noticed that the ones long-beaten whimpered and cringed like long-beaten dogs, tucking their tails between their legs. Others will recoil but not with such terror.

Theresa opened the file once more, looking for alarm bells. When abused women took action, most men let it go, ran away, changed or adapted. Only a few of them persisted. There were no indicators in this file, so she left it on top of her desk, planning to look again on Monday, revisit it, try to smell the evil and see how much it stunk.

She was reluctant to act after her last intervention.

Raul, her best friend in the office, came tapping at her door, shaking his hips at her. *Drinkies*, he mouthed, *time for drinkies*, so she locked her office and left the troubles there.

She would not be back on Monday.

Saturday morning she slept in past her hangover and then went shopping. She'd promised the kids some things for the playroom and it was sale time and she had not much else to spend her money on. She did well, emerging with arms full of soft toys, cheap electronic games she knew would be broken in a week, a sack of handballs.

She shoved them all in her car and decided to take them to the refuge, where she could spend an hour putting them away without feeling as if she had to see clients.

As she pulled up, she noticed a group of bedraggled ghosts clustered together by the doorway. She shook her head at them; *nobody here for you.*

A tall, tanned man stepped beside her and the ghosts rose up, mouths open, hands reaching for him. His shoulders were broad, his smile kind. It took her a moment to recognise him from his file; this was the man who had threatened to make it so his children never thought of their mother again.

"Those are for my kids, are they?" he said, soft and sweet, gentle. She momentarily wondered: *Was I wrong? Is he a good man and she was lying?* Because the thought was never far from her. Although she had the help of ghosts, things could always be misinterpreted.

She held up the arm full of soft toys. "Yes, your kids are sweet."

19

"They are. But they're being ruined by their mother." His fists clenched, the ghosts flew around his shoulders and back to nudge Theresa. She took a step back, felt for the door handle. "You know that. I know that. You need to tell me where they are."

"I'm sorry. I can't."

"Can't? Won't? Are you sure?"

She shook her head, nodded, and he took her. The soft toys cushioned the first blows, but her head hit the curb with a crack. She felt the thrum of footsteps, heard cars drumming past. The curb, the mess around her, the shouts of people by the river. Riverside city; pretty, pretty city. She felt sweat blur on her skin. She saw the sun squinting over the top of the office buildings, or was it the sun reflecting off hundreds of windows? Either way, her head hurt as this man kicked her.

She knew that nobody would step in and save her. They would look after her later, but nobody would risk their lives for a stranger, especially not in front of a centre like this one. So, broken and bleeding, she curled up into a ball over her backpack. He kept kicking, kicking, but that was okay because she absorbed those blows, and he was weaker, the force of his anger spent.

She thought, *It's okay, it's okay, he's getting me because he can't get to her*, but then it came.

He said, "That fat slag's dead. Fucken slaughtered, bitch. And I'll get my kids, too, I'll fucken get them when I find them. So fuck you bitch. Fuck you and your putting thoughts into her head," although the thoughts were already there.

Theresa wanted to open her arms and legs to him and let him kick her to death. She thought she heard breathing close by and opened her eyes to see the ghosts of beaten women squatting around her. Slumped shoulders, torn ears, weeping wounds. They clustered together, like attracting like.

She'd seen them before, those bitches, when Ben died. Then,

they'd been shaking bottles of pills at her, eat me, eat me. Theresa lifted her head. "I'm not like you," she whispered to the ghosts. Whistled. There was a gap in her teeth. "I'm not a beaten woman," although beyond the smell of sea and sand she thought, *I deserve this.*

The ghosts came even closer, staring into her eyes as if searching for something.

"Look," she thought one of them said, "look at us, our long wet hair, our fish-bitten lips, our white swollen fingers. Drowned, every one of us, and you too."

"I'm not going to drown," she said, loud enough that her attacker heard and he nodded, grabbed her by the heels and began to drag her towards the bridge.

It was then, at last, that the crowd reacted. They closed in on him; he dropped her heels and ran.

Theresa hurt in every part and she lay, gazing up at the sky and at the faces of the strangers who'd saved her; breathing, breathing, and watching as the drowned women walked away, disappointed. She wanted salt. She licked at her arm for the sweat.

"Piss off," she called after the ghosts. "Fuck off, piss off, fuck off out of here."

The paramedic put his hand firmly on her shoulder.

"It's okay, Theresa. We're not the enemy. We're helping you."

He carefully peeled back her shirt to look at her bruises. He felt every part of her body, but she felt no physical response and she sensed nothing from him.

"Okay, you've got a lot of nasty injuries I can see but nothing that won't heal. You're going to be okay. We'll get you a bed in the hospital, though. They'll sort you there. Do you have someone to look after you?"

She wished that Ben was alive so she could name him, say she had a husband, because they would have been married by then for sure. This was not a healing thought. This was a dangerous route to a dark place. She thought of her happy place; hot sun on hot sand, the gentle burn on the soles of her feet.

She never knew the name of the paramedic. Or the one who called for the ambulance, or the woman who held her hand and then disappeared. The stranger who rescued her from drowning when she was five. These were good people.

She heard clicks, people taking snaps of her, and she thought, *I want a copy of that.* She had pictures like this, at home. Photos of things other people may not find pleasant. But to her, it acted as a contrast. *This is how bad life can get. Your life? Not so bad.* The photo would remind her that she had weak moments. That she could be got. And she could show her clients so they could see she understood. But she would never allow it to happen again to her.

Theresa awoke in hospital, her mother by her bedside flicking through a magazine.

"Mum?" she rasped.

Her mother looked at her. "You're awake."

Theresa's throat was so dry it felt as if she'd swallowed glass. "Thirsty. Thirsty."

"I'll see if they'll let you have water. They don't when you've had an accident."

"Not an accident," Theresa said, but the pain of it made her stop halfway through.

Her mother stood, graceful as always, her silver hair in a loose bun, her clothes flowing and soft. She walked to the door. "I'll see, shall I?"

Theresa closed her eyes, feeling tears come. Sympathy, she wanted sympathy, she wanted someone to be kind to her for a change, to tell her it was all right, that none of it was her fault. Words she used all the time with other women.

Her mother returned with a jug of cold water. Her shoulders

were hunched and she had her eyes squinted half-closed, as if not wanting to see the room, or Theresa.

"You can look at me, Mum. I'm not that bad."

"You are, actually. You look terrible." There was a catch in Lynda's voice then, and Theresa felt gratified she'd moved her to emotion. Lynda helped Theresa sip some water.

"I don't feel so terrible. Just thirsty. And a bit dizzy. That's all." But saying the words tired Theresa out, and she sank down, her mother's sweet perfume in her nostrils, comforting her.

She awoke to a different kind of smell. It was rubber; it was heavy woollen sweat; it was familiar and it took her back to her childhood and also, strangely, made her think briefly of Ben, but she thought of sand, the beach and the warmth of it filling her.

Prudence, Theresa thought.

Face painted red, balloons banging at her ears, Theresa's aunt-by-something stood over her and said, "He didn't look like a monster. You are not the only one at fault," which did not give Theresa any comfort.

Her left arm was slashed to the bone, her throat bruised, her right ankle aching. She couldn't move the fingers of her right hand because three of them were broken. Her ear was torn. She'd lost all the toys she'd bought. She hoped they'd gone to a good home.

Theresa had not seen Prudence for many years, but she looked like she always had; greasy hair clumped into rats' tails, covered with bright red powdered dye. Her broad, lined, flat face (she was almost featureless) was covered with thick, red makeup, as was every part of exposed skin. Her face was streaked with grey ash.

Her layered clothing was red. Her toenails were painted red and they were long and curled backwards over her red, weathered sandals.

Two dozen or more balloons, tied around her wrist with dis-coloured string, floated above her head, nudging the sharp bright lights.

23

"And you are such a monster yourself. Always helping. Always wanting to hear 'good girl' and 'isn't she a darling'."

"I'm not a monster," Theresa said. She thought, *How could she say such a thing to me? Who does she think she is?*

Theresa wondered where her mother was. Her father. She wanted them to come and take Prudence away.

"My dear little fairy god-daughter. Monsters like you, you only die one way. Each monster, one way. For you, it must be drowning in shallow salt water," Prudence said, her balloons bouncing colourfully against the bed head.

Her words made Theresa thirsty, as if she'd been swallowing that salt water and was dehydrated. She reached for the plastic glass by her bed.

They heard Lynda's voice outside, heard her laughing with someone, a stranger. She didn't laugh like that with Theresa.

"I'll be back. I'll be back to watch over you," Prudence said, her shoulders twitching. "We won't miss another monster."

Theresa heard her in the corridor, handing out balloons.

When Theresa awoke again, her whole body tingled and she felt heavy. She sat up in the bed and reached out her arms to test them, and then pulled back the covers, dropping her legs over the side.

She felt shaky but strong. Stretching her toes to the floor, she stood up, balancing herself against the side of the bed until she was steady.

Her clothes sat in a pile beside the bed, though not the things she'd been wearing. Her parents? Her sister? She reached for the pile as a nurse entered the room.

"They were hoping you'd be up and about. How are you feeling?"

"I feel fine. I don't want to hog a bed."

The nurse took her arm. "Let's take a walk up and down the hallway, see how you are. You're a tall one, aren't you?"

They took it slowly. Theresa hated hospitals, not only for the smell, the lights and the noise, but for the ghosts. She could see them outside half the doorways; some of them blue in the face, choked. Some of them crushed. All of them staring into the rooms, waiting greedily.

"I feel fine," she said, scrunching up her eyes.

"Headache? We can send you home with some ibuprofen for that," the nurse said. "Let's get the doctor in so she can release you."

They walked back to the room and Theresa slowly pulled her clothes on, needing help with the short tartan skirt, the striped stockings. She felt conscious of her tattoo and wondered what the nurse would make of it; it was an intricate design; a leafy pattern with the letters BENRIP woven through it.

"How'm I going to manage at home? I need to take you with me!"

"You'll get used to it. Everybody does." The nurse bustled about cheerfully and Theresa wondered why there should be a ghost with its shoulder bitten out standing in the doorway.

"You should be careful of dogs," Theresa said. "And sharks. Anything with teeth."

"Oh, I love my dogs! Wouldn't be without them!" and Theresa knew that at least she'd tried. She'd become fatalistic over the years, because who would believe her? Who would listen?

Theresa's left arm was aching and heavily bandaged, as was her right ankle. Her right hand had been splinted but the breaks were clean. Her ear had been stitched and felt thick and strange. They'd fixed her tooth; looking in the mirror she could barely tell work had been done. She felt as messed up as if she'd intervened and saved her client. And yet she'd done nothing.

H er father collected her, pacing anxiously around the room. "There you are!" he said lightly. He hugged her fiercely, causing her to grunt in pain.

"Dad, I'm fine, but not if you break my ribs." He had tears in his eyes. "Dad, don't cry or you'll set me off."

"Come on then. You'll stay with us for a few days. We'll make some popcorn and watch a movie, ey? One about princesses and horses?"

Theresa laughed, although it hurt to do so. "Dad, I'm 24. Not 4!"

He drove cautiously, silently, to her childhood home. She noticed his hands tight on the wheel; he was usually a relaxed man.

"All right, Dad?"

"Not bloody all right. No. This bloody shit who did this to you…" Phil rarely raised his voice and she didn't remember him ever losing his temper with her or her sister Giselle. "This arsehole…." Unused to articulating his rage, he let it sit.

Theresa looked out of her window. "What about her? Dad? His wife. My client. Did he really kill her or was he just saying it? Tell me he was just saying it. Tell me she's okay."

Phil said nothing. His mouth opened, shut, as if he couldn't bear to talk.

Theresa started to cry. She'd cried a lot in hospital, alone in her room, letting the starched pillowcase soak up the tears. Here it seemed strange and out of place and in the silence her sobs eased.

"It's all right," Phil said. He'd stopped the car. He patted her hand, squeezed her fingers gently. "It'll be all right. I didn't mean to upset you."

She saw ghosts around him; men of close to his age, squatting, slumped. Pants down. One of them holding a newspaper.

For fuck's sake, he's going to die on the dunny, Theresa thought.

It started raining.

"Bloody idiots!" Phil said. "Look at them! People always go crazy in the rain. It's like they think driving faster gets them home and out of the rain faster, and they're horribly surprised to find themselves in an accident."

It was a three car pile-up. Clearly one dead; Theresa could see the mangled ghosts of previous victims. She watched as the ghosts gently reached in together and hitched out the new ghost, lifting it carefully out of its wrecked body. They rose with it, leaving the devastating scene behind.

"Did you see that?" Theresa whispered to her father. "Oh, it was almost beautiful."

Her father shook his head. "I see nothing. Nothing at all."

"You look after yourself, Dad," she said as he drove on.

"Why?" His face looked startled. Frightened. And she realised that he believed absolutely in what she could see.

Two blocks from home, Phil said, "There she is again."
It was Prudence, selling balloons on the street corner, her red face blurred amongst the brighter of them.

"I don't want to talk to her," Theresa said. "She came to the hospital and freaked me out."

"She's odd. No doubt about it. We'll try to keep her away. It's been years, hasn't it? God knows where she's been, but I wish she'd go back there."

"She told me I was going to die drowning. I don't even like the water."

"You never did," he said, although she had.

She'd loved it before she'd almost drowned when she was five, and had to be rescued by a stranger leaping into the water fully clothed. Her mother and father on the beach, oblivious. There had been fallout for that, Theresa remembered, and she knew that her sister Giselle blamed her, as if she'd deliberately fallen off the pier

27

and nearly died. She'd never been keen to swim again although she loved the beach.

"She's always been obsessed with you. She sent you a present every year, Teese, remember? Your fairy Godmother, she called herself. Didn't bother with Giselle, which caused problems, didn't it?" Theresa remembered clearly. Each year a present would appear, something Theresa would fantasise as magical. Tiny flying pigs, dice that transformed into jewellery boxes, a chocolate bar that never ended.

But every year it was something useful; books about water safety, floating devices and life vests. Novels that started with drownings and ended the same way.

Theresa's mother would put the gifts in the cupboard to donate them to the school fete.

As a child, Theresa thought Prudence was an imaginary friend because she was so weird and scary. And Theresa's parents never talked about her. She was one of the many family no-go zones.

"Theresa means reaper," Prudence told her when she was seven. "But it doesn't mean you have to be like that. You don't have to be a parasite. A vampire. You can be a strong woman, a fighting one." Prudence was the one who convinced Theresa to ask to do karate classes, and join the debating team, and learn boxing. All things she'd given up after Ben died.

"Well, we'll keep her away from you now. You're not strong enough to deal with a crazy woman like that. She's poison, your grandad always said. He wouldn't let her in the house."

Phil fussed getting Theresa inside and settled on the couch. Giselle had been to her house and packed some things for her. She'd done a terrible job; not enough underwear, too much sleepwear, lots of the ugly stuff Theresa had been meaning to give away. They'd decided she needed babying. Theresa gave into it, although she knew there was much work to do, for the clients and for herself.

Her job had been her release for a long time. Hearing terrible stories made her feel grateful. Helping other people made her feel worthwhile.

"I have to keep my little girl safe," Phil said. "I'm ready to smash him with a sock full of sand if he comes here."

Theresa laughed, but stopped herself when she saw Phil's face. He left the room for a few minutes and came back with a filled sock and a tomato. He put the tomato in the centre of the coffee table, wielded the sock and splattered the fruit.

"That's…effective! Different if it was a person, Dad." She picked up the sock, feeling how heavy it was.

"You know I was in Vietnam, Teese."

"Yeah, but I thought you were a desk jockey. Ordering in supplies or something."

"No. I was there."

"Part of the job?" Theresa said. "Did you kill people?"

"I'll tell you about it one day. Not today. I know how much you hate the nasties. You're a gentle soul."

"I'm always seeing nasties."

"And yet you remain gentle and kind."

"Like a child?" she said, but this made her feel as if she was acting like her mother, bitter, so she smiled at him. She hadn't seen her ghosts since her attack.

They heard Lynda entering through the kitchen door, the rustle of bags, the smell of Thai takeaway. Even carrying plastic bags her mother was graceful, and Theresa felt like a great lump beside her.

"Our girl's here," Phil called out.

"Which one?" Lynda walked into the room. "Oh, Teese. I forgot you were coming."

"I'm not hungry," Theresa said.

Lynda served out the food for three of them anyway, washing

up the containers as she went along. "Love the takeaway," she said. "Your father makes such a mess of the kitchen when he cooks. And when he makes jam there's no room for anyone to do anything."

Theresa took a sip of Tom Yung Gung and winced. "I feel awful. My throat hurts."

"You look better already than you did when I saw you in hospital. How did this happen? After everything you've seen, all you know?" Blaming her. Lynda hated failure of any kind.

"You're the only one who agrees with me it was my fault. I can't stand to think of those kids left without a mother."

"I imagine that would have been her dying thought, knowing her kids would be left alone."

The cruelty of this, the truth of it, made Theresa suck her breath in. She should have tracked down that tall, tanned man and fucked him up, before he had the chance to kill his wife. The ghosts had let her down.

"You must be used to it, in your job. Surely you're used to people being awful to people. At least you'll know he's locked up. He won't be able to get to you."

"Thanks, Mum. Hadn't thought about that."

She wished her mother would hold her hand and tell her everything would be all right.

"It's a shame you've got no one else to help you right now but us."

"I've got plenty of friends to help me. You don't have to worry," but even as she spoke she wondered who she'd call. Which of her acquaintances she could ask to help.

Her mother hurrumphed, looked at her watch. "Too many friends, not enough close friends. It's that job you do. I've always said so. This helping people nonsense. Help yourself, I say, and that way you help the world. And you won't be at risk. Every day I worry about you. Every day I expect a phone call, and I wasn't surprised when it came."

"I've gone a long way without this happening, you know. Been in plenty of circumstances where it could have happened but didn't. This took me by surprise."

Theresa felt glad now that her mother had no sympathy. Any kindness would make her collapse.

"We should be quiet now. Save your throat." Lynda was tired of talking; over it. She moved into the kitchen where she brewed the herbal tea no one else would touch.

Theresa slept well in her childhood bed and could almost imagine she was nine again, or ten.

Raul called her and she had to shut herself into the study to talk to him, because the sound of her voice seemed odd in the silence of the house.

"The funeral is tomorrow. I'll come with you if you want to go. No one else is going but I think it would be okay if you wanted to."

"You mean because it's my fault she's dead?"

"How is it your fault? She's the one who married the man. All you did was try to help her."

"All I did was get her killed. That's all."

"Listen, if you're going to talk like that I say don't go to the funeral. It won't help you and it won't help anyone. So what do you think? Talk to me, T. You can."

"I hate talking about myself."

"And that's what makes you such a good listener. But you should talk."

As Theresa dressed for the funeral, Phil called through her door, "You shouldn't go. It'll upset you."

"There's nothing wrong with being upset. I should be upset. She deserves that, at least."

It was an awful affair, sparsely attended, the children up the front with a frazzled relative who seemed unsure of what was going on. People turned around at every noise and Theresa wondered if, like her, they feared the husband would show up with a rifle.

There were a lot of police in the room but not for protection, Raul said. "He's actually a cop. Did you know that? That's how he got the info. It's gonna go hard for him in jail."

Theresa got the sense she would not have to intervene for the children's sake, that jail justice would take care of it again. She wanted to comfort the children, who recognised her and turned away. She hadn't expected a thank you for finding them a place to live, but she'd thought they'd say hello. She wished she hadn't lost the toys she'd bought; she could have given the children gifts. She felt gratified that her beating had saved them. If not for that, their father would have been on the streets and able to find them and who knew? Who knew what he would have done?

"Oh, the poor darlings," she whispered to Raul. "Where are they going to live?"

"T, don't worry about that. Someone's taking care of it," he said, meaning, *this is not your file any more. Not your business.* "They're not going to be homeless."

He'd been homeless himself for a long time and never forgot. Theresa thought cruelly that he still looked as if he lived on the street most of the time, with his scrawny, greasy hair, his floppy hat. He was always dirty-looking and skinny. An ex-drug addict, he was so filled with compassion and understanding Theresa felt like a better person being near him, as if the reflected glow of his pure need to help shone on her. Some people were like that; improving you by their presence.

"I'll be back at work in a week," she said. "I'll take the file back then."

"We miss you. I miss your coffee. Everyone else stuffs it up." He touched her shoulder. "You have to wait till you're physically ready, at least."

"At least? You mean mentally I won't be?"

"You'll be fine," he said, but he wouldn't catch her eye. "But last time you...weren't well, you took no time off at all, and you were exhausted."

Theresa knew they all thought she felt responsible for the death of Client D; that she was too emotionally attached. They didn't understand that she was not just responsible, but she had caused his death, and that the aftermath had been a vicious attack of shingles which left her distressed and in pain.

Raul and Theresa went out to eat after the funeral. He held her hand. "You did well. I'm glad you went."

"Me too."

"I was worried you'd get angry and all worked up and make decisions not in the best interests of everybody."

"Thanks, Raul! Glad to know you trusted me."

For another week, Theresa ate comfort food in front of the TV with her parents or on warm days, in the backyard, newspapers and magazines piled on the table in front of them. Giselle brought over old magazines, hag rags going back six years. Theresa hadn't read one in a while and found the world of celebrity gossip a relief. The dates were hard to cope with, though, once she realised how far back the magazines went. This one was the day she and Ben had walked up a mountain. This one they'd read together, laughing at celebrity lives, feeling superior in their ordinary existence.

This one was the day of Ben's death. She remembered people reading to her, wanting to distract her. And, she thought, testing her facilities.

After Ben died, Theresa couldn't move for five days. Immobilised by the tranquilisers they fed her, she lay trapped with her thoughts and if she could have willed herself to death she would have. Those ghosts, shaking bottles at her, tempting her.

"My fault," she'd tried to say, "MY FAULT!" But no one listened to a griever. Not even her counsellor, relentlessly cheerful, full of advice.

"We have to keep you busy," the counsellor had said, and this made sense, because Theresa felt useless. Helpless.

She was not alone in this feeling. The counsellor had taken her to a session with other grievers, all of them talking in a circle, waiting for the other to finish, then jumping in with their own tragedy. Their own failure.

All of them, "If only, what if…" Especially the accident victims, where 'what if' was a real alternative. None of them, "From now on." If only he was arrested before this had happened. What if we'd left. If only I'd had a place to go. What if I'd stopped him from swimming. If only I'd intervened."

The ghosts in the room were palpable, but not overwhelming. When the counsellor talked, in his calm, helpful voice, the ghosts subsided even more. A grey-eyed man of fifty, he said, "Remember, people. Always have a happy thought ready. A memory not associated with your loved one. Anticipation of a future event, a pleasant smell or taste you remember. Something you can turn to when unwanted thoughts of your loss come to you."

They had all nodded, murmured.

"And if that thought turns stale? Get yourself another. Fantasy is your friend."

Theresa's place was the beach. She loved it; the infinite grains of sand, the starting anew with each tide, the wiping clean. It meant warmth, relaxation, time to be alone.

Ben had disliked the beach; found it dull, too hot, too sandy. So there was no connection with him, an added benefit.

After the first session, the counsellor had taken her aside. He said, "You have a natural talent for listening, and asking the right questions, Theresa. You have an empathy I don't see very often; an understanding of the suffering of others. An affinity. Have you ever thought of social work?"

That's where it began. Theresa took a job finding shelter for those abandoned and afraid. And she intervened for the first time.

She called Giselle anyway to thank her for the magazines and invite her for a meal.

"No, the kids are sick. I'm exhausted. I'm not up for looking after you."

"I don't need looking after! I'd like to see you. And the kids."

"And Nolan?"

"Him too."

"We'll see how the kids go. Enjoy the magazines." Giselle was always terrified she'd be asked for more than she was willing to give. "Enjoy Mum's cooking." They laughed.

Lynda liked to experiment with food, and even when they were children she'd fed them adult food. When they were younger, they'd grown adept at secretly disposing of scraps of undercooked meat, of salty fish, of shredded, uncooked, too-spicy potato. Theresa ate adult meals from the moment she had teeth; steak Dianne, curries, pasta with anchovies and olives. She liked to visit friends' houses for the plain food that was served up, which wasn't hard because kids didn't like visiting her. Lynda abhorred noise in the house, and some kids found her scary.

Theresa said to Giselle, "Dad's been doing the cooking. Mum's full on with some letter writing campaign. She needs plenty of wine to help her sort it."

"We might be able to come when the kids are better."

"I'm bored."

"I sent you all those magazines."

"They're old as! What, did you clean out under your bed? What else did you find under there?"

"They're not that old, are they?"

"They're old. Like the CD collection here. It's a joke. Three quarters Sol Evictus, one quarter Beethoven. I'm stuck with talking to Dad about plants and trying to get Mum to talk about anything."

"She says she's proud of you for not giving in, not letting it destroy you."

"She hasn't told me that. And anyway, I'm no Mrs Ellis," Theresa said.

"No, you're not. That poor woman. Now SHE was one who used to love Sol Evictus. Don't you remember? Whenever the husband was away that crap would be blaring out over the street."

Theresa had always wondered what they could have done for Mrs Ellis, a battered neighbour. If she'd only needed a friend. Or a rescuer. If helping her might have saved her. But Theresa had been too young to do anything and Lynda, her mother, was not a helper. "Life's too short," she often said.

Theresa looked out of the side window at the house next door, now lived in by an elderly couple who hung out clothes in brown, grey and pink. Even looking at the clotheslines gave Theresa the shivers.

Mr Ellis was still alive, and many times Theresa had considered tracking him down. But she knew it would be revenge, not intervention. He'd been badly disabled in a car accident and was cared for full time by a nurse.

"Hers were the first ghosts I saw. Did you know that? When I was like, nine or something. Pathetic women, all weak and cowed. I had some hanging around me when this shithead bashed me. They thought I was going to die."

"You were never going to die."

"That's what Prudence says. She says she knows that I'm going to die by drowning. She says she knows how all monsters die."

"She says you're a monster?" Giselle laughed. "You? Saint Theresa?

36

You only ever do good. You've never done anything monstrous in your life."

"Not without good reason," Theresa said, and Giselle laughed again.

"If you're so bored, you can always go home. If you're well enough to be bored, you're well enough to go look after yourself." Giselle's voice took on the tone it sometimes did; *get over yourself. Don't you know I have children? I'll show you problems!* Theresa let her sister change the subject. They didn't talk about the ghosts in her family.

In the end it was her parents who left her behind. They started packing for an overseas jaunt and they didn't invite her to join them. They never did.

"You want your own holidays," her mother said, little caring what sort of holiday Theresa had. "You're a grown woman now," although Lynda had always treated the girls that way, as if they were grown. "Even if you wanted to come on holiday with us you couldn't. You need to get back to your job before they give it to someone else. You can't let a work place down again."

"Again?" She knew Lynda thought she'd coped badly when Ben died and it was true that she never returned to her part-time job at the RSPCA. "They told me I could have as long as I needed."

"They probably don't even want you back. Maybe they think you won't be able to do your job any more."

Phil, who was packing the last of his preserves to store under the house, called to Theresa for help. Handing her a carton, he said, "I feel bad leaving you. But this trip has been booked for months."

"Don't worry, I'll be fine. I'll house-sit. It'll make me feel useful." The idea of going back to the large house she shared with six other people made her feel exhausted.

"I don't like to think of you on your own. Think about your uncle's offer."

Theresa tilted her head at him, unsure what he meant.

"Didn't your mother tell you?"

Theresa shook her head.

He sighed. "She was supposed to. He's offered for you to visit. If you want a break from that refuge place. He'd be happy for you to work with him."

"What uncle? Uncle Scott? I barely know him."

"Well, he heard about what happened to you and he sent us a business card. Your mother's got it. Lynda!" he called out. "Give Teese Scott's card! She wants a look at it."

Her mother came heavily down the stairs. "Teese wouldn't know about it if you didn't tell her," she said. She handed a grey business card to Theresa. Lifted her hand over her eyes and squeezed.

"Scott's Stamps" it said. A bright Mauritian stamp in the corner. An actual stamp, which Theresa thought was clever. And on the back, "Call me if you want a job. No excitement, guaranteed."

"I've only met him like twice in my life. Grandpa's funeral was one of them. And I was only tiny then. And I remember him at one of Giselle's birthdays, and he was there when you had your graduation thing, Mum." She counted on her fingers to annoy Lynda. "Did you tell him what happened? How did he know I was...sick?"

"He found out. I don't know how."

Theresa flicked the card against her fingernails.

"Stamp collecting, ey? I loved stamps when I was a kid."

"Loved them? You were obsessed. That was all we heard about for a while there. I thought he was a lawyer, but he sent that, saying, *send her to me*," Phil said. "It'll be perfect."

"Not sure how much use I'd be. My hand isn't fantastic yet."

"It'll be a clean break. Get it? Clean break."

"That's awful, Dad. Scaring me into a drastic decision with bad puns. Not very fatherly."

"It's not a drastic decision. You do it for a while, you see how you go, and things clarify in your mind. Nothing is final."

"Stamp collecting might be about my speed at the moment."

The scar on her arm was healing, though it would always be there. Her throat was healed, as was her ear, but her ankle and her fingers still twinged now and then, and she felt as if she would never write comfortably again.

Phil said, "Why don't you let someone else decide for you for once? Let someone else help you for a change. Life's too short."

"What's he like, this long-lost uncle of mine?"

"We used to be good friends. When I first met your mum, Scott and I were good mates. He and your mum had a falling out, though. I haven't spoken to him for years, but he was always a good bloke," Phil said. "You'll probably find him a bit dull. They had a daughter. Amber. But don't mention her. Something happened and I think it's better if you don't ask about it."

"What happened?"

"Look, I don't know. You know we've barely been in contact…don't ask, Theresa. Better that way."

Denial is always the best policy, isn't it, Dad? Theresa thought. There had been a massive falling out between brother and sister. It was never explained or discussed, and Theresa was too young at the time to remember it. All Theresa knew was that suddenly they didn't see Uncle Scott any more and no gifts arrived.

She and Giselle had been sorry about that part.

"It sounds tempting. But I have obligations. I do need to get back to work. People are waiting for me."

She felt guilty about her clients, although she knew they had other case workers. The conversation spurred her to call Raul and tell him she was coming in on Monday; the recuperation time was over.

Following her usual routine on Monday morning, Theresa walked three blocks to work after getting off the train a stop early. She hated the underground train loop. Its hot wet stink. Its metal and steam, compost. The faces she saw in the dark. She always got off at the station before the tunnel and walked.

She saw three regular beggars every day. Fifty cents each she gave them, every day. The young guy, "God Bless You," he'd say, but he didn't believe in God. He wasn't the type. He didn't know her from day to day. Not the slightest glimmer of recognition, not even any idea that every day someone gave him 50 cents.

The old guy, quietly playing music, always smiled at her, always said, "Good girl," fatherly and kind. He sat cross legged on a woven mat. When her father sorted out his clothes for the stuff he didn't want anymore, Theresa took a bag of warm things to the old man. From then on, cold weather or hot, he'd be wearing something of her father's. "There's the good girl. There she is."

The young woman was the worst of them. She was aggressive, always tired to the point of fury, and smelly. She stank of park sex, car sex, train station sex. Sometimes her hair was washed but mostly it wasn't. She came at Theresa, grabbing at her. "Come on, share it out. Poor little rich girl. Give us a bit of Daddy's money." Theresa handed over the usual 50 cents.

"You know this is bullshit, right!? Bullshit amount. Nothing I can do with it."

"I give you $2.50 a week. Plus those other guys. It adds up."

"Not for me it doesn't," but still she kept the coin.

Raul met Theresa at the door with coffee. She could tell he hadn't showered for a couple of days; his hair was lank and his clothing hung on his frame as if slightly damp. He smelt stale but not sweaty. He rarely exerted himself enough to sweat. Still, she welcomed his kiss on the cheek, his smile. Her heart beat faster as they entered the office and she found it hard to breathe.

"Don't have a panic attack on me, T," Raul said. "I'm not equipped."

He walked with her to her office, where there was a month's worth of files and messages. An avalanche. The files screamed at her and she couldn't tell if she was imagining it, or if it was the ghosts screaming at her, *get out get out we can manage on our own.*

She looked at the files and thought; *I can't do anything about any of this.* She felt a deep sense of exhaustion, of failure, a lack of ideas.

She looked at her appointments for the day; nothing. That would start the next day. So she made coffee. Her workmates avoided looking at her. *You're one of them, now,* she knew they were thinking. *You should be sitting on the other side of the desk.*

She thought, *I'm not like that, I'm not a beaten woman.* The men she knew didn't turn on her. She hadn't chosen this.

But she felt herself cringing at the thought of big, aggressive men and she hoped she'd still have the power to stand in front of one and tell him to fuck off, as she'd done many times before. There had been many small interventions; a file gone missing, a phone call made. Small things to help effect big changes.

She hoped she'd still be able to help and that the ghosts hadn't deserted her.

The court case was held a month later and her attacker charged with his ex-wife's murder. Theresa's assault was tacked on at the end, giving him another year in jail. He stared at her malevolently, as if she'd caused it. As if it was only her presence that caused his life to fall apart.

The look didn't bother her. She'd been looked at like that before. As her supervisor liked to say, *It means you were doing your job.*

Like a scab that itches; it means it's healing.

He said in court, "Ruby would be alive today if it wasn't for that interfering bitch." A gunman blaming his rifle.

Theresa saw fat ghosts with bloody eyes leaning up against him but she felt no compunction to warn him. She had her own ghosts to worry about; those wet-lipped, bedraggled women tugging her to swim, put her head under for a minute. *He should have been my fifth intervention;* the thought roiling in her head. She wanted to bite her veins till they bled.

As she sat alone outside the courtroom, the idea of going back to work exhausted her. She thought, *Half an hour. I'll sit here half an hour and then I'll go back.*

She felt assailed. Every woman who came out of the court room, and most of the men, were followed by ghosts. She couldn't differentiate good from bad, true from false, saved from doomed. The stress of it made her stomach rise.

"Take the afternoon off," Raul said, touching her shoulder. "Do something for yourself."

The foyer seemed misted, so full of ghosts Theresa could hardly breathe. What was it? Who? Who here was attracting these ghosts?

They concentrated around one young man, who sat slumped, his shoulders hunched. People gathered around him, whispering, but Theresa thought, *Don't go near him! Don't let him hurt you!* Because she could see how much the ghosts loved him.

"Who's he?" she asked a middle-aged woman next to her.

"It's that boy who lost his family in a car accident."

Theresa thought that it was no accident. That he would drive again, and that no one was safe from him.

There was something about him that reminded her of Ben, which made her head ache with remembering, with not remembering.

The young man swung his car keys around a finger and she thought, *He's going to drive. No, I have to stop him, intervene this time. He's going to crash, kill them all.* Because the ghosts were damaged, all of them. It wasn't until after she'd thrown herself at him, knocking him to the ground, that she thought through the logic. He couldn't hurt all these people with his car unless he drove it into the building. Up the stairs, through walls, along the hallway.

Raul pulled her away, and people laughed. But the ghosts subsided and she knew that something had shifted.

Her supervisor knocked on the door. "Theresa," she said. "We've been happy to have you back. But we've had reports in and from what I can see, you need more time off."

"I've had time off. I'm fine now," Theresa said, though she yawned and stretched and felt numb from the neck down.

"You're traumatised," her supervisor said. She closed the door and sat down, crossing her legs and leaning forward. "It happens to almost everybody. You've got a physical response to trauma. Your senses shut down. Take some time off, a lot of time off. Do something different, stress-free. Don't help anybody. Heal yourself."

These words, the words a mother should say, broke Theresa down.

"What if that bastard was right, though? What if it is my fault she's dead?"

"If it wasn't you, it would have been one of the others. All you did was help her. He killed her. That's it."

"Would they have pushed it like that, though? Would they have convinced her to leave, like I did?"

"We all would, Theresa. The day we don't do that, we're finished. It is not your fault. You have to remember that. Nothing is your fault. It's out of your hands."

Theresa took a sip of the cold coffee on her desk. "I know that."

"I know you do. I have every faith in your responses. But we do need to watch your reactions to others. To the people you may put into place as ciphers for your own sense of guilt."

Theresa recognised the tone of voice. She used it often herself, when she was lying to make someone feel better.

"I wish I'd read him better. I should have intervened. I was too easily distracted."

"You can't be right all the time."

Theresa didn't talk about her client's excited ghosts, how if she'd listened to them, watched them properly, she might have been able to warn her. Although sometimes warnings made things worse; warnings never made them better.

"This is the job I'm meant to do, though. It always has been."

"And you've been good at it."

"But not any more?"

"I'm talking about a break. At one time or another we all need a break, a change, then we can come back refreshed. My feeling is that at the moment, what happened to you is fresh in the client's minds."

"But they'd think I understood now. I thought it would help."

"They like the idea that we don't understand. That's something I figured out early on. If they can say to you, 'You can't understand,' it makes it easier for them to let you help them."

Theresa thought of the mounds of files on her desk, all the people she felt unable to help.

"And then there is your…reaction at the courthouse. There is an element of the unpredictable about how your emotions will direct your behaviour. And we need to manage that."

"Maybe you're right. A short break."

The supervisor shook her head. "A real break. Find yourself."

Theresa thought of the files, the people who needed her. But she agreed.

Sitting in her parent's small but sunny backyard, Theresa closed her eyes, letting the warmth fill her and the bright orange light glow through her eyelids.

She smelt rubber. Heard the soft banging of balloons.

"Hello, Prudence," she said.

"How are you, my dear? All right?"

"Alive, as you can see. As you said. That was a great pep talk you gave me when I almost died." She closed her eyes again.

Prudence whispered, "You're so tired. So tired."

"Oh, God, I am. I can't even imagine not being tired."

"You need a change of place."

"Pace, you mean."

"Place. Place. You need a change of place. Get away, have a break. Try something new."

"Maybe. Dad wants me to go to work with Uncle Scott. Do you know…?"

Theresa couldn't keep straight how the family worked, who spoke to who.

"You should go," Prudence told her. "He will save you from yourself. They are good people. They are better people than others you know."

"If you mean my parents, they're fine."

"Fine. You say fine."

"Why do you talk about them like that? Mum's your niece or something. You should have more trust in her."

"Trust! Hmph!" The woman snorted. "I will come with you. I will keep you company."

Theresa found that strangely comforting. But she said, "I can't afford to pay for you. And you can't live with me. I want to live alone for a bit."

"You don't have to worry about me. You worry about you, and you stop being a parasite. That's what I tell you. You stop it for a while."

"Parasite! What does that even mean? Why are you calling me that?"

"Because you feed off helping others. You feed off their despair. That's why you help them. You are a parasite because you live off their helplessness and need. Who are you to decide who needs your help?"

"That's harsh. What about what happened to me? I got beaten up, you know. For trying to help."

"He will stay locked up. You don't need to worry about him," Prudence said, echoing what Lynda had said but in such a kind way Theresa felt like crying.

She was right about one thing: Theresa needed to leave her job completely, leave behind the memory of her clients and their filthy men. Go to work in a place where no one knew her and she could start again in a new city. New people. New friends. Be the person she was now, not the person they remembered, the one she was before.

She could reinvent herself. There would be no more interventions. She would ignore the ghosts. Choose not to see them, look down, always look down, and she would not help anybody except herself.

The Sixth Intervention

Theresa emailed her uncle Scott, thanking him for the invitation and accepting. She kept it brief; she barely knew him, and felt nervous about presenting herself properly. She had her hair cut and coloured and momentarily regretted her decision when she thought of finding a hairdresser in the new place to keep the look maintained.

Her workmates took her to lunch. She knew that once she was out of their sphere she'd cease to exist but that was okay. If she'd needed them, she'd remind them. She'd forgotten others in the same way; workmates mostly vanish once you don't see them every day. On her card, someone wrote, "You won't be able to leave. You're too obsessed!!!!" with tiny hearts for periods.

Raul offered to come with her, help her settle in. "You're about the only person who gets me," he said. "It's gonna be really hard without you."

"Can you come visit later? Once I'm there?"

"Yeah, yeah, once you've got a new life. You won't need me then."

Her share house was full of noise as she packed boxes by the dozen to put into storage at her parent's house, a favour they considered greater than she thought it deserved. No one helped her carry the boxes down; they waved goodbye to her as if she was going for the day.

She stacked her belongings in her parent's basement: her books, her clothes she'd kept from childhood, her knicknacks. A box of things that made her think of Ben: napkins and scraps of paper with lyrics and ideas for band names all over them. He never did anything about it; waste of talent. Over the phone, from Paris, her mother said she kept too much.

"You should give that stuff away, Teese. Ridiculous to keep these things. None of them mean anything."

"They don't mean anything to you, but they help me to remember."

"Remembrance is over-rated. Stick it all in the recycling bin. You focus too much on the dark side of life, anyway."

Her mother was talking about her newspaper clippings; going back a decade or more, evidence of outrage and offence and atrocity. Constant proof of how awful the world was.

The file was large, now, having grown over the years with a creeping insistence. Clippings of children beating children to death with barbed wire. Of fathers impregnating daughters and watching them die from home abortions. Of the grandmother who poisoned her whole family one Christmas day because she didn't have enough money to buy them Christmas presents. Theresa used to keep the clippings in a wooden box given to her by Prudence, but they outgrew the container. Now she had a five drawer plastic filing cabinet.

"You want me to fly home, come with you? Get you settled?" Phil called out. Lynda snorted.

Theresa hated the idea of that. She looked forward to the eight hour car trip. Silence or music, the road, anonymous meals.

Driving, Theresa avoided the ghosts. It wasn't hard. She saw a large man in a smooth and shiny red car, noticing the car, not the man. As she drew closer, she saw it was full of them, ghost faces squashed against the window pane, and so she pulled over, waited for the danger to travel far ahead. She drove a different way, not wanting to see the wreck he was in or see his body lying there when he'd been so full of life before.

Stopping along the way for petrol, for tyre checks, for oil, she felt self-sufficient and capable. Men offered to help her but she shook her head, *no, I'm fine.*

She arrived after five at the beachside bungalow Scott had told her she could use. Their 'little place by the beach', actually a three bedroom house overlooking the ocean. Bright and clean. Theresa wondered at people who were so casually wealthy. She supposed it came with habit. She was tired from the drive but suddenly filled with energy and excitement at this new chance.

There was a slight mustiness about the house. She'd half-expected they'd be there, waiting. Or have left flowers and chocolate, or a note. The cupboard had Vegemite, sugar, bad instant coffee and an opened packet of rice she threw away. She thought of a happy memory; the smell of the hot sand on holidays.

She unpacked quickly, wanting it done and to be settled. She'd bought fresh groceries on her way, knowing that once she was home she'd want to stay there. When she was showered, fed, she emailed her parents to let them know she'd arrived.

Giselle had texted her to say *Good luck*, and *I bet it's QUIET there.*

She texted Scott to say she was there, inside, okay. No response, though she wondered if perhaps he was a non-texter. She'd find out once she met him on Monday.

She called Raul at the office and talked with him and the others for thirty minutes or so, being passed from staff member to staff member. She checked up on a couple of the clients she was worried about, and made sure Raul knew where all the files were.

Then she walked on the beach. There were dogs running free and every one of them came up to sniff at her. Dogs were so kind.

On the morning of her first day at Scott's Stamps, Theresa arrived feeling as nervous as she had been going back to work after her enforced break. The office, on the second floor above a French bakery, carried no signage. Theresa wondered how fat she'd get with all that temptation downstairs. And if it smelt good upstairs in the office, like fresh baked bread, or it would be old cooking smells that rose.

She bought a tray of small cakes, something working with her clients had taught her. If you have food, especially sweet food, everything goes more easily. An elderly woman struggled with her shopping and Theresa helped her to her car.

"Thank you, kind girl," the woman said, and Theresa felt a small buzz of pleasure.

The door was locked. Theresa checked her watch. Five to nine. She sat propped against the wall and waited. She felt stupid with her tray of cakes. Ignorant about the family, self-absorbed. She didn't even know if Scott liked cake.

At 9:15, she heard footsteps and stood up. Scott, his mouth full of almond croissant, his fingers sugar-dusted, looked at her in surprise. He resembled Lynda enough to be recognisable as family. Grey, slightly curly hair. Pale brown eyes. He was taller than her, though not by much.

"Therese! You've grown!"

"Theresa," she said.

He blinked. Shoving the rest of the croissant in his mouth, Scott dusted his fingers on his pants and unlocked the door. It was dark inside.

"You'll have to excuse the mess. We don't get many clients in so don't bother," he said, turning on the light. She could see chairs askew, stacked boxes, piles of paper, plastic bags, buckets and

51

magazines. "You see why I need help?" he said. *Kindly*, she thought.

"Yeah," she said. "I bought cakes."

"Well done." He cleared off two chairs and they sat, eating the pastries greedily. "So, how's your mother?" he said. "Your father? And your sister?"

"All fine," Theresa said, thinking that she couldn't give him 20 years of updates on the first morning. He didn't ask about her injuries and she was glad. She wanted her uncle to like her, not pity her.

"So it'll mostly be the two of us. Your Aunt Courtney doesn't come in often. She's not keen on having a stamp collector for a husband." He seemed pleased by this.

"Courtney sounds sensible."

"Weeell…yes, about this she is, I suppose. Yes, she is. She doesn't like to go too far from home, but she's…sensible."

They didn't talk further. Theresa wanted to avoid discussion about what had happened to her, so kept things shallow and amusing. No Lynda, no unfortunate daughter, no childhood. Scott reminded her he'd given her the first stamp album, and had shown her how to soak the stamps, and she could remember it, if she thought hard.

Her first job was to tackle some of the mess, get it sorted and neat. She pulled down the thick, heavy, filthy blinds. Cleaned the windows. She and Scott stared out. The room was lighter, and warm.

"I don't suppose we need anything on the windows. Not like anyone can see in up here."

There were no tall buildings opposite. "You'd have to be determined to stare in. Maybe if you stood right down there, next to the shoe shop, and tilted your head," she said. They stood, pressed up against the window, heads tilted.

"I'll try it tomorrow on the way in. See if I can see," Scott said, and they smiled at each other, sharing the small joke. She threw the old blinds into the dumpster down in the alley.

Theresa found peace in learning about stamps. Which to collect, which ones there were thousands of and therefore almost worthless. She learnt that she was a mediocre collector at best, that others were so obsessive their collections were their lives. Scott wasn't like that. He said he got into stamps because it was quiet and clean, and it was certainly that. Even when they spent the day soaking stamps off envelopes. Scott said, "Of course we don't have to do this; we can get them pre-soaked. But I like doing it. There's something satisfying about the moment the stamp floats to the top."

Theresa agreed. She enjoyed being around a man who lacked aggression and was devoted to his job. His attention to detail made her think of her dad and his jams.

They played music in the background, though not the kind of music her mother liked, she was relieved to discover. He liked heavy metal, all variations, so sometimes they'd hear a full philharmonic orchestra playing Black Sabbath. It rested her, this music. It had little emotion but a lot of passion. No sadness. It was about power and control and she liked that. It made them laugh to hear classic metal lyrics sung soft and low, like hymns.

They joked about finding the rarest stamps amongst their piles of mostly low value ones. "It's a lucrative business, this one. You have to know what you're looking for, though. Know how to price things. Good to be expert in something, don't you think?" Scott said. He told her about the Z Grill Stamp, with tiny squares to absorb the ink, last one sold for almost a million US Dollars. They laughed at the idea but still, both of them thought it was possible.

"It'd be good not to worry about money," Theresa said, although she didn't care.

"You won't have to while you're here, Therese."

There was a lot of down time. Scott didn't mind if she did other things when it was quiet. She'd read, or research which stamps she could collect to make her money. She and Scott talked, but mostly they worked in companionable silence. Sometimes his face would change; he'd stop, gaze away as if he was alone. His lips would move, his eyelids flutter and she knew he was elsewhere.

She didn't ask him where that was.

Sometimes her fingers stuck out when she was sorting stamps. They'd never be quite straight again, the doctor had told her. Scott didn't say anything. He wore t-shirts to work because he never saw clients face-to-face. Theresa wore client-appropriate clothing for a while. Her matronly, non-threatening office wear, ready to answer a call at any moment. Within a fortnight she was in jeans and a t-shirt too. She called Raul at the refuge, to tell him what she was wearing. Raul used to tease her about her clothes, how she dressed for work like a woman twice her age. But the clients liked it. Trusted it. And Raul? With his baggy pants saggy at the knees, his patchwork vests and his "Homeless kids matter" t-shirt?

"So it sounds like you've settled in okay," Raul said.

"It's okay. Weird being away from you lot, and from the files. But I like it that no one knows me. There are no familiar faces."

"You'll know them all within a month and you'll be bored," he said. "Then you can come back."

"I'm not coming back till you've visited. You have to come and see how fat I'm getting. Work is so easy, and there's no stress. And there's this amazing bakery downstairs, and Courtney's always sending in muffins and biscuits." Courtney had walked in so Theresa said the words loudly to make her smile.

"Hang on, who's Courtney?"

"My aunt. The gorgeous, talented Courtney. Gotta go."

Courtney kissed her cheek. They'd met before, at the office, and

Theresa thought she'd figured Courtney out. Courtney dressed young, as if she was 18, not 48. Wanted to treat Theresa like an equal, a friend. Theresa wondered what her daughter had thought; was she embarrassed, or did she like it?

"Love your shoes," Courtney said, tapping her toe to Theresa's dark green pumps. "Good for dancing. We should go out some time. It'd be fun. Leave old grumble-bum behind," Courtney said, opening her eyes wide. "Sometimes he makes my life a misery."

Theresa didn't think Scott was a grumble-bum. Courtney had no idea how miserable a man could make a woman's life. An angry man. One 'suffused' with anger. Her dad had almost been that way when he saw her injuries, but not quite. Most men don't have it in them. Client E's husband had.

"I used to love to dance."

"What do you mean, used to? You're 24 years old! There's very little 'used to' about you!"

Thinking of dancing was a blank space; *we don't go there*, her mother's voice in her head.

"Don't talk about me!" Scott said. He kissed Courtney. Patted her behind. Their intimacy made Theresa feel pleased for them, but also envious. She thought about the smell of the sand when she was a kid.

Courtney talked a lot, non-stop. *To avoid any chance of questions or real conversation*, Theresa thought. She'd had clients like that, who didn't draw breath in case you asked them something they didn't want to answer. Courtney seemed brittle, full of no-go topics. But there were no ghosts floating around her.

They ate the muffins, Courtney pulling a corner off one and nibbling it. "I'm so fat," she said, although she wasn't. She was far too skinny. She made Theresa think of sticks in a bag.

"I don't get out much, can you tell?" Courtney said, high-pitched, almost hysterical. They laughed together, but Theresa felt like she was encouraging something that shouldn't be encouraged. Scott was busy with paperwork and barely listened.

Courtney stayed for half an hour, and then swept up the crumbs, kissed Scott and said, "It's so stuffy in here I can hardly breathe."

When she left, Scott and Theresa quietly sorted stamps. The silence seemed large between them.

Scott coughed; poured himself some coffee. "She's got a bit of agoraphobia, so she doesn't get out much. Then when she does, sometimes she finds it hard to breathe. You were kind to her," he said. "You're a kind person."

"Aunt Prudence calls me a parasite."

"That old bag? I'm glad she lives away from here."

"I wish. She got here yesterday. She followed me. She follows me everywhere." Theresa pointed through the window; there she was, all in red, standing by the discount shoe table, selling her faulty balloons to children. She had made no attempt to talk to Theresa. Where she slept, how she ate, Theresa didn't know. She found it strangely comforting to know Prudence was out there, but she didn't want to talk to her. She was enjoying her visit to the other world, the place where monsters didn't seem to exist. She liked the simplicity of it. She still received thanks on a daily basis, but it was for finding a rare stamp, or passing the sugar, or allowing someone to go first in the queue. Handing coins to beggars with a smile, not a sneer. Small things that bolstered her and took nothing from her.

"Look at her, with her awful balloons. What do you mean, follows you?"

"She's always hanging around back home. She came to see me in hospital and she was a complete bitch. She called me a parasite. And a monster. She thinks I'm awful."

"You?" Scott laughed. "You're so sweet and kind. Who could possibly think you were awful? She's more than a bit loopy."

Sweet and kind, she thought. Yet there she was with her list of five interventions, and the others, too, the word said here, the recommendation there. None of it she was proud of; none of it she regretted.

"She says to me, 'Each monster only has one way to die,' and she's talking about me! She makes me feel guilty even when I haven't done anything."

"She freaks Courtney out. She lived around here for a while, ages back, and caused shitloads of trouble. Courtney's going to be pissed off she's here. She is crazy."

Theresa didn't wonder then, but she did later: did he mean Courtney or Prudence?

"What sort of trouble?"

"A couple of times Amber ran away to her. Well, I say ran away but it was only an hour or so. She seemed to think Prudence had something we didn't. But she'd discover no, there was nothing." Theresa was startled by the use of his daughter's name. It seemed he was, too. Changing the subject, he held up a stamp. "Hey, look, I think I found a British Guiana 1 cent Magenta. That'll get us a million US."

He had her for a moment; she looked up, eyes wide.

"Sorry. My mistake. It's a fifty-five cent-er from New Zealand. Not from 1856 at all."

"How many of them are there?"

"Only the one found. By a schoolboy! And owned by a murderous billionaire. You see that anything is possible, Therese. Anything at all."

They packed up the office and walked downstairs. Prudence stood in the entrance to their office, pushing her balloons at them.

"Ignore her," Scott said. "She'll go away."

He shielded Theresa with his broad shoulders, as if protecting her from paparazzi. He walked this way until they approached the pub, when he turned with his back to the door. Theresa had noticed him doing this before, and wondered what he was avoiding.

"She's the one who told me you'd been…hurt. Sent me this odd little postcard. Hadn't heard from her for at least two years before that. Might have been three. Strange."

Theresa looked back at Prudence.

"I'll see you tomorrow," he said.

"You and Courtney should come eat at my house. It is your house, after all."

Scott nodded. "Yeah, yeah, good idea, we should. In a while. She's organised all these things for us, I don't know till I get home where we're going, so I'll let you know."

"Dad sent me with some good bottles of wine. He's a bit of an aficianado."

Scott's cheek twitched. "I'll let you know," he said.

She thought perhaps this wasn't the usual way a family behaved. She didn't expect to be an instant close family member, but she thought they might feed her once or twice at least. She should know about Scott and his life, but she knew nothing. Her grandparents had separated early; he'd gone with their mother, Lynda had gone with their father, so they'd each grown up with that pressure, of hating the other parent, that negative noise in their ears.

Her mother had never told funny little stories about things he'd done, or complained about his faults. Lynda tried to pretend he didn't exist. When Theresa asked, Lynda said, "We don't go there." So much the family didn't talk about. Theresa thought this was one reason she listened so well.

Were there secrets? Things her mother thought she shouldn't know, things Scott would rather kept quiet? Theresa knew that most people had a dark side and she liked to know what it was. To be prepared.

She could find out what she needed to about Uncle Scott, if she wanted to. And about her cousin Amber, the unmentionable, the pretend-she-never-lived. If she started to ask questions, to track down the information, she knew she wouldn't be able to stop, though. Still, she called Raul and asked him to look into Scott's background and Courtney's too. Not out of any moral high ground, but because she needed to know who they were. What secrets they held. He knew what to look for.

The next morning, she watched from the office as Prudence sold a balloon to a young boy walking with his dad. The boy looked up at his balloon in wonder. There was something unusual about Prudence's balloons; they seemed to grow and glow. Theresa watched as the boy and his father walked along the street, the boy with his eyes on the balloon, fascinated. He clutched the string, but the balloon came loose from its moorings and floated away.

The boy cried, the father shook his head. *That's what balloons do*, he would say, because Theresa's father had said it to her. *They fly away*. This balloon floated back to Prudence, who reached up and tied it to a new piece of string. There was a smear of grey ash across the bright red of it.

Theresa wanted to shout at her that she was a cheat, that she shouldn't treat children that way, but the father had noticed. This was impressive; so many adults would not have done so.

Prudence offered the boy another balloon; the father shook his head, holding his hand out for the money to be returned. Then, as if that movement had caused something, he clutched his chest and fell to the ground.

Prudence turned to look at Theresa, as if she'd known all along she was being watched. She waved her arm; *come down. Come down.*

Theresa shook her head. Prudence pointed at her again; Theresa said *no*. There were people with phones, calling for help. She wasn't needed.

Prudence nodded. She put her hands together; *Please?* Theresa gave in, walked downstairs.

"You see his ghosts?" Prudence said.

"No, I don't see anything."

"I guess he's okay then. It must be heartburn. They complain a lot, these men."

Nearby Prudence were thin ghosts. They looked tired, and hungry. Theresa thought perhaps these were people who died of hunger on the streets. She reached out to touch Prudence's bony arm.

"Are you eating enough? You have to eat," Theresa said.

"Is that what you see? Those ghosts?" It was as if they spoke to each other every day.

Theresa thought about lying but went for avoidance instead. "A lot of people don't have any ghosts around them at all." She felt stunned that Prudence understood and accepted what she saw.

Prudence gave the boy another balloon. His father rose unsteadily to his feet and was helped by strangers to a nearby seat.

"Not all deaths can be seen. You see the victims. I see the monsters. Your mother...sees the shadow."

"But how do you know who is a monster? Who are you to decide? Like you say to me. Who are you to decide?"

"I don't decide. I see. You don't decide who is a victim, do you? Each monster only has one way to die. There are no rules. You need to know the monster to kill it. One, he sucked words from people as if they belonged to him. Ate words like snacks, crunch crunch salty or sweet, leaving the victims numb-tongued and speechless. He was killed by this." She drew her finger across her throat. "Every killing lays a curse."

The son and his father walked away, the son far more interested in his balloon than in his father.

Prudence was covered head to toe, layers of clothing. Theresa thought, *You must be hot. So much clothing. What scars do you have? Have you sold a kidney? Perhaps you sold your appendix for a meal. What sort of person would buy an appendix?* It was hard to tell where she was from, or what her skin colour once was. Ash covered her face.

"I've seen a lot of monsters," Theresa said. "People are awful."

"You think I don't know that? What do you think I see, sitting on the street like this, invisible? I see more than you do. Then I'm not invisible sometimes and that's worse."

Prudence closed her eyes. Her eyelids fluttered and Theresa thought, *Her life is passing before her.*

Prudence said, "How is your uncle? And your aunt? How are they both?"

"They treat me like a daughter."

"Like a daughter, yes. Like a dear, dead daughter."

"They don't talk about Amber. It's kinda weird. No photos of her, no mention, nothing. I wish someone would tell me. Did you know her?"

"Ah, Amber. Amber. A dear, dear girl." Prudence made an odd rocking movement with her arms, as if she held a baby.

"She was my only cousin. I'd like to know what happened to her."

"They'll tell you when they're ready."

"Scott said you were the one who told him about me. That he invited me here because of you."

She nodded. "I thought it would help you both. All of you. You needed to come. They need help and you are the best monster to help them."

"Help with what? I don't want to help anyone. I'm having a break from helping."

"They'll tell you when they're ready. Soon. Spend your time sorting that place out." Here she gestured up at the office. "Help them to get that in order."

"I am! Have you seen the shit up there?"

"They are distraught with death and changed, but they are not monstrous. Even in their depths. They tried to destroy themselves but not each other or others."

"Neither of them have ghosts hanging around. Not even small ones. I keep expecting to see them dancing around Courtney, at least."

"She likes you. She might be a friend to you. She trusts you. Most women don't."

"It's because of what I see. So many of them are victims and I can't help myself. I don't like to be around victims."

"They are sad people," Prudence said. "They have loved deeply."

Theresa thought of sand, sun, water on her toes, sun hat, lovely warmth, hot, hot sand.

Prudence began packing up her rug, her begging bowl, her shoes. Theresa watched, unwilling to touch any of it.

Scott was deep in a phone conversation, so, as directed by Prudence, Theresa set to work.

She began in the storage room of their small office and she would wonder, later, if Prudence had known that she would find the blood stained newspaper in a pile of recycling there. She would wonder; *how much does she know, and how much does she direct?*

The newspapers were oldish, three or four years, and Theresa looked at each one before she added it to the recycling bin in case it was marked 'keep'. In the middle of the pile she found a dark brown stain covering an issue.

She took the paper to Scott because they were both bored and needed distraction.

"Look at this!" she said. He took the newspaper from her, ran his fingers over the stain. His desk was covered with flowering shrub stamps; some collectors are specific.

"What is it; coffee?" he said.

Most bosses would tell you to get back to work, but Scott was relaxed. He used to be a lawyer. The office they sat in was a full-on, rush-rush, rich-clients, save-the-falsely-accused kind of place. She found it hard to reconcile with his being so placid, so sleepy. She couldn't imagine him rushing anywhere or, to be honest, saving anybody. It took him half an hour to hang his coat and settle into his desk sometimes; he was slow, ponderous, easily distracted and prone to gazing into space. He hadn't brushed his hair that day. She wondered what he would have been like, then. And if she could have worked with him. Because she liked the quiet cocoon of their office.

She'd never asked why it wasn't that kind of office any more.

"I think it's blood," she said. She raised her eyes in a ghoulish way, looking to entertain him. "Maybe someone was murdered."

"Blood?" Scott said as he stood up to take the newspaper from her. He touched the date. "Where did you get this?"

His voice was quiet. He was pale.

"There's a pile of newspapers in the storage room. I guess we haven't cleaned up for a while in there."

He pressed the paper up to his face and Theresa thought, *I'm watching someone lose it, right here.* He dropped the paper. He was crying soundlessly, tears pouring down his face.

"Scott." She did the things you're supposed to do when people are upset. She said, "I can go down and get some brandy from the bottleshop. Is that what you give people?"

He recoiled from her. She thought, *Shit, shit, recovering alcoholic— that's why the booze avoidance.* She made tea instead and as she handed it to him she read the headlines on the front page. *Six Dead in Freak Auto Accident.* And *Government Silent on Fuels Emission Policy.*

"What is it, Scott?"

"My daughter. Your cousin Amber."

She looked at the headlines again. "The car accident?"

"The blood." He said it so quietly she almost asked him to repeat.

The blood. She took the paper from him. It was crumpled now. She touched the bloodstain. She thought, *Oh, shit. Don't tell me she cut her wrists. And here I am blabbing on with murder stories for entertainment. He must hate me. Hate my guts.*

"The store room was where she did it. I guess we never threw out the papers and more were piled on top. We had a lot of people through here afterwards." A familiar look crossed his face. She'd seen it many times since she joined him. He'd lose focus, his mouth would drop, his eyes would look into the middle distance for a moment.

Now she knew it for what it was. Fleeting thoughts of his daughter.

How did I not find this out before I even came here? My bloody mother. I should have asked harder.

But Lynda made Theresa tired. Her defences were impossible to break through. That was why she hadn't questioned more. And perhaps her parents didn't know the details, only that something 'had happened'.

"This is her blood?"

He nodded. Picked up a handful of stamps and began sorting them by colour. Theresa helped.

"Three years ago? How old was she?" Theresa hated herself. Her fingers twitched; she wanted to clip this, add the news to her collection. She had to know, had to ask the questions.

"Sixteen. She did it with a Stanley knife. I found her in there. I had five clients clamouring for me and another eight people on the phone wanting quotes on this, quotes on that. She'd been gone, what, an hour? I thought she was out getting lunch or something. I thought she was reading a book or getting lunch. Then I knew she'd been gone too long, I hung up the phone and called her. And searched the office. Until I found her in the storeroom."

He added a pile of stamps to another pile. "We blame ourselves. Why else would she do it here, for us to find her?"

"Maybe she felt safe that way. Knowing it would be you."

"She must have hated us," Scott said, not listening. "She must have blamed us, done it because of us."

"No," she said. This was a different man, stiffened with grief, nothing but grief and guilt and she wondered if the Uncle Scott she'd come to know was a fake. "I'm sorry. I wish I hadn't shown you the newspaper. Reminded you."

He smiled. Patted her. "I don't need reminding. It's always there. Only time it wasn't there was when we were hammered. We tried to drink ourselves to death. Courtney came close, really close, and that's when we realised we didn't want to die."

"That's good," Theresa said, so very inadequate.

"We were like *Leaving Las Vegas*. You know that book? And there was a movie. A guy who wanted to drink himself to death, keep drinking till he died. Courtney bought nice cupboards to keep our booze in, as if that made it better. Like antique, art deco or whatever. Beautiful furniture full of poison."

Theresa couldn't see any ghosts around his head, and she knew what men who'd died of alcoholism looked like. Skinny. Stick legs.

"How did my mother not tell me, how did we not help you?"

"We've never been close," he said, and there was a world of history in that sentence.

"I lost my boyfriend five years ago. I know how you feel."

Scott smiled at her. "Grief is hard," he said. "Guilt is hard, too."

Theresa understood what he was talking about. She knew what guilt felt like, when the waves quietened.

She understood grief.

"I can't believe we didn't know about this. I feel awful."

"Look, we weren't there for any of your things. It's not that sort of family. Your mum wanted nothing to do with us, and you know, that's fine."

"She was my cousin, though. I would have liked to know her. I don't have any others."

"You would have liked her. She was clever. An artist."

"What did she paint?"

"She did these incredible portraits. If she'd lived she would have been famous."

"Do you have anything I can see?" Theresa started a pile of mauve-flowered stamps.

He shook his head. Tipped out another bag of stamps.

"I think those are mostly deciduous," she said.

"An art collector took all her work before we even came out of shock. Said she was contracted to paint only for him."

"He sounds like a total arsehole," Theresa said, and Scott laughed nervously.

Theresa found another glassine bag of shrubs. They sorted for a while. "Are you sure he was right? That he owned the paintings?"

"We weren't up to any arguments. He didn't come in himself, sent his lawyer, a guy I'd heard of but never dealt with before. He was way out of my league. I was looking after property, a few small claims. Busy enough with it, but I wasn't spending weeks in court. We never wanted that life. We wanted a family. We wanted our daughter to know us both."

He held a stamp up to the light. "We have a couple of sketches she did at school. And pottery and things. That's all. And one she did before…she did it while she was in the storage room."

"I'd like to see it."

He nodded; reached down to the lowest drawer of the desk and pulled out a large client ledger.

The sketch Amber had left behind was disturbing. She'd done it on the back of the ledger, and had run out of space so continued on the inside pages. She drew a sprawling mansion, a house looking almost alive. Faces in the walls, doors and windows in strange places. A nightmare home, a tortured building. In the centre, like a vortex, was a dark hole. A broken doorway or something; it was hard to tell. Theresa thought that hands reached out of this space but she couldn't be sure.

So, so disturbing.

There were thin lines rising from the bottom of the page and from the top and it took Theresa a while to realise they were eyelashes.

They were seeing Amber's vision, her view of this place. As the pages went on, they travelled inside, into the rooms.

"Do you know where this is?" Theresa asked Scott. She handed the ledger back to him, not wanting to look any more.

"I don't think it's a real place. Is it? Her friends probably know but they wouldn't tell us. They might think they're protecting us from something. Or, I don't know, maybe they hate us for letting her down. We haven't seen any of them for ages. We stopped looking for answers because time and time again we had to confront the fact she was dead, that we had failed her and she had killed herself. It was too much for us. But it drew me and Courtney closer together. That doesn't usually happen. That's what people have told us, anyway. Most marriages are destroyed. We're like the poster children for a happy marriage." That twitch in his cheek.

They walked out for sandwiches. "We knew her friends well. We used to have an open house. A hang-out place, I guess. We didn't let them smoke or drink, but they could play music, whatever they wanted. And swear. We didn't care about that. And the girls told Courtney stuff. The boys didn't tell me anything, thank God. I didn't want to know."

"Seems weird, you and Mum being from the same parents," Theresa said. "Mum hated noisy kids in the house."

"I think she might hear more noise than the rest of us do."

"Giselle and I used to roam the neighbourhood. The Crash Sisters, we called ourselves. No, we didn't actually. But we did spend a lot of time out of the house. Crashing at other people's houses."

"We always liked kids in the house. We liked Amber around us, and her friends were fun and smart and didn't seem to mind us. But they don't come around any more. And Courtney..."

He paused. "Courtney. I like people to know about Amber before they meet Courtney. That's why we haven't had you over. And why we haven't been to your house. It's a hard thing to talk about, but I don't want people judging her without knowing what happened."

"I think Courtney's lovely. Even without knowing."

"You are kind. Where did you get it from?"

"Dad."

"Do they get on well, your parents? I remember him as being a quiet man. Understanding."

"I guess they get on well. Mum can be mean. But he seems not to mind."

"Maybe she's scared of what happened to our mum. Dad was awful to her. He didn't understand her at all; you know she was a medium? He thought it was all bullshit. All evidence in her favour, but he didn't want to believe it. Best thing to happen to all of us, them separating. Except it meant Lynda and I don't know each other as well as we could."

"But you still invited me here. You still knew I needed to get away and come here."

"Yeah, I did. Blood ties, Therese. I'm glad you're here. You're helping."

"Except I've made you think of Amber when you didn't want to." She turned away from him, not wanting to see his face.

"No. No. We should think of her sometimes, shouldn't we? It doesn't make sense to pretend she never existed."

"Without her art, maybe that's like a part of her is gone. I can't believe they took it all from you. Do you ever think about it?"

He finished his sandwich, started on cake.

"All the time. She didn't leave a diary, or letters. Her computer's got barely anything on it. We were quite strict about who she contacted online. I wish we had her art. Something to show people, something to keep. We could leave it to an art gallery or something. Courtney's always talking about opening a gallery for upcoming artists. Take the snobbery out of it all. She's obsessed with art. She buys truckloads of it. I have no idea if it's worth anything, but it keeps her occupied. I guess she's trying to replace Amber's stuff. But it just sits in the spare room. We don't even display it."

"Why haven't you tried to find it? Get it back?"

"I don't know. Mostly because I can't face talking to Courtney about it. And this lawyer was very aggressive. He freaked Courtney out. Said something like, 'You don't want to look too closely at what your daughter was painting. You may not like what you see.'"

"What did he mean?"

"I have no idea. I told you, we weren't questioning anything. We were in shock. You know what shock is like. You must have felt it. You must have felt it when...you were attacked."

She didn't want to talk about that, but some moments couldn't be avoided. She knew this. "I guess I was in shock. But mostly I was scared. I don't get scared often, but I was terrified. I had no idea how to save my own life. I didn't think anyone else was going to either."

"Who was he? Someone you knew? Or someone random?"

She told him. As she spoke, she realised she was trying making herself look good, wanting him to like her, good girl, unable to stop herself.

"You're coping so well. Incredibly emotionally stable. I can't tell, looking at you, that anything happened."

"My fingers still hurt, sometimes. But this isn't a tough job!"

"No scars?"

"One on my arm." Sometimes she'd touch it, run her fingers along the smooth surface. "The thing that won't heal, ever, is the fact that my poor client is dead. I remember it every now and then. I didn't save her. I probably helped get her murdered."

"Was she a friend of yours?"

"No, no, not at all. But I'd dealt with her three or four times. I knew her kids. And I do feel responsible. I said I'd help her and I didn't. I hate myself for that."

He shook his head. "I think you helped enough. Her kids are safe, aren't they?"

She nodded.

"No way was her murder your fault, Therese."

"Maybe," she said. The sun went behind a cloud and the office darkened, but neither rose to turn on the light. "I hate him. I hate that I hate him. Does that make sense? I don't like having that in me."

"Where is he now?"

"He's in jail."

"You should go look at him. See how much he's suffering."

"I suppose. But that would be about revenge. The only thing I'm interested in is intervention. Stopping a thing before it happens. And I failed with that." Scott let his mouth hang open, as if unsure what to say.

They stood in silence for a few minutes, until Scott began to awkwardly sift through some bags of stamps. He held one up, flicking at it, and then knocked the rest of the bags off the table.

"We should get them sorted," Theresa said, her gaze fixed on the scattered stamps. "At least get through a couple of orders."

So they sat and worked quietly for a while.

"I wish Courtney was as resilient as you are. I wish she could feel secure again. She's lost a lot of weight in the last three years. She hardly eats. And all that booze, all that poison. You know she mostly wears Amber's clothes? I hate to look at her like that. She likes to be thin so she'll fit into them. So she doesn't eat. If we were any kind of parents, we would have never let her Amber's art go."

"I can find stuff out if you want. You know, about where her art is. And why. Maybe even why she did it."

He was silent. "That's not what nieces do. Uncles are supposed to do things for nieces, not the other way around."

"That's for people who've lived around each other for ever. We haven't had that. We're blood alone, Scott. Not experience. It makes a difference."

"Why don't we see what Courtney thinks? Come for dinner. She's been harassing me to ask you. She says it's been too long, she feels bad. We'll ask her about the artwork then. I warn you though; there'll be a cast of thousands. She always invites half the country."

Theresa called her mother, wanting to tell her about Amber, share the shock, the sadness.

"Oh, that's awful! I had no idea. That poor little girl. She was so sweet when she was a baby. What happened to her, do you think? What went wrong?"

Theresa thought, *Bullshit. She knew this shit and still she sent me into the mess.* "I don't know, Mum. Scott feels so guilty, I can tell. Imagine if your kid killed themselves."

"You would never have done such a thing. We didn't bring you up that way," her mother said, and there was so much wrong with that statement, at so many levels, Theresa was speechless. Her mother didn't seem to notice. She went on, "Maybe you should come back home. They sound as if they are needy and I'm not sure it's your place to fill that need. Why should you? You don't owe them anything. And as usual, people are at you. You shouldn't let them. All those women at you."

Theresa hadn't thought of the office for a couple of days. Now, images of her clients, her women, came into her head.

"We'll see, Mum. I'm going there for dinner on Saturday. Any messages you'd like me to give them? Belated condolences for Amber, anything like that?"

"No. That's all right. I'll call them myself." But they both knew she wouldn't.

"Is there any mail for me?" She was expecting thank you cards from her clients. Birthday cards. She always got those.

"There's nothing we haven't sent on to you. I wish you'd get a forwarding thing at the Post Office."

Theresa hung up, feeling empty. She'd wanted her mother to be as upset as she was about Amber, but there was nothing. She dialled Giselle, who was serving up an elaborate dinner to family and friends.

Giselle sent her a photo of a table laden with food. "Look what we're eating. Your niece has decided she's a baker. Look at the pies!" It was pigeon, and duck, with raisins and macadamia nuts. The pastry looked solid.

"Lucky you," Theresa said. "All I'm eating is grilled gourmet sausages, fresh baguette and a gentle cheese." She felt sad. Was this all they had in common? Food? "Hey, I found out about our cousin Amber. But now's probably not a good time for you."

"No, it's fine. These people bore me shitless. Let me go into the other room."

They talked about Amber and her death for thirty minutes or more, Theresa wishing they were in the same room. Giselle was called away, but before they hung up she said, "I wonder if it was the white nights for her. When you can't sleep at all and all your horrors come to visit you."

"You don't have those sorts of nights."

"Everybody has those sorts of nights."

Saturday evening found Theresa nervously navigating her way to Scott and Courtney's house. She hoped they weren't going to match her up with some poor hapless man. She'd have to be polite to him and he'd realise she wasn't going to sleep with him, and he'd get angry, as they did, and she'd have to talk about Ben, and he wouldn't care and... She hoped there was no hungry single men there.

Their house was lovely; large, but not ostentatious, with a huge native garden surrounding it. At least she could talk about that; perennials and soil condition, she'd ask a question and off they'd go. People who gardened were like that.

Scott greeted her at the door. "Therese! You're late. Everyone's here."

Courtney bounced up, dressed in short shorts and a t-shirt saying, "Call me Princess...or else."

"Theresa! At last! I feel bad it's been so long," Courtney said, the exact words Scott had used. When they were together they sometimes seemed to move as one person.

Does he have a dark side? How does he cope with his crazy wife? She's one of these women who can look 25 from behind if all the skin is covered up, Theresa thought, wishing one of her bitchy workmates was with her so they could whisper this nasty stuff together.

She wanted to turn and leave. The house was full and she didn't want to meet anybody.

Courtney made a fuss about some non-alcoholic grape juice, fussed about pouring it for Scott, too, telling him he was too slow for words. "For you, Theresa? Or are you more a wine kind of girl?"

"I'll take a glass," one man said. He tilted, clearly well into his wine-drinking.

"Take him outside, would you?" Courtney said to the room, and someone did.

"That's Darrell. He's a playwright," Scott told Theresa, and the guests nodded as if this explained something.

Theresa had brought a bottle of Phil's wine but it sat, unopened, on a beautiful red art deco side table. She stared at it, realising how stupid she was. They didn't drink. How much did Scott try to avoid alcohol? She'd bought Zinfandel, a grape Ben used to drink. She thought about the sea, the smell of the sea when she was a child. How the salt would sit in your nostrils, stinging but feeling so fresh and clean.

"Lovely, thanks. The juice." Theresa felt as if she was being tested.

She wandered the house, feeling out of place. The rooms were cold, barren, the walls bare. There was nothing there to indicate Amber's presence. No evidence she had ever lived there.

She caught Courtney looking in the mirror, practising teen-speak/laughter/boredom.

"If you didn't know me you'd say I was how old?"

Theresa took these questions often from her clients and she knew what was needed. "I would have said 25. Only a couple of years older than me, I would have said."

"I knew I liked you," Courtney said, squeezing her. Scott came to stand beside them, smiling.

When she thought people weren't looking, Courtney moved slowly, with her head tilted sideways, a slight wince on her face. Theresa thought she looked as if she had a bad hangover; couldn't eat, bad head, bad memories.

When people were looking, Courtney bounced up and down to the loud music she played. It was an odd movement, as if she was forcing herself to be lively and youthful. She liked the same music as Lynda did; Sol Evictus, a crooning singer. Full of charisma, they said, but Theresa found him and his music dull. She had plenty of friends who loved him as well, but she figured they enjoyed a nostalgia for a place they never knew.

"Mum loves this guy," Theresa told Courtney.

"Oh, I do too. He's so smart."

Scott snorted. "This guy isn't smart! All he can do is sing."

"He is a patron of the arts, don't you know? You always misjudge people, Scott. He is a patron. He shares his money. He's a comfort, so be quiet." She turned the music up louder and two of the women started to dance. Courtney took Theresa's hands and tried to make her sway.

"Courtney, leave her! Dance with me. I'm the one who loves you," Scott said, singing the words.

Theresa hated dancing. She always felt ungainly. Wrong. And dancing to Sol Evictus felt like an old person thing to do, although there were guests her own age enjoying the music. She found an odd languidness about it, not the passion that often shows in intimate dancing. Finally Courtney stopped to rest.

"It's a stunning house," Theresa said, feeling nervous, tongue-tied.

"We had a mansion at one stage, didn't we?" Courtney said, as if it was a happy reminiscence. "We were going to have a dozen kids or more. But it wasn't to be. We were judged and found wanting." Loudly, over the top of the music.

"No!" Scott said. "That's not it. Not judgement. Biology."

"Biology!" she said quietly. "Did you ever notice that the more precious the child, the more careful the care? Scott and I could not have been more cautious with her. But we had to let her have friends. Everybody said so."

Theresa started to ask about these friends, but the other guests filled in the empty space. Noise and nonsense.

Later, the man who'd been introduced to her as a playwright said, "We don't talk about Amber. One mention of her name and it all falls to pieces. You don't want to see that." It seemed he'd sobered up in the cold, or realised that people didn't find him funny.

"But this isn't real, then. How can we pretend?"

"She thinks of Amber every minute. We try to give her some respite from it. That's why we're all here. Keep the noise going, the clutter. They're private people, your aunt and uncle, but they do like to have their friends around. Come and see what's for dessert," the man said, as if she could be distracted, like a child, or like Courtney. He was older than her and smelt expensive.

Part way through dessert, Courtney screamed and pointed; Prudence stood at the window, staring in.

"Get that woman away from me and keep her away from me. Please, Scott."

"I'll move her on. Ask her to leave."

"Don't ask! Tell! Order!"

"I'll talk to her," Theresa said. Outside, she called Prudence away from the window.

"I'm glad you're with family. That's who you should be with," Prudence said, looking at her happily. "This is how it should be."

"Maybe so. But Prudence, they don't want you here. You hurt them. You can't be around here. You're not wanted."

Prudence lifted her shoulders up to her ears, a defensive reaction. There were tear streaks on the ash on her face.

"I don't meant to be harsh, but I don't think you'll accept it any other way. You were the one who let Amber run away to you. You are the one they blame for that."

"I'm a lonely woman." Her skin seemed even redder. "Who am I to turn away company?"

"It's not company if it's someone else's child."

The corners of Prudence's eyes filled with a clear, reddish liquid and she squeezed them shut.

"I'll listen to you, I will. Today I will listen to you because you listen to me."

Theresa said, "Wait here," and she collected a paper plate full of food.

Prudence took it with pleasure. "It will feel like I'm eating with the family," she said, her voice soft and child-like.

Theresa went inside. "It's okay, I killed her, cut up her body and fed her to the dogs."

Scott laughed. "Don't worry, Courtney. Theresa has a macabre sense of humour Seriously macabre."

"I am. I can tell you jokes about Near Death Experiences, Last Rites, Last breaths…"

"Did you have enough to eat, Therese? You should eat more," Scott said. He gave her a quick shake of the head; she wasn't to talk about the truly macabre or the things their family could do.

"We're all stuffed to the gills," the playwright said. He closed in on Theresa, causing her to back up to the bare walls. He leaned over her, his broad hand above her head.

"Piss off, Darrell," Scott said.

"Yes, Darrell, piss off," Theresa said. She twisted to get away from him, leaving him standing foolishly leaning on the wall. Even if she were blind drunk she'd have nothing to do with him.

Darrell pursed his lips, annoyed.

Her hair caught in a picture hook and she turned to untangle it.

There were hooks in many places. Were they waiting for Amber's art, or did they take down their paintings so they wouldn't think of her?

Theresa made a questioning face at Scott.

Courtney stepped in. "Oh, I know, bloody ridiculous, isn't it? Here we are, millions of dollars of art, original. All of it in storage. We discovered a few people before they were discovered. I was always good at that. And my grandmother left me some pieces; there's a Pro Hart, some others. There's one worth twenty or thirty grand, at least. But…I like the bare walls." Courtney's voice squeaked like a teenager's. "I like art. But it makes me sad, now. You know?"

"I know. Did Uncle Scott talk to you? About the art?" She didn't want to be the first to say Amber's name.

"Amber's art. Yes. She had such a sense of humour, did you know that? Every picture had a joke. The ones she did at school. Most of the little jokes were meant for us, I always thought, messages of love. But she wasn't very good. Not all that talented."

Courtney's hand made a movement to her mouth and Theresa thought she imagined a drink there. She thought they would have been awful to know as alcoholics.

Scott put his arm around Courtney, concerned, Theresa thought. Always aware of how Courtney was feeling.

"Would you like me to find her pictures? See if I can get at least some of them back for you? I've done stuff like this in the past. Tracked people down and that. It's not hard."

"If Scott thinks you should." Courtney reached out and touched Theresa's shoulder. Her voice lowered as she spoke; she sounded like a woman. A mother. "I wish you two could have met. Why do families hurt each other so?"

Theresa thought her aunt and uncle both looked fragile, on the edge of something. She knew the look of it from her own face. They tucked into each other and Theresa backed away, desperate for a glass of wine. There was a slight shimmer to the air about them, as if merely talking brought the ghosts forward. None were clear, though.

The playwright said to Theresa, "I can already see it on the stage, can't you? I'll tell you. I'll tell you a story. About the lovely, lovely people who turned ugly. They couldn't handle the booze. Some can't. Some..." He lifted his glass. "Some, it improves vastly. They didn't eat a proper meal for months at a time. They became unwell."

She poured herself a glass of wine and swallowed it quickly, and then another.

Telling the story, he sounded fatherly; she wanted to lie down on the couch and fall asleep. He leaned into her, thinking himself sexy, young. She wanted to know about her aunt and uncle, things they wouldn't tell her themselves.

"They look well now," she said.

"Now. Then, they didn't want to eat. They went out to the pub at 5 or 6, or 4 in the afternoon. They drank. They bought potato chips, or cheese twists. They maybe ate a pub steak if someone bought it for them. They. They. There is no 'I" with Scott and Courtney. They are the grieving parents, always together, clinging to each other. Flesh appearing merged. 'How are you?' people said, looking at their feet. Not wanting an answer. They avoided friends and family for a long time. Too many reminders, a graduation comes, a daughter is caught smoking, a son passes his driving test. Amber won't. Will never do those things.

"Mostly they made new, momentary friends. They travelled to different bars each night so every night they could be strangers.

"The younger drinkers were impressed by their stamina. Sometimes, though, often, as the night closed in and booze brought truth, one of their new friends would say, 'I hope like fuck I'm not still a pisshead at your age.'

"The response was always another round.

"They never drove. Much as they wanted to die, they didn't want to take anyone with them. They had enough guilt.

"What stopped them from destroying themselves? Who knows. Maybe a trip to the doctor. 'At this rate you'll be dead in five years.' 'That's too long,' they would have said.

"They never seriously contemplated suicide or an overdose. This way, boozing themselves to death, they could claim no responsibility.

"He found her crying in the back yard. A pool of vomit at her feet. She was so pale. Her clothes hung off her. He said, 'If you're crying, you need a drink. You're feeling. You don't want to feel.' She says, 'I think I do, though. I don't think I want to do this anymore. I haven't for a while.' He says, 'Why keep going, then?' She says, 'For you. Because you want to.' He says, 'But I don't either. I feel as if I'm full of poison and I'm tired of it.'

"The booze tasted like poison. They drank so much. Irreversible damage. But from that day they've never touched another drop." The playwright swallowed, spittle and wine. His eyes had glazed over as he spoke, as if he was transported. He leaned closer to her, his grey, spit-flecked lips pursed.

"Of course I can't use a word of it. It's my own, secret Broadway hit."

She saw no ghosts near him, which surprised her. Perhaps his drinking was occasional, or contrived.

"Thanks for sharing," she said. "That is good to know."

"Always at your service, always, my dear," he said. He gave Theresa his card, a soft-edged, plain piece of cardboard. "We should keep in touch. You have a touch of the poet about you; I can sense it."

"I really don't!" she said, laughing.

She watched Scott across the room; he laughed as if carefree. Their helplessness and desperation, their love. She would never have love like that, not now. She thought of the smell of sand when she was a child. How it felt between her toes, and if she didn't wash it all off and shoved her feet into her shoes, how the sand would scratch and irritate all the way home.

Theresa wondered how Scott stayed patient throughout it, how he didn't take his grief out on Courtney or those around him. He must have been tempted to lose it, yet he didn't.

A conga line formed, with Courtney at the centre, screaming with laughter until she wasn't. Scott moved people out quickly. This was clearly not the first sudden ending to a party. Everyone was sent home; Courtney was tired.

"We don't like visitors overnight," she said. "I hear the noises and I think that Amber is back, even when I know she's not."

She stumbled upstairs, her toes dragging as if she was sleepwalking. Darrell the playwright was driven home with no discussion, another thing that apparently happened often. Scott gave Theresa the ledger with Amber's drawing in it. "Take it home," he said. "I don't even like to look at the book, thinking about what's inside. What was in her head. I can't bear the thought that she was so haunted."

Theresa knew about haunted. She knew about ghosts. Most of the children who came through her workplace carried ghosts with them like the smell of garlic on the fingertips.

"Did she always paint or whatever, draw like this?" Theresa asked Scott, as they stood on the kerb near her car.

"Up until a year or so before she died, it was beautiful stuff. Honest portraits, but she always found something beautiful. Even when she did my bitch mother-in-law. Amber showed her surrounded by pottery mugs she'd made herself. Her cheeks glowing. Holding a cat too tightly; you know that look cats get when they want to get away and you won't let them? Like that. Her art teacher thought she had real talent. You should talk to the art teacher. And Annie. If Annie will talk to you. I'll call her mother."

Annie had been Amber's best friend.

"And the other friends, the ones who don't talk to us anymore."

From upstairs, Courtney shouted down, "Those people are not her friends."

Scott said, "She blames Amber's friends for the suicide. When she's not blaming us. This has brought back a lot. Made her think of things. Like the future, you know? What Amber might have done with art. She wants to pretend Amber had no talent. It makes her not regret things as much."

"You should come with me, to introduce me to the art teacher. And Annie. It'll be weird me just showing up."

"It'll be okay. Less weird than if I go."

"Are you sure about this? Courtney seemed a bit fragile about the idea."

He put his hand on the ledger. "She wants it, but she doesn't want to know about it. So we'll go ahead and she'll pretend it's a nice surprise at the end. I've never shown her this and I don't want to. And listen, don't worry about the money. Money is no object, as they say."

Theresa spent the weekend at home. Early morning walks on the beach before the sand was sullied with footprints.

She had started picking up the rubbish she found on the beach the weekend she moved in. She piled it at the top of a rise, hoping someone would take it away, but now the dune-top had become a rubbish dump with others adding to it. Someone had added a filthy mattress overnight. The sight of it made her angry with human selfishness. She hated the self-absorption she witnessed every day.

She thought about the search for Amber's art. She knew that once she embarked on the search for the missing artwork, things would change. Scott would owe her, rather than the other way around. He would be quieter around her, knowing the things she could do and was willing to do.

She thought about Scott and Courtney and their guilt and loss.

Theresa was filled with gratitude to them for helping her to make the break from her other life. She could mostly forget what she had and hadn't done. Who she'd helped, who she'd helped to die.

She'd do anything to help Scott and Courtney feel better.

Curled up with coffee with her "Suicides" file and the ledger, Theresa found nothing in her files about Amber. Nothing about greedy art collectors, though she'd snipped a couple of clips about thieves dying on the job under suspicious circumstances.

She looked up the case online, unable to restrain her curiosity any more. All she found was *Girl, 16, dies*. No suspicious circumstances.

The long eyelashes Amber had drawn in the ledger looked pearled with tears. Water drops. *Around the edges, on every page, were further water drops, and water swirls, and cascades*, Theresa thought. There seemed to be many rooms, and a long hallway covered with what looked like graffiti; this part was blurred, as if by spilled water. In one room, Amber had drawn clearer graffiti. "Haunted" she wrote, the letters all twisted, faces drawn in the *a, e* and *d*. In one corner of the room, Theresa thought she could see a woman, tied and twisted, her head tilted back so you couldn't see her face, her legs spread, dark shadows wreathing around her, claw-like. The ceiling in the most detailed room was covered with stars. The walls were covered with small paintings of children, babies, animals; all happy, all safe.

On the floor Amber had drawn detritus: a gin bottle, what looked like a CD, a book with the word "Dreams" on it. A wilted daffodil. A rainbow painted on the wall. Below it, the word "Eternity" in beautiful, flowing script. There was a massive anchor in the corner. Ribbons tied around a post. Musical notes, and the song, *Tie a Yellow Ribbon* came into Theresa's head and wouldn't leave for days. A ladybug. A line of ladybugs, wings tucked in. A robin, 'Number 1' written above it. A sparrow. And a dove, flying with an olive twig. Amber had drawn the room four times, each time adding further items. In the fourth drawing were three teenagers amongst these things. One with arms out, bleeding blackly from the veins. One with his eyes bulged, his hand clutching a jar of pills. One swinging from the ceiling light. All three drawn cartoon-like, as if they weren't real. It was one of the most complex works of art Theresa had ever seen.

Theresa hung the newspaper bloodied by Amber on her wall. She'd had it framed; she thought it would inspire her, and there was something about the pattern of the blood that made it beautiful.

Theresa took a while to decide what to wear to visit Annie. Should she look older? Or try to look younger, to match the younger woman? In the end she stuck with jeans and a band t-shirt.

Annie's mother, tall, middle-aged, answered the door. "Scott called and told me you were on your way. How is he? He sounded exactly the same on the phone. You're here to see Annie? She'd love that. Annie? Annie? Someone to see you. A young person!"

There was no answer. The mother's shoulders slumped. "Nobody comes any more and if they do she refuses to see them. She doesn't even spend time on the internet. She cuts pictures out of old magazines until her bedroom is teetering full of clippings. Can I ask you in?" The house seemed unnaturally quiet. Deadened.

Theresa, already desperate to leave, nodded. She sat with the woman, drinking hot brewed tea, eating home made biscuits, and they talked about the Australian Women's Weekly, and shoes. They talked about drinking water. There were unframed sketches stuck to the walls with sticky-tape.

"Is Annie an artist, too? I've heard that Amber was clever."

"Oh, she was. The things that girl did. Annie was always a bit jealous, to be honest. I always say she's talented, but she hasn't done anything since those ones, years ago." She waved her arms at the walls. "It's mostly about patience, isn't it? Persistence. That's what I tell her. Most people who are gifted at something improve at it because they're patient and work hard."

"I think that's true."

The mother put down her cup. "Annie!" she called out. "Annie? I don't think she'll come down today. Was it something in particular?"

"I'm…trying to help my aunt and uncle. Amber's parents. I

don't suppose you know what happened to Amber's pictures?"

"No. Annie doesn't tell me anything any more. The only person she'll talk to is her sister. Sometimes. Maybe you could ask some of the others, from their art class. Annie didn't see much of her school friends once she started art class. I sometimes wonder how those girls are getting along. They don't call anymore. And I don't blame them, I really…" She tidied up the tea things. "If you want to know about her art you could talk to Mrs Cook, the art teacher on the weekends. She might be able to tell you more. She calls every now and then, but Annie doesn't want to see her. I'm not sure she was a very good teacher. But she did seem to love and admire the girls."

"Thanks for the tea," Theresa said, standing. She'd never learnt her mother's skill for extricating herself easily.

"You come back again, won't you? Next time she'll talk to you, I bet. She'll be ready by then. Please come back. And tell Scott and Courtney I'd love to see them. Although they may not want to see me. I feel like a bad friend. I let them down when Amber died. Couldn't face them." The woman hugged her. "Thank you," she said. "Thank you for coming and talking."

Theresa called the art teacher, Mrs Cook, and arranged to meet her and the other students at her studio.

Mrs Cook's fingers were covered with paper cuts, her clothing with clay and paint. Walls and easels covered with brightly coloured slightly surreal paintings. Theresa liked them and said so.

"Very kind. I can tell you're part of Amber's family. She was a kind and talented girl too. The others all thought so. And prolific!"

"I've seen none of it. Her parents don't have her work."

"Oh, but that doesn't make sense!"

"I'm trying to track down where it might be. Who might have it."

"I do know where most of it likely is. She had a patron," Mrs Cook said, her voice sinking even lower.

"A patron?" Theresa asked, wondering why this made the teacher feel guilty.

"He commissioned a lot of her art, and told her he wanted everything. She was flattered. Artists are so desperate for approval. I was right behind it. I supported it all the way. It's an artist's aim to find a mentor." She brushed her hair behind her ears.

"Do you know anything about this man? Or where she worked? Do you think it might have been here?" Theresa showed her the ledger.

The teacher shook her head. "Horrible looking place, isn't it? Amber was a genius at capturing mood. I knew very little of what she was doing. She gave the impression she disliked her benefactor. I told her we can't always be choosy about our mentors. We take the support and inspiration where it comes." The woman shuddered. "I didn't pick her as suicidal, not for a second."

"You can pick some of them?"

"Sometimes. Rarely."

"That's not your fault," Theresa said. "You can't blame yourself for that. Everyone is in control of their own destiny. You can't let it run you." Theresa felt hypocritical saying this, knowing how she had let her client's death affect her.

"I know. I do believe you. I only wish I had advised her more along the way, though. Been more of a mentor. Though I don't know how many an artist needs. Her poor parents. They must feel devastated. And to not have any of her work..."

"What did you think of her parents? Did she get on well with them? With her dad? Did she ever talk much about him? Fights or whatever?"

"You'll have to ask her friends about this when they get here. I do hope they come. They seemed keen. We've talked about Amber very little and I'm not happy about that. I've let them down. I know how devastated they were by her death. I'm not sure what they'll tell you, though. There seems to be a lot of secrets with teenagers. Not that they are really teenagers anymore. But I still think of them that way. They'll be here soon, I hope."

The students arrived; three young women and a young man, all around the age Amber would have been. One was taller than the others, and too skinny. Theresa had a habit of nicknaming people to remember them; this girl she called Lurch. One was dressed all in black with an ugly, amateur rose tattoo on her wrist. Rose. One smelt of cigarettes. *Cancer the Crab*, Theresa thought.

The girls managed to look different from each other but sound and act the same. They laughed at the same things, they used the same words. They reminded Theresa of girls she'd been to school with. The ones who'd called her Saint Theresa.

"There was nothing bad about Amber's parents. Never. And you know which dads are the sleazy ones. He's not sleazy at all. And her mum was always friendly. Bit flaky, but. A bit wishing she was young like us. That kind of thing. A lot of mums do that but she believed it more than others do. Amber didn't know how lucky she was. Well, she saw what the other parents were like, like my bitch mother, so maybe she did know. But if she did, why kill herself? That's what I don't understand," Rose said.

"Who can understand Amber? She had a secret life her family never knew about. We didn't, either. One of those kinds of girls. You know them. All sweet and innocent and that but lots of secrets." Crab, who kept going out to stand on the kerb for another cigarette.

"Like what?"

"Like she had some older boyfriend. We never saw him, but we heard about him. Gave her presents and that. You'd have to ask her real friends. Like Annie. But Annie isn't talking to anybody," Crab said.

"We always thought it would be Annie, if anyone killed themselves. She's the sad one. She got a lot worse once Amber died, too," Rose said. "Did you talk to Annie? We kinda gave up."

"I tried to talk to Annie. She's not doing too well."

They all looked at the floor as if seeking lost coins.

"We thought this boyfriend must have got her into drugs. She always looked tired, didn't she?" Crab said.

"Yeah, and she didn't want much to do with any of us anymore. Who wouldn't? We were the most fun she could ever have. She was always too serious," Lurch said. "Never smiled much. Used to shit me. Here she was, with this rich good family. Here I was with my shitty little box of a house and my shitty useless parents and my shitty useless brother, and I managed to smile."

"You held it all together," Rose said. "Not!"

"Thanks a lot. Thanks a fucking bunch." They all laughed.

Theresa said, "The thing I want to talk to you about is her artwork. Some guy took it all away and I really want to get it back. Her parents need it."

"It sucks that her parents don't have her art. That sucks."

Theresa pulled out the ledger. The three girls looked at it, and then at each other. They sipped their soft drinks, not catching Theresa's eye.

"Does it look familiar at all? Remind you of something?

They all shook their heads, but she could see it did mean something to them. Lurch clenched her eyes shut as if trying not to see, and Crab coughed abruptly, a hacking noise that made them laugh.

"Give it up!" the teacher said. "I've been telling you that for years. You're too talented to kill yourself…"

She stopped, and all of them let the horrified silence sit.

"What about you, Mrs Cook? Do you recognise this place yet?"

The woman took the ledger. Touched the pages. She shook her head. Blinked tears away. "So sad. I can see the symbolism rife throughout. We talked a lot about symbolism, didn't we? All those images of hope. Of peace."

The others nodded.

"It's horrible," the teacher said. "No wonder none of them want to look at it."

Theresa felt queasy from the smell of paint in the room. She wanted to get out of there and they were ready for her to go.

"It's no place," Rose said, her voice tight.

Theresa felt as if she'd done something to offend them. She'd thought art students would be tough to offend.

Theresa thanked them. She told Lurch, "You've got a lot, you know that, don't you? You've got more than you think you have. Use it. Don't waste it like she did."

She couldn't help being Saint Theresa.

The girls sidled towards the door like a puff of smoke. Only the young man in the corner, curled up with a large notebook, didn't seem ready to leave. He'd said nothing. Hadn't even reached for the ledger.

"Tim, we're heading off now," the teacher said. He folded his sketch pad over and tucked his pencils into his pocket.

"Show me," he said.

"Don't, Tim," Crab said from the doorway. The girls hadn't acknowledged his presence until now. "It's not worth it." She sucked on her cigarette, blowing the smoke away from the room.

He looked at her, as if surprised that she'd spoken to him.

He reached out his hand for the ledger.

He looked at the drawing for minutes, tracing his fingers over the lines. His mouth moved as if he was trying to speak but couldn't.

"I don't know it," he said.

"None of us know it," Crab said. She coughed; left.

Theresa thanked Mrs Cook, saying, "Let me know next time you exhibit. And if you can think of her benefactor's name, or how I can discover it, please, call any time."

"Were you close to Amber?" Theresa asked, as she and Tim followed behind.

"You sound like her," he said. "When I closed my eyes in there, I could almost imagine you were her."

"Really?" Theresa hadn't heard that from Scott or Courtney. She wondered if he'd tell her more than the others had, if she could use her voice to convince him to open up.

"Have you got time for a coffee or something?"

"Not now. But how about tomorrow?"

Tim waited at a café, as they'd agreed. She walked in, thanking a young man who held open the door as she entered. Tim read some kind of gaming magazine, holding it with both hands up to his face.

"Sorry I'm late, Tim."

He looked up and nodded. "Coffee? The froth here is good."

"Sure." She sat with him. Once she'd mentioned his name, Scott had told her this young man had been a good friend to Amber, had been a huge help with the funeral. His mother not so much.

They talked for a while about online gaming, pizza and a local gallery. The coffee was too strong for Theresa but he drank it like water.

Finally, she pulled out the sketch. "Have you thought about the drawing?"

He took it. Blinked. "No," he said. But he said it like the others had, as if he knew far more than he was admitting to.

"More coffee?" she said.

"I'm kinda outta money," he said. "Starving artist and all. I'll be rich when I'm dead so that'll make my kids happy. Not that I've got any." She laughed, and he softened, seeing her understand his humour.

"I'll get us the coffees, don't worry," she said.

Once they'd ordered, she handed him a twenty dollar bill. "I'm happy to pay you to spend time with me. I don't want you rushing off anywhere." She thought this way at least it was out in the open. "But I need your help. Scott and Courtney need your help."

They drank coffee in silence for a while, and then talked about the coffee, until Theresa talked a bit about a mythical ex-boyfriend; *weak man*, she said, *weak and I spent six months frustrated with him.*

Guys like Tim liked to hear about how weak other men were. She'd picked him already as the friend, the guy women felt safe with. She thought of Scott calling him 'a dear friend' and wondered how Tim felt about that. She also wondered if Amber had been using him. Teenagers often used a 'nice guy' as a cover for someone unapproved.

She ordered sandwiches too, fat toasted sandwiches full to dripping with ham, cheese and tomato.

He wasn't starving but she could tell he hadn't eaten for a while.

As he wiped his hands, she opened the ledger in front of him. He touched the dark hole Amber had drawn in the centre of the building with one finger and shook his head.

"You sure you haven't seen it?"

He closed his eyes, tilted his head away from her.

"You have seen it."

"No, I haven't seen it." She thought he was lying but didn't call him on it.

"But you know what it is. You recognise it. Don't you? The others knew, but they didn't have the guts to tell me. Fear is a rope around your neck, I reckon."

"It's...this is not something we talk about. Like my mum has a parking spot in town but she won't tell anyone about it because she wants to be able to park there whenever she wants."

"Who's we?"

"Anyone who knows about it."

"So how do I get to know about it?" She shifted her chair so that their arms touched, and she leant so close to him she could smell coffee on his breath. "Please, please talk to me. Scott and Courtney need us to do this. I know you care about them. They care about you."

"They were good to me. They paid for one of my terms at art class. Actually, two terms."

"So please, help me. Help me find this place. I think this drawing is a message to her parents. That she wanted them to know about it."

"Maybe. Nobody would want to know their kid was there, though."

"Is it that bad? What, is it a make-out place, what, teenagers go there to have sex? Amber went there, did she? With a boyfriend she didn't want them to know about?"

He flinched and she thought, *I was right. He's covering up for the boyfriend.* "So she went by herself? What sort of place is it?" she asked, thinking he'd rather talk about that than the boyfriend.

"It's not a place for old people. It's a place for kids."

They drank more coffee. He'd opened his eyes momentarily; now he shut them again.

"So what sort of place is it, then?"

He shook his head. Theresa felt like punching him, throwing him to the ground—she knew she could—and hitting him around the face until he answered her.

"Tim," she said. She put her hand on his and squeezed.

"It's not something you can unknow. Once you know it. You can never unknow it. You don't want it in your head. It's like…it's physical. It will be a physical presence in your head."

"I've seen a lot of bad stuff, Tim. I was a kind of social worker.

I've seen bad things and there's no big lump in my head. I had an x-ray last week." She smiled.

"How often a day do you think about killing yourself?"

That surprised her. "I don't."

"Not even at 3am when you haven't slept?" he asked.

"Not then. My sister calls those white nights."

He smiled; he knew what she meant.

"Okay, what about this: Do you think sunlight means safety?" he asked her. She held her hand out to a ray coming in through the window.

"Depends on who you're talking to. Or where you are. Or what you are. Why do you ask?"

"Because it's lit with solar power. Lights are always burning. But that doesn't mean it's safe."

"What's not safe?" She held up the ledger. "This place?"

"Don't tell the girls I told you. Promise."

"I won't tell. What is this place?"

"That's The Falls," he said. His voice cracked on the last word.

She turned the ledger back towards her and looked at it. "I can't see any waterfall. Only what she's drawn in the margin."

He didn't answer her. She realised that she was breathing faster, matching his. There was a sense of panic about him.

"The building. We call it the Grief Hole. It's Paradise Falls. Some people call it The Falls."

"The Grief Hole?"

"That's what Amber and I called it. That's what it is. It's like the hole that you fall into and you can't get out again. It sucks away all your good stuff. We only went there because Mrs Cook said we should experience life."

She touched his hand when he paused. This kind of man wanted to be liked. They were needy for attention. They had low self-esteem and needed less flattery, were easily manipulated. Especially those who wanted what was beyond them, and she wondered if that was the case with Tim.

They were good men, usually. Kind men, with good intentions. All they needed was some ego-boosting.

"It's a suicide place. They crawl through the hole and they kill themselves." He ducked his head as if ashamed.

"A place where kids kill themselves? And Amber went there?"

He nodded.

"But she didn't kill herself there. What made her change her mind? And why did she draw this picture."

He scratched at his jaw. "She sketched there," he said, his voice tight and strange. "For that benefactor person. She sketched the faces of teenagers about to kill themselves."

"You're kidding. That's sick." Theresa had thought she was beyond horror at human behaviour. She'd been submerged in it, surrounded by it, and risen above it, day by day, in her job. The contrast of THEM making her feel like a better person. She'd seen or heard the worst of it, the lowest. They'd share stories in the office, about the baby battered beyond recognition and put into a backpack for disposal. Left in a school ground, for children to find.

Prisons were full of these monsters.

But to ask a young girl to draw the faces of suicidal teens? That was something new. "Why would she do it? He must have paid well."

"He did. But he also told her what he'd do if she didn't do it. To her parents."

"She loved her parents?"

"She did."

"Why force her to do it? Why not find someone happy to do it?"

"She had a special gift. Like a different kind of gift than other artists."

"That's what her dad says. I wasn't sure if it was just dad-talk."

She felt a sudden craving for her own dad's jam, on toast, with him sitting there, engrossed in the morning paper folded and leaning against the sugar bowl.

Tim shook his head. "No. She was a genius."

"So you never told her parents about the Grief Hole? Or about the benefactor?"

"I think we thought they'd feel bad. To know that she knew this man. He's…powerful. I wouldn't want them to know she had anything to do with him. If I was a dad and my girl even breathed the same air as a man as sick as him, I'd want to kill myself."

Shadows drew around him; his ghosts, rising and falling. Holding their arms out to welcome him, blood dripping from wrists. So he was serious; it was something he'd thought about.

"Not him? Not kill the man?"

"He can't be killed. That's what she used to say. It was creepy."

"Every man can be killed. So who is he?"

"She never told us."

"Seriously? That seems weird."

"She never wanted any of us to meet him. Or even hear his name. What I said to you, she said to us; you can't unhear it."

She leaned closer to him. He was the sort of guy easily played by anyone with a vagina. Very led by hormonal scent.

His mouth opened slightly, and he closed his eyes, leaning in.

"Can you show me this place? Paradise Falls?"

"No one's supposed to see it and live."

Theresa almost said, "Amber did," but realised that wasn't true. "I'm looking for clues, Tim. Her parents want to know why."

"We're not even supposed to talk about it."

"I'm not as old as you think I am. I'm 24. Not that old! I seem older because I've had to look after myself. It's been lonely, Tim."

Tim gave her a sidelong, curious look.

"That's why I want to help Amber's parents. I get loneliness. She was my cousin, you know? I want to track this down for them. If you show me the Grief Hole, maybe there'll be hints as to who the art collector is."

She couldn't understand why this wasn't in the news. Why hadn't she heard of it? Perhaps the media and the police had joined to keep the secret.

But Tim said, "For some of them, it's like they vanish. Like they never existed. They go in there, and they don't come out. Or they get carried out when no one can see them. And people look for a while but not there, and then they're forgotten."

She ordered more coffee and two massive apricot muffins. She didn't want to wait for another day, knowing that he was almost convinced and if she let him off the hook now, he'd talk to his friends and change his mind.

"You have to take me there. Or at least tell me where it is."

"If you get close, you get sucked in and I don't want to."

He finished his coffee. Slowly, without real appetite, Theresa ate her muffin.

"Tim, you are not the type to kill yourself. I can tell that by talking to you. You're looking forward to the future too much. You're an artist. You want to see what happens next. You're strong."

"Do you think so?"

"Only you can really know, but I don't think you're risking your life by coming with me. You're stronger than that. Please. Come on. Please. For Amber. If you were her friend, you owe it to her."

He blinked at her. "Do you think so?"

She did; she wouldn't lie to convince him to go with her. She wasn't a monster, regardless of what Prudence said.

He stood up, grabbing the last of her muffin. "All right, let's go then. We can drive to a few blocks away and I'll wait in the car. Okay? I don't want to get close."

They stood at the counter while she paid.

"So, what do you do?" he said, making conversation to avoid

any chance of having to hand over money, Theresa thought.

"Now? I'm working with my uncle in his stamp business. Back home, I helped with women's housing. You know, for battered women. Help them get away from the arseholes. I help find them places to live."

"Right. Right. And now you're here. Long way from home."

"Hearing about another arsehole."

"All men are arseholes, right?

"Not all men! But a lot are. And a lot of women can't manage those arseholes, so I help."

"Help them get away, and what else?"

"Not much else. There's only so much I can do."

She drove for thirty minutes from the busy, popular area where the café was to an almost hidden suburb. Tim directed her without giving clues where they would end up, and he talked a lot. He was quite entertaining. She wondered if he was trying to distract her, to change her mind.

"You should get a GPS. You'll never get lost," he said.

"Really? What about those guys who ended up in a whole wrong country, following a GPS?"

"Yeah, they were stupid. But I heard that they set up a camping ground in the place they ended up, called it Lost Souls. They're booked out."

He joked with her, made light comments about the things they saw around them.

"Do you always chatter like this?" Theresa said, laughing. "Seriously, you can pause for a minute if you like."

"You have to fill yourself with hope and happiness before you go in there," he said. "Seriously. And if you're not scared, it's because you haven't listened. You don't believe me." He waved his arm in her face. "Park here," he said, pointing to a space in front of a bakery. It sat between a small deli, a newsagent and a fruit shop. She pulled into the parking space ahead of an elderly man, who waved at her in a friendly, accepting way. The pavement was busy with parents and prams, young children in bright clothing, and older people, neatly dressed, chatting with baskets on arms.

"This seems like a safe area," she said. "Are you sure this is it?"

"It's a bit of a walk but we don't want to park close to the place."

"I'm not worried about the car being stolen. No one will pinch this old thing."

"It's not about the car being stolen. It's about the ghosts. The ghosts of suicides sometimes hitch a ride. We might get back to the car and find it full of crazy ghosts," Tim said. He grinned, opened his eyes wide. She wasn't sure if he believed in the ghosts or not, or if he was playing with her.

The thought of ghosts in her car freaked her out. She liked them away from her, attached to other people. She grabbed her backpack and locked the car. "You shouldn't joke about ghosts. They're very real for some people."

"Yeah, I know. I knew one guy..." He looked at her. "Like, for you?"

"I don't want to talk about it. Should we get going?"

"Hang on a tick." Tim ran into the bakery and came out with a meat pie. She stared hard at it until he said, "Oh, sorry, did you want one? I'm not used to having enough money to shout people."

"Yeah, sure. Get me a meat and potato." She was suddenly starving; fear, perhaps. This act seemed so normal it almost shocked her. "Buy a frozen six pack for yourself for later." She gave him another twenty dollars.

She liked being generous, even if it was with Scott's money.

Tim ate his pie in three bites.

"You like to eat, don't you?"

"Yeah, I guess. These are good pies."

"How do you stay so skinny, then?"

"I don't always get pies. Sometimes it's Vegemite in hot water for a couple of days. You know how it is."

But she didn't. She'd never really been poor, not like that. She'd never had to worry about where her next meal was coming from. Even in her first year away from home when she was seventeen, she always knew she could go home and eat. She'd always be fed.

"It's good to be happy," he said. "You need to go there on a full stomach, all satisfied and happy and that."

She saw a hint of ghost in the distance but couldn't get a clear picture. She didn't always, and she thought this meant his death was a long way in the future.

They walked straight for four blocks past increasingly deserted houses. There was no sense of menace, more a sense of decay. Vacancy. Lawns unmowed, windows fixed with masking tape.

There were a couple of people sleeping on the streets here and they made her think of the beggars she used to help on her way to work. The old man in particular. She'd asked her dad to drop some money to him. She felt bad that he was without the meagre bit of income she'd added to his week. She fumbled for coins and handed them out; the people looked stunned.

They turned right. Houses in this street were small and dark.

"You seem to know the way. I thought you said you'd never been here before."

He paused before answering, confirming to Theresa that he was lying. "We all know the way. It's like a popular movie that you never see but you know scene by scene anyway, because people talk about it so much. People talk about how to get to the Grief Hole. You don't want to get lost, once you decide to go."

They turned left. It seemed to darken. She wondered briefly if he was leading her into a trap. That would be too complex, though. Not worth it.

The street was deserted. As if the whole world was empty and they stood alone at the end of civilization .

"Does anyone live around here?"

"They used to. But most moved out once this thing started building." He lifted his arm and pointed, otherwise she would not have recognised it.

It was only three storeys tall which surprised her—in the drawing it had looked enormous. The front doorway was bricked up, as were the lower windows. There was a ladder propped against the front face. Theresa supposed that no one ever thought to take it away. Those who climbed it didn't need to climb back down again. It lead up to the dark hole.

She pulled out the sketch. This was it. That was Paradise Falls.

Along the roof, ornate ironwork hung, looking like frozen water. The walls were blue with swirls of white, an attempt to create a water scene.

"People think this place doesn't exist any more. It's like a ghost building," Tim said.

"It looks abandoned. Newish and abandoned." She took a photo with her phone.

He nodded. "And check it; see how it sucks in the light? The heat and the light?"

She shivered, although she thought his imagination had taken hold of him.

There were two cars parked on the road, a Mitsubishi long-since abandoned, covered with parking tickets, and a new BMW, clean, with no rubbish or leaves built up around the tyres.

Theresa glanced into the windows of the first car. The windows were filthy and inside was a mass of rubbish, many years' worth. One of the windows was open and that, Theresa thought, was where people deposited their crap. The car smelt like an alley corner; beer-piss left to dry on the street.

It was dark in the car, but she thought she saw two or three ghosts, cringing from her. She shuddered. She had only seen attached ghosts before. These ones could catch onto her, creating a death in her she didn't want.

"This car isn't going anywhere," Tim said. "No point those ghosts hitching a ride."

Now it did seem as if the building absorbed the light. *Fanciful*, Theresa thought. But it was definitely darker and colder. Apart from the size, it looked like Amber's drawing; sprawling, clearly abandoned. The dark hole opened half way up the building.

There were dogs in the street, ten, maybe twelve. Snapping, yowling. Tim thrust his hands deep in his pockets.

"Are you scared of dogs? You need to let them know you're in charge." Three thin dogs snarled as Theresa reached down to check their tags.

She loved dogs. She'd done some work after school for a while at the RSPCA, in another lifetime, it seemed. She'd liked it. Helping animals rather than helping humans. Finding the dogs homes. Dogs were loyal.

There were dogs around the base of the ladder. Sad dogs, their heads on their paws. Starving dogs.

"They're waiting for the owners to return."

"Why would they bring their dogs?"

"They say that the dogs guard you, prevent people from stopping you. That you will be able to finish. You know what dogs are like. They'll sit and wait forever if they love their owner."

"Seems hard on the dogs."

"Hard on the teenagers, too."

"But surely the suicides didn't bring their dogs here and abandon them? These dogs must have found their way."

Tim didn't know, and he didn't seem to understand why this worried her. What sort of person leaves a dog like that? She'd known hungry men give half their food to a dog.

"This is a mourning place for them, a place for them to howl."

She thought she should call the RSPCA at least. She felt like crying, seeing these dogs hanging around, waiting for owners who would not return. They didn't deserve to be left like this. Dogs didn't deserve most of what they got.

When she was little, her own dog had bitten a man who, her mother said, would have done nasty things to her. The man had kicked him, kicked the dog so hard his back legs were broken. Her mother had the dog put down, although her father had told Theresa her dog had run away to find an old lady to care for, that dogs were lovely to old ladies.

Tim rocked on his heels.

"I'm going in," she said, wanting to get it over with.

"I'll wait here. Have to make sure you come out again." He smiled weakly.

She knew that all their banter, all the foolish talk, had been about staving off this moment. She realised he was terrified.

"I'll be as quick as I can. Tell me what I'm looking for."

"Amber said the room she painted in had bright green walls or something. She said it was right at the end of a hallway."

Theresa patted the ledger, which was like a map. "I should be able to find it."

"I haven't told you the rules yet."

"Come off it! This sort of place doesn't have rules."

He clutched her arm. "Don't try to save anyone in there or you'll have to take their place. Once a suicide's that far gone, it's too late. If you don't take their place, someone you love will. Whichever one will hurt most."

"Is that why Amber killed herself? Because she convinced some-one not to?"

"I think she looked into those souls and didn't save anyone. I think it was guilt. Or she did save someone, and she had to take their place. Or she fooled us all and was full of dark despair." He let go of her arm, grazing his fingers on her cheek instead. "Look, don't touch anything, okay? And don't push open any doors that are shut. Those are the only rules I know. There are heaps but I don't really know them. You shouldn't even be going in there."

He searched around on the ground, finding a broken piece of glass. "And take this in with you. If you want out, you give yourself a small cut on the finger. Or the arm, or somewhere. Okay? This reminds you that you have a body and that you want to stay in it. This is to get you out again. Some people cut. Some will give themselves a small burn. Something physical, a short shock."

There were swirls around his head, ghosts sniffing him out to see if he suited.

"I'll be fine." Her ghosts were in the distance, waiting suddenly on the street corner.

She shook his hand off her shoulder and started to climb. She felt stiff, out of sorts. Her left arm was not as agile as it once was, and her fingers couldn't grasp the rungs as well as they should. Her right ankle didn't feel as strong as it used to. She cursed the man who'd beaten her and wished him all awful ghosts around his head.

There were marks up the wall. Some initials, some dates, the oldest going back twelve years. There was a smiley face, a rocket, a dog with big ears.

A large hole at the top had been cut through the door.

"HELLO?" she called into the building. Her voice echoed back.

Tim shook the ladder. "Don't shout here. Don't draw attention to yourself. Don't interfere."

His words made her think of her mother. Lynda would laugh at this; she wouldn't believe for an instant that such a place existed.

"Helloo?" she said quietly. Only the echo came back. She was relieved; the idea of making small talk in here was terrifying.

She climbed through. It was very bright, which made the shadows sharp. She stood at the end of a long corridor, wide and airy. She started to head for the stairs she could see at the other end.

There were some doors wide open along one side, leading to small apartments the size of hotel rooms. Some had stone figures in bed, unmoving. There were many closed doors. She saw thin ghosts sliding in and out of one door and she thought, *Is someone starving to death in there?* She didn't think this could be possible.

There was a massive mural running along the full length of one wall. Professionally painted, it was so realistic Theresa reached out and touched one gaunt face, almost expecting it to be warm. It showed a queue of people. Children squatting, adults weeping, waiting. One little girl had torn stripy leggings. One of the women was tall and stooped, as if she was trying to make herself shrink.

At the head of the queue, near the end of the hallway, the artist had painted a man who held out one small apple to the mother at the front. His face looked kindly, hers filled with despair as if she knew that she and her children would be dead before they reached the front of the queue again. He had a sunny aureole painted around his head. He was so much the hero of the picture Theresa took out her phone and snapped a picture of him.

Maybe it's a magic apple. Like the magic pudding. You bite and eat and it's never finished, Theresa thought, but she knew it wasn't.

She thought of Amber's drawing, how she had depicted this wall. Blurry, unclear. As if she had squeezed her eyes closed as she passed it.

At the end of the hallway, a hole had been knocked in the wall. Theresa climbed through it. She walked through rooms and holes until she reached a small, green-painted room, the walls outside covered with names and dates.

As she entered, she felt as though all sound was numbed, as if she sat in the eye of a storm.

It smelled dry and stagnant, like a museum, with an underlying odour of old sweat, or old plastic.

The room was full of the detritus they left behind. Empty water and soft drink bottles, empty wine bottles, empty whiskey and gin bottles. Wallets. Notes. Empty packets of chips. There was evidence of last meals. There were shoes. In her mind she catalogued it, sorted it. *This is where she sat. She sketched here*, Theresa thought.

The music was louder. The room was different to the one in Amber's sketch in small ways; there was no anchor in the corner. No rainbow on the wall. No daffodil. The walls were covered in graffiti, not even 'eternity', or sweet paintings. No ribbons, no egg shapes, no ladybugs. No birds.

There were no dead bodies, either, but she could see remnants of these in stains on the floor, kick marks on the wall, and understood they really had been there.

She could feel a sense of hopelessness in her. She hadn't expected to feel this way so soon.

There was poetry written neatly on the walls. Theresa scrabbled out her notebook and wrote down some of the lines:

> *Still I rise*
> *Up high enough*
> *Until the smell*
> *Of the air*
> *Is pure*

The words made her feel dizzy. She squeezed her eyes shut because the writing didn't look like hers, it looked like Ben's. And it wasn't a notebook she held, it was a paper napkin. He'd scribbled lyrics on a napkin as they sat eating hamburgers—no, it was pasta that time, remember he'd told her not to get the cream sauce, that the tomato was better. Remember how he squeezed her thigh and she'd liked that he knew food and knew that the cream sauce would make her feel ill. Clever man, kind man beach sand water.

She felt it: the napkin between her fingers, could smell the garlic of the bread, hearing the tinny Italian music, the love song playing.

She wished she could hear Ben sing; his voice wasn't good, but she loved it. There was faint music, she was sure, but it wasn't Ben. It was muzak, elevator music, faint but irritating. Also, the sound of running water, and she wondered if there was a tap left on somewhere. She thought she heard footfall. She could smell Ben, the hair product he used. His aftershave. She didn't want to turn and find him. She couldn't bear such a thing, to imagine him there, and then remember him gone.

She tried to smell the sand, the hot sand when she was a child, so hot it burnt your feet but that was good, it was a good thought, but the good thoughts were gone. She felt an attack of memory, of all the things she'd denied. The thought of sand made her think of her cabin by the beach and how much Ben would have loved the place. He would have had the windows open all night, and music on. He'd be tugging at her hand to go down to the sand and he'd pull a surprise bottle of champagne from the boot of the car. He had loved surprising her. She could taste the champagne; she knew what he'd buy. He'd loved expensive food and she smiled, remembering how he'd laugh at her when she bought cheap cheese, how he'd grate it and use it in a pasta sauce, teasing her, feeding her. But he hated the beach, she remembered. Hated it.

She could hear him breathing.

But she stood alone in the room. The debris, the emptiness, the sense of ending.

She heard noises: things dropping, humming.

She wondered if she should sit down for a minute or two, read the lyrics again, listen to the music. She wondered how long Tim would wait for her or if he was already back at her car, shitting on the bonnet, Surprise!! He hated her already, she knew that. Amber would have hated her too. Scott did. Scott thought she was an idiot. He probably talked to her mother and they both couldn't understand how Theresa could be part of the family. Amber would have found her boring, too big, gauche, ugly, uncreative, dull.

She pushed her way to the door, feeling as if she was walking through jelly. Or as if a powerful vacuum stopped her from moving. It was like every sleepless, self-hating night she'd been avoiding in her lifetime had come to haunt her.

Rain, rain, go away.

She HAD had white nights, she realised. Dark hours of self-hatred. But she chose to forget in the waking hours. Because she was pathetic. She ignored everything important, she forgot things. She forgot the truth. And Ben would have left her if he'd lived. She would have tricked him into getting her pregnant and she would have been a terrible mother. And she had failed him, she had not intervened. If she had he would be alive today and he and Client E would have gone off together, they'd be fucking now, right this second, and laughing at her.

She kicked a long knife. If it was sharp it wouldn't actually hurt to cut with it, she was sure. Sun came in through a window at the end of the hall and she could sit there, be warm, and not worry anymore.

It would all be over. She wouldn't feel guilty anymore.

Her phone buzzed. She didn't want to answer it. She didn't think she ever wanted to talk again. But Tim texted her: *Come out. Now. The dogs need you. Come on. The dogs are out here and they need you to come down.*

She shook her head, understanding it was time to leave, surprised at how the feeling had taken her.

The piece of glass in her pocket; she took it out, but didn't feel as if she needed it. She could leave without it; she wanted to leave, and that was important.

And there was a pencil, HB, soft and blunt sitting beside the knife. She put that in her pocket. She could feel bite marks on its tip.

A s she walked back to the entrance, she thought she saw a moving figure up ahead. He climbed down ahead of her and she raced to catch up, sure it was Ben, sure she'd been dreaming that he died and he'd be waiting at the bottom of the ladder for her.

She stuck her head out of the entrance hole to see Tim standing below.

"Oh, fuck," he said. "Oh, fuck. Thank fuck."

She felt both massive disappointment and huge relief to see him. Once she reached the ground, she hugged him and he hugged her back. It was strong, sexual, and she thought for a minute she could drag him into an alley, and…there, right there.

He shivered. When he put his hands over his eyes, she noticed a small white scar on his thumb and this was proof he'd been lying to her.

"You have been in there, haven't you?"

She didn't ask him why he'd lied; she could understand it. She hated the idea of ever talking about that place, of admitting she'd been in there.

"Once. Never again. That place sucks. Literally."

"You didn't think I'd come out."

"I knew you would. But I sent the text just in case. Did you see Amber's room?"

"I think so. It was green. I'm glad you sent the text. It was… hard in there."

He lifted her hands, inspected them. "You didn't need the jolt, though, did you? Didn't need to shock yourself out of there. You're strong."

He held her. Didn't press up against her. She liked that.

He said, "So, did you find what you wanted?"

She leaned against the old Mitsubishi – the BMW was gone. Her legs shook and she wished her car was there. She wasn't sure she could walk.

He glanced up the ladder and she did too; was there a shadow up there? A face?

"Come on. We shouldn't hang around here for long. Dogs. And deals being done."

Suddenly she wanted to get as far away from the place as possible. Vietnam occurred to her. Or Hawaii. She wanted sunlight.

A dog snapped at her and they panicked, running to the end of the street, dogs at their heels too weak to catch them. They stopped at the corner, panting, laughing at themselves.

"Hey!" they heard.

They turned to see a child, maybe fourteen, his hands on his hips, staring at them. "Whydya go in there? Did you take anything? That's mine, what you took."

"I only took a pencil. That's all. Do you want it?"

Theresa guessed this kid was homeless. There were no ghosts about him, though if she squinted in the distance she could see some figures hanging from a tree branch and wondered if they were his.

He took the pencil and examined it. Handed it back. "Nuh. That's junk."

Theresa put the pencil back in her pocket. "Did you see me inside? I thought I heard noises."

"I'm allowed in there. I got called. If you get called you can go in." He put his hand to his stomach and winced slightly.

"Are you okay?" Theresa said. She wanted to flick through her phone, find her local contact, get this kid somewhere to stay. "Would you like something to eat? We're going to a café, aren't we?"

She nodded at Tim. This was good. She needed this boy, after the despair of Paradise Falls. Needed to help.

Tim looked at the boy with suspicion. "Yeah, yeah, we should eat."

They walked the three blocks to the car, the boy following a short distance behind. Theresa felt shaky, unable to talk. The child wasn't talkative either, and Tim seemed nervous, as if he regretted the whole thing.

They argued briefly about where to go. Tim wanted to head for the mall; he craved a greasy hamburger. Theresa hated crowded shopping places; she often couldn't tell ghosts from people, they were so pressed together.

"I can't believe you're hungry, Tim. I don't think I can eat," Theresa said. But even as she spoke, her stomach twinged. She was starving.

"You'll want to eat. I don't know what it is. But I was starving after I came out of that place."

"I'm always starved," the boy said. "'Specially after being in there."

Ignoring Tim's suggestion, Theresa drove them to Passing Strange, her local café. She wanted somewhere familiar, safe. She wanted to breathe the sea air, to feel it inside her, to remind herself that she was alive.

Sunny, bright, salty food, expensive wine, the sea rolling nearby, the birds. All of this made her feel full of life, clear. It took all sense of despair from her.

They sat at a table and Tim ordered a plate of chips with gravy. The kid—"I'm Andy"—asked for chicken nuggets and tomato sauce.

Theresa looked at the chips, glistening with grease.

"I'll have the salt and pepper prawns, and that spinach and fetta pie."

Sometimes, when the memory was too strong, she needed salt. She'd sniff a seashell if she had to. Because she didn't want to think.

They ordered milkshakes and coffee.

As they waited, the silence became uncomfortable. Andy took a pen out of his pocket and began sketching on the paper menu, tiny faces, miniature houses.

Tim stood up and came back with a bag of doughnuts.

"Did you see who drove away in that car? Was there someone else inside while I was in there?" The idea panicked Theresa.

"They were around the corner. People get drugs and stuff there," Tim said. He ate a doughnut.

Andy took two doughnuts, pushing one into his pocket. "I hate druggies," he said. "My mum's a druggie and it sucks. They should all kill themselves and give me their money."

Tim looked shocked, while Theresa asked, "What would you do with it? If you had lots of money?"

"I'd buy a fancy house with room for all my friends. Only if they're not druggies."

"I bet that car was full of ghosts. I bet they were hanging off each other," Tim said. He drained his coffee and turned his shoulders slightly, as if distancing himself from what Andy had to say.

Andy nodded. "Hitching a ride." He shoved four chicken nuggets in his mouth, and then squeezed another two in.

"Hitch a ride to where?"

"I dunno. Some of them want to get away from where it happened, I guess. They want to forget what they did. Remember it as an accident."

Theresa took a bite of her pie and realised how hungry she was.

"They must feel bad, after," Andy said. "When they think about how much they've hurt people. It sucks, actually."

He ate most of the chips and gravy and Theresa bought him an orange juice. The owner came over with a brown paper bag. "Anyone want this sandwich? Was ordered but never collected." She offered it to Andy.

"What's in it?"

"Roast beef and potato. Gravy."

Andy nodded. Took it casually. Sank his nose into the bag. Sniffed deeply, came up smiling.

This was reality. This was life. Not that filthy dark place of quiet and cold.

Theresa ordered a piece of cheesecake.

Andy slurped the last of his milkshake. "What'd you go in there for, anyway?"

"Why does anyone go in there?"

Andy shrugged. "They go in if they don't want to come out. Some go in 'cos they wanna feel better when they do come out."

"I was looking for something. Maybe something a cousin of mine left behind."

"I can look next time."

"I don't know how you can keep going in there," Tim said.

Andy shrugged again. "Everyone else is too gutless. 'Cos of who you see or whatever. Like this one kid, he saw his grandfather, and if you'd heard the stories about that bastard you'd be shitting yourself. This kid, he was all marked up and shit. I don't care what I see. I score the stuff."

"What sort of stuff do you get?"

"Sometimes I get some really good shit, sometimes it's crap. I look for cameras or whatever. Or drawings or shit like that. I take photos of the wall if someone's drawn on it or written on it."

"Art like this?" She showed him the ledger.

He nodded. "I never knew who painted it or drew it or whatever. They told me if I find art, it's for the boss. Not for me. I know someone who tried to keep one once."

"What happened?"

Andy shook his head. "Dunno. We never saw that dude again. Possible he went home, but he wouldn't. Hey, did you see the rats in there? They totally went wild when they started clearing the land to build. All the ones who used to live in the wastelands, and the fall-down homes. Once they got flattened, the rats took over the other houses. It was totally freaky, I heard.

"Sometimes it's poison but they told me not to touch that. Sometimes it's a body and you can take what you want from it." He gave her a sidelong glance and she wondered if he was making that part up to impress her.

"Have you ever touched one? A body? And what happens to them? Do the police come or whatever?"

"Dunno. They're gone next time I go back. Like, disappeared. Someone always comes in and cleans the place up. It's prolly not the cops. They hate this shit. Scares the shit out of them. That's why the dealers like it."

He rubbed at his nose. "The dude doesn't care about anything but the art, anyway. I get to keep the rest."

"The dude?" Theresà tried to stay relaxed. This was the information she needed. "Have you met him?"

"No one's met him. Not even me. But I know what he looks like. And you do, too. He's the old bastard handing out apples in that mural."

"He was creepy," Theresa said, glad she'd taken a photo. She showed it to both of them.

"Is it a Saint? It looks like Saint Jude," Tim said. "Patron Saint of the Hopeless Case. I had a teacher at school who used to tell me he was my saint."

"Nice teacher."

"He was charming. It could be him, with the sun all coming out of his head like that. He's the patron saint of despair as well, so that would fit."

"Patron Saint my arse," the café owner said. "That's Sol Evictus! How do you not recognise him? Here, I'll chuck some music on for you."

Soft sounds came from the speakers; it sounded like Mozart. It was peaceful and for a moment Theresa could pretend that all was ordinary and all she had to do was go home and worry about what to eat that night.

She tapped in *Sol Evictus* and *Collector* to her phone and came up with a result. "He does collect art. It could be him. What do you think?"

"I dunno," Andy said. "He doesn't care about what I draw, that's for sure." He stood up. She wanted to ask him a dozen questions but she couldn't keep him there. He tipped the sugar packets from the bowl into his coat pocket. "I gotta go."

"Tim, give him one of your sketchbooks. I'll get another one for you." She jangled her keys. "I can drive you somewhere, Andy. I can find you somewhere to stay."

Andy looked at Theresa as if she was an idiot. "Yeah, nah," he said.

"Where can I find you if I need help?"

"Dunno. I move around heaps." And he was gone.

Theresa sighed; she felt as if her soul was released in that sigh. She and Tim drank coffee. He watched her carefully.

"I'm okay, Tim. It was weird in there, though. I've never felt like that before. I had no idea."

"Some people feel like that a lot. They don't even need to go into that place."

She folded napkins. Kept her eyes downcast.

"I told you it's like a living, breathing thing in there."

"I get it. I don't want to go back in there either. I don't want to see that again."

"What did you see?"

"I felt like Ben was there. My fiancé. Ex. Late. Fiancé."

"Like a ghost? Is that the ghost you were talking about?"

She shook her head; she hated this moment. "No. I see the ghosts of people who've died in the same way. They hang around, waiting. They get closer when death is closer and they go away when death is a long way in the future."

Tim shivered. "Jesus, that's awful."

"It's not the best. A lot of people have them hanging around. I see a lot of beaten women, but I also see car accident victims. Stroke victims. I've seen burnt up ghosts, wet ghosts. Mashed ghosts. I saw a ghost with a stick through his eye, floating on his back after…someone I loved."

"Oh…did he die? That person?"

"He died."

"Oh."

He looked over his own shoulder. She knew what was coming; hated the inevitable question. *What are my ghosts doing?*

"Who did you see in there, Tim?"

He shook his head. "No one. I didn't see anyone. That's the thing. If you don't see someone, you're supposed to stay there."

"Another rule."

"It's the truth."

"Truth. What about Sol Evictus, ey? That'd be a shocker."

"Jesus Christ, Sol Evictus. My mum loves him," Tim said. "And the art girls. And half my mates."

"Whose mum doesn't? I need to contact Sol Evictus, make sure he's the one who has the art. I'm sure when I explain about Amber and her parents, he'll give it back. Easy."

"This is the man who we think commissioned this nasty shit in the first place, don't forget. He was the one who asked for it. Why would he give it back?"

"Maybe he didn't know where it came from. Who knows? Let's wait till I meet him before judging him."

"How do you think you're going to meet him? He's famous, don't forget. People want to meet him all the time and he tells them to fuck off."

"He says fuck off?" Theresa said, smiling.

"Well, maybe not like that. But he has people around him, I bet, who stop people like you getting near him."

"Maybe I'll be a different person, then. Not 'like me'."

"I don't think it matters who you are, Theresa. He doesn't deal with fans."

"I'm not a fan. I'll think about the collecting part of him rather than the singing part. Courtney and Scott are tapped into the art world. We can try to figure out what he wants and get to him that way."

Tim rubbed at her cheek. "Dirty spot," he said. It was almost nice, being touched like that, but she'd stop him if he went any further.

They sat for longer, talking and by turns silent. The owner didn't care. She was a poet, who sold chapbooks along with coffee and cake and used her customers as material.

"I'm going to let the police know."

"You shouldn't. It'll come back on you. And they don't care."

"Still."

So she made a call, and Tim was right: "Were there any deceased?" the polite policeman said.

"No, but…clearly there have been."

"Thank you for your report. We'll put it on record."

"I told you," Tim said as she hung up, without much apparent pleasure. He closed his eyes. "I wish she hadn't done it."

"Amber?"

"Yeah. Why didn't she talk to us? Why didn't she ask for help or something? Why didn't we stop her?"

"You didn't know where she was at. No one knew, not even her parents. You know you can't blame yourself." Theresa said this a lot to clients, even though half the time she thought they should blame themselves.

A balloon floated up towards them. Then another. The café owner's fingers flickered. *She wants to write it down. The words are already forming*, Theresa thought.

Prudence crouched in the sand when Theresa and Tim looked over.

"That's not a good place, where you went," Prudence called up. "You stupid girl."

Tim made a face, wrinkled his nose. He leaned his head on Theresa's shoulder; she moved slowly away. "Come on, I'll give you a lift home."

She knew that later, when she was alone, the sadness of the almost-Ben would take her. She'd pull out his t shirt, fold it into her pillow and sleep that way, with his smell in her dreams.

Theresa picked up a newspaper to take home. She was in the mood to add to her atrocities files.

She was exhausted when she reached home, and the idea of telling Scott what she'd seen filled her with such deep weariness she decided it could wait until they were in the office.

Theresa sat on her balcony, allowing the comfort of the ocean to reach her.

She thought about the possibilities ahead, and what she might be losing by proceeding. It meant she gave up the idea of stamp sorting and moved back to the idea of hunting arseholes. She missed hunting arseholes. She wished she'd started younger. When she was nine. She wished she'd started with the man next door, Mr Ellis.

Mrs Ellis carried the first ghosts Theresa saw. Theresa was home sick from school, enjoying her day, when she and her mother heard, "Lynda! Are you there?" Mrs Ellis calling over the fence that divided their houses, knowing full well Lynda was there, hanging out the washing. Theresa brushed her hair in the sun.

"Look at that golden thread," Mrs Ellis said. She'd climbed up on a box so she could look over. "Such beautiful hair, Theresa. Such a beautiful little girl. Charmed life for you. You'll never have to work if you play your cards right." She laughed, then winced, and then smiled. Theresa thought there was a mist around her head but it wasn't cold.

"Of course she'll work, " Lynda said. "Why wouldn't she? She's smart and talented and the world needs her."

"But she won't HAVE to, is what I'm saying."

Mrs Ellis had worked for five years as a receptionist before she met Mr Ellis.

"My job is my family and the house," she often said proudly.

Lynda once responded, "Most of us manage family, house and a career."

Mrs Ellis had looked pointedly at Lynda's kitchen. Full of quick fix meals and grubby around the handles. "Yes, but I'd rather do less but do it well."

She was an irritating woman. Theresa knew her mother's fingers itched to slap sometimes. But Theresa's parents never slapped. Never raised a voice, never kicked, pinched or slyly pushed.

Theresa had felt annoyed with Mrs Ellis too. She was enjoying her day home from school with her mother and this silly woman was ruining it.

Theresa saw that mist around Mrs Ellis was actually women, ghostly women, stoop-shouldered, bandaged, averting their eyes but stroking her shoulders gently.

Mrs Ellis had a lot of make-up on. Theresa's mum sometimes wore a bit, if she was feeling old.

"Time for a break? I could murder a cuppa," Mrs Ellis said.

"We're doing the washing. Lovely day for it." Lynda rolled her eyes at Theresa, who was mesmerised, frozen with horror at ghosts she saw. "I can cliché with the best of them," she whispered.

"Pop over for a cuppa once you're done. I've made a batch of raspberry scones I want to try out on an innocent victim."

"We'll see how we go. Theresa has to tidy her room first, don't you Teese?"

Theresa, horrified, shook her head. But Mrs Ellis understood the need for tidy rooms.

"All the more for me, then! Send Theresa over for a play on Saturday. And din-dins. Jenny is always on at me and I know Theresa likes my cooking." Her head popped down.

"I think she wanted us to visit," Theresa had said, distracting herself from this disturbing possibility.

"I'm sure she did, Teese, but life is too short to visit people simply because they want you to. People are not like the dogs you drag home all the time."

"Can we get another dog?" Theresa said. Taking any opportunity as she always did.

"One is enough!"

"Why were there women hanging around her head? Floaty and not there."

"If they weren't there, they weren't there," Lynda said.

"No, Mum, they were there but they were ghosts. They looked bashed up and awful." She knew what ghosts were; she loved scary stories.

Her mother stopped hanging out the washing. She sat down next to Theresa. "It's better not to see those things, Theresa. If you try really hard, you never have to see them again. It's not good to see them. It will only make you unhappy."

"Do you see them too?"

"I see something different. I used to. I don't now, because I don't want to. You think of favourite things. Clothes and books, and a musky perfume. Think of those things. It's a choice. You can feel everything with great intensity, or you can see the ghosts. You can't do both. Ghosts numb you. Or it could be your eyes. Maybe we need to get you to the eye doctor."

"No, Mum! I didn't see anything!" Theresa said, cringing from this dreadful suggestion.

Three nights later, Theresa went to dinner at the Ellis' house. Her friend, Jenny Ellis—Jellis, Lynda called her—always did what Theresa said. Jenny's brother Jaimie was older and he made Theresa nervous with the things he said and the way he looked at her. Their little sister Jilly was only four years old and quiet, adoring of Theresa. Theresa preferred going there to visit when Mr Ellis wasn't home because it was quiet and calm and all the kids paid attention to her. When Mr Ellis was there she was too frightened to speak. She wanted Giselle to go with her but Giselle pretended to be asleep.

"Mrs Ellis went away," Mr Ellis told her when he opened the door. "So it's meat pies and chips for dinner. Chocolate icecream for dessert. Why is it the mothers don't like chocolate icecream? It's good for you, isn't it? Go on, tell the truth."

Theresa almost turned and went home again. He was so jovial and welcoming, friendly and wanting to share. It frightened her. It seemed desperate and forced.

Jenny and Jamie sat watching TV. Jenny's face was streaky; she'd been crying. Jilly was curled up between them, pretending to be a cat. Mrs Ellis' ghosts (Theresa thought of them as the beaten women) flew around the room, and she didn't think anyone else could see them, although Mr Ellis ducked without looking up as they flew past.

There were seven or eight distinct faces. They flew at Mr Ellis as if to attack him, but pulled back, unwilling or unable to follow through.

Then the women flew at Theresa, beckoning her. She didn't want to follow, raised her arm to shoo them away. They recoiled like dogs afraid of a big stick. Even Theresa's dog, spoilt and fluffy, would run away when they played cricket. Scared of the bat, although he'd never been hit or even shouted at. Theresa could see marks on their faces, blood patches, limbs swinging at odd angles. Two of the women had blood trickling down the inside of their thighs.

Theresa stood up. "I need to go to the toilet," she said. She squeezed her eyes shut; she tried to think of perfume. Her mother said the ghosts would go away if she wanted them to and she did want that. These women were horrible and she felt so scared her legs shook.

"Thanks for letting us know. Would you like me to alert the newspaper? They might like to send a photographer," Mr Ellis had said.

His son snorted but Jenny said, "Dad!" She blinked at Theresa. "He has no idea."

"Neither does my dad. He brought me home a present the other day. Do you know what it was?"

Jenny shook her head, already laughing. They were used to laughing at their fathers.

"It was a golf book!"

"Speaking of driving, Jaimie, I think it's time you went for driving practice. Off you go. And that's no joke."

"You're supposed to come with me," Jaimie said. He often had a whine in his voice; Theresa would recognise it in men she met in the future. These men responded well to sympathy.

"Girls, you'll be fine on your own for a bit? Look after Jill. Don't let her fall down the stairs."

The girls looked at each other, knowing Mrs Ellis would never leave them on their own. They were only nine.

"Okay," Jenny said.

Jilly wailed and held onto her brother's leg, but Jenny tempted her with a piece of chocolate.

When the car drove away, Theresa said, "Where's your mum?"

Jenny shook her head. "Dad says she went away. But her bedroom door is locked. And as if she'd go away and not take me with her."

The ghosts flew up and down like they were riding waves.

Down the hallway and back, down and back.

"Let's knock on her door," Theresa said. Jenny looked terrified. "We won't go in."

There was no answer, but the ghosts slid under the door and flew back out, like Theresa's dog trying to get her to go for a walk.

Theresa tried the door. "I think it's got the same key as my room," Jenny said.

"Go on, then."

The door opened. The room was in disarray: a spilt glass by the bed; bed clothes in a clump. Drawers open. The smell of vomit.

The smell made them run from the room.

"Mum never has a messy room," Jenny said, and Theresa took her hand and said, "Let's go to my house."

M rs Ellis was never seen again. Theresa told people what she'd seen but she was a child. Invisible. Word was Mrs Ellis had left her husband for another man.

"What other man?" Lynda raged about Mr Ellis. "That bloody pathetic man. Weak, pathetic man."

Theresa wondered what would have happened if they'd visited Mrs Ellis more. If she'd had someone to talk to. Some days Theresa would look over the back fence at the clothes line, always empty. No one to do the washing now; it was all sent out.

It was big news in the neighbourhood. Theresa realised, years later, that Mrs Ellis must have been alive while they ate their meat pies and chips. Locked in the boot of the car, perhaps, but still alive. Because the ghosts were egging Mr Ellis on; *come on! Come on!* Not wanting to let her slip from their grasp.

A s she drove to work on Monday, Theresa kept thinking, *I've seen the place where kids kill themselves. I've been in the Grief Hole;* the echo a part of her. The idea of telling Scott, of him knowing, scared her, but she couldn't hold it back.

She told him everything, including the possibility of a secret boyfriend.

"Well, he's some kind of arsehole if he does exist. He obviously didn't care about her. Didn't care less. He didn't even go to the funeral."

"At least be glad that Amber never knew that."

"So this is where she did those sketches? This place they call Paradise Falls? I used to hear Amber and her friends talking about it, thought it was a club. Or a place, you know, outside. Like an actual waterfall. It sounds so innocent. I always thought it as a good place for her to go. But this…"

"This is awful. It's a terrible place."

"And my little girl went there once."

Theresa shook her head. "It was more than once. I'm sorry. I don't know how many times. But a lot. She was there a lot."

Scott sat, his fists clenched, and tears spilled. He made no sound. Theresa thought, *Men cry so rarely, they forget how to.*

"You shouldn't have gone in there, Theresa."

This was the first time he'd called her by the right name.

"It sounds dangerous, and you don't even know this guy, Tim. I mean, he always seemed okay to me. But why take you to a place like that? I'd never forgive myself if something happened to you. It'll be on me."

"I made him. I wanted to see where she'd created that art. The stuff Sol Evictus took from you."

He sighed, his mouth open. "I don't believe she'd go into a place like that. She was so sensitive when she was a young girl. She'd cry if she saw a bird out of the nest, and we had to take detours on trips so we didn't go near cemeteries. She wouldn't go into a place like that, no matter what Tim says."

But he knew; she could tell that he knew it was the truth.

"It was creepy in there. I'm not usually bothered by things like atmosphere or whatever, but while I was in there I hated myself. Really despised myself. And I don't."

"So what did you see in there?"

She hadn't actually seen anything; she'd imagined Ben. That was all.

"Anything of Amber's?"

"No, I don't think so. Only this pencil." She pulled the HB out of her pocket.

He turned it over in his fingers. "Did she bite her pencils? She used to, when she was a kid. But I don't know. I have no idea if this is hers or not. I should know, shouldn't I? I should have a feeling. I should know. I might not know any of her things if I saw them."

"You shouldn't have to know anything like that. You're not a psychometrist."

"Well, don't go back. I think you've done enough. Where is it, anyway?"

"It looked like it might have been an expensive building once." She described it for Scott, told him where it was.

"I think I remember about that. I thought it'd fallen down. I remember jokes in the paper, you know. Calling it Paradise Fallen. Paradise Falls, your safe haven. Even at the time we all thought it was stupid. They tried to sell it as an exclusive hotel. All solar power. Like the White House. And Skylab. All Feng shui and open living. People joked about building a place like that in a suburb like that. The developers were sure the area was up and coming. They sold it like: *get in early! Before the prices rise!*"

"I haven't looked it up yet. It must have been special when it was first built."

"No one bought any of it. They had squatters right from the start. But even the desperate wouldn't stay there. Even they kept moving out."

"There's no one at all living there now."

"I remember it because, you know, tall poppies and all that. We love to see this kind of thing fail, don't we? But there was a lot of crap in the place, I remember. The water supply. And the area is shit, isn't it? No one wanted to live there. Not even the junkies."

Scott's eyes were wet and his movements slow.

"Scott?" she said.

He lifted his head heavily. "I'm thinking of that place. Of my little girl feeling so sad she had to go there."

"Oh, crap. Oh, crap. No," she said. She covered her face with her hands. "God, I've told it badly. He made her go there. This collector, who I think is Sol Evictus, he wanted her to draw what she saw. She hated it there. I'm pretty sure she hated it. Did she have any cuts on her fingers? Any you noticed? Because that's a sign that even when she was in there, she wanted to leave."

"She always had paper cuts."

"That's good, then. That tells us something. That she didn't want to stay there."

He lowered his head, wiped his eyes; gave a small snarl. "God, this boyfriend, though. Do you think there was one? Why would she go out with such an arsehole? Is that what we taught her? Because a man like Sol Evictus...I don't know about that. It seems impossible. God, how are we going to tell Courtney? She loves that man."

"You're the one who's going to have to tell her. Not me. And she might be kinda happy. It's an excuse to get in touch with him. She'll like that."

Theresa called Raul. She talked about Paradise Falls, and how she hoped she'd never have to go in there again, and about the dogs waiting outside. Sometimes, clients had to abandon a family pet, and the dogs were always the worst. Often, the only home Theresa could find for them wouldn't take animals.

"God, I still cry about that gorgeous big brown bitzer we had to have put down. He was so young and healthy. Remember him?"

"Yeah. I don't know why we couldn't find anyone to take him."

"People are bastards. Selfish bastards." This was not a new conversation but one they both found some comfort in. "Raul, you should come visit. Come see my place. It's so cool, right on the beach. You need a holiday."

"Can you imagine me asking for time off now?"

"Busy?"

"Always. What about the friend, this Annie? She sounds as if she could do with some counselling. Is anyone helping her?"

"Her mum feeds her. Lets her sit in the garden. If you were here we could visit her together. See if we can help."

Raul laughed. "Nice try! If I can wrangle a long weekend, I'll come out. There's nothing on either Scott or Courtney, by the way. Except for a few large donations. They're into childhood disease, as far as I can tell. And repairing eyesight. And there was a big one to cystic fibrosis."

"What about my cousin? She killed herself. Is there nothing there?"

"You didn't ask me to look at your cousin. Do you want me to?"

"See what you can find."

"I will if you'll promise me you'll help Annie if you can."

Annie's mother met her at the door. "She doesn't know you're coming. I don't bother telling her anything anymore. She's decided to waste her life. Waste it away."

The woman was sick of it, it seemed.

"It's all those wasted years; that's what upsets me most. All that careful learning how to cook, the walks, the reading, the friends we made. The boring coffees I shared with boring women so she'd have friends. And how she sits there as if her life was over. She's still at Uni but she's only going through the motions."

"Maybe if she sees me, it might help."

"Maybe. Do your best. Get her off that chair. I'm making apple pie for afternoon tea. I had the urge, had the apples, off I went. I could make scones instead."

"I love apple pie," Theresa said. "And I only like scones with my dad's jam."

"What a clever man he must be."

Annie sat, wrapped in a blanket, in her sunny, flowery backyard. Her long, smooth blonde hair shone. Theresa wondered if her mother washed it for her.

Annie shivered.

"We can't warm her up," her mother said.

Theresa sat beside her for a few minutes, watching her rock slowly from side to side. Then she started to talk. "Y'know, Annie, it was easy getting up the ladder because I didn't know what was coming. You can't be warned about something like that. All those names along the walls, though. All those kids, stopping to sign their names, then climbing inside."

Annie stopped rocking. "What are you talking about?"

"You know what I'm talking about. Paradise Falls. I went there. Tim took me."

"He shouldn't have. He should have asked me. I would have said no. Then he should have said no. This is not for people to know about and he knows it. There's no reward. He'll get nothing."

"Reward? What sort of reward would there be?"

"Rumours went around that if you took people in there, or told them about it, you'd get something back. Money, or whatever. Some kind of good luck. But it never happened."

"Did you ever go there, Annie?"

Annie didn't want to answer. Then, "I went once. It was …cold. Smelt bad, like BO. But I didn't want to leave. It was only Amber dragging me out. And all those dogs…"

"There are still dogs. Breaks your heart."

She thought, *If I go back, I'm poisoning those dogs. Putting them out of their misery. I hate to think of them suffering.*

"You shouldn't go back. You shouldn't have gone at all. It's like a bee-sting if you're allergic. It gets worse each time. And those who don't come out, for some of them, it's like they never existed. People forget they ever lived."

"I probably won't go back. But I can't promise anything." Even saying that, she felt temptation. As awful as it was, as much as she knew whatever form of Ben was there was not real, still she was tempted.

"That's your choice. But if you can avoid the Grief Hole, you should. And if you can't, don't blame me."

Annie sank into herself again, as if she'd had enough.

"I saw something in there. Well, no. I smelt. I heard. I almost tasted."

Annie tilted her head.

"I thought it was Ben. He was my boyfriend. My fiancé. And he's been dead for five years."

"You saw him?"

"Smelt his aftershave. Remembered him like I was watching a movie." Theresa's eyes filled with tears. She wiped them away.

"That's what happens in there. I saw my baby brother. Crawling and crying. Mum thinks I don't remember him but I do. Pretending he doesn't exist doesn't make him vanish."

"I guess it works for some people. Did Amber see anyone, do you know?"

"She was too busy looking at the real people in there. We walked in on this kid. Maybe sixteen. Seventeen. Older than us. He sat in the corner and stared at us till we left. His face—Amber drew it on the wall outside, wanting to remember him. Soon after, she was hired, and making money. Buying the beers and burgers. Her parents never knew. How are they? Still alive? Or crawled into a hole and died?"

"They're better than they were. They feel guilty."

"It wasn't their fault. It was mine. My fault about the Grief Hole."

"It wasn't your responsibility to save her life. You know that. You need to believe that. But, next time? Intervene. Say something. That's my motto."

"There won't be a next time. I don't have any other friends to help." Annie lifted her head, looked at Theresa.

"You need friends of your own age," Theresa said.

"That's what I keep telling her!" her mother said. "Look, I found this picture of you and Amber and Alexis, remember her?" Annie's mother said.

Annie took the picture. "We used to get called Triple A until Alexis moved away. I liked her but she was a bit of a bitch. All this is a long time ago, though." Annie's voice was quiet.

"It's three years."

"You don't think that's a long time?" Annie looked at Theresa in astonishment. "Maybe time passes more quickly as you get old but this photo…This is like another lifetime."

Theresa thought about the years after Ben's death, how each day seemed to take a month. "Help me. You know her parents are good people."

"They used to be good. But they don't give a shit about me."

"I guess you make them think of Amber and they can't stand that," Theresa said, wanting to defend them, provide a reason why they had not kept in contact.

"Yeah. Yeah, I know. But still. It would have been good to have them around, you know? I wanted to comfort them somehow or other. Make them feel better. You know how making someone else feel better makes you feel better? They wouldn't let us do that." She shivered. "I don't think they would like the art."

"You mean the stuff Sol Evictus had her create?" Theresa threw it in, wanting to shock her with the name.

Annie choked, although she had nothing in her mouth. "A fly," she said, "a fly down my throat."

Annie drank a glass of water and another. She closed her eyes, as if wanting to sleep, get away. But the name was like a password; using it opened Annie up.

"You shouldn't talk about him," the girl said, and Theresa realised she was terrified. "You shouldn't say his name unless you love him."

"I'd like to talk to him at least. About the art."

"A lot of it is brilliant. She was so gifted, you hated her for it. But the ones he commissioned…" Annie shivered.

"Sol Evictus?"

Annie nodded. "Those pictures…they were evil before he touched them, but after…"

Theresa knew from past experience there was often more in the pauses between the words. Annie was seeing images she didn't want to see. But Theresa needed her to see them.

"What did he do? Destroy them?"

"He…breathed them. Not the fumes, because they were mostly drawings, not paint. What Amber said was he had her capture the last breath of hope in her drawings, and that's what he sucked up."

The girl exuded a scent, and the smell made Theresa think of Paradise Falls. Like hopelessness, and how destructive a lack of hope is. There were no ghosts around her, though.

Annie shivered again. "I've felt cold since Amber died, but it's getting worse. How do I get warm?"

"You move. You live. You're only going to get colder, sitting there."

"I don't want to move. That's the point. Look at Amber. She got sadder as the time went on and darker and hard to talk to. I used to like being friends with her but she got kind of angry and mean. I didn't know why. I think it was because of me, because I'm so boring and awful to be around. That's what I think."

"You know that's not true," her mother called out, so wearily it made Theresa tired.

"That's not true at all. It wasn't you. It was the Grief Hole. And the paintings he made her do there."

"He's got two collections, Amber used to say. One open to the public, that everyone knows about. And a secret one. With cruel, awful fucking stuff in it. That's where Amber's work is. I reckon he would have fucked her there if she'd let him."

"God, did she?"

"She never told me. Would it have been any worse than what was already happening? Seriously?"

"Didn't her boyfriend do anything?"

"She didn't have a boyfriend. There was only Sol Evictus."

Theresa was ill to the point of vomiting.

Annie put her headphones on and started listening to music. It was loud; *must hurt her eardrums*, Theresa thought.

She left Annie's mother crying, the girl staring blankly away. There were no ghosts around either of them.

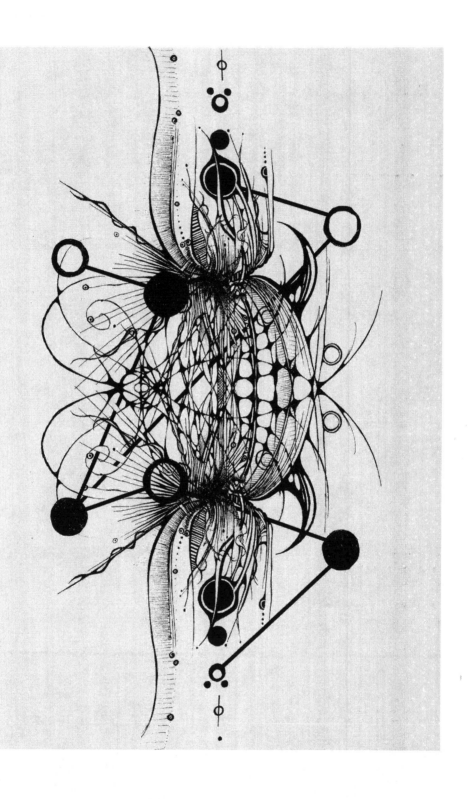

Sol Evictus was playing on the CD player when Theresa went to see Scott and Courtney that night. Up loud, Courtney singing along at the top of her voice. It would have been a coincidence if Courtney hadn't always played his music.

While Scott made coffee, Theresa sat with Courtney and listened, wondering who he really was. His voice was beautiful, there was no doubt about it. And his music was accessible, so someone like Courtney could sing it without feeling as if their voice could shatter concrete.

"You should never forget
What you have done
Or when you remember
You'll remember it wrong"

"Come to the kitchen with me, keep me company while I make dinner," Courtney said. She turned up the music so she could hear it throughout the house.

"Courtney! Do we have to have this shit so loud?" Scott said. It was the first time Theresa had heard him be even remotely negative.

"It's pretty schmaltzy music, you've got to admit!" Theresa said.

Courtney laughed. "Well, who do you like?"

Theresa named some artists; Dixie Chicks and Billy Bragg, people with stories to tell and a world to change. She loved the truth of what they wrote about, the barriers they broke down. No balking with them. They sang about pain and how to deal with it.

"You should listen to something relaxing. It'll make you feel better," Courtney said. She kept talking until Scott said, "Come on, let's eat."

They sat on the veranda, staring out into the gum trees. Sometimes Theresa thought the trees came to life. She thought they had their own ghosts who whispered and called in the night time.

The meal was too salty; a simple pasta sauce Courtney had overseasoned. The taste of it took Theresa to her quiet place, her safe place, her beach memory. She didn't want to go there.

She drank a lot of water.

Courtney talked almost without cease, boring stuff that had Scott surreptitiously flicking through a newspaper and Theresa wanted to throw a bread roll at him to make him stop Courtney's flow of words.

"Would you like any more, Theresa?" Scott asked. He nudged her gently. "Anything else to eat? Drink?"

"No. No. Sorry. I was drifting off."

"She didn't notice," he said quietly. He took Courtney's hand and kissed it.

"Did our playwright friend Darrell ever call you? I think he liked you," Courtney said.

Theresa shook her head. "Not my type. Nice guy for a playwright, but..." She felt frustrated, wanting to get it over with, so she reached over and took Courtney's hand. "I've learnt some things in the last few days. Do you want to hear it?"

"Of course. Of course we do," Courtney said, but Scott's face looked stricken, as if terrified of what she might say.

"Tell it from the start. I've told her some, but she should hear it from you."

"Are you sure?" Theresa said.

"Of course, we need to know," Courtney said, but she stood up and walked to the beautiful red art deco side table where the alcohol used to be kept. As if she thought a ghost of the booze might still be there.

"Not everything if you don't think so," Scott whispered to her. "Whatever you think is good to hear. She knows what I know. I filled her in. It wasn't pretty."

"None of it is good," she whispered back. She felt let down that he asked her to decide what to say. It was weakness on his part.

Courtney came back to them, and Theresa plunged in.

"I saw Annie. She's not too good. She feels as if she's lost you guys as well as everything else."

"She must be so different now. We'd barely know her," Courtney said, as if that excused them from seeing her. "And she must feel so guilty for what she did. Or didn't do. She knows Amber would still be alive if it wasn't for her."

"That's not true," Scott said.

"I think she'll be okay in the long run. I can't see any ghosts over her shoulders so she's not dying soon."

Theresa said this without thinking. She felt comfortable with them; they were family. She forgot they didn't know what she could do.

"Ghosts?" Courtney said. "Do they give you messages from the other side?" She clutched Theresa's arms.

"No. Not like that."

Scott shook his head. "It kinda runs in our family, doesn't it? This idea that we can see ghosts."

"It's not just an idea," Theresa said. She didn't want to talk about it if he wanted to avoid it, but she didn't like being dismissed as 'having ideas'.

"Sorry, didn't mean it that way. I meant the concept. The knowledge."

"I don't usually talk about it. Mum hates to talk about it."

"It's one of the reasons we're not in contact anymore," Scott said. "That denial. I wished I had the skill but she got it and refuses to use it."

"I'm not even sure what hers is. Mine, I can see the ghosts of future death."

They nodded like a mirror image.

"You already knew that?" This surprised her. She wasn't sure she liked them knowing so much about her, and keeping that knowledge a secret from her.

"We knew you could see something. We weren't sure what it was."

"Is that why you got me here? You thought I might be able to see Amber's ghost? I can't. Mum might be able to but she won't."

"We asked you here because we thought it would help you," Scott said, but he looked down. "And...yes. We did think maybe you'd see her. Maybe you could tell us what she looks like now."

Courtney squeezed Theresa's hand. "Where is she? Is she happy? What is she doing? Is she with my grandmother? She'll be okay if she's with Granny. Is she eating well?" Courtney's voice rose to a screech and her fingers dug deep and hard into Theresa's arm. "Where is she? Where is she?"

"She was happy," Theresa said. "Loved." Mollifying words.

Courtney leant into her, calling into her face as if she could contact her dead daughter that way. "Amber? Are you there? Amber?"

Theresa pulled away, backed away to the other side of the room. She leant against the wall. Tears filled her eyes, and she shook.

"Leave it, Courtney. She can't do that. I told you she can't."

"She should be able to, shouldn't she?" Courtney froze in place, staring at Theresa as if seeing her as a real person again. She sat down. "Sorry, sorry. God, sorry for frightening you. I thought I'd be able to talk to her again. Tell her how much I loved her. I'm sorry. I shouldn't have."

"She knew you loved her. Jesus, she knew it, okay?" Scott rubbed his hair. He sighed, a deeply weary sound, as if he'd told her this a thousand times; their daughter knew she was loved.

Theresa sat on the couch, curled her legs up, hugged her knees. She felt useless. Pointless. "I wish I could see her. But all I can see is future death. I can't even save people; I only see it when it's inevitable. I've tried. But I can't do a thing to help anybody, not even you. Sometimes I can intervene to stop something else happening, but I've never really saved anyone."

"You have already helped us and you know it. Not with the ghost thing, but you've found out about Amber, and you're going to tell us about it." Scott spoke quietly and she felt as if he was being kind to her, like an uncle should.

"What about us, then? What do you see?" Courtney said, her voice almost cruel. "How are we going to die?"

"I don't like to tell people that."

"But we might be able to avoid it."

"I don't know. I think once I see it, it's set."

"Tell us," Courtney said. "Please. So we know."

"From what I can see there's nothing around you, Scott. Around you, Courtney, I think they might be people who died of liver damage. But they are faint. And I don't often see them. But your ghosts become clearer when you talk about Amber. Like now."

"Maybe those are the times I'm thinking about drinking. When I'm wishing I was blind drunk and not caring."

Theresa told them all she had learnt about Paradise Falls. About Tim, and about Andy, the street kid.

"Is he okay? That poor kid. Where are his parents? Where did he go? Did you give him money or something, Theresa? You should have brought him here. He could stay till he gets settled."

Scott humphed in surprised. "Courtney, we're not having a strange kid in the house! I'm sure he's okay."

"I offered to find him somewhere to stay but he didn't want that. But he's got ghosts. More than any kid his age should have. He's got so much crap in his life. He knows a lot. He said that this is the collector." She found the mural photo. "Tim thought it was Saint Jude at first."

"His mother is one of the bad Catholics," Courtney said. "She was so awful when Amber died. Lots of stuff about eternal hell. Horrible woman."

"He does look like a saint!" Scott said.

"Show me," Courtney said, and then she squealed. "He is a saint. He gives heaps to charity. And he's a patron of artists. It is Sol Evictus, for sure. He is an art collector. I've got his art catalogues."

"Of course you have," Scott said. He sounded like Theresa's father did sometimes; indulgent. Loving.

She laid out the material on the table.

"Is there anything of Amber's?"

Flicking through the catalogue, Courtney said, "Nothing. He's a good man. He's a poet."

Theresa pulled out her notebook, checking the poem there. "Do these words look familiar?" She showed them the note.

> *Still I rise*
> *Up high enough*
> *Until the smell*
> *Of the air*
> *Is pure*

"Of course. That's one of his songs."

"These lyrics were written on a wall at Paradise Falls."

Music seemed to fill the room.

"Well?" said Courtney. "If it is him, of course he'll give us the art back. Oh, we could invite him over! Why didn't Amber tell me she knew him? She knew how much I adore him. How could she keep him to herself? He would have been very kind to us, I'm sure."

"I don't know about a man who collects this sort of art," Scott said.

Theresa thought of her own choice of art, the bloodied newspaper. She worried they'd see it and what they'd think of her if they did, and decided to hide it in the second bathroom before they came to her house.

"We'll invite him here. If he bought Amber's art, it's because he thought she was talented. Had a big future. I'm sure he'd want to meet her parents." Courtney breathed heavily, as if trying to control herself.

Scott shook his head. "He's huge, Courtney. We'd never get to see him."

"What about at his public gallery? We could make some enquiries there. We might have to buy something, though, in order to talk to him," Theresa said.

"That's okay," Courtney said. "We've got plenty of wall space. And he has impeccable taste. This is lovely stuff; look, lots of poor artists he's supporting. Look!"

There was a quote from Sol Evictus on the catalogue: "I love to support the struggling artist, but I'm also self-interested. I'm only going to buy what I think will be huge one day. Never out of pity. These artists are here because I have faith in their futures."

"It seems so weird to think of Amber's art in Sol Evictus's house!" Courtney said. "I didn't think she was that talented, that a man like him would want her work. I'd love to see it. To see what she was working on. To remember it."

Courtney didn't seem to understand or accept that some of it was created in a hell hole, a terrible place. Theresa had no desire to make it clear for her.

"Well, I think I've figured out one thing. Amber was sending you a message with this last drawing. Paradise Falls. It's...a sad place. A place she didn't want to be." Theresa pulled the ledger out. "But you see here, here, here, here...heaps of symbolic messages of hope. None of these things are actually in this place. Never were, as far as I know. I think she was saying to you that she was not filled with despair. That she still had hope."

Courtney slumped. Her colour changed; it was as if she'd turned to stone.

"Time to go," Scott whispered. "She's falling in."

Theresa thought a lot about Ben and all she'd lost. She felt cold and tired, empty. She felt as if anything she tried, each step, was backwards.

Theresa felt lazy, her muscles atrophied, so she found a fight class and she took her first lesson. It made her ache all over, but she was glad she'd done it. She didn't talk to anyone, didn't make friends. She only wanted the physicality of it.

Theresa and Courtney decided to go to Sol Evictus's gallery, called Solace, without Scott or Tim. Courtney said that Scott was too cynical about art, that he would make comments and ruin it. She hadn't seen the works collected before and she wanted to do so in peace.

Theresa picked Courtney up at ten. They'd talked about what to wear, wanting to look the part and not be noticed. Theresa had flat black shoes, a knee-length houndstooth skirt and a zip up sleeveless blouse, thinly pin-striped. She tied her hair back and wore a dark red lipstick.

Courtney emerged from her bedroom with skin tight jeans, high heels and a t-shirt so small her breasts popped out of it. Scott stood in the doorway, shaking his head.

"You look very sexy, Courtney."

"Thanks!"

"But did we want to look sexy? Or did we want to not stand out?"

Courtney looked in the mirror. "Do you think I'll stand out?"

Theresa wasn't sure if she was so unaware, or if she was doing it deliberately. "Think matron. Think decent to the point of dull." She didn't add, *We went through all this.*

"Do you think I should get changed?"

"Oh, I don't know. I'm not the boss! If you feel comfortable, then wear it."

"Well, I do. But maybe I should put a wrap on or something. I don't want Sol Evictus staring at my boobs, now I think about it."

But she winked at Theresa as if to say, *That man can stare all he wants.*

Theresa waited in the car. Closed her eyes and rested.

The door opened and a fresh waft of perfume came in. Courtney liked to use young people's perfume as well, and it suited her. Theresa knew that Tim would say her older person scent mutated it but he was wrong. She was now dressed in a neat grey dress, button up, with closed court shoes.

"You look gorgeous," Theresa couldn't help saying.

The gallery enjoyed a lot of press coverage, mostly because of its owner.

One newspaper wondered, "If you could slit the canvasses from their frames, would you find other works concealed?" There was speculation about the nudity in the collection, and doubt about the age of some of the models. All this did was cause more adoration of the man, his fans coming out to call him a true believer, a patron, a genius.

The gallery was in a large, circular silvered building. Floor-to-ceiling windows reflected the street back at itself and the doorway was concealed in a large, abstract mural.

They'd expected to walk straight in, but people were only allowed in in groups of ten at a time. The guard at the door was one of the angriest men Theresa had ever seen. Caucasian, with straight white hair he tossed every minute or so, he snarled at people in the queue. "Any of you here for the view, you should fuck off," he called out. "This is a place for art-lovers. Sol Evictus IS NOT HERE."

He was huge; he made Theresa nervous. She never used to worry about a man's size, before it was used against her.

Three people peeled out of the queue. The guard's face crinkled. A weird, stiff smile on his face, rictus, as if the muscles were stuck in place.

"Yeah, fuck off," he said.

"We've got every right to be here," a middle-aged man said. He carried a briefcase; his hair was perfectly combed. He shook his head at the guard. "You have no right to keep us away from Sol Evictus."

"Listen, faggot, this is not the place for you. Fuck off now before I do you some damage."

"We're not at a night club, you know. We are sensible people who simply want a glimpse of a man we admire."

"He's not fucking here. Okay?"

The man pushed forward. "You have no right—"

But the guard wasn't interested. A fast right hook had the man's nose bloodied.

The crowd gasped; many covered their eyes. The guard spun the man around, pushed him.

"Hey!" Courtney said.

Theresa grabbed her, pulled her back. "Leave it, we'll get hurt. I hate violence." Even as she said it, she thought, *Most people do, you idiot.*

"Anybody else here for the man, not the art?" the guard called out. He nursed his right hand in the palm of his left.

The queue shook their heads, scuffled their feet, looked at the ground.

"All right then. You two. Lovely pair of ladies." He pointed at Theresa and Courtney. "Lovely ladies are welcome in to see the works of art. Lovely ladies are works of art." He stepped back, gesturing, all charm and presence.

They were given name tags and small bottles of champagne with a straw. "Sol Evictus says looking at art should be intimate. Like you're in someone's home," Courtney said.

On the polished wood floor, which was speckled with sparkles, were calligraphically beautiful quotes, spaced out amongst the art works. Theresa had to pace the whole gallery to read them all.

"What art offers is space – a certain breathing room for the spirit." John Updike.

And *"For me, painting is a way to forget life. It is a cry in the night, a strangled laugh."* Georges Rouault.

And *"When painting, an artist must take care not to trap his soul in the canvas."* Terri Guillemets.

And *"Art is a powerful solace: by means of it one gets through many a bad night."* Friedrich Nietzsche

The artwork on display was uniformly beautiful. There was nothing dark or confronting; it was like a room full of pure good fortune. The walls were sun yellow, and the room designed for people to revolve around the room like planets in orbit.

"You see what a lovely person he is?" Courtney said. "Oh!" She stopped by a lake scene, bright pink flamingos flocking. "Look at the colour. Doesn't it feel like you're there? Camping? I can almost taste the billy tea!"

Theresa said, "Buy it. Take it home if it makes you feel happy." But she thought there was a shadow in the painting, as if the artist loomed over it.

She read the description. It ended, "The artist died tragically young."

Sad, she thought. She read the other descriptions.

Every single artist; dead. Some young—these were always 'tragically'; some old—'peacefully'.

"He's not helping any living artists," she said, but Courtney seemed so euphoric she didn't want to bring her down.

"Oh, look at these tiny ones!" Courtney said. Then, reading from the catalogue: "These are replicas of the so-called kit-cat portraits, by the artist Sir Godfrey Kneller. Each one a member of the Kit Cat Club. This club had very low ceilings, so the portraits were so designed. He painted the subjects until they died. Each of these, a man passed on with his portrait incomplete, which he hung unfinished."

Theresa left Courtney to her viewing and looked for the gallery manager. She smiled. "Do you have anything by the artist Amber Stephens?"

"I'm not sure that we do, but let me check. It may be a recent acquisition." The impeccably dressed woman tapped at her keyboard. "No, nothing, I'm afraid. I'd offer to track something down for you but I see no record of her works at all. Is she upcoming?"

Thankful she had asked the question while Courtney was looking at the artwork, Theresa said, "No, she's passed on."

"Oh, what a shame. I'm sure Sol Evictus would have taken an interest."

"Maybe he has it in his private collection?"

"Private and public are one and the same thing. What he buys, he shares. He's a generous man."

"A benefactor." A polite cough made Theresa step aside to make room for Courtney.

"Will we get to meet Sol Evictus if we buy something?" Courtney asked the gallery manager.

"Sadly, no," the woman said, with no trace of sadness at all. "He doesn't meet our patrons. Most understand that."

"Oh, we understand," Theresa said. "But what if we have things to sell?"

"He's not in the market and if he is, he has all the contacts he needs." Theresa wondered if the woman was deluded. Did she not see that Sol Evictus collected dead artists?

A tall man, red hair, wearing the same suit as the guard at the front door, watched over them. "Like the tattoo," he said to Theresa. She instinctively lifted her hand to the ink on her bicep. "Benrip. Who's that, like a dead guy or something?"

Theresa summed him up in a moment. He wore a wedding ring which he twisted, so he wasn't interested in her that way. But he licked his lips as he looked at her and she wondered; death? Is that what he's interested in?

"Yeah, dead boyfriend. I don't like to forget. Sometimes you forget the dead, don't you?"

"You should never forget."

Courtney started humming, a Sol Evictus song, Theresa realised. A club she didn't belong to.

The guard touched his finger to the tattoo, blinking. "It's a good song, that one. Feels sad. Sol Evictus, he'd like that kind of thing. Death makes him sad but sad isn't always bad, is it?"

"Yeah?" They stepped sideways, into a quiet space. "I like stuff like this, too. People say I'm macabre." She was making this up on the fly, although she wondered if the bloodied newspaper might be something he'd be interested in. It was the personal history that made that work, though. "I've got some items he might like."

"You never know what he's after. Give me a call if you like. I might be able to hook you up."

He handed over a card. Pale red, it said: Peter "Red" Jones with his phone number beneath.

"They call you Red?"

"Better than Bluey," he said. "So you give me a call, we can talk about rewards and benefits."

He fiddled with his ring again and she wondered if he was thinking about spending the benefits; buying his wife diamonds, a family holiday, expensive schools.

"Thanks, Red."

She saw, watching her from the doorway, three drowned ghosts. They hovered there, not coming closer.

Courtney bought the painting she'd admired. Theresa thought her whole body shook as she did so, and she wondered how close to breakdown Courtney was, and how much this purchase could help to stave it off.

Scott welcomed them with relief.

"See, none of Amber's work at all. I told you. Sol Evictus is an angel," Courtney said. "No man who can buy and sell work like this can do any wrong."

"I don't think that's all he buys and sells. One of the guards gave me his card. The thing is, if we can find something Sol Evictus is interested in, I might be able to get to him. Something..." Theresa looked at Scott. "Something Courtney would hate. The sort of thing he commissioned from Amber. Stuff that's dark. The guard hinted that death is his thing."

Scott nodded. "I can ask around. Collectors know other collectors. Leave it with me for now. Maybe you should take a break. Go home, visit your parents. I'll shout you the trip."

"Are you sacking me?"

He looked surprised. "I don't think that's even possible. I'm gonna shut it down for a while. Look for a masterpiece. I mean take a long weekend, go see them."

"I wouldn't mind seeing my sister."

"So see your sister."

In the end, Theresa just wanted to walk on the beach. Be alone. Eat salty food, but no amount could take the memory of the Grief Hole from her. The sound of it, the smell.

She Skyped Giselle. Their parents were visiting.

"Mum's holed up in the bathroom. She can't cope with the kids," Giselle said. Theresa could hear them, screaming for the sake of screaming. Theresa felt grateful to be the aunty.

"Dad's so good with them, though."

"That's our Dad."

"Here's Mum. Talk to her for a while, then I'll have a turn."

Lynda sighed into the screen. "You'll have to speak up, Teese. I can't hear you."

"I haven't said anything yet."

"Well…how are you? Are you eating well? Not too much fried food? Are you all healed?"

"I don't think about it except when my fingers hurt. My throat is better, although sometimes it hurts when I drink straight vodka."

"Theresa! Why are you drinking straight vodka?"

"Mum, you are far too easy to tease."

"What about the scar on your arm? Is it still there?"

"Of course it is. How do you imagine scars go away? By magic? I quite like it, actually. It makes shop assistants feel sorry for me and they serve me straight away. My ankle sucks, though. I can't run very fast. Have to plan not to be late for a movie or whatever. My ear is fine and so is my tooth."

"Lovely." Lynda sounded distracted already. She looked at her fingernails.

"So I saw Ben."

"What? What do you mean?"

"I went into this kind of haunted place, and I saw Ben. He was clear as anything. Well, I didn't see him. But I felt him. I smelt him. It was bad."

"You shouldn't go to places like that, Theresa. You should keep away from them. You're too sensitive, you can't cope. What were you doing there?"

"I've been trying to find out about my cousin. It's all kind of mixed up with your singer. Sol Evictus."

"Ooh, I love him! Did you know he's doing a show next month? Your father won't come with me. I'd love to see him. What charisma that man has. Seriously. I don't think there'll be a woman in the audience not secretly in love with him."

"Not so secret!" Phil called out.

"I still keep clippings of him for you," Theresa said. "Courtney loves him, too. Scott's wife." She knew her mother had distracted her, but let it go for the minute.

"Does she?" There was a pause. "You should both come with me. We'll pay for the airfare. They've done so much for you."

"That's why I want to help them. That's why I went into this place."

"You know Ben would have left you, anyway. It was only a matter of time."

Theresa turned her shoulders, blinking away the tears. She heard her father call, "Your Mum's had too much to drink. Ignore her."

She turned back to the screen.

"Try not to listen to her, Teese," her father said. He'd shuffled Lynda out of the way. There was little argument from her.

"Why is she so cruel?"

"She doesn't mean it."

"She does, Dad."

"She's had a few too many. You know what she's like. Sometimes she sees things too clearly and she has to block them out." Behind him, the squatting ghosts.

"Tell her I don't want to go to the concert and neither does Courtney."

Giselle came into view. "What's up?"

"Oh, nothing. Mum's being a bitch as usual."

"Don't worry, I'll leave her with the kids for an hour. That'll sober her up. What were you talking about?"

"I was talking about Ben. I saw Ben."

But the kids were screaming and Giselle had to go. Nolan, her husband, came on. He'd unbuttoned his shirt; he always took the flirtatious brother-in-law thing too far, and Theresa hated it.

"Hello, Nolan," she said. She could see Giselle in the background, being relentlessly cheerful with her children, as if desperate to avoid any sadness.

"You look tired. Is everything going okay out there?"

"It's fine, Nolan. You should all come out."

She waited until Giselle returned and said, "I've been to a place you don't want to know about. Our cousin went there and it's part of why she killed herself."

"What sort of place is it?"

"They call it different things but the one that resonates with me is the Grief Hole."

Giselle told Nolan it was his turn with the girls, and to shut the door.

"Theresa…"

"What?"

"That's…it's a perfect description."

"Have you seen the place?"

"No, no it's…it's what I see. Don't tell Mum. But that describes exactly what I see when I look at some people. A black hole of despair and I feel it. I'm always feeling it."

"But…you're always so up. So cheerful. And your kids; you're so happy with your kids."

"I'm terrified of a grief hole forming in them."

The sisters sat in silence.

Giselle said, "That's why I never rated what happened to you when Ben died. You've got no grief hole. So I thought you were faking it."

"I wasn't faking it," Theresa said. "I don't think. He was perfect."

"He was. But by now? He wouldn't be so. And in another twelve years or something, he would have been as ordinary as everybody else in the world. As flawed. It's because you only saw him as perfect that you thought you lost so much."

I've been in the Grief Hole. I've been in there. The thought kept coming to her every now and then.

"My turn, my turn," Lynda said. She was drunk; drunker than she'd been even twenty minutes earlier. "So how is your new mummy Courtney going?"

"She's not anybody's mother!"

"Oh, yes, poor suffering Courtney with her fucking dead daughter."

"We should have been there for them."

"Those arseholes should have been there for me. I lost a child, too."

"Bullshit," Theresa said. She couldn't help herself.

"I did, Teese. We never told you or your sister. We had a stillborn baby when you were five and Giselle seven. I'll show you where she's buried one day." She opened another bottle of wine and threw down a full glass. "I see her every day," Lynda said. "Most days. I used to. It was stronger before I started to pretend it wasn't there. I see her growing up, along with you two. But she doesn't get to achieve anything. She doesn't get married. Have kids. A career. She doesn't get to meet anyone at all. All she does is grow up. I can't bear looking at her. I can't bear it."

"Do you mean really see her?"

"I really see her. Every single day. Unless I try hard not to. If you try hard enough, the ghosts go away."

"No, they don't," Theresa said. She thought, *No wonder Mum doesn't want the gift. No wonder she tries to ignore it. Deaden it.*

"You haven't actually tried."

"I can't pretend they are not there, even if you can."

"They aren't there. She isn't. I don't see her any more. And you should think about that, too, if you want a normal life."

"Normal?" Theresa laughed. "Normal is a mother giving comfort to a daughter. It's not having one daughter you like and another you hate. It's showing up when you're needed and not pretending that the world is something it isn't."

"My Dad wanted it to have never happened. The shame. And Mum was as useless as ever. And Scott. He did nothing. None of them helped in anyway." Her hand shook as she poured another glass of wine and drank most of it in one tilt. "It was only you two who got me through. You were so sweet. And your father. He is a dear man, isn't he?

"You shouldn't make me talk about it. You're being a bitch." She finished the dregs of her glass. "That baby? We never talk about it again. You understand me? It is never to be mentioned. These things change us. Like you, when Mrs Ellis was murdered. You were never the same. Where's more wine. Phil, where's the wine? You know Sol Evictus has a winery. 'Solace', it's called. Did you know that?" Lynda slurred her words slightly. Theresa realised this was often how she spoke.

She took solace herself in remembering all she'd done. The people she'd helped. Reminding herself she was a good person.

She was fixing herself some soup when she heard a scrabbling sound at the door.

Prudence stood below the front door step, hitching her bags, her balloons, looking tired. Theresa stared at her. She shouldn't want the woman in her house. She should want her gone, a long way away. But there was comfort in the honesty of being with her.

"Do you want to come in?"

"No, no, I don't like it inside. You die inside that's where you stay. True true story." She cocked an ear. "What's that music you've got playing? It's nasty."

Theresa laughed. "It's Sol Evictus! Most people think he's amazing." She listened to him at the office, in the car, at home, until she knew every lyric. Every note.

"Don't be fooled by him. He's a monster. You keep away from that man."

"What makes you say that?" Theresa said, thinking, *She'll know. Mum's right. She'll know.*

"He sounds terrible. He's got a terrible voice!" Prudence cackled, laughing at her own rudeness.

"He seems charming."

"I'm sure he is. He's not what he seems, though. You know that. He's lived a long time already. Longer than you can imagine."

"He doesn't look that old. He looks good." Theresa sat down on the step. "What else do you know about him? Do you know how I can get to meet him?"

"You don't want to meet him. He's not nice up close."

Theresa decided to leave that for now. She made big mugs of tea and took them outside. They sat together on the step, looking out at the beach.

"I'm worried about my dad. I don't think he's well."

"You think he's going to die? Is that what? Death is not so bad." Prudence could be relied upon to say the oddest things.

"I saw someone die in a carcrash. It was almost….peaceful at the end."

"And the spirits? You saw the spirits?"

"I did see the spirits. They lifted him out of his body, carried him away. It seemed right. Supportive. Comforting."

"Yes, that is how it is. Like that."

"I guess it's like, the more people who do something the more normal it seems. If one person wants to drink blood, that's insane. But if a whole neighbourhood is doing it, that's the norm. The ghosts want their deaths to be right. Normal. So they gather in packs of like."

Prudence nodded. "You understand. Such a clever girl."

And they sat together peacefully, drinking their tea.

Scott pretended to be a collector of a certain kind. Most sources had Sol Evictus collecting paintings by the people without hands and by elephants, by struggling street kids full of natural talent, by old men struck by lightning. But Scott and Theresa knew what they were looking for. The underground stuff, things not seen in public. The locked room art.

Theresa listened to Scott work the phone, watched him work the internet and realised he must have been a brilliant lawyer.

She filled their existing orders and took the few new ones.

They found a series of paintings from men on death row, a large portrait depicting a dead, lamented grandmother as a child, a painting of a pet cemetery, with the animals sitting, ghostly, on their own headstones.

None of these interested Red or the man he represented. "Think outside the box," Red said. "Art can take many forms."

They found the last will and testament of a man who'd shot eighteen children at a shopping centre play area.

They found shoes last worn by the victim of a human vampire, and a collection of toys from a children's hospital, guaranteed last held by a dying child.

These were unsuccessful, although Red said, "Some good thinking here."

Then Theresa came upon what she thought was the perfect thing. A genuine piece of Staffordshire pottery, one of the *Murder Collection*.

It depicted the *Moat Farm Murder*. Samuel Herbert Dougal, the greedy killer standing over the blood-soaked body of poor Camille Holland. It's said that in the time after her body was discovered, there were so many lady visitors come to see that it was like a carnival. Oranges and nuts for sale, vendors of souvenir postcards, liaisons behind the shed.

There were others in the series and Scott had his finders on the lookout for them.

Theresa called Red and set up a meeting. "You come alone. He doesn't like a crowd. He'll take a look and see what he thinks. Try not to disappoint him."

"What I've got is shit hot. I swear."

Theresa could see ghosts around Scott now, as if the more he knew, the worse he felt. He was usually the level one but now he seemed in the need of care. His ghosts were blue-faced, as if they'd gassed themselves. She knew they needed resolution soon. Without trying to make a point, Theresa talked to him about Giselle, and how focussed she was on her children.

"Sometimes I feel like she's got a mask on, this serene face. But underneath she's screaming."

"Being a parent can be a bit like that. Courtney did most of it. I was busy working."

"You spent plenty of time with Amber. You've told me yourself."

"I guess. I wonder if Giselle and her family will come visit? We could find them somewhere to stay. I'd ask them to our place, but you know Courtney and overnight visitors."

"They could stay with me. It'll be a squish but having the beach will help."

He spurred her to send Giselle a text: *Found a recipe for acorns mushed up with marshmallows. Want it?*

Giselle texted back: *Kids won't eat marshmallows. Can I use cough lollies instead?*

She took a photo and then bubble-wrapped the *Moat Farm Murder* plate carefully

"Maybe I should go. Man to man, that kind of thing," Scott said.

"I've made the contact with Red, and I've done the negotiating. I think it should be me."

"How about I go with? We'll dress up in suits and look like lawyers."

It was an option, but Red, on this request, refused.

"Send in the dogs if I'm not back in a day," she said to Scott.

Theresa called Tim over and they sat on her veranda, drinking vodka with orange juice and eating beef and pepper flavoured potato chips.

Her hands shook.

"Here," Tim said. He brought her a fresh drink, fruit pieces speared on the edge of the glass. "Look, I'm a cocktail waiter."

She laughed. He started to spin glasses, trying to catch them, dropping them. Playing the fool. They talked about empty things. Cartoons, TV shows, food.

"You are so cool," Tim said. "You've got it all. Gorgeous, funny, smart. If I had half what you'd have, I'd be something famous. Or something. Not a big nothing like I am."

"You're not a nothing," Theresa said. She didn't feel kind, though; she felt annoyed. "If you want to do more, do more. It's not hard."

"Yeah, but you, you are so good at everything you do. And you're so likable. I'm not likable."

"Why are you doing this? Sucking up to me?"

"Is that what I'm doing?" He looked surprised. "I thought we were hanging out. I thought it was mutual." He shrugged.

"Are you disappointed? Sorry."

"It's okay. I guess I'm the kind of guy people want to be friends with. I can live with that."

Theresa looked at him, considering. "I decided a long time ago that I would never pity fuck. It's no good for either person. Don't you think?"

"Yeah, yeah, you're right."

But they drank more, and later in the evening he tried to kiss her.

She said, "Listen, I'm sorry, but I don't do this any more. Not since Ben."

"But that's five years!"

"I know. But…he died because we were together. And I think that if I sleep with anyone, they'll die too. That's all it is. I assume they're going to die."

"That doesn't make any sense. But even if it did, maybe it's better to die before you get old."

He looked away, and she knew then. She knew that he had no intention of becoming elderly. She wasn't sure if she should try to save him. If it was up to her. Or if that was his business and she had other things to do. People to save. His ghosts were barely able to be seen; far enough away that she could see them at the end of the veranda if she squinted. "You're not going to die for a while."

"What were you looking at?" He twisted around to see.

She considered him. She hated her mother for her silence and her lies, so she told him about the ghosts.

He took it well. He said, "I could paint that. You describe it, I'll paint it. We'll be rich."

She liked his rush of passion.

There was a loud car horn and there was Red, in limousine painted with suns, to pick her up.

"You're not driving?" Tim asked.

"They didn't want me to."

"Be careful. Seriously. God. Maybe I should follow you."

R ed barely spoke on the forty-five minute drive, beyond saying, "Don't panic, stay calm. He hates panicky females."

She'd sobered up by the time he drove her through the heavy, wrought iron gates that opened at his command. The curved driveway led them through an ornate garden of citrus trees, to a solid brick mansion painted in a clean white that reflected the sun and blinded her.

He pulled up gently. "Hop out and give the door a knock. They know you're coming."

She climbed out, holding onto the *Moat Farm Murder* plate, reluctant to leave the safety of the car. It was warm in there, and Red wanted nothing of her, and if they drove forever she wouldn't mind.

She thought she could hear the squelch of her ghosts, their wet clothes and hair, their soggy socks. Hearing them made her feel stronger; there was no water here. She couldn't drown.

She knocked on the heavy oak door. She waited ten minutes or more and began to wonder if it was all a trick. A camera above the door moved as she did but she resisted the temptation to do a tap dance for the watcher's amusement.

Finally the door opened. A tall, bald Japanese man with sunglasses and an unconcealed gun nodded at her.

He handed her a note. *Phone please.*

She handed him her mobile phone. He gave her another note. *Follow me*, it said. Walking behind him, she saw he had a large shiny lump on the back of his bald head. She wondered what was inside it.

"Do you speak English?" she asked him.

He reached into his pocket and pulled out another note. *I do not speak*, it said. He pointed at a chair at the foot of the stairs; *sit.*

The entrance hall was large and circular, the walls painted a bright, sunny yellow.

"I should have brought my sunglasses," Theresa joked, but the man's only response was to hold out his hands for her parcel.

She was reluctant to give it to him. "I'd rather show the collector myself," she said, not wanting to use Sol Evictus's name, wanting to pretend this was still anonymous.

The guard shook his head sharply and pointed at the chair again; *sit down.*

There was a large water bowl in the entrance, and a chewed toy bone. Theresa thought, *He can't be too evil, he's a dog lover.*

Around the walls was a border of clean, white stones.

On the walls hung a series of watercolours; nothing memorable. She looked closely at the one nearest her; it was a river scene, willow trees hanging over the gently flowing water. Sunlight dappling through. Nothing sinister. There was nothing by Amber, she didn't think. All of it pastoral, peaceful. Bright. She didn't know the artist.

"D'ya like art?"

Theresa turned to see a tall, broad, handsome man, curly hair cut short. He held his palms open to her and she knew this gesture; a man showing he was no threat. His hips thrust forward slightly, he smiled at her. "I have no idea myself but they tell me he's got some good stuff here."

"It seems nice."

"You let me know if you need anything," he said. "Carter. I'm Carter. You don't want to know my first name. Women hear my first name and they don't want to sleep with me."

He smiled, and she laughed with him, for the sake of peace. She didn't think he was funny at all.

The Japanese man returned, carrying the bubble wrap and a note for her: You've misunderstood my needs. It isn't the macabre itself. It's the look in the eye. I will keep your gift, although disappointing. Do not balk in your searching. Goodbye.

"Harsh, Takehiro," Carter said.

Takehiro handed her the bubble wrap and the *Follow me* note again and led her out.

The car took her home. As he dropped her off, Red said, "He'll give you one more chance but he won't be interested after that."

S he texted Scott. We have to keep looking. That didn't work.

Scott called her straight back. "I thought he'd go for it. What happened?"

"He kept the bloody thing, but he wouldn't pay me for it. He called it a gift. I didn't speak to him face to face or I would have asked for money."

"Don't worry about the money. You use what you have to use. It might be to our advantage if he thinks you're weak and malleable."

"He said, 'It's the look in the eye.' It made me think about photography. Like a photo of the eyes as close after death as possible. Or, you know, lenses actually removed, photo taken through them."

"We'll look. We'll find something. This is not a whole lot of fun, though. Dealing with these sellers makes me feel dirty."

"I'll help," she said, and those words calmed her for the job ahead.

T heresa missed the simple, pleasant days of stamp sorting. Life felt darker each day, searching, looking at death, at grief personified, at cruelty and insanity.

"I'm glad we're doing this online," Theresa said. "Thing with online is, you don't see a person, they don't seem real. Meeting a creep like that in person would be disgusting."

Scott was lost for half a day when he found a website called *Suicide notes*. Theresa thought he was following leads, but he was reading note after note after note of lost souls, found souls, angry people and devastated people. She finally realised that he had barely moved for two hours and walked to his desk to see what he was doing.

"She didn't leave one," he whispered. "They all say if they leave one, they love you; if they don't, they don't."

Theresa put her arms around his shoulders. "That's such bullshit. And she did leave you a note. The drawing. We're figuring out what it means, that's all."

He nodded, clicking out of the site. It led to another, and another; it led them to the item they both knew instantly Sol Evictus would want.

Ten minutes, twenty-four frames per second, separated. Thousands of frames, blown up. The long, violent and bloody death of a morbidly obese young woman. It was truly an obscene thing, the white globs of fat under her skin glistening, the focus on the loss in her eyes.

Theresa sent one frame to Sol Evictus, a freebie to apologise for wasting his time with the murder plate. She offered him the second, and the third, the first twenty-four, one second of footage, so he had an idea of what he would be buying.

While they waited for a response, they went back to parcelling up stamp orders and talking about generalities; food, drink, movies.

Theresa got the call at home a week later.

"Bring the film," Red said. "Be ready. I'll be there in an hour."

Theresa gave Takehiro her phone and he led her down a long bright hallway and opened the door to a large room.

"I'm allowed inside this time, am I?" she said.

He gave her the *I don't speak* note as if she'd never seen it.

It was a small room. A coffee table sat in the middle, with a bowl of chocolate coffee beans in the centre and a stack of art books. On the walls hung art work that was much darker than that in the entrance.

There was an adaptation of Millais' *Death of Ophelia*. Her wrists were slit, deep, dark cuts, and blood trailed into the water around her, surrounding her, a crimson crowd. In the water reeds, Theresa could see leering faces, eyes wide, watching Ophelia die.

Ophelia's face no longer resembled that of a saint. It was lined, and she seemed to be snarling. Theresa was entranced by it, wondering what sort of artist would twist the nature of a work like that. Takehiro pushed a large painting—actually, a door. In the next room, the other three guards waited. Red, Carter and Blondie, all three with arms crossed, in front of Sol Evictus, who sat with a large book on his lap.

None of them smiled but then she didn't expect them to.

Up close, Sol Evictus was handsome for a man in his sixties; his hair silver, his face lined in the right way. When he smiled, as he did whenever he was interviewed, whenever he sang, his eyes widened and you could see their deep, deep blueness. He didn't smile now. He had a dog at his feet; it rested, head on paws, eyes watchful.

He had a broad, flat face. Pale, bloodless lips. High forehead, pale silver hair flat and shapeless. You were not supposed to notice him and you didn't, until he got onstage with his microphone and the world stopped breathing.

There were no ghosts. Floor lighting forced a glow around him

"Thank you, Takehiro. Efficient as always." He beckoned her with a forefinger. "Look at your hair!" he said, his voice quiet. "Shiny and black, like a record. Like an old LP record, remember those?"

Instinctively, she stroked her hair.

Red said, "This is Theresa Clarke. She's the one who brought the plate last time. She has the film this time."

"Ah, yes. I believe I know your uncle. We have had some small dealings in the past, yes? At a personal level."

She nodded. He wasn't going to deny the purchase of Amber's art, then.

"What's your favourite of my songs?" he said. His voice was creamy. Of all the things she expected to be asked, this was not amongst them.

"My mother likes *The Woman Who Got Away.*"

"You mean *The Woman Who Slipped Away*. And you?"

She felt blank. If she named a song, and he asked her to sing it, there was no way, no way she could even remember a chorus.

"I'm actually not a fan. But my mother is. And my aunt."

He smiled. "I thought as much. You have an internal strength about you that my fans don't always have. Some of them...you know one of them cut off her own finger to send to me? Set it in resin and thought I might like it. I don't allow them in my home."

He hummed a tune; she recognised it as something Courtney had hummed, and other women on the street, humming mindlessly, a particularly sad note.

"I know that song...my aunt hums it too."

"Your aunt, your mother...you say I appeal to the older women, do you?"

"I'm sure..." She couldn't think of anything polite to say. Blondie glared at her. "I know a lot of younger people who like you, too. They adore you."

Blondie whispered to Sol Evictus.

"He doesn't like people to talk about how old my fans are. You see how they protect me?"

"They seem very efficient."

He laughed. "Oh, they are. Especially Red. He has an eye, this one, or a nose. He can sniff out my type." Red's skin looked painful; peeling as if he'd had a bad sunburn.

The guards laughed. "They laugh because I tease. I mean my type of art. He can sniff out my style. Is there anything we should know about you, Theresa Clarke, before we begin our dealings?"

She knew she had to answer without hesitation but she gave a charming smile to give her a moment to think. "The only thing you need to know is that I don't trade sex for deals, but I am an easy drunk."

He laughed at that and poked Takehiro. "You hear that, Takehiro? Get some sake in."

Takehiro remained impassive, though he lifted his hand and rubbed the large lump at the back of his head. She thought it was larger than the first time she'd seen it and wondered if it was cancerous. Or filled with pus, or spiders. Theresa wondered if he didn't honestly understand a word of English or if he was seeking an edge like everybody else. They guarded with constant motion, circling around him like the planets around the sun. Sol Evictus watched her carefully.

"You seem to have been in the wars lately."

For a moment she was confused, and then realised perhaps he'd noticed her slight limp and the stiffness in her fingers. Or perhaps he knew everything about her.

She said, "You shoulda seen the other guy."

He laughed. "I was impressed with the sample you sent me. What can you tell me about it?"

"It's a special series. It has a story, truth. It's unlike anything you see at ordinary galleries, with their happy faces, their happy endings."

He nodded. "People do like a happy ending. Why are you selling it?"

"I thought I could handle it, the emotion of it, but I can't. I feel as if the spirits of the dead stay with it. I feel as if I can look into that celluloid face and see a thousand deaths. As if this is the moment, the last moment, the last breath. The angel chorus. It's too strong for me. But I thought it would be perfect for your collection."

He looked at her without speaking for two minutes, maybe three. "What do you know of my collection?"

"I know that you are a collector of unusual items. I'm a collector too. I collect photos, letters, wrappers, people, jokes, cutlery, stamps, clippings..." She pressed her left heel into her right big toe to stop herself from talking more.

"All right. You'll give us a few moments to have a look at the next frames you've brought to show me. Will you be able to occupy yourself here?"

He lifted his arms to encompass it all; the art, the books, the treasures.

"This room is amazing. I could spend hours here," she said, looking around and stepping forward to reach out. The walls were covered with large, detailed historical paintings. "A novel in every one."

"Ah, an appreciator," Sol Evictus said. "Not everyone understands. I'm assuming that you won't take anything personal of mine and sell it. People will buy and sell the most remarkable things."

"I saw that people offered money for some of your hair, or an envelope, a spoon, empty packet of something you've used. Anything. Don't worry. I'm no thief."

He turned and wiggled his arse at her. "Perhaps they'd like you to capture a fart!"

They all laughed, guards included. Takehiro wiggled his arse as well, and Theresa felt part of the team. One of them.

She wasn't sure why this made her happy. She'd always been able to win people over with a smile, but in the charisma stakes, Sol Evictus beat her hands down.

She was fascinated by him. Strong, manipulative, magnetic. She was not sure how to play him. It was a challenge. She'd never met anyone like him before.

He left her in the room full of temptations; carpet fluff, hair strands, torn slips of paper. It was clearly a test. Theresa knew that, and she had no problem with it. She lost herself in the artwork.

She had no idea of the monetary value of what she was looking at, but these were clearly great works. The one entitled *The Appian*

Way depicted the 6,000 slaves crucified along that road. Somehow the artist had captured the immensity of it. Theresa felt dizzy looking at it, as if she might tilt forward, falling amongst rocks and the dust. She felt like a voyeur. Was this what the artist intended? This sense of guilty observation?

It was so warm in the room, direct heat, and looking up she saw sunlamps, warm and glowing. She felt sleepy, and happy. It was a stark contrast to the way the Grief Hole had made her feel.

The five men re-entered the room. Sol Evictus smiled at her, held out his hands. She took them; they were surprisingly firm and smooth.

"You've brought me something special indeed. What do you know of the young woman?"

"She's over eighteen. That I'm sure of. I imagine she was not an innocent."

"Do you think the innocent die harder? I do. They aren't ready, or deserving. They think, 'But what could I have done with my life? How could I have helped?' They are futureless." He was dramatic, whispery, stretching his fingers out like a magician displaying a trick. "It is superb. Let my man know how much you want for the entire film. We are reasonable people, aren't we?"

"Of course," she said. She stretched her fingers, mimicking him. Flicking the hair he admired. "Perhaps we could consider a swap."

"Swap?"

"Trade. For some of your pieces."

"Ah. I'm not sure that will be feasible, Theresa. My pieces are chosen very carefully. Part of a puzzle, I need them all to complete the picture."

She reached down to stroke the head of his spaniel, come to sniff at her feet.

"You like dogs?"

165

"So long as they don't bite."

"Oh, I bite, you know. You need to keep your arm from my teeth." He snapped them at Theresa, and Red laughed. He carried a stick under his arm; he tapped it now, as if preparing to beat the dog.

"I have other dogs. Like this one." He showed her a picture a muscly brown animal with a black snout. Its face was lifted, its eyes closed. "He's a Papua New Guinean Singing Dog. Have you heard one? Oh, it will break your heart. Snap your heart in two. I listen to him for inspiration, sometimes. These dogs, they say, harbour the souls of the dead. Their living relatives can communicate by singing along with the yowling."

She thought of the dogs waiting at Paradise Falls; these singing dogs belonged there.

"I use his voice in some of my tunes. He doesn't mind. You won't be able to miss hearing it, now you know."

"Is he happy? He doesn't look unhappy."

"Oh, he's happy. He has plenty of mates. Some of them stuffed, I admit. I have a penchant for the stuffed dog. You can look into their eyes for an image of the last thing they saw before they died."

"Don't stuffed animals have glass eyes?"

"Yes, clever you. They do. But my taxidermist can capture the images. He paints them in. Something to see indeed. Strangely human, don't you think? I've seen such expressions on prisoners who have lost hope."

Theresa tickled the spaniel's ears and his tail wagged wildly. "I must get a dog soon," she said. "I've only recently moved and I'm not settled in yet. I won't feel right until I have my own dog."

"I'd offer to buy you one but I think dogs should be chosen by their owners. I'm a strong believer in that."

"Mostly the dogs choose us, don't they?"

"That's true. Now tell me, why would you go to so much trouble to sell me such a piece? You've been here before. Why are you so keen to sell to me, that you'll keep searching till you find something I want?" Sol Evictus said, watching her.

She felt a buzzing in her ears. A flicker of fear. "I know you're the perfect person for it, and I know you'll give me the right price."

"No one else would buy it. The price is mine to name."

"You are not the only one interested in this," she said, and by the flicker of his eyes she knew this was true, that there were other collectors like him. "I want to see your collection. Your true collection. With an eye, as I said, to a possible swap."

"What makes you think I have more than this?" he said, but he smiled. "Perhaps when I know you better. Is there something in particular there you want to see?"

"There is," she said.

He held his hand up to her. "Don't tell me! We will discover what that thing is. In the process. We surely will. Next visit we will show you more if you bring me more. Goodbye."

With that, he lifted his hand to direct the guards.

Red drove her home. She sat in the front seat with him, leaning over to press against him as she put her seat belt on. She turned to face him, asking him questions about the car, how fast it went, how long they'd had it. Lulling him, making his tongue loose.

At a red light, she touched his wedding ring. He drove one handed, the other resting on his thigh.

"What does your wife think of Sol Evictus?"

"Why, what do you think of him?"

"He's very charismatic."

"Do you like that, or what?"

"I like strong men. Charming men." She thought briefly of Ben, who could charm anybody, from a mean old lady at the bus stop to a drunk in the wrong place at the wrong time.

"He is that."

Her eyes felt gritty with sand. "You must work long hours. What does she think of that?" Pushing him because she sensed he wanted to talk.

His cheeks reddened. "She thinks very highly of him indeed."

"It must be hard, doing this job and having a family. Both so needy, aren't they?"

"It's not called needy when it's your wife and kids. A man's job is to keep his family happy. But yeah, it can be hard because they want so much of you."

"Your family, you mean?"

"Yeah, yeah. You haven't got a family? Then you wouldn't get it. Life is free and easy for a girl like you."

The light changed and he drove on.

"You wouldn't change things, though. Even if you could?"

He clicked his tongue. "I love them and resent them. And sometimes they piss me off. Any family man would say the same. If he was honest. I wouldn't have my wife and kids if it wasn't for him. I would have been long dead. Or a skeleton sitting in a jail cell. Or buried up to my neck in some shit or other. So I'm grateful. Couldn't be more grateful."

He arrived at her street and pulled over. "You make me talk too much," he said, but he smiled.

As she walked up her driveway, she realised she was looking forward to telling Tim what had happened. That she knew Tim was interested in what she'd discovered, and that he would be anxious for her to be all right. It was nice to think of him waiting at the house. He liked her place better than his; his flatmates were grubby and loud and barely noticed his existence.

She didn't have many friends. She thought perhaps she didn't have any friends. Yet Tim, who was connected to her only by the death of her cousin, seemed to be one.

He'd cooked spaghetti bolognaise, a huge pot, and set the table for two.

She felt relief and a sense of normalcy as she told him of her visit.

"He's almost hypnotic to be around. Odd, interesting, charming."

"Don't get sucked in by him, Theresa," Tim said. "He might turn out to be completely innocent, but let's not give him the benefit of the doubt."

She ate more pasta than she thought possible, and then she texted Scott that she was home. He replied; *I'M COMING OVER.*

He was at her door within thirty minutes, and he held her at arm's length, as if seeking damage.

"I'm okay. It was fine. Strange, but fine." She ran through what had happened. Tim had already heard it, but he listened quietly.

Scott said, "I want to meet this man. And we know that Courtney does."

"He doesn't do that. It's hard to get to him and we don't want to jeopardise anything at this stage."

"But you said he was fine! And his house was clean and all that. She'd be happy to hear that, wouldn't she?"

"Yeah, but we know that's not his reality. We know he has another house wrapped in this one. The real house. Like he has his real self wrapped up."

"What did you talk about with him? Amber? Did you ask him about Amber and Paradise Falls?"

"Not yet."

"I want to see that place. Courtney, too. I want to meet this man and see that place." He stood up, patting his pants pocket as if checking for his wallet, his keys, as if ready to head out the door immediately.

"I don't know if Courtney should go. It's a sad place. She doesn't cope with that stuff well."

"She doesn't cope. No. But she's going through Amber's things. Actually giving stuff away. So I think there's been improvement. She'll never get over it but if she can let go… I want to understand what made Amber feel such despair, and maybe I'll be able to see a mark of hers. Something personal you wouldn't notice or understand."

Theresa felt terrified at the thought of going back, but could see how deeply Scott needed to see the place. How he could confront his grief there. She also wondered if she would see Ben again, smell him, glimpse him, and was tempted.

"Let me think about it, okay? It'll be on me forever if I take you there and it destroys you." She looked at Tim, who looked down. "Tim knows he shouldn't have taken me." Scott's ghosts hadn't entered the house, but she could see them hanging around his car.

"Why, how does it affect you?"

"It makes me sad, thinking of Ben. And all the kids who've gone there. They've all left some kind of mark, like you say. I don't know if you'll see Amber in there."

Scott's eyes widened. "I could actually see Amber?"

"Not actually her, Scott. The memory of her. The thought of her." Though Theresa wasn't sure.

"I didn't see anyone," Tim said. "Although I think I smelt my grandmother's perfume. She always wore it stale. Mum said she used to buy it at the op shop, the last remnants of other people's expensive perfume. I could smell that in there."

"Were you sad when she died?"

"I was only eight but I remember crying a lot. She was a sweet lady. But I never want to smell that old lady smell again."

"So it's not only those who die violently we can see," Theresa said. "Because your grandmother died peacefully, didn't she?"

"In her sleep. Holding a hot water bottle."

"So, then. There are the peaceful as well as the disturbed."

She could feel how dark the silence was; how much both men wanted to ask her about Ben.

Her throat constricted at the thought of it.

"You saw Ben in there?" Scott prodded gently.

"I sensed him. I hope the fact I smelt him in there might mean he's forgiven me. That he really loved me and doesn't blame me for his death."

"For what? Therese, I hope you don't blame yourself for anything."

"I failed to intervene is what happened."

She wondered if telling them the full story would help. They would use the right words afterwards. Absolve her.

"It was a picnic at a creek with a bunch of his friends from work, and everyone was supposed to drink, and swim and eat all the food. Ben told me I had to act normal."

"What?" Tim said, and she thought it was sweet that he didn't find her abnormal.

"You know. Look people in the eye. Don't keep my eyes on the ground all the time. He didn't understand that looking down means I see fewer ghosts. But then he didn't really get the ghost thing.

"It was quite fun, nice people, no one seemed to think I was weird. Of course I didn't tell them I could see ghosts splashing in the water and waving at me. *Come in, come in.*

"I did go swimming. I thought I'd be fine, forewarned means extra careful. And I was. But it turns out..."

Her throat dried out and she could barely breathe.

Scott gave her water. "Don't tell us if it upsets you, Therese. I'm no fan of talking for the sake of it."

But she'd started and no thought of the beach, the sand, the warm sun, could take away the truth this time.

"Turns out they were Ben's ghosts, not mine. I sat on the water's edge, drying off. It was a gorgeous, sunny day. Someone gave me a vodka drink and I felt so ordinary sitting there. I imagined the ghosts were mirages, not real.

"Ben sailed off in an inner tube. They were all taking turns on it, floating down around a bend where the water was choppier, then dragging it back for the next person. He sailed off. The ghosts went with him and I should have said stop. I should have waded out and dragged him in if he didn't listen to me. But I felt so normal. The women were talking about boyfriends and including me. I had drink. Ben sang at the top of his voice and everyone laughed. He was really popular. 'He's a catch,' one of the women said. 'He's a keeper.'

"He turned the corner, singing. Singing. Singing. I thought his voice changed, became weaker and reedy, but someone asked me about the RSPCA where I was working and I was so busy talking about cats and dogs that I did nothing.

"The singing stopped. That I noticed. I looked down to where he'd gone and there was something….a clotted mist. 'Where's Ben?' I asked, and they were good; they all reacted, running along the creek side to reach him.

"But it was too late. He'd tipped out. Banged his head. He was under, well under, and had been for a while."

"So…who was singing?" Tim asked.

"Those fucking ghosts. Do you see what I mean?"

Tim put his arm around her. "I think you're amazing. I think you are absolutely amazing." He kissed her cheek lingeringly, until she pulled away.

"It wasn't your fault. In no way was it your fault," Scott said. "I'm sorry we weren't there for you. We should have been. We could have helped. We could have understood what you were going through." Scott had his head in his hands.

Theresa wanted to move on; she didn't want to stay in this hole. "What happened with you and Mum? Why you don't talk anymore? Why am I only just getting to know you?" She wondered if his version would differ from Lynda's.

"Our family is special in different ways, like you and your ghosts. Not me. I didn't get any of it. But your mother did, and she always hated it. That's the truth. I was jealous of what she could do and would have loved it; she hated it. Typical, isn't it? We all want to be what someone else is and someone else wants to be what we are. Then there was a time that was hard to her, a terrible thing."

"She told me about the stillbirth." Saying the words made Theresa want to be with her mother, to force her into a hug of comfort.

"Yeah. Yeah. God, if I knew then what I know now, about the pain of losing a child and all…She felt like she should have done something about it. Kept her baby from dying. Our father gave her a hard time. Blaming her, calling her a witch, saying it was punishment. I didn't help her. And I didn't back her up at all.

"She decided she wanted not to be part of our family after that, and she cut off contact. She wanted total separation, I suppose. It was a pain in the arse, to be honest. Leaving me with all the family duties."

"She leaves me with a lot of it as well. She's like that."

"She let you come here, at least. That was a breakthrough."

"It wasn't her idea though, was it? It came from Prudence. I think my mother didn't want to deal with me there. She couldn't cope with how I looked, all beaten up. And why. She thought it was my fault, I think. Like I'm a failure, weak."

"Surely she doesn't think that."

"I don't know."

After Scott and Tim left, Theresa watched three dogs running along the beach, rolling in the sand and the contrast of their happiness with the mournful waiting of the dogs at the grief hole gave her the idea of what to do to wipe the thought of Ben from her mind.

She needed to help those dogs.

Standing in the shadow of Paradise Falls, she was momentarily tempted to climb the ladder, to see if Ben was there. If he wanted her to stay with him. But she remembered how much self-hate she'd felt in there, and she didn't want that.

Theresa fished in her backpack for the mince. The dogs were at her heels, some of them too weak to jump, but knowing she had food in there and wanting it.

She threw handfuls of it and watched them eat.

"There's no point feeding them. They'll starve tomorrow instead," Andy said. He looked grubby, his hair in clumps, as if he hadn't washed in days.

"They won't starve," she said.

The dogs ate voraciously, all except one, a large, black, strong-looking male, who refused to eat. He followed her instead sniffing at her ankles, barking softly.

"He wants to go home with you," Andy said.

"I can't take a dog."

"Why not? You've got a house, haven't you? He wants to go with you. You can't be a bitch and leave him behind."

Andy looked almost puppy-like as he spoke and she wondered how she could convince him to let her help him.

"I couldn't look after him alone. I'm out of the house a lot. I'd need someone to feed him, take him for walks sometimes."

"I can't. I don't know where you live."

"It won't be often. And I'll pay you. For getting there, and for feeding and walking."

"Maybe." He looked up at the entrance to Paradise Falls. "Are you going in again?"

She could. It would be easy to give in to it. "Not today."

He nodded. "That's good."

"Have you been drawing? Do you need another sketch book?"

"It's okay."

"I'll bring one next time I see you. A few of them."

He reached into his backpack and tore a page out of the book Tim had given him. The drawing was clever; The Sun, with the planets in the background. All of them anthropomorphised.

"Is that your mum?"

It wasn't a lucky guess; the Sun was wild-eyed, black-toothed, with 'Mother' written over it.

He laughed. "She'll kill me if she sees it."

They spent an hour with the dog, taking him to a park away from Paradise Falls, feeding him dog food Andy bought from the small supermarket nearby. They threw a stick to each other and the crazy jumping of the dog made them laugh.

"What should we call him?" Andy said. Theresa liked the 'we'.

Sleepy. Theresa was so sleepy. She dozed on the couch after she settled the dog; woke up at three in the morning, stiff, her throat sore. The dog curled up on her feet, numbing them. She stumbled to bed and didn't wake up until late in the afternoon. She hadn't slept like that since she was a teenager.

She was woken by a phone call from Red. "Sol Evictus wants to see you again. Have you got something else for him?"

"Yep. I've got the next frames he wanted to see. And some more murder pottery; he might like it if I can explain it to him."

"And he says something of yours. You said you collected weird shit. He wants to see some of it."

As she spoke, a call came through from Raul. He'd left some messages; there was a job opening. In the area. Perfect for her.

There was nothing about the offer that enticed her and she wondered; do I really not give a shit any more?

Theresa dressed in the sort of clothes she knew Sol Evictus liked. Shiny, no fibres hanging loose. Neat.

Prudence, her balloons bright and full of gas, said, "You

shouldn't go back. He is not a good man."

"He's not all that bad. Old. A bit flirty."

"You don't know how monstrous he is. You don't know that. He wants more from you than you should be willing to give. You listen; listen to me."

Theresa listened, but there was little Prudence could tell her. "I can find out. Let me find out before you see him again. Let me watch this monster."

"I haven't got time today, Prudence. You do it, though. Tell me next time."

Prudence had a point, though. What was she willing to trade for Amber's work returned?

She called Tim to let him know she was going again, saying, "Call in the dogs if I'm not back in 24 hours."

Sol Evictus was dressed in a shiny grey suit. It was silver, tight, like a skin. He looked, Theresa thought, a glistening, skinny fish out of water.

"You look beautiful today, Theresa. I can see the effort you've put in. So many of the people I see come here with no thought of how they look. All those people who want to get close to me, but they want to do it on their terms, don't they? Never mine. You, I think, understand. You understand the artistry of how you present yourself."

Takehiro brought out a plate of crisp fried white bait.

"It's the Moat Farm plate!" she said.

"Ah, yes. A handy dish." Sol Evictus took a handful of fish and poured it into his mouth.

"I didn't get the chance to tell you about it last time."

"I'm sure it was tragic," he said, looking away.

"The victim was an amazing woman. Really tough, really smart. But this guy got under her skin. She was over fifty when she met him. Never been married. As soon as he moved in, he tried to seduce the maidservant. But she wasn't having any of it and Camille stood by her, told him to leave, and he killed her. She must have died hard, I think. She must have been totally pissed off. She'd survived on her own, never been fooled, and yet this creep gets her in the end."

Sol Evictus smiled. Nodded kindly.

"The thing is what happened after. There was an absolute media frenzy. And the public; they hung around too. They tried him in the barn for some reason, although not everyone talks about that. So there were a lot of people around. Feeling the dirt in the ditch where the body was found. Ladies sewing little bags, as if they were for lavender, then filling them with dirt from Camille's shallow grave."

He nodded. "I've seen such things."

"The newspapers talked about 'all sorts of goings on', as they called it. Horrified, people were. Ladies at it, gentlemen, all stirred up with the passion of murder."

"You can't see that in this piece, though. Can you? That is my only issue with it."

"I wish I could tell you some of that grave dirt was mixed into the ceramic."

He smiled so sweetly at her, she felt as if he loved her.

"Camille had no one to grieve for her," Theresa said. "I find that sad. Only the maid cared and she didn't care much."

"Grief is not the only emotion," he said. "And it can in itself bring great solace."

"It is a powerful one, though. I've been in a place which is so full of grief, you can smell it. It smells like old plastic."

"Ah," he said. "I'm sure there are many such places. I have been in some myself. Do you come out gentler? More understanding? Do you come out with words filling your mouth, ready to be sung?

"Have you been to Paradise Falls?"

Blondie stood beside Sol Evictus. Head tilted sideways, always listening.

Theresa wondered if he told people what he heard. Around his feet, squatting, were ghosts where she hadn't seen them before. Young, old, male, female, but all of them surprised. All of them with knives in their backs.

He leaned into Sol Evictus, who was humming. She wished she could photograph him, wanting to capture that sense of absolute devotion.

"I'm sorry, you spoke? Sometimes the music takes me and I hear nothing, nothing at all, beyond it. I'm lucky, I think." He took her hand. "Thank you for the film, Theresa. You do understand me, now. I admire a woman who learns so well."

Sol Evictus breathed deeply, his nostrils flaring.

He lifted the film to the light, his lips parted. He stared for minutes.

"What are you looking for?"

"That moment of knowing."

"I am gradually collecting them all, but the owner is reluctant. He is very attached."

"I can imagine," Sol Evictus said, and he started to hum as he thumbed through the film panels.

"Next time, bring me more," he said, sighing. "Bring me the ending."

"I've got something else to show you. A small collection. It's not the kind of thing I show most people. Last lover I showed climbed out the window to get away from me."

"Sounds enticing."

She spread some photos on the table.

"I hope there are none of you on stage as Little Red Riding Hood? You, Christmas Day, holding a baby doll? You, dressed in tight jeans, arm around your clearly disinterested first boyfriend?"

Theresa laughed. "None of those! Look."

His lips kissed out as he flicked through the pages. He nodded.

Photos of a baby dead at birth. A woman so badly beaten her face was only recognisable as such because of the hair around it. A man, standing in his underwear, leaning on a baseball bat. You could see the dark stains on the tip. And his underpants dirty.

"You're quite the photographer," he said.

"I didn't take all of these. Some of them. Others I've picked up here and there," she said.

He waved his fingers and Red brought a plate of tiny biscuits with slices of smoked oyster on them. Sol Evictus sucked up five, six, before offering the plate to Theresa. He licked his fingers. "Try one," he said.

When her mouth was full, he said, "What do you see in these photos, Theresa?" he said.

"You mean...beyond what we all see?" Crumbs fell from her mouth and she collected them into her palm. "Here, I see nothing. Only what you see, although I can imagine each story clearly."

"But you do see beyond, sometimes, don't you?"

"Not in photos."

"Not in photos, no. But I've seen how you look at people. That woman at the department store last week. Remember?"

Theresa felt momentarily frozen. She had not been with Sol Evictus that day; they had never met outside this home. He followed her; personally followed her.

"Which woman?" she said, to buy herself some time.

"Ah, you know. High heels she walked well in. Firm calves. Skirt perhaps too short for her age, but why not, don't you say? You looked at her as if you were already mourning her death."

Here, Theresa realised how brilliant Sol Evictus was, how well he could read people. "I..."

"I'd be interested to hear about what you saw."

"Perhaps we can exchange. My story for one of your artworks."

He smiled. "A businesswoman ever standing. Was there a particular piece?"

"There is a particular artist."

He nodded. "Make your suggestion and we will see."

"Her name was Amber."

She saw that he was not pleased about this. His mouth drooped sadly, as if he'd been emotionally hurt.

"I don't have that artist in my collection. Come on, I'll show you some of the work I own," he said. "Perhaps something will take your fancy."

"You're talking about your ordinary collection."

"Yes, yes, ordinary is all I have," he said, but he lifted his cheeks, part grimace, part secret confidence.

Holding her arm, they walked through corridors and rooms, till they reached his gallery. The floor was painted with a circular maze; he loved his circles. In the centre the sun, and the planets in orbit around.

They saw paintings from the Impressionist era. There was modern art and small sculptures, built into crevices in the wall.

"I have my special pieces, Theresa. But these others; there is tragedy in all of them. This marble of a young man holding a ball? He had hopes and dreams never met. He has been sculpted standing but in fact he could not. He was a cripple from birth. No strong thigh muscles. No firm calves."

She touched the cold marble. "You have a lot of art."

"Yet there is still so much more I'd love to own. Some wonderful Victorian pieces. This is only a copy of the wonderfully tragic painting called *The Sempstress*, by Richard Redgrave. Did you know that Saint Theresa's mother was a sempstress?" He looked at Theresa, not the painting, as if wanting to see how she reacted to his story. "Famous for her work. Look at this poor woman; she sews and sews as the night passes, her eyes swollen with tiredness. Gazing up at the ceiling; perhaps at her child awake, perhaps at God, beseeching him for a helping hand. I don't know. I will own the original one day. You see that the house next door is also lit up at this late hour. What do you think is going on in there? Things a lady doesn't discuss."

Theresa peered closely at it then said, "Sewing? Maybe they are competing, each to complete the most shirts. Or handkerchiefs. Whatever it is they are sewing." The more they talked about the art, the less he would try to delve into her secrets.

"Could be. But what is being sewn? What memories are being created, do you think? Created and forgotten. I think she is sewing her own funeral shroud. That her children sleep upstairs but rather than be close to them, making the most of the short time she has left, she is sewing. She knows her hour of death and her terror increases as that hour approaches. 'At least the children won't have to sew my shroud,' she sings to herself. Her swan song. Her last song on Earth."

"That's so sad." Theresa felt her voice break slightly.

"It is sad, I suppose. But she also looks forward to that beautiful moment of death. The moment of knowing, as I said. When all the questions are answered. When she will know. Imagine the solace of that.

"She looks so tired. Almost zombie-like. She's been sewing forever. She's wearing a silver thimble. An heirloom, do you think? Ah, the tiredness of working people through the ages. The drudgery of continuing. Having to feed themselves. No food in the cupboard, day by day struggle, if I don't finish this my children don't eat. A hard life for the working people." His sigh was so deep she felt a wash of breath over her. Theresa had never heard anything like it.

"You've never had to work like that?"

"I've been lucky. I've worked for pleasure for most of my life."

She wondered how long that life was. "That is lucky. I guess I'm the same. I've worked hard and helped people, but I've never had to work or starve.

"It would be like a curse.

"And even harder if you have children to feed. You have not had to worry about that with your income. Your children will never have to starve."

"I have no children," he said. "Not a single one. Never blessed in that way. You will not be, either, I don't imagine. Not a child to be had."

Theresa was shocked by this. She was in control of her decision not to have children, but the way he said it made it sound like a curse.

"Am I right about this, Theresa? Theresa of the wonderful child-bearing hips?"

"We'll see," she said. "But I do think the world is an awful place for children. I don't want to feel a child's pain. I don't want to fail to protect my own child."

"But what about your husband? When you meet, fall in love, marry?"

"I don't think that's going to happen."

"We can be surprised by love," he said. He tilted his head at her. "But you have already loved, haven't you? And lost?"

She shook her head. She couldn't bear the thought of talking about Ben with him.

"I am working on an album of children's music, hoping to help them to a state of grace. Do you think it's possible? Is it possible for us to understand a child's pain? But without a family, you will need some kind of replacement, then. Women do. Have it ready for when you accept the truth, that you will be a lonely old lady. Art, perhaps. You know that Nietzsche says that art is a powerful solace."

After seeing the quote on the floor of Sol Evictus's gallery, Theresa had looked it up. "He says that about the thought of suicide."

"Ah, is that it? Well, then, good friends. A protector to watch over you. An obsession."

She almost laughed, but realised he was serious. He puffed out his cheeks as he said this. Like he was blowing up a balloon.

"Though I think perhaps I don't need to talk to you about obsession." He tilted his head to one side. "Shall we move through?"

They walked together down a softly lit hallway. Flocked wallpaper she ran her fingers along. It felt velvety. Like a kitten's fur.

Theresa pointed to a painting of a corrupt clown. "The art is much darker here."

"I call this the moonlight gallery," he said as they entered the silvery glowing room. "I'm not unknown for me to sit here with music for hours. It's inspirational, isn't it?"

Theresa didn't say anything.

"You brought up our mutual acquaintance," he said. "I'm sorry about my reaction before. When you mentioned her name I had a mental blank. Of course I know her. I knew her. It's tragic. Ah, the sadness of youth, the sorrow, the debacle of it all."

"I never actually met her. Our families are not close."

"Ah, families are funny things, aren't they? You are the first to come looking for her work. Her parents were happy for me to have it at the time. Do you think it made them sad? I can understand that. How sunk in grief they must have been, and how they wanted to divest themselves of all reminders of her. Of what she could have been."

"They were in a state of deep mourning," she said. He was so persuasive, she almost believed they had willingly given up their daughter's artwork.

His mouth turned down; *how sad*, he mimed.

"Actually, now, they would love to have her things back. Her art. They feel as if they could understand her more if they had it."

He looked out of the window. "I do appreciate your honesty, Theresa. I do like an honest person. But I like to know the price. I will have to consider. You understand you are asking for far more than the worth of what you offer?"

"Think about it," she said. "You know you want to know what I see. That I can offer you something unique."

"Most of us think we are unique, Theresa, but very few of us are. I'm sure there have been many like me in the history of the world, although people tell me otherwise. The media!" He smiled broadly, as if making an hilarious joke. "So, as an indication of your faith: What did you see when you looked at that well-dressed woman? Why did you mourn that living person?"

Theresa nodded. "We can discuss that. We definitely can. There is more to it than you might imagine."

Takehiro leaned over and whispered in his ear.

"Ah. Yes. This way, Theresa. We must make our way back."

Theresa was glad Takehiro led them. She had lost all sense of direction, with the circles and curves and turns. She saw nothing she had seen before and could not even imagine the size of this house.

They stopped in a large, warm room.

Sol Evictus said, "You must excuse me. I have another visitor coming. Another sort of visitor. I know you understand me now; we know each other. We have secrets, and secrets are strengthening for a friendship. I'm sure you understand that better than most."

He shucked off his suit as if it were loose skin. Naked beneath, he nested himself in the large velvet beanbag in the corner. He slapped his thighs.

Theresa looked at Red, horrified.

He shook his head; *Not you.* She thought dry skin flaked off his face.

A young woman dressed only in a thin dressing gown came through the door and walked sinuously to Sol Evictus. Her eyes were unfocused and it seemed clear that she had taken something to deaden feeling.

She straddled him. She held onto his shoulders. Her head tilted back, her blonde hair reaching almost to the floor. No black roots.

Blondie lent forward and slipped the robe off her shoulders. She lifted herself up, down. His guards watched, not concealing it. Sol Evictus held her hips and his face was filled with concentration rather than pleasure. Her hair flew, static electricity. Theresa looked away but thought, *I'm only going to imagine it. That's worse.*

He grabbed the girl's hair and sucked on it, hard, as he came. All of them watched him. He grunted, red-faced. She whimpered gently.

He flicked his hand, shaking off a wet handful of hair. Later, Theresa watched Red collect it and wind it around his stick.

He slapped her bottom, but kindly. "Good girl," he said.

Carter gave Sol Evictus a cloth to wipe himself. This was thrown straight into the fire after use.

Takehiro passed him a robe. It was like the girl was invisible to Sol Evictus now. Blondie held out the robe to her and led her out.

"Soap," Sol Evictus snarled. "Bring me soap. Only women with short hair from now on. This is not rocket science." Theresa noticed for the first time an angry scar across his throat.

He smiled at Theresa.

"You see what we have shared?" he said. "You can see how much I rely on my staff? How trustworthy they are?"

She wondered if he was testing her yet again.

"Will she be all right?" Theresa said.

His men surrounded him, cleaning him, dressing him.

"What a team I have. Selection of staff is artistry," he said. "Making sure you have a team that looks impressive. Is varied."

It was as if the girl had never been in the room.

"How many do you have altogether?" Somehow in his presence the things he did seemed right and good. Later, she would remember what she'd seen and wonder how she could have stood quietly.

"Oh, dozens. Dozens. You can't always tell them apart, though. You understand the importance of that? Five redheads. Five Japanese. That sort of thing. Some help are grown from birth. You want them to be docile but also able to act immediately if need be." He cracked his knuckles. "My team is fully devoted and I don't expect them to let me down."

"A bit like zombies, do you think?"

He squinted at her. "Nothing at all like zombies. Although they will do whatever I say. As will their families. We are a close-knit group."

Theresa sensed movement near the door. Red stood there, eyes squeezed tight, shoulders hunched, as if he didn't want to hear or see. The other three guards were impassive.

Sol Evictus called for food, and he ate, and she did as well. They ate mounds of garlic prawns, the buttery juice dripping down their chins. It made them both laugh. The guards ate, too. Carter sat at the table, knees spread, elbows wide. His food was grey and even from where Theresa sat, she could smell it. Old meat. She saw one ghost sitting beside him, a man with a grossly distended stomach.

"Now, you must tell me. It is time for you to tell me things I don't know. What can you do? That's what I want to hear. I can't show you my real collection until you do. I can't trust you until I know it all."

"I can't tell you until you trust me!"

He laughed. "Will you take a drink? I like a cocktail myself," he said. Red handed him a large glass full of a frosty fruity drink. "Thank you, Red. For a family man, you are a good zombie. I mean guard. Team member."

He slapped Red on the back, as if the joke he'd made was hilarious and Red would share it with him. Red smiled with his eyes closed.

"Not for me. I'm not much of a drinker," Theresa said.

"Ah, yes, I remember. You are a cheap drunk. You told us that. Are you one of those people who suffer from *in vino veritas*? I rather like those people. Drunken confessions are often the best kind."

"It's more that I hate drunk people. I've seen violence. I've lost clients to it. These men, they wake out of it with no memory of the violence at all. Some of them actually don't remember beating their wives to death. They don't feel guilt. Some of them, you have to inflict physical pain for them to feel anything, and even then they try to laugh it off. Some of them you have to go all the way."

He reached out and took her hand. His palm was soft, like a child's.

"All the way? Tell us. Tell us. What have you done?"

She felt her pulse race. She knew what he wanted to hear; that she had been violent, had killed for what she believed in.

"I've only ever helped to move things along. Nothing more than anybody else would do, given the circumstance." But she was suddenly desperate to tell him of her interventions, about the men she'd led to arrest. The ones she'd thwarted by keeping their women safe.

"I think there's more. You are the best kind of good woman; the kind who will take action. Tell me, Theresa. Tell me what you've done. I need to hear your artistry."

She laughed.

"Tell me about these men. Did you enjoy their suffering? Or is the helping of the others that makes you squirm with delight?"

"It's not only men. Women, too. One mother who would have killed her kids before they were teenagers; I chopped her voice box. Because she was a charmer, could talk her way out of anything. Into anything. Even with her girls sitting next to her, deformed because of the way she neglected them. So I took her voice away from her."

Theresa stood up, into a karate position, arms out. Red stepped quickly to Sol Evictus's side, protecting.

"I'm not going to chop him!" she said. "There was one man; I don't what he would have done, but I could…see the results of it. He filled women with a sense of worthlessness. I have no idea why. But I introduced him to some men far stronger, far more violent."

Tremors ran through Sol Evictus.

"They never expect anything from me. They assume I'm weak. Some I leave alone, like the guy I saw who had the ghosts of dead drunks around him. I knew he'd die of liver-damage. Painfully."

"Is that what it is you see? Ghosts? What sort of ghosts?"

"I see the ghosts of people who have died in a particular way. And the person they haunt will die in that way, too. The closer the ghosts, the closer the death." Even as she spoke she thought, *Oh, fuck. I've given it away. Given it to him for free.*

She felt stupid. Used.

"Is that what you saw about the woman we discussed? With the high heels and the short skirt? You saw how she would die?"

"I saw beaten women and it surprised me. It still surprises me, who will become a victim."

"Who do you see around me?"

"No one. No one at all. Not close, anyway."

"And him?" He pointed at Red, who leaned on his stick and rubbed at the skin on his face.

"When we're driving, sometimes I think people wave at him. Old, old men who can hardly stand."

She felt panicked, idiotic, trapped. She looked at the door, at Red, wanting to run.

He had taken what she wanted to swap for Amber's art.

"You are an astonishing woman. Unrelenting. Such drive to help. To make things better."

Takehiro nodded and tapped his watch.

"Ah, time for the show. You should watch from offstage. We'll talk soon about cost and value. Price. Bring her in the other car," he said to Red.

He walked out, leaving them alone.

"He is shithot on stage," Red said. "You'll enjoy it."

"I've seen him on YouTube. I know."

"This will be even better. You'll be close up. You'll be able to smell his sweat."

"Do I have a choice?"

He smiled at her. "None of us have a choice," he said.

Theresa didn't like the sight of the crowds queuing to get in to the vast theatre, but at least they seemed orderly. She'd expected them to be all middle-aged women, but everyone was there. Teenagers, people in their twenties, male and female. All of them on the balls of their feet, chattering with excitement. Ghosts amongst them, pawing, sniffing, rolling.

"Take your fucken time," Blondie said, waiting for them at the stage door. Red winked.

Red on one arm, Blondie on the other, Theresa felt like the bright-eyed lucky one escorted backstage by two handsome protectors.

Hunched over, angry ghosts plucked at Blondie's shirt.

"You be careful," Theresa whispered to him. "You watch your back." He glanced quickly at Red. "I don't know who. How. You be careful."

"I will, if you say so."

She had two of them onside now.

Red handled and groped her into position side stage. "You ready for this? You might get weak knees."

Inside, people settled in to their seats, chattering, the noise of it clanging in her ears, and even at a distance she felt closed in.

The lights dimmed after twenty minutes. There was a hush. The theatre went completely dark for a blink, and then a spotlight revealed Sol Evictus, standing centre stage with his arms stretched out to the audience.

The crowd roared.

Dressed in a dark grey suit with an open-necked, pale-blue shirt, he seemed taller. He glowed.

"Clever lighting," Theresa whispered, and Red winked at her.

"Hello again," he said, and the entire audience swooned. He led into his first song; even Theresa knew it.

"He always does *You Are the Sunshine of My Life* first. Highlight of my existence," Carter said, bopping sarcastically. He did the bump with Theresa, letting his hip linger on hers.

When the song ended the audience cheered for a minute or two, and then hushed.

"I'm not bad for my age, am I?" Sol Evictus said, and they all screamed again. "You know what my secret is?"

"Tell us, tell us," the women screamed.

Sol Evictus bent over his microphone as if he was telling a secret. "Deep breaths," he said.

He sang for almost two hours, telling stories in between. The crowd was euphoric, adoring. When he lifted his arms, the people rose. Higher, higher. Theresa felt like she was watching a room full of balloons, and the ghosts lifted with them, rising to the ceiling where they played like dolphins.

She didn't feel any desire to join the audience. There were too many smells. Too much perfume and hair gel, too much hormone-infused aftershave.

Red was right; he was amazing on stage. His presence was almost blinding. Was she the only one who heard the words? Who listened to what he sang? The music was bright and uplifting, but he sang of heartache and hopelessness.

They didn't listen.

> *I am Soul Ace*
> *The one and only Soul Ace*
> *Come to me for Soul Ache*
> *Come to me for Soul*

Sol Evictus said, "This is a song I call *The Woman Who Slipped Away*." He had to wait for a couple of minutes for the cheering to fade. "You know those times when you hear a success story and you think, that coulda been me if I'd tried harder. Those times you think, I've failed. I'm a failure, I shoulda done better? The day my true love, the woman I shoulda married, the day I read she was marrying someone else was one of those days. I wanted to run to the church and carry her away, tell her she was making a mistake. I wanted to lock her up till she saw the good in me, till she understood me and adored me.

"But I didn't do any of that, you'll be relieved to know." He had to pause again. The audience found this very funny. "Because I knew deep down he was the man for her. That I had lost her because I didn't deserve to have her in the first place. This is the song I wrote to explain how I feel. It's a clumsy effort but I hope you'll forgive me." The music started, an easy listener as he often had.

> *I said the wrong thing and I said it again*
> *But looking back now*
> *I can see it was wrong*
> *And I wish I could call back the words*
> *The tone*
> *The meaning*
> *Call it back and shift it around*
> *It wouldn't take much*
> *Then I wouldn't upset you*
> *And you wouldn't hate me*
> *And we would be married today.*
> *I am to blame.*
> *I am always to blame.*
> *Because we are destined to fail.*

"Do they know what they're hearing?" Theresa asked Red.

"It makes people think harder about the way they deal with their loved ones," Red said. "He makes better people."

"It's never enough," one fan called out. "I've never done enough."

> *Do you feel regret?*
> *For some of you it is too late;*
> *The loved one is dead*
> *Or gone in some other way.*
> *Your murmuring is like the ocean,*
> *Gentle and rhythmic and, under the heat of the lights,*
> *Your eyes close,*
> *And think of that lost one, that dead one,*
> *The one you let go.*

Theresa imagined herself at the beach, the smell of the sand, the feel of sunscreen.

He sang,

> *Look back and think*
> *About the things they did*
> *And wonder if it was out of love*
> *Or hate*
> *Or disgust.*

He sang about grief and sadness and loss. He sang to them,

> *Too much grieving*
> *Can anchor a person here.*
> *Make ghosts of them. If you feel a presence,*
> *You're grieving too hard*
> *And that's your fault.*

She watched him work his magic, watched the audience rise and sink, watched an almost physical euphoria settle over them.

They stood as one, arms in the air or wrapped around themselves. Swaying, swaying.

Someone in the audience called out, "Gloomy Sunday", a song he'd covered early on in his career.

He shook his head. "I don't want to make you sad!" he said. "That song is the saddest song ever written. Don't listen to it alone! Listen to it with a friend! It's a beautiful song but it will make you cry…"

Red stepped forward to stop a dark haired woman from entering the stage. His button caught a large clump of her hair. She tugged forward, tearing her own hair out by the roots and turning to glare at him.

He nodded at her, but didn't smile. Blondie pushed her back as Red wound the hair around the etched stick he carried.

"Is that what's at the end of that thing? I thought it was horse-hair."

He shook his head. "I collect it. He hates hair. My tiny bit of power. If he ever comes for me, I'll wave it at him."

"What, he hates all hair?"

"Once it's off your head. I've got an eye for it. I see it, I wind it."

The opening chords of *Gloomy Sunday* began with Sol Evictus saying, "That's what other people think about this song. That it's the saddest song in the world. Do we agree? No, we don't. Other people think this song caused hundreds of people to commit suicide. I think if you hear this song, you'll know it brings hope, and the joy of love. This song shouldn't make you feel like dying. It should make you feel like living."

But, Theresa thought, *of course it didn't. It broke your heart to hear it and it filled you with a deep sense of almost irrational sadness.*

Red said to Theresa, "He has to have sex as soon as he comes off the stage."

"He just had sex," she said. "He was having sex two hours ago."

"Nonetheless." He smiled at her. "If you would choose to be waiting I'm sure he'll look fondly on your deal. On this art shit you want."

"What, I stand back stage, undies off, skirt up?"

"Something like that," he said.

"Do I have a choice?"

"None of us have a choice."

"He's not real good with women, is he?"

"He leaves them happy. He dumps them and they have no memory of even being with him. But they're happy. He leaves something behind, though. He always says he likes the idea of women alive with his mark on them."

"What, like a brand?"

"Exactly like a brand. And sometimes seed."

"What, children?"

"He hates children."

"Did one of his children die? Is that it? He's trying to replace a dead child by having so much sex? Oh, no. He told me he didn't have any children at all."

"He's got so many children he'd barely notice if one died. You have no idea."

"What? Six? Seven?"

"Dozens. Dozens we know about. If she's fertile, she's pregnant. Doesn't matter if she's on the pill. I know two of them, at least."

"I can't get pregnant, though. Will that bother him? Those bits don't work for me."

"Cancer?" He moved closer, sniffed her. "Was it cancer? Is it all removed?"

She pushed him away. "Not cancer. It was my choice. They do miracles these days with implants, you know. I want sex but I don't want kids. Is that a problem?" Lying, because there hadn't been a man since Ben.

"Tell ya what, if he turns you down, I'll fuck ya," Carter said.

"I thought he'd asked for me?" She felt a ridiculous disappointment.

"He might, Theresa. You have to be prepared. Or he might go some other way. Some nights we have ten of you, all lined up," Red said.

"By 'you', you mean women?"

He nodded, a confused squint in his eye. He didn't take her point at all, and she thought, *I guess he doesn't meet too many feminists.*

Blondie watched them. He made a whipping gesture, mouthed "Pussy whipped."

Red mouthed, "Fuck off." To Theresa, he said, "That guy's such a loser. Sol Evictus would be better off without him."

Sol Evictus crooned on stage, all sweet and loving, causing tears. He lifted them up, made them love him, and then he'd sing about what he thought was true, how shutting the door doesn't make it better, make it go away. He sang it light and lively, as if he was telling a joke. Theresa saw the audience smiling, but lips twitched as words sank in.

"That's a man whose going to live forever," Red said.

"He does have ghosts, though," Theresa said. Lying. "Faint, there at the foot of the stage. But I can't see what's wrong with them."

Theresa felt increasingly claustrophobic, the press of bodies took her breath even though she wasn't amongst them. She tried to focus on Sol Evictus but kept thinking of what would happen if there was a fire.

Sol Evictus sighed. It filled the room. "I'm so sorry. I have to go." The audience sighed with him.

He walked into the wings and didn't even see her. Carter met him with a girl from the audience; red cheeked, dressed in hot pink, her hair tied back tight in a bun.

"Don't go too far," Red said. "He's gone for this slut but he'll wanna talk to you. I know it. He likes you. He'll kill me if I let you go. He hasn't said goodbye to you yet. Never leave until he says goodbye."

"I'll wait outside. I need some air."

Theresa sat on the steps leading to the backstage entrance. She felt exhausted, drained and had no real idea what to do next. She'd lost her one small bargaining chip; information about what she saw, the ghosts she saw, although there were always more ghosts to see. She could smell sea salt but did not see her ghosts.

The audience took a long time to file out, as if they didn't want it to end. They came out weeping, many of them, and exhausted from two hours of ecstasy .

Dozens of women clustered at the back door, desperate to be close to him. Theresa listened to them, wondering if any had been changed by the concert.

They all clutched Sol Evictus CDs.

Blondie stood high on the steps, calling, "Send him a fan letter, ladies. He likes those. I promise you he'll answer every one with a photo and an autograph. No doubt there."

Next to him, Carter, reached out to touch the women, to take gifts from them.

"I bet that guy'll do all right with the ladies. Look at him! I bet he's telling them he can get them in, and then he'll fuck them and forget them," a middle-aged man said to Theresa.

She was shocked, and stepped away from him.

"No doubt," he said loudly. "He'll fuck their brains out then beat the crap out of them. I can imagine it."

The woman beside him opened her mouth, her eyes; she seemed shocked at his words as well. "Why would you even think that?"

He shook his head as if he wasn't sure what she was talking about.

There was a small scuffle, two women and a man fighting for space near where Sol Evictus might emerge. One woman was pushed to the ground, cutting her palm. Another gave her a handkerchief and mopped up the blood.

"Here, let me take that. I'll make sure Sol Evictus gets it," Carter called out, and the two guards laughed. Theresa filed this away. She wasn't sure what it meant yet, but she'd figure it out.

"Sorry, ladies, Sol Evictus went out the other door. Next time."

There was a collective moan of disappointment.

"Come on, Theresa," Red said. "This way."

They left Blondie and Carter to manage the slowly dispersing women and walked to the car.

"He'll be a while. He likes to clean up afterwards. He wants us to go home with him, though."

"He must be exhausted."

"I dunno."

"Those poor women. I wish I could help them, but all they want is him."

"You can't help everybody."

Theresa flicked through the music magazines she found in the seat flap; all of them with marked articles about Sol Evictus.

The door opened and he slid in. He'd changed again; he was in jeans and a loose, green shirt. His hair was washed, slicked back, his face glowing. He seemed small again.

"What did you think of the show, Theresa?" He clapped his hands together as if applauding himself.

Carter opened the passenger door and sat down. He and Red spoke quietly together.

"My aunt will be so jealous when she knows how close I was to the stage."

"Ah, your aunt. Such deep, deep grief that only a mother can feel. Perhaps we can spend some time together. One day. Although you know my feelings on fans. You didn't say what you thought of my performance."

"You know how to play an audience. Every last one of them is thinking of lost love, whether they've lost loves or not."

"Ah, it's a form of magic, isn't it? It's all about distraction. Having the audience focus so completely on one thing they fail to see what you are hiding from them."

"What are you hiding?"

"The fact that my voice is rather weak! Did you think of lost loves? Like the maiden ladies whose one great love died in the war." He didn't say which war. "They lost their one true love and never recovered. That's what you remind me of." As if he had known such women personally.

"You think I'm like a virgin old lady?"

"Ahh! Aahhhh!"

Theresa realised he was laughing. "Is that what I am?"

"Ahhh! Aaaah! I think we both know this is not the case!" He tapped the back of the driver's seat. "Let's get a move on, Red."

He sat back. "I couldn't do it if it wasn't for the pleasure and sustenance I take from my artworks. They give me strength enough to help all those people to happiness."

Theresa wasn't sure what he meant.

"For the greater good. Small sufferings for the greater good," Carter said, as if he was used to filling in this gap. He passed Sol Evictus the bloodied hanky; Sol sniffed it and tucked it into his sleeve.

"Tell me what you saw in there, Theresa. Ghosts galore, I imagine? Ghosts by the thousands?"

"There are always ghosts."

"What do you see around my favourite guard?" He spoke *sotte voce* and pointed at the passenger seat.

Theresa looked hard at Carter. "His ghosts look sick to me.

198

Thin, but with a distended stomach. Some kind of illness which makes people not eat."

Carter glanced at her in the rear view mirror, his eyebrows raised. She'd seen him with his meat. His health bars. She saw how little he ate, how he patted his stomach sometimes, feeling its tautness.

"Or perhaps the cannibal disease."

Carter laughed, surprised and, she thought, guilty.

"Really?"

"Naaah, I'm kidding. All your guards are clear."

"And her? That woman over there, with those ugly shoes and the fat ankles, her little dog on a leash."

"There's nothing around her. The plain woman next to her, though, the one you wouldn't notice? I think she'll be hit by a car. Or she'll be driving a car and cause an accident. I'm not always sure."

"I know that feeling." He opened a bottle of bright green soft drink and sank back in his seat, his eyes closed. "I'm tired, worn out. Fill me with solace, Theresa, while we travel. Tell me more of your adventures, your…"

"My interventions."

"Tell me about them. The ghosts. Tell me everything. Then perhaps I'll show you my collection. My real collection."

It had been a long day. Theresa wondered if Tim was keeping an eye on the time; she'd jokingly told him to send the dogs in if she'd been gone longer than 24 hours. It was now past midnight; close to 1:30am, she thought. She didn't want to take out her phone to check the time. It seemed rude and something he wouldn't like.

"You're not tired, are you? People are never tired around me," Sol Evictus said.

He spoke with his eyes closed. He waved his fingers at her gently. "Tell me. I know you want to. You can't tell anybody else. But you can tell me anything."

She felt an intense rush of desire to talk. She knew he'd understand; that he'd admire her.

So she told him. She spoke until she barely had the energy to move.

Sol Evictus sat by her, not touching her, but his breath washing over her, his eyes so intent on her she felt anchored to him.

Sol Evictus said, "You have seen death and it hasn't destroyed you. But it has changed you. You will never be the same because of it. But you don't run from death. You embrace it. You are fascinated by it. You want to know it intimately."

They had been parked in his driveway for some time. "Come inside," he said.

The thought of it exhausted her. "I should make a quick phone call," she said. "I've been gone a while!"

"Who is it who cares?" he whispered, his eyes widened. "Who is it who will worry about you?"

"A friend. He knew Amber. Sometimes I think he sees me as a replacement."

He smiled at that, waved his hand at her. "Make your call. I'll wait."

He leaned back in his seat.

"Hi, Tim? Yep, it's Theresa. I'm having a good day. Night. Listen, don't worry about me. I'll be home in a while. I'll call you when I get in. After I have a sleep. Okay?"

"Answering machine?"

She nodded.

"I'm curious to know why he would worry. Why you say, don't worry?"

"He's that kind of person. He's a bit of a control freak, actually. But some friends are like that, aren't they?"

"That poor boy. What a childhood Tim had. Those old ladies and what they did to him. He hasn't told you, has he?" Sol Evictus shook his head, tutted. "He doesn't like to think of it. But try to make him remember, if you become close. Help him remember so he can understand why he is a failure. It is because he is a victim in his heart."

"How do you know that? And what can I do to help him?"

"Oh, Theresa. Oh, beautiful, beautiful goddess of grief. You give your life to the suffering of others. You are suffused with it, engorged, your cheeks flushed and warm."

He put the back of his hand to her cheek.

She felt as if she were burning up. He reminded her of Client D, the fourth intervention. The one she misjudged.

Silver haired and charming, you can't imagine there was anything but kindness about him.

He lead her through a door she hadn't noticed before. "You have secrets," he said. "I like that about you. I don't trust anyone I can't blackmail." He threw his head back and laughed.

She said, "You have a huge house. I think I could come here a thousand times and still not be able to find my way around."

"I have many rooms. There are not many who take in interest, so there are very few who have seen this much of it. Those who have can be...disturbed by it."

She wasn't sure if this was a challenge or a warning.

He began to hum, and then to sing softly. *He's trying to seduce me, to draw me into his world*, she thought. He wanted her to understand him.

As they walked, he talked. He told her the stories of his paintings, told them with such glee and delight she felt ill.

"This one," he said, "is Alfred Konrad's *Summer Afternoon*. They think they have the original in the New Jersey Museum, but this is it. I commissioned this one from him. Why would I give it to a museum?"

A large, white house dominated the painting. It seemed to loom over the people sitting, stone-faced, at a table in the overgrown garden in the foreground. Around them, behind them, between them, were ghosts; pale, transparent figures.

"He painted what could have been. The ghosts of children who died. This family had a history of miscarriages. I had him paint those dead babies grown up. These are the adults they could have become. They are futureless. He is almost unknown, now. It's a shame about his dead career. He was a talented man."

"You've commissioned a lot of portraits. Over a lot of years."

He smiled. "I'm a lot older than I look. I credit freshly-squeezed orange juice." He smiled at her, looking like a boy of ten making a cheeky joke.

He must be over a hundred years old, she thought. She could hear him creak as he moved. Today he looked forty.

"You and I understand grief, when we look at a sad painting. We have suffered such loss."

"What loss have you suffered?" she said in the voice she used for clients; kindly, designed to extract information.

"Ah, like you, it pains me to talk of it."

He led her to a small gallery room. The room smelt faintly antiseptic, and there were chairs in the centre, lined up like in a doctor's waiting room. The art in this room was graphically medical. Theresa felt her skin twitching, her organs throbbing, as if what she saw was being transferred to her body. Bulbous growths, distorted brains, deformed foetuses. Syphilitic penises. Cancerous blobs. She could almost smell the disease.

"What do you think of the medical profession?" he said. "Doctors and surgeons? I think we give them so much respect in society, yet what are they after all but dabblers? Experimenters? One of them gave me two years to live on the day I was born. Others...

five in all…others failed to see what should have been seen in a lady I adored. All failed to diagnose a fatal disease."

"Did it end badly?"

"It could not have ended in a worse way. I lost myself for a while, Theresa. When I lost my precious one. Can you imagine? I know you can. I've had little faith in doctors since."

Takehiro brought them both a drink, circling Sol Evictus as he always did. Theresa was tempted to poke or squeeze the lump on the back of his head to see what was inside it. He didn't catch her eye or smile.

She'd said to him, in English as he let her in, "I'll pay you a thousand dollars to fuck my dead brother," to test him, to see if he was faking. He handed her the note, "I do not speak" so either he was a brilliant actor or he hadn't understood her.

"That will quench our thirst." Sol Evictus sipped his large brandy and dry ginger.

"How did you climb out of your grief hole? If you have the secret to that, you could be rich."

"I am rich! As Croesus, as the saying goes. I didn't climb out. I built underneath myself with song and healing. This is the healing I offer those who listen to my music. You've felt it yourself. An unidentified comfort, perhaps. A feeling of well-being. I almost died soon after my lady died and by the time I woke up, I had been forgotten. I didn't find that pleasant." He sighed. "Doctors."

"I can't remember the last time I went to one," she said.

"Some people have the right disposition for doctors. Malleable and weak. Not you. You would cure yourself with a thought." He gestured, tapping his temple then pointing at her.

He breathed deeply, so that he almost lifted off the ground. Theresa saw his skin change colour; almost become blue, like a victim of gas poisoning.

There were paintings of artificial limbs. "All taken from dead men and women. This is Carter's favourite part of the gallery. Red prefers the so-called Body Art area, where I display the work of the knife-wielders. You know, he is the only one of them with family but I'm not sure how well his wife understands him. He is a kind of artiste, better than the others. I recognize that. Cutting is an art and it can be beautiful. If you use an unfeasibly sharp knife it's painless."

He breathed deeply, sighed the air out.

"Look at this," Sol Evictus said. On the back of a picture of a decayed leg, hidden in the frame, was a pornographic photo; a one legged man and a woman with breasts so large her back was curved.

"I believe this couple died in an horrific car accident the next day. Horrific."

It was shocking, but mostly Theresa thought, *He looks like a good man. He has his hand on her shoulder gently, and there is a tender look on his face.*

She loved that.

He scratched gently at the painting with one long fingernail. "You see? A hair. You know when you're painting a wall, sometimes a loose hair will stick to the wet paint? One of yours, or a bristle. You understand the information contained, don't you? What we could learn?"

Theresa realised that all of the paintings had a hair. Even the drawings had hairs trapped under the glass. She didn't like to think about who owned the hair. Red held his stick firm, walking with them. She saw his fingers clench around it.

"Ah, there is power in capturing hair. Power in keeping it safe. You know I have a strand of hair from a 90 year old woman who never cut it? Her entire life is in that hair. Takehiro took it from her head as she lay in her coffin. She didn't feel a thing."

"You have an interest in hair?"

"I have a disgust for hair. A phobia, you might almost say. But I think strength comes in confronting these things, don't you?"

She nodded.

"Then you will be impressed by the next room." His voice wavered slightly. "I call it the Hair Loom Room."

He stood in the doorway and gently pushed her inside.

"That one has the hair from Marie Antoinette, taken from her guillotined head. And this one has hair from the tail of Phar Lap. You know he was poisoned."

"You hate hair, yet you're surrounded by it. Even your guards are hairy!"

"Ah, yes. You're right. How is that?"

He slumped as they walked through this room, dragging his left foot, he slurred his words, sounding as if he'd taken his teeth out. "Let's move on," he said.

"What else do you have in your wonderful collection?" Theresa asked. Being kind, distracting him.

"Would you like to see more? Are you ready? Would you like to see my Dina Gottliebová collection?"

She wouldn't, she didn't, but she had to. She had to see it. If she stopped now, she could convince herself he wasn't so bad, he was a strange old man. She could almost convince herself of that. But she knew this wasn't true, and that she was the only one who could see it clearly and be willing to act on it.

"I call this the Room of Woe." She thought he was joking but he wasn't and she despaired of ever knowing when he was joking and when he was serious.

"He never jokes," Red had told her.

"But he smiles."

"Not a joking smile."

She wondered if he could see her thought processes.

"Through here." Hard, swivelling chairs, so you could always face the painting you were looking at.

They were brilliant and sickening. "Your Amber loved these,"

205

he said. "She was moved to an almost physical response, you know."

Theresa shuddered at the thought. Surely not.

"Gottliebová painted children in the concentration camps. Her work echoes Amber's in that way. Look at the detail. Here, and here. Dina took great care with the hair colour, even when the child was out of patience. We talked about it; the children would have been lethargic; lack of food, lack of sleep, maybe they knew that their mothers would not be able to save them. We always think our mothers can save us but they can't. She must have known her portraits would be the only real record of these futureless children. Their name would be on a list and one day perhaps a memorial, but no one would remember them. That's why Amber used to say she had to get the hair colour right. To remember them truthfully."

Theresa wanted to burn them. There was no true memories here; there was exploitation. Abuse.

"This is not simply historical. Not simply a record. It is an understanding of human nature, our cruelties. A reminder of who we are at base level, that no one is above this. I am not alone. Many others have this fascination. This…scholarship. People don't resile from death in art as they do in reality."

She didn't feel faint or weak and would not ask for a seat, but she was so tired she could curl up on the floor and sleep, regardless of the cold and the artwork. She was so tired. She tilted until her shoulder touched his as if she was magnetically drawn to him.

"Have you had enough?" he said. "You are coping well. I don't remember a woman coping more impressively. Or a man, for that matter."

"There's more?" she said.

"There's always more. My gallery is endless. We look until we are tired. I've disappeared for weeks in here, haven't I?"

Red nodded.

"It's why the cabinets are stocked with food and drink. Why the couches are so comfortable. More?"

She nodded. "More."

He pushed open a solid mahogany door. A musty smell hit her. And darkness, so dark she almost felt she could cut it.

"Red?"

Red flicked a switch and gaslight filled the room, flickering and weak.

"Some ancient treasures in here. Very old deaths. Some I collected myself, or I inherited. Some I took. You would not have liked my grandmother." The smell in the room was like an old jewel box or an ancient painted roman coin.

He said, "People have died with these items in their hand. This coin travelled the world a hundred times, maybe more. I bought it from an air hostess, gorgeous thing she was. Long blonde hair but neat? You've never seen neater hair. She pulled this from the pocket of a man who died onboard. Choked on vomit, she said. Nasty!"

He placed it in Theresa's hand and reached for a goblet. "This one is not old at all. A few years. It's a replica; someone thought they'd fake the holy grail. The last sip of a holy man. This one was used at the death beds of a number of relatives before I bought it. A family heirloom, one might say. A lucky family with such mysterious deaths."

They walked on. He linked his arm through hers. "You must have seen some terrible things. Terrible ghosts."

Theresa knew she should bargain with him. Demand Amber's pictures in return for her stories. If he was a weaker man, this would be happening. She understood that she was a bully too; that she could beat men she thought weak, but not the ones who were strong.

"I saw the ghosts of beaten women around a teacher once. It was shocking. I couldn't imagine a woman like her beaten. I know different now."

"You thought she was too smart?"

"Smart, strong, tough. But those women get beaten too."

"Not all teachers are good people, you know. I had a terrible teacher when I was a child. He took away all hope from me, day by day. How do you survive without hope? It was only through music I rediscovered hope. That's the music I share with my fans. My lovers. Music I shared with that teacher, to help him heal."

"I see the ghosts of men killed by prostitutes. Saw them around my father's best friend, a man I called Mr Respectable because he was the epitome of it. And others. Saw the ghosts of prostitutes killed by men. I can't help them all, can I?"

"You can't help any of them. Not in the end. But it makes you feel good to try."

They reached the end of the hallway. "So many gaps," he said, sighing his deep, deep sigh. "So many portraits I should own. Like the Mona Lisa. What do you suppose she is looking at? A pool of blood. A baby splashing in it. That's what I imagine."

"You have a very vivid imagination," Theresa said, and they laughed together.

"Show her the pillowcases," Red said.

"The pillowcases?"

"She knows the lady."

"Do you, Theresa? Know the balloon lady, the red one full of tragedy and failure?"

Prudence.

"Ah..."

The men watched her and she thought, *They will find out, anyway.*

"She's a relative. A distant relative. We've had very little to do with her but she follows me around sometimes."

"She is riven with guilt, I think, and wants to save you. She's lived a sad life, that one. She lost her daughter in a fire. Other children, as well. Burnt her own skin clean off trying to save them, but still four of them burnt to ash."

"Oh, God, is that what happened? Poor Prudence. It's terrible.

That ash…she wears that across her face."

"You didn't know this?"

"My family doesn't talk about the bad stuff."

"Those children all dead in a fire. They left an impression on these pillow cases." They were framed, the material still bright although marred with burn marks. "I do like fire. It is so definite."

"Where did you get these?"

"Where do I get anything? People sell them to me. I asked your cousin Amber for a memento of this family tragedy and she brought me the pillowcases. Clever girl."

She looked at the death impressions of her cousins. Second cousins? Her relatives. Prudence must have been devastated to lose the pillowcases. Therese felt sickened by it all. By how much Prudence had suffered, and how little people cared.

"Your family disowned poor Prudence after that. She wasn't to be trusted.'

It made her think again of the bloodied newspaper she had hanging, and she decided to take it down when she got home.

"What are you thinking of?" he said. "I'm greedy. Tell me what's in your mind. You're thinking of something lovely."

"It's nothing. A piece of art you'd have no interest in."

He pursed his lips.

"It's a bloodied newspaper. I'll tell you the story next time you need calming."

They reached a silver closed door. "This is what you want. This is what you are here for. This alone."

He seemed angry.

"Amber's work? I came here for that. But that's not why I'm still here after so many hours. I'm fascinated. Bewildered. Tireder than I've ever been. I want to be asleep but I'm not. I'm in a state of fugue with your art, your collection, spinning around me. I'm changed in 24 hours. Different."

"But you still want to see the work. You still want to bargain with me for it."

"Yes," she whispered.

"Then in we go."

Theresa drew in her breath. *He showed me the pillowcases first, to soften me up, make me more vulnerable to this.*

"My God," she said. Sketches and paintings covered the walls. Sketch pads lay open on two low tables.

Mostly they were portraits, people Theresa didn't recognise, although she thought the pear-shaped couple nestled in a butterfly cocoon were Scott and Courtney. All of the pictures had a certain element about them, deeply-etched lines on their faces, all of them with a crease between the eyes.

Sol Evictus stood close to her. He smelt like her father, when he hadn't before, as if he now exuded the same aftershave from his pores to make her trust him. "What do you think?"

"Brilliant. To do these from imagination is incredible." She wanted him to confess where the drawings had been made. To tell her the circumstances.

"A talented young woman," he said. "As you well know." He winked at her, and felt as if all her life had been a lie. He knew it all; the lies, the mistakes, the shame.

"These children, these teenagers, every one of them dead. Moments after Amber drew them, in some cases. They killed themselves. Gave up. Gave in." He sighed deeply. "They gave themselves to the perfect solace of death, the comfort, the glorious sleep in Paradise Falls."

Theresa looked closely at one of the drawings. In the corner, she could see a dove. All of them, she saw, every one, had a symbol of hope. She thought, *Anything but look at him.*

Theresa thought of Scott's description of Amber's grandmother's portrait – a cat held too tight, wanting to be free. This was the look on many of the faces in Amber's work.

"Where did these things happen?"

"Do you like the work? Are you proud of your cousin?" His voice was deep and gentle, full of quaver and sadness.

She touched some of Amber's work, feeling tears welling. "She was talented," Theresa said. "These drawings are incredible. I'm jealous."

"Jealous of a dead girl?" He'd caught her. At that moment she did envy Amber. Sol Evictus clearly admired this.

"Her parents would give anything to have these back. At least some of them. They've lost her, and this is all that remains."

"People say, 'I would give anything' but they don't mean it. And tell me; if this physical depiction is all they have left, did they really love her? Do they really remember her, did they really know her? And are they ready to climb out of that dark hole they so clearly find comfort in? Besides, they have nothing I want." He flicked his hand, as if flicking them away. "You, however. You have a talent useful to us. You can see things no one else can. Luckily you're also an attractive one. Makes my job easier."

"Your job?"

"Self-employed! Self-described! But how good for us to talk about this girl of incredible talent. Talk with honesty and truth about what she gave to me. Talk to someone who knew her well. And you're so delightful to look at." Sol Evictus shucked off his jacket. She hadn't seen him change his clothes, but he was now wearing a tight grey t-shirt. He had the torso of a much younger man.

He showed her a portrait of himself. "This is the one she did for me."

Theresa almost stopped breathing at the beauty, the perfection, of the portrait.

"Can you see the resemblance?" Sol Evictus said, and if eyes can be said to twinkle, his did, like Santa Claus with a sweet secret.

"It's so different from the others she did, isn't it? Around the eyes."

"Ah, because I'm not dying. That was her talent. She didn't know the cause of death, or the method, but she did know the time. You can see how it works together. Like a jigsaw puzzle. Each piece needs to be on the wall for the picture to be whole."

The next wall was full of tiny drawings, most the size of a standard envelope. They were all drawn in purple ink.

"My artist who followed Amber." Sol Evictus whispered. "She died."

The purple line drawings were clever, but lacked the pathos of Amber's work.

"How did she die?"

"Train wreck," Sol Evictus said briefly. He moved her to the next display: seven photographic-like portraits of teenagers portrayed as angels. "She was replaced by this artist. Such an idealist, as you can see. But slow with her work. We had to let her go, only recently. I don't suppose you know of any brilliant young artists? I don't like to be without an artist in residence."

"You mean sleeping here?"

"They often would. You know it's a lovely home. Anybody would think so. And those, like Amber, who are tired of the confines of living with their parents, find it a great freedom. We have no rules here. Apart from the ones of basic civilization. So, a name? You have a name?"

He peered at her so intensely she gabbled nervously. She felt as if he knew her exactly, knew what was in her mind. *Annie,* she was thinking. *It's Annie he wants. Or Andy.*

"Amber had a group of friends she studied with. They can all paint."

"Ah, yes. I know the girls you mean. They are not all doing as well as expected."

"So sad."

"I've heard sadder stories," he said. "We will call them in. Don't you think? We will see who is right for the job."

"There's Tim, as well. You'd probably get on well with him. He's doing an amazing series of paintings. Inspired by ghosts."

"Ones he sees?"

"No. Ones I see."

She thought of Andy and his feverish sketching, but kept *Tim, Tim, Tim* in her thoughts. Choose Tim, choose Tim. Tim didn't care much anymore. He thought about suicide often. He had far less to lose.

Andy was just a kid. She had to keep Sol Evictus from him.

They entered a small dining room. Table set for three.

"We must eat," Sol Evictus said.

Theresa wasn't sure what meal they were up to. She hadn't heard him give out the instruction for food, but supposed he must have. She felt shaken from what she'd seen. So much death. So much pain and loss. This man feeling intense joy in his collection, taking strength from it.

Worst of all, she felt a kinship with him. She shared his fascination.

It was breakfast, a lavish, British affair with kippers, toast, eggs in many varieties, marmalades and bacon. Theresa ate voraciously, making Sol Evictus laugh.

"Oh, there is something very, very special about you after all. I did see it; even your famous murder plate showed me that. And your mother..."

He held her face, spoke right at her. "I can help you to understand her. Your mother knows more than she tells you. Your mother sees everything. She was trying to protect you. You probably can't remember." Sing-song, in his beautiful voice.

Theresa said, "What do you mean? What does she know? Tell me. I can't ask her."

"She doesn't want you to know."

"Tell me."

He led her to one of the comfortable couches. Reached to the small fridge and pulled out a lime. He cut the lime, poured small shots of tequila, opened a cupboard and pulled out a box of salt. "Here," he said. They drank. She twisted her face at the taste.

"You don't like tequila?"

"It's okay. But drinking it makes me feel like I'm drowning. It's the salt I don't like."

"Drinking is good. Drowning can be good momentarily."

She thought of Scott and Courtney, who had almost drowned in drink. "Some people find it hard to drink a small amount. They get lost in it. They get sucked into it."

"Some of them sing about it," he said. "Some of us sing."

He crooned to her, and she thought, *There are millions who would kill for this.*

> *You should never forget*
> *The actions you've taken*
> *Each action deliberate*
> *Each aftermath chosen*
> *You should never forget*
> *Your interventions*
> *Those times you said no*
> *Those times you said yes*
> *Those times you stepped in*
> *To change someone's life*
> *To break someone's heart*
> *To make something right.*
> *You are good, a saint*
> *A goddess of good*
> *You are good, a saint*
> *And you should never forget that.*

With that, he poured her another tequila and helped her drink it, his touch so light and sweet she could have cried.

"Did you write that for me?"

He nodded. "Inspired by you. And I know my fans will love it. It's the sort of thing they beg me for. They all want to believe in their own goodness. No one ever wants to believe they are a monster. And yet…"

Theresa held his gaze, but he began to hum and she felt her eyelids flutter. She was nauseous, exhausted, and there was something like a butterfly in her brain, a flickering memory of truth or lies.

Then she blinked, and time had passed.

"Theresa, you must take pity on an old man now and let me sleep. If you want payment for the film you brought me, ask Blondie. He'll give you money."

"I don't want money. I only want Amber's paintings back." She was full of satisfying food and honest words seemed right. "And Blondie…I don't like talking to him. I don't trust him. He's full of fantasies I don't want to know about."

"I'm sorry you don't like him. I haven't heard that before. He's such a smiley fella. I will keep an eye on him. Thank you for your honesty. Many are too scared to tell me the truth, but I'd hate to think my fans are frightened of my team. My lawyer does do checks on all of them and I trust his judgment completely. He is behind many of my decisions."

He whispered, "You threw yourself in. When you were five. Only your mother knows you wanted to die." So quietly she thought she imagined it.

He nodded to Red, who took her elbow.

"I thank you for a pleasant evening, but now I must sleep. Tomorrow more preparations. Prepare always. Goodbye." He tilted his head at her and left the room, saying, "Show our lady out," to Red.

As they walked to the front door and climbed into the car, Red said, "So she was your cousin? Shame you weren't here, then. You mighta been able to help her. She couldn't get out on her own." He had a child's drawing on his dashboard, a sunny picture with four smiling people.

"Did she want to?"

"That kid fought against doing the shit he got her to do. Some of the others don't care. They take the money and get pissed, don't think about it."

"I'm glad Amber fought against it."

"Yeah. The next one didn't. She got pulled in. She lasted, what, a year? Then the last one, a month ago you would have seen her."

Theresa felt her skin burn. "So it's true, then. He's had more? Girls who draw for him? I thought maybe he was trying to shock me."

"He's always got one on the go," Red said. Casually, as if it meant nothing. He pulled to a stop at the red light, took out his knife and shaved hairs off his arm, creating art himself. "I hope my girls turn out like her. Like you. But he's been at them for a long time. Who knows what he tells them while they're sitting on his knee? Uncle Sol. Uncle my fucking arse."

Theresa had a moment of clarity.

"You were talking about the two children you knew for sure were Sol Evictus's. Do you ever see them?

"Mine," he said. Voice low. For a moment, his eyes were clear and he seemed to be a different person. "He'll kill them if I don't keep this up. He doesn't care. Kill my wife, too. She'd let him. She'd lie back and take it across the throat as if he was fucking another baby into her."

"But can't you run? Take them away somewhere?"

"Nowhere to run from him. You can only kill him, and you can't kill him."

"No way at all? People have tried?"

"No one's tried. Who the fuck would dare? We're all blinded by devotion. We've been with him a long time. We owe everything to him. I was a mess when he found me. I would have killed and been caught without Sol Evictus. It's the fucking call of the blade.

"One kid is still in primary school but it won't be long before he's talking to her and do I want her to hear what he has to say? Do I? I feel like the other one is already lost."

He drove. She saw old men ghosts, waiting at the side of the road, thumbs out, as if expecting him to pick them up.

As he pulled into her driveway he said, "Call me if you need to talk. No one else understands."

The day was beginning for most people. Her dog would be starving. She felt deeply exhausted and sadder than she ever had in her life,

She fed the dog and ate a banana. There were messages from Tim, from Raul, from Courtney and Scott, notes under the door. She made quick calls to each of them to say she was okay.

Then she slept for twelve hours.

Theresa woke up with heavy legs; the dog lying flat across her. Watching her patiently. When she sat up, he leapt off the bed and spun in circles.

"You want a walk?" she said. Of course he did.

Unsure whether it was lunch or dinner but ravenous anyway, she cooked pasta with bacon and broccoli, lots of cheese, and she ate two huge bowls. The dog ate the rest, and then dragged her out the door and up the road. They walked for half an hour; Theresa heading towards where she thought Prudence would be selling balloons. She bought coffee and croissants from the café to take away, the dog waiting patiently outside. She'd planned to sit in but three large men were in there, and they made her nervous. She felt out of sorts, so much so that the café owner said, "You should listen to some music to make you feel better. Some feelgood music."

As if this was something no one had thought of before.

The café owner held up a Sol Evictus CD. "My husband calls him Mr Feelgood. We throw on some Sol Evictus and we feel better. He has the voice of an angel. I'll agree with him on that much."

"He sings like an angel, but he doesn't sing pleasant things," Theresa said, testing the waters, seeing if simply telling people would make a difference.

The café owner looked at her as if she was crazy. "He provides solace to those who need it."

Theresa watched as Prudence slowly walked along the street. She had a limp which made her roll from side to side, and her balloons bobbed up and down.

Prudence stopped when she saw Theresa and her dog. "You waited for me?" she said. She smiled. "First time, you waited for me." She had her balloons covered with a dirty cloth, as if she thought she could hide them. "You look sick."

A drunk teenager came up to ask for a balloon and she snarled at him.

"I'm tired."

"You poor, poor girl, poor tired lonely girl."

Theresa wanted to reach up and wipe the ash from her face, to say, *I know. I know what happened to your child and it's terrible.*

"I've got coffee. I've got croissants. Would you like to sit with me and share them?" The dog sniffed at the bags she carried, wagging his tail.

They sat on a bench, looking out over the water. "You've been with that man again, haven't you?"

"I haven't!" Theresa said, thinking she was talking about sex. "I haven't been with any man since…."

Prudence squinted at her. "You were there. I saw you."

"I was. I went. I saw his art works. I saw Amber's artworks."

"Oh, that poor, poor darling. Such an innocent. So much ahead of her."

"And yet she ran away from her parents. Maybe there's something wrong with them after all."

Prudence shook her head so hard sprinkles of red powdered ash flew through the air. "You know who saved you from drowning when you were five?"

"It was a stranger. He disappeared before my parents could thank or reward him."

Sometimes, if her family felt happy together, they'd talk about how lucky they were, and about what reward the stranger deserved, ever-more extravagant things like a boat or a small island.

Once, when the girls were bitterly fighting over something, Giselle said, "I hate that stranger for saving you." The punishment for that—a trip alone to Grandmother's house—meant she never said such a thing again.

"It wasn't a stranger," Prudence said. "It was your Uncle Scott."

"It can't have been."

"Scott saved you, and he carried you to the car, and then off your parents drove with a live child instead of a dead one. He put you on his towel. Had Coca Cola written on it? You have that at home?"

Her mother did. It was used for dogs, or cleaning up spills.

"Scott saved me?"

"You were all together. A family day out. He hadn't met Courtney yet."

"God, my mother." All those times her mother said, "Imagine if that stranger hadn't been there." Lies.

"You don't blame your father?"

"He's her victim. Why don't you call her a monster? All the things she's done? Hasn't done?"

"She has her own death. Don't worry. A monster's death awaits her. There are so many different kinds of monsters."

"Why don't you follow her around, then?"

"She doesn't see me any more. I'm invisible to her. You ask your mother about it."

"Sol Evictus said I was in the water because I tried to kill myself."

Prudence hummed; didn't answer.

Theresa thought about telling Prudence about the pillowcases in Sol Evictus's collection. She was curious about the story and this would be a way to bring it out. But Prudence had trusted Amber; this would hurt her more than help her. She'd leave it for now.

A text came in; Raul from the refuge. Theresa waved her hand at Prudence, who tucked her balloon strings up and walked away. Raul said they were going out to lunch. Did she want to come? She laughed. Missing the simplicity of the life she'd had there. Who was good, who was bad. It was clear and obvious.

Save me a spot, she texted back. *And order me a spunky waiter.*

He texted, *got some info re: numbers. Will call after lunch when I'm pissed.* He added; *Nothing on your cousin, BTW.*

What about Sol Evictus?

Not much going on there. Can't find out about his early life, but that's not unusual. Nothing on the record, though. Nothing concrete, if that's what you're looking for.

Thanks, Raul.

Theresa phoned Lynda. "I can tell from your voice you're not getting enough fibre."

Theresa thought about all she'd seen and heard. How helpless she felt.

"Yeah, fibre. That's my main problem. How are you doing, today, Mum?" Theresa had felt far more kindly towards Lynda since learning about the baby she had lost.

"I'm okay. Busy. Always busy."

"We're busy here, too. Lots of things happening." Theresa waited, but Lynda didn't want to hear it.

"Your father wants to know if you're all right. " Lynda had a mouthful of food.

There was no way she could talk to her about Sol Evictus and what he'd shown her. Told her. Made her feel.

"Mum, Prudence told me something interesting. About that time I nearly drowned. She says it was Uncle Scott who saved me."

"Well, she wasn't there, so she wouldn't know." Lynda's defensiveness gave something away. She didn't want Scott to get the credit. She didn't want him to be the good guy. She preferred him as the enemy.

"I know my uncle saved my life. I know the truth about that."

"There is no truth."

"So it didn't happen? He wasn't the one who saved me? You're denying it outright?"

"It was a long time ago."

"It doesn't make anything else different, just this. If he saved me, he saved me. It doesn't affect the fight you had or anything else."

"Don't believe everything she tells you."

"Did I jump in, Mum? On purpose?"

"You were five years old. Nobody wants to die at that age. You fell. We weren't looking and you fell."

"I heard about what happened to her. Why the family hates her. And it's not fair. Can I tell you?"

"Honestly? No. I simply don't care, Theresa. Please don't inflict that woman's dull story on me."

And she hung up.

Tim had left another three messages, but hearing him say his own name made her feel guilty. She'd never tell him she'd offered him up to Sol Evictus. Or maybe she would, if it made her happy.

"You can come over," she said to him on the phone, and he was there within half an hour, wasting thirty dollars he couldn't afford on a taxi.

He tripped on the front step and that about did it for her. He was too pathetic, too weak, too forgiving. He'd be perfect for Sol Evictus but he wasn't for her.

She led him on a long walk on the beach. "I'll give you one kiss. If you don't change my mind, if I don't feel anything, then this will be over. All of it."

He kissed her, and it was awful. He tasted of salt and vinegar chips, and he smelt faintly of bananas, and he gripped her arms too tight.

"Theresa," he started, but she put her fingers on his lips, thinking he'd enjoy that level of drama, of romance.

"We can't," she said, and she left him on the beach.

Two days later, Scott knocked at her door, carrying a box full of baked goods from Courtney.

The dog ran around the house sniffing, investigating. Went outside to piss, which relieved Theresa.

"We've been worried. We haven't seen you. And you're always odd on the phone." He touched her cheek. "You look pale, Theresa. This is not doing you any good," He didn't look so well himself. His blue-faced ghosts were leaning against the wall.

They sat on the deck eating their way through the biscuits. Scott seemed at a loss for words, as if he wanted to push her for information, but felt guilty doing so.

"Prudence told me something kind of amazing."

"She's full of amazing things."

"She said that you were the one who saved me, when I was drowning."

That he didn't ask, "When?" told Theresa this was true.

"That was a long time ago." He looked embarrassed. "And all I had to do was pull you out of the water. You were a tiny little doll. No big deal."

"They never told me it was you."

"That's weird. I kind of left soon after, but I thought they would have told you."

"They didn't. Mum always said it was a stranger."

"Weird." He put his arm around her. The comfort, the kindness, the sense of protective love she felt from him made her feel almost sleepy. "Best thing I ever did. Apart from having Amber, of course. I met Courtney about a week after that, I think. It's one of the first things I told her. It meant a lot to me. I've never forgotten the feeling of you breathing in my arms. Alive. That relief."

She thought, *Yet another reason I owe him.*

"Thank you. I'm glad you saved me, even if my mother isn't."

"Of course she is. But your mum is a weirdo. We both know that."

"I've seen the paintings. He's got them all displayed. He loves them. Adores them. It's going to be hard to take them from him." She wondered at her own word choice. *Take them?* Had he won her over so completely she believed the work belonged with him?

"I can't bear to think of Amber there, time and time again. Time and time…and that Sol Evictus using her like that. She was so stubborn with us. How did he get her to do these drawings?"

Theresa poured another cup of tea. "He's a charismatic man

who likes art. And I like being with him. It's like you're more alive."

"Are you always a good judge of men? I mean, you got beaten up. That didn't work out."

Theresa was shocked. Was Scott trying to hurt her, punish her for taking him into Paradise Falls even though he'd begged her to?

She knew he didn't mean that she'd asked for it, or deserved it. She understood that much at least.

"That guy blamed me for his loss of power, I guess. A lot of weak men are like that. Easy to bully, easy to anger. Strong men rarely get angry, I reckon."

Scott. Her father.

"Did it do any good at least? Is he in jail?"

"He is, but it doesn't make it any better for his wife. He killed her." Saying the words, hearing them aloud, struck home. Theresa started to sob, and it wasn't for all the ills of the world, for her own grief and sadness. It was only for this woman, this poor dead woman and her lost children, left with only a murderer for a father.

She cried for five minutes before she felt it ebb away from her.

"Better?" Scott said quietly. She nodded. "It's amazing this stuff doesn't fill you with despair. How do you manage that?"

"I don't know. We spend so long pretending not to see, maybe it helps us not to feel as well."

"Let's go to my place. Courtney wants to see you. It won't be enough me telling her you're okay. She'll want to see you. She's sleeping a lot. And listening to Sol Evictus when she's awake. I don't like it."

"I see you've got the flamingo painting put up. The one you got from Sol Evictus's gallery." It looked odd on the bare walls, and Theresa was sure the artist's shadow was looming even darker over it. It was a benign painting, yet it had a sense of despair about it.

Courtney hugged her, hard. "You look so pale. You need to sit in the sun more. Much harder to be sad on a warm day." Yet her own sadness could never be lessened.

She made iced tea and mint tea, adding to the table laden with fruit, cheese, biscuits. Theresa thought, *This will make us feel happy and healthy and lucky to be alive.*

"I should learn to cook," Theresa said, as she'd often said before.

This time, Scott gave her a pile of cookbooks and magazines.

"Life isn't so bad," he said, and she thought she must be looking very down for a man in his position to feel he had to cheer her up.

"Life is so bad," she said.

Scott took her wrist. "I don't think we want to hear."

"We have to hear," Courtney said, her voice stronger now. Determined. "We have to know."

Theresa felt angry for a moment that she was the one to talk about this. She shouldn't have to do it. She should be skiing somewhere. Shopping. She should be on her wedding night, on a hike, climbing a mountain.

This should not be her responsibility.

"This is not your secret to keep," Courtney said.

"I've seen Amber's work. It's beautiful. And it's terrifying. If you get it back...when you have it back, you may not want to show it."

"How could Amber paint anything like that."

"We know this, Courtney. Theresa told us. Sol Evictus forced her."

"What does that mean? Where? What does it mean? Forced? How? He wouldn't do this. Not Sol Evictus."

Theresa wondered if one of the reasons Courtney failed to recover from grief was that she listened to Sol Evictus, all the time. His words in her heart.

"The man you love so much, Courtney, is about as cruel a man as ever I've met. And I have met some cruel men, even though you won't believe me to say that. I think he tired of her work and that he planted the need to die in her. That's what he does. He plants the need to die. He builds self-hatred. He gives you the idea that suicide is solace. I think Amber tried to save some of those teenagers, and herself. But in the end the guilt was too much for her."

Courtney said, "You sit there blaming a good man. But you have the power to save lives. You see these ghosts, why don't you save people?" She was angry, standing over Theresa. She'd be threatening if she wasn't dressed in a mini skirt and tank top.

"I'm sorry I was too late to save Amber. I'd give anything for that, now. But I'm never sure what the ghosts are telling me. Things change quickly and I don't know what effect I'll have. The ghosts are not good guides for saving lives. And I think I only see them when death is inevitable. I do try to save them but it doesn't work. I can't stop it." She'd thought Client E's ghosts were telling her to keep her away from the husband. Not offering a warning of what he was capable of.

"The man sings like an angel. No one who sings like that could be so evil." Courtney said.

They cried together, she and Scott, two middle-aged people who had cried a lot. Tears prickled Theresa's eyes, too, but she didn't think she deserved to cry. She hadn't known Amber.

"He can't be a bad man. He makes us feel so good."

"I wish that was true," Theresa said.

"Then we can call him a murderer. Do you think? And we are, too. We killed our own daughter because we didn't know what she was doing."

They slumped together, breathing heavily. It sounded to Theresa like a death rattle, as if they were last breaths.

"You couldn't keep her in your sight forever. She made her own choices. But this man took advantage of her, as he does of everybody. He is made of sorrow. Maybe he thinks this will lessen his burden. I don't know why else he would do it."

Courtney poured coffee, brought out a plate of lemon tarts. She had baked a lot.

"I haven't been into the office for a while. This might settle us." Scott cleared the table and pulled out bags of stamps. "I love sorting stamps. Love the feel of them. Smooth, most of them, but some still a bit sticky, still a bit of residue left behind. Those are the ones people picked out of the water too soon. They helped it along by sliding of the wet envelope paper, didn't they? You should wait until the stamp floats off itself. The envelope sinks, the stamp floats; did you ever notice that?" Scott asked, as they started sorting out the large delivery. "And did you know that an Empress Dowager stamp in Hong Kong sold for a million pesos? The old man who'd bought it and kept it safe for decades turned in his grave, they said. They hate their stamps being sold. They want to keep them forever. But what's the point if no one cares? If the children don't share the obsession? You can't force an obsession on somebody. You can't make them want to."

Theresa let him talk without interruption for some time. It became too much, though. The pretence of it all, the civil discussion, the blandness of the stamps, when beneath was dead Amber, Paradise Falls, the art and the filth that Theresa felt was inside her.

"It's how he makes people feel when they listen," Theresa said to Courtney.

Courtney nodded. She seemed controlled. She pulled out her Sol Evictus CDs and a notebook. Determined. Focussed.

"We've got this now. Scott is going to be a lawyer again, aren't you, Scott? Now that we know for sure. He'll get our things back legally. And I'm going to think about him, this man, and what he has to say. You, Theresa, will concentrate on getting well. Have a weekend away with Tim. He loved Amber so much. He always wished there was more between them, I think. But he wasn't her type. She was more like you than you can know."

Theresa thought that even if she was replacing Amber in Tim's mind she didn't care.

She thought Amber would be a good person to be.

Theresa yawned.

"You get some sleep. Forget about this for now."

"I'm fine," she said, but she was tempted.

They could forget about the art, and she could act as a replacement daughter to take their minds off it. Forget about Sol Evictus, forget about Paradise Falls and who waited there. Sort stamps, hang out with her aunt and uncle sometimes, being spoiled by them. Walk on the beach, play with her dog, eat food she'd cooked herself and that her mother would approve of. Send presents back home to her niece and nephew. Remember to say thank you. All of that sounded tempting and easy.

The time she spent with Sol Evictus seemed dream-like, far from reality. She ate out at restaurants with Tim, she cooked for herself following recipes precisely, she drank till she was numb, she read vast numbers of magazines. She didn't listen to music, she didn't think about art, she filled her mind with crap.

Then Red sent her an email. *He wants to see you.*

Theresa felt like screaming at the idea.

Will he see my uncle instead?

Lol! No, he'll see you. He doesn't like dealing with parents. He reckons they're irrational. He told me to say, 'Bring me something special. Something real.'

What does he mean?

I think he probably means you, Theresa. But you should bring something else along as well. In case he doesn't.

What if I am the offering? What will I do?

That will be up to him, won't it? We'll collect you when he's ready.

When will that be?

An hour? A day? A week? Time means nothing. And think about a haircut. He's gone a bit whacko with the hair thing so it might piss him off if you have your long hair. He's sent you something he says you might like. Courier'll be there shortly.

It was a beautifully written letter, on thick, cream notepaper.

Theresa, it said. *You ask me about my lost loves and for whom I grieve. I give you here a list. I cannot speak these names aloud; even writing them down gives me pain.*

My mother, Gloria Brenda Brennan.

My father, Joseph Adam Sheen

My siblings, Mark, Douglas, Benjamin, Deanna, Celia, Shaun, Tim, Warren and Ryan.

My wives, Jean, Sarah, Susan, Cornelia, Cathryn, Lusi, Kristy, Indira, Maria, Victoria and Raki.

My children, there are too many to name. I mourn them all though, all those who've died.

My grandchildren.

My great grandchildren.

All the generations of children I've lost.

This is the great loss I feel, Theresa. This is the grief, the Grief Hole I live in.

Now do you understand?

Goodbye.

There would be no time to find a new item, and Theresa felt certain he didn't want anything anonymous, anyway. He wanted something special. Something real. There was the bloodied newspaper, but Theresa didn't feel right handing that over. She felt as if that would complete him, make him more powerful than ever and it wasn't hers to give. She'd left most of her personal belongings at her parent's house and there was no way she'd ask them to look through them. The only thing she had with her…

Theresa looked through the small suitcase at the back of her cupboard. In there were a couple of diaries she couldn't bear to throw out but didn't want her mother finding, some tickets and programmes from shows she'd seen with Ben, and there was a shirt.

His shirt.

Someone had placed it over his face after they dragged him out of the river and lain him amongst the stones and twigs on the riverside. He was covered with blood, so much so you couldn't see his features.

They placed the t-shirt over his face to stop people screaming.

Imprinted on the t-shirt, in blood, was his face.

The shirt smelt of Ben and of blood. She'd taken it to bed a few times. More than a few. It was crumpled. Dirty.

And, she thought, there was the smell of rubber, and then, *Was Prudence there? Has Prudence always been there?*

She folded it neatly and put it into a linen shopping bag. Looking at herself in the mirror, she was a wild-eyed woman. Hair awry. Her head felt heavy and she thought, *I can win him. I can convince him.* Running her fingers through her hair she thought, *Why not? It needs a cut anyway.*

R ed and Blondie came to collect her the next afternoon. They had both shaved their heads. It threw her; they were nicknamed for their hair and now they didn't have it anymore.

"Don't bother with your underwear. It'll be fucking, not art this time." Blondie smiled; he always smiled.

"What if I don't want to?"

"You'll want to, by the end. They all do. He's put it in there." Here the man tapped his temple. "You'll come when he calls. We both know that. It'll only upset you to fight it. But you can try. I wouldn't mind."

His face flared and Theresa knew there was no way she'd fight him, not with what she knew of his strength, his anger and his lack of remorse. His hands were clenched and his mouth, too. Teeth pressed tight together.

"Is everything all right?" she said in the car. He sat in the back with her while Red drove and they spoke low. "Something happened to piss you off?"

"None of your business," he said. She had to bite off a laugh at this childish response.

"No, sorry. It isn't."

"Things could have worked out differently, that's all. I should be in a position where I'm not the babysitter." He looked at her, grinned sideways. "Or the pimp."

"I don't want to think about what that means."

"Most women are desperate to think about it. And we get lucky too, sometimes."

"Well, lucky, lucky you."

His stabbed ghosts were still there. Angry ghosts. Fists clenched. *Join us, join us,* they'd say if she could hear them.

"Yeah, lucky. We get to mop up, don't we, Red?" he said, raising his voice. "Especially those who say no. Not that there's been many of those. And not that we can do much for them."

Theresa tried the car door, thinking, *I can jump out, run. I don't need the artwork, Scott will understand. If there's a choice, I know what he'd choose, he wouldn't want this.*

But the door was locked. "It's too late," Blondie said. "Too, too late. He's decided and that's it. Don't worry. We'll mop up."

Red hadn't spoken. She wondered if he wished this wasn't happening but didn't dare stand against it.

Red drove her to the door. "Takehiro'll let you in. You'll be seen in the Inner. I'll be there shortly. Blondie and I have to sort out a couple of things."

The inner. She hadn't heard them mention it and she hated to think what it was. She thought bowels of the building, deep inside, many doors, many passages.

And that was right.

Theresa was attracted to many elements of Sol Evictus. This filled her with self-hatred. But he could change her life. He could change it completely and part of her felt this would be a good thing. He had the power to help or destroy many.

She waited in the hallway for forty-five minutes, until Takehiro led her deep into the house to the Inner.

Sol Evictus, in a dressing gown, leant back. A young man gave him a pedicure.

The room was red velvet, curtains, carpet, walls. Red stood beside him; Theresa wondered what he'd sorted out. There was no sign of Blondie.

Sol Evictus waved the boy away. He looked, wide-eyed, at the shopping bag she carried. "You've brought me something heart-breakingly personal this time?" She looked away as he pulled the shirt from the bag and unfolded it carefully. Gasped. "My God, that's a face. That's a face."

"It's my boyfriend's face. That's Ben. He drowned, remember? After hitting his head. Blood everywhere. That's his face."

He held it up, his mouth open. He didn't blink.

"It was over his face when he died."

"Over his face, you say?" He clutched it to his face and breathed in. He seemed to writhe, almost, and a low moan escaped him. "This has a lot of meaning."

He tapped her knee with his fingertip. He turned the shirt over in his fingers. Laid it out on his lap. Smoothed it. Smelt it.

"Is it a good likeness?"

"I think so. It smells of him. It looks like him."

"It smells of the moment of knowing. This makes me happy. I wish there was something I could give to you. But what could match this? What possible thing?"

"You know what it is," she said. "You know but you don't want to part with it. How about this, then? You make me a promise."

"What sort of promise?"

"Don't send anyone else in to Paradise Falls. Close it down."

He smiled. "My goodness, you are a saint, aren't you? Always thinking of others. Anything for you. Consider it done. You are good to me. In my time of need."

"Are you not well?"

"I feel the pressure of the world harder some days than others. I feel the hairs of the world in my throat. To be given this gift, and to hear what you want in return, fills me with joy. Let us pray this joy lasts a while. But you. You seem sad. What can we do to lift this sadness from you?"

"Your promise will lift the sadness. I'm sure."

He cupped her chin, leant forward and kissed her gently on the mouth. Then harder. His lips were flaccid and cold. He caressed and squeezed her knee, rubbed his fingers up her thigh. Stroked her arm.

Red fidgeted slightly. Sol Evictus smiled at him, shiny mouthed. Wet-lipped.

"You wanna watch, Red? You a bit agitated?" He smiled at Theresa. "You know I like to have my guards with me. They know that if I'm ever hurt, they should instantly kill the perpetrator, no questions."

"I'm not here to hurt you!" she said.

"I know, I know. I'm explaining why my man Red is here. Some women can get over-wrought at being alone with me. Others don't like an audience."

"Whatever makes you happy," she said. She felt suddenly

euphoric, desperately in love. She wanted him, she wanted him to be happy, she wanted to be the one to make him happy.

Sol Evictus left to 'prepare', he said.

Red said, "You need to be careful of him. He can trap you."

She stroked his cheek. "Trap me? Does he trap people?"

"He'll trap you in a box."

"Like, a real box?"

"No, doesn't need that. He'll keep you trapped until he's bored with you."

"What does it matter to you?"

"He hasn't had people like you here before. You make me look at life and wonder."

He wore a bracelet made out of drinking straws; a daughter's project.

"Sorry."

"You are sitting very close to each other," Sol Evictus said, treading softly into the room. He was dressed in a silk dressing gown with tiny stars on it and Theresa had to close her eyes not to laugh at him. He looked like a cliché, a joke. He'd brushed his hair, wet it down, and it sat neat against his skull. He'd poured on some scent; something expensive, she thought, because it didn't hurt her nose. He'd washed his hands; they were still damp. He had soft slippers on his feet.

"Sorry, sir," Red said. He stepped away. Stood with his face to the door, only a metre or so away from it.

"Who do you see around him?" Sol Evictus said. He almost purred.

"I see men with their throats slit. Fingers broken. No wedding rings," Theresa said. It was the first time she'd lied about the ghosts to be cruel.

"Red," he said. "The curtains." Red drew back the heavy brocade to reveal a large four poster bed, made with pale pink bedclothes set with flowers and gold stripes.

Sol Evictus reached his fingers out for her throat and stroked. "Like silk," he whispered. His hands smelt of expensive soap. The smell of a clean man.

He stroked her cheek, her chin, her neck. His fingers were soft, as if he used hand cream every night. Men didn't usually have soft hands like that. But then he hadn't worked physically for most of his life. He'd sung. He'd worked at that and she wouldn't deny that was hard work but not the graft that some…she realised her mind was babbling, taking her elsewhere. She'd done this before. There were times. She'd taken herself out of it, let her mind babble.

She wasn't even sure if this was worth it, if she would gain anything at all. But she felt as if she had no choice. She wanted it; she wanted to try him. See what sort of a lover he made.

"It's lovely," he said. "Oh, you smell so good."

He kissed her. If she closed her eyes, concentrated on how he smelt, she could imagine he was someone else. Even Ben. The aftershave he wore smelled a lot like Ben's.

"Do I smell good?" he said. "What do you think?"

"You do. I love it."

"Do you know the scent?"

"It smells a bit like the one Ben used to wear. But that was a while ago. I'm not sure."

"You never forget a smell. I bought this scent from the man who cleaned out his work desk."

She stood up. Horrified. "You're wearing Ben's actual after-shave?"

"Did you make love before he died? Had you made love that week, before he left? Or did you have a fight and never got that last one, that farewell love? What a loss. What a shame."

He kissed her again. This time she breathed deeply and he did feel like Ben, his body shape and his face. Had he changed? Was he different? She reached her arms around him and pulled him closer to her. He grunted, pleased.

She put her hand against his chest and she felt his heart beat faster, as if excited.

She tilted her head back to display her throat. He kissed it, licked it and she shuddered. His breath smelt like musk. She put her hands to his shoulders and they were firm, smooth.

He led her gently to the bed. He drew his fingers over the scar on her arm and touched her ankle. *He sees beyond the obvious,* Theresa thought.

She kept her eyes closed and he didn't seem to mind. Some men liked your eyes open, so you could see them. Some men didn't care. She went through lists in her brain; of the food she had in her cupboard. The stamps they had on the 'ordered' list. The clothes in her wardrobe.

"Call me Sol," he said.

She went through the top ten list of music downloads, the last Oscar winners, she went through anything at all.

He whispered, "We may never meet again."

There were ghosts hovering around the bed, hers or his or Red's? She wondered if they were her potential lovers, all the men she could have slept with, and she put faces to them, imagined them as real people, watching over her. All the good men she hadn't slept with, all the men who could have loved her.

And he whispered in her ear, "I knew your grandmother."

His smell though, and the feel of him, the first man since Ben. He let her keep her eyes shut, thinking of Ben, Ben, Ben…

She awoke alone and cold. The bedcovers bunched at the bottom of the bed, only the sheet draped over her. Red stood at the door, still facing it. She wondered if he'd moved.

"Red?" she said.

"Are you okay?"

"I…" she sat up. She felt fine. It hadn't been so bad. There was no pain. It was intense and strange, but she wasn't hurt. "I'm tired."

"He drains you, doesn't he?"

"I guess so. But it was okay. As you know. You must have heard everything."

"I try not to listen."

"I think I'll get dressed. Don't turn around."

When she was ready, she said "It's okay now."

He turned. Looked at her quizzically.

"I'm fine. Seriously. I don't feel trapped at all. I'm sure I can walk away."

"Yeah, well. Sometimes it sneaks up on you. My wife was fine for ages, but now I can't even get her to cook the dinner. She's on about warming up soup or shit like that. Kids and I need to eat."

"There must be something you can do."

"What, quit? He doesn't like quitters."

"I don't know, report him or something. Fight him, knock him down. He's only a man."

"He's not that easy. That thick scar across his throat is from a slashing. We all saw it. His throat cut, and jeezus fuck, how much blood was there? Like a man emptied. And yet he didn't die. God, we shat ourselves. He lay there and then he sat up, holding his throat, as if it was like a scratch or something. Then we knew we couldn't go anywhere until he said we could."

She picked up her dress.

Theresa felt something dark and cold inside her, as if a baby was forming, a devil. She knew this wasn't possible, but still she felt his seed in there and it changed her. She felt darker than she had ever felt, even after the loss of Ben, even in the Grief Hole. She felt hopeless, wasted.

They walked to the car. Red helped her.

"I'm shattered," she said, her legs weak.

"You'll be right. He likes you. If he didn't, if he wanted to get rid of you, you'd be chucking yourself under a truck right now."

Theresa curled herself up in the back seat, thinking of the men she'd damaged and the woman and how detached she was from their final ending. How she'd set things off but not pulled the trigger herself.

She didn't notice where he was driving, too caught up in her own ball of flesh.

"Anyway, he's real happy with his new artist."

"Has he found someone?"

"Yeah, a young kid. Knows the Falls so doesn't have to get used to it, if you know what I mean."

Andy. He means Andy.

She felt a loud buzz of ghosts she couldn't see.

Theresa knew then she couldn't let it lie. She had to intervene. She couldn't let another child die. It didn't matter that his music helped; the way he made his music, by sucking in the despair of art, was not worth it. A life should not be sacrificed.

At home Theresa showered, showered again, ordered the grossest, cheesiest pizza on the menu, took the delivery, managed to smile at the delivery boy. Ate it all, greasy cheeks, full stomach, and then she showered again. She made toast and slathered it with her father's jam, something she'd been doing since the age of three. Making a mess on the bench and usually her dad would wipe it up, pretending to be cross but happy that she loved his jam so much.

She sat with her dog, holding him until he wriggled free then came back to her for more.

There were three messages on her machine, two from Courtney.

"We're worried about you. You seem different."

If I seemed different then, imagine what they'll think now, Theresa thought. She knew she'd been odd with them, that the grief hole would always sit on the edge of her consciousness.

One from Tim. "Are you okay?"

She couldn't cope with kindness, so deleted the message.

She showered again. She felt his saliva on her as if a snail had crawled across her skin. She felt his fingers in her hair and she wanted to shave it off but thought he would think she'd done it for him

She searched her body for his mark. His brand. She found a small star-shaped mole she didn't think she had before, above her right hip. It felt slightly tender to the touch.

She remembered that he had told her he had no children.

She dressed and went to Passing Strange, her café. The owner's husband was redesigning a wall, outlining a mural. The owner told him, "It's gonna look great," five, six times in the thirty minutes Theresa was there.

"Artists need a lot of reinforcement," the woman said, smiling at Theresa.

"As do poets," her husband said, and they crossed hands, the intimacy of it filling Theresa with deep envy for what she would never have.

She drank black mugs of a spicy brew and ate chocolate chip cookies. Her dog sat at her feet, snuffling up the crumbs, sniffing at the other customers.

"He's such a sweetie," the owner said. "Look at him. I think he brings good luck to the place."

It was as if nothing had happened. As if Theresa was the same person she had been a few days earlier, could interact as she would have then.

Her phone rang. Scott. She couldn't talk to him yet; she felt shame about what had happened, she didn't want to face him, didn't want to tell him what she'd done. Courtney, she didn't want to tell her either. Courtney would feign jealousy and that would be embarrassing, she'd gone on about how she'd do Sol Evictus in flash. She answered the phone, faked a hangover. Scott understood hangovers.

Theresa walked naked around her house, trying to recapture herself. She read his list of lost loved ones, to understand him, make him seem lovable. Her list had one name on it. Only Ben.

"Mum?" She'd called her on a whim. Called her for help. "Mum? I'm feeling lost, I don't know where to go next. I don't know who to trust." It was the answering machine and her mother didn't call back.

She called Raul, telling him the same: I don't know who to trust.

"You should know. You should know by now. I can't tell you. But if you're not sure if you can trust someone then you probably can't."

"I don't know. I feel damaged. I feel changed."

"Change can be for the better. You don't want to stay the same all your life."

"This is more damage than change. This is unwilling."

"What's happened?"

"It's Sol Evictus. There's something about him."

"He's got the magic, all right. Isn't he too old for you? Or not. I have no idea how old he is. He does have a beautiful voice."

"I know. He's too old, he's too strong. He's too full of shit."

"So you've answered your own question." She recognised his tone of voice; she'd used it on clients. It said, *I've sorted you out, move on.*

She showered. She thought she would never have sex again; that

240

her sexuality was wiped clean. She felt no desire, no interest. The dog whined at the bathroom door, not wanting to be apart from her.

She ate salads and vegies, expensive steak cooked fast and hot. She ignored the phone and the texts that came through.

She walked with her dog on the beach.

She showered.

Prudence sat selling her balloons by the shore. "Ah, there's my poor little girl. My poor, dear girl."

The sympathy, the acknowledgment, broke Theresa. She sat on the seat beside Prudence and cried.

"You're scaring away the customers," Prudence said. "You'd better cry around the corner." But she put her arm around Theresa and held her. The smell, so long unwashed, of this woman, stopped Theresa. The physical contact wasn't pleasant.

"I don't know what to do. Is this man a monster or is he an ordinary man? He feels like a monster. But I want to be around him. But I know he does damage. But he says he helps."

"If you don't stop monsters, you remain one. He is a monster, but the death I've seen doesn't make sense yet."

"I don't see any ghosts around him at all."

"Maybe that's because no one has ever died the way he is to die."

Prudence shuffled towards a customer. She allowed her balloons to droop, to trail on the ground. Theresa thought, *You say her name, Prudence, with a puff of air. Puff of air to blow the balloons and every time you say her name you inflate her balloons. She gains strength by her malevolent balloon tricks.*

Prudence shuffled back and settled her red mat, her begging bowls. They sipped tea.

"I found the first balloon in my daughter's bed. Covered with ash. They can be dangerous if a parent isn't a good parent. Every balloon a weapon to choke a child if a parent isn't vigilant. If a parent is a failed one."

She gave the balloons a shake. How many were there? 50? 60? If they were gas-filled they would have lifted a child but Theresa doubted anything could lift this woman.

Prudence started to cry. Tears streaked her red make up even more. "Oh, you. Oh, so bad for you."

"Be quiet. It's none of your business."

"You are my family and I don't want to see this. You should not be near that man at all. Not any more. It is not up to you to stop him." She cried noisily. "Oh, you are not such a bad girl. You are okay. You are better than the rest of them."

"The rest of who? The family?"

She nodded. "They don't talk to me."

"Why don't they talk to you? Or about you? Why do we keep you a secret, anyway?"

Prudence sniffed, a shuddering sniff which made Theresa feel ill but stopped the tears.

"Because you can see the deaths of monsters?"

"And you can see the deaths of victims."

"Sol Evictus says he has been a victim, too. He says he has lost many, many loved ones."

"I don't know about his losses. I only know about my own. And the losses they say I am responsible for." Prudence rubbed at the scar tissue on her arms. "This is why they hate me but it wasn't my fault. Wasn't my fault and I couldn't stop it."

"Sol Evictus talked about it. He told me he knows about it. But he didn't tell me what happened."

"They always took advantage of me. Thought I was slow and only good enough for looking after the children. I had my own little girl and they thought I did a good job of that. Kept her alive, at least."

"What children?" Theresa said, thinking, *The fire. She's going to tell me about the fire and I'm going to have to tell her about the pillowcases Amber stole.*

"The cousins. Not your mum or your Uncle Scott, they had good parents to look after them, but their little cousins, and another one as well. Belonged to your grandfather because he couldn't keep it in his pants, could he?"

Theresa had been terrified of her grandfather, a blind man who seemed to see more than any man should.

"My girl was a beautiful perfect girl. Beautiful face and curls but nothing could move below the waist. You know I was only 21 myself. Close to a baby. Exhausted by all these screaming, needy children.

"Other mothers would talk about the future, about the day when their child would be independent and live their own life. I knew that wasn't for us, that nothing would ever change until I died and she was left to rot in a bed somewhere. She looked at me with such love but she was always in pain, every minute of the day.

"'Rock me, Mummy,' she'd say, because movement would make her feel better. 'When I close my eyes I think I'm on a train and we're going to Paris,' she'd say, that dear little dreamer, but she'd open her eyes and they'd be full of tears because she knew she'd never go. Although she didn't talk because she was only one.

"I was out buying some milk. I did take longer than I should have; I had to pick up some work. I didn't sell balloons, then. I sewed hems and seams, fitting skinny clothes onto fat ladies. I worked with a woman...yes." Prudence stood up and did an odd little dance. "That is the answer. That's what I saw. The Lacemaker. She was brilliant."

"Who?"

"Ah, soon."

"Okay, so what happened? After you bought the milk?"

"The oldest of the cousins was thirteen and I trusted her, paid her to keep an eye on the others. I gave those children cold snacks. Never anything warm till I got home because that old oven was a vicious thing, it was like it snapped out and bit you. I reckon it's eaten children, burned them to ash and caked all their fat onto the wall. I got it from the tip for a song but I swear there were children baked in there and what do you do when you have four children, all of them needy and wanting more than I have to offer but not one able to do a darn thing, never would. The thirteen-year-old was all right. She could at least pour a glass of water. They never paid me enough to look after them. No one had enough.

"I smelt smoke from two blocks away. I didn't run at first because I had six bags of shopping and didn't imagine for one moment that it was my house burning. How could that be? I got close and the bags were heavier, I imagined the children coming out to meet me and carrying a bag each. It'd help! And sometimes they did come out to meet me if they were hungry enough.

"This time, no. I struggled on. At the end of my street I saw it was my house burning and I dropped the bags without even thinking about them and ran on.

"I'd say one of the neighbours made a golden find because all that food disappeared. The mince, potatoes, milk. I'd even splurged on a small treat for the kids, one of those tiny animal chocolate bars each. Didn't matter; we couldn't eat it anyway.

"The fire department was there, angels every last one of them but I couldn't wait, they didn't know she couldn't even crawl by herself and never would have, beyond dragging herself like a commando so I raced in there. I had to force past those men. But I don't know if they even saw me. People never saw me much even then. The firemen had rescued three bigger kids. All carried out and jumping up with excitement. They saw me pushing through the front door. 'It's okay,' they said, 'we've got the kids.' I said, 'No, there is a one year old, my little girl,' and I ran through the door. The kids had been playing house with her, they sometimes did, and there she was, all wrapped up tight, in the cupboard they used for a play house. I was burnt by now but not feeling it, tucked her into my clothing and I ran. Outside, there were the three kids, but they were the wrong three kids. 'Where's Mark,' I said to them, 'and Douglas, and Deanna?'

"I couldn't make any sense of it. Who were these kids? 'These are the wrong ones,' I said 'These are not my children.' Those kids were crying and pointing.

"They'd had a play party. Nobody asked me but nobody cared about that later. They said I left seven kids alone but I didn't there weren't that many when I walked out the door. I was on fire, burning, and screaming, 'Get the others, get the others.'

"It was too late for the others, though. Terrible. Terrible. Their little faces burnt sad forever. This world is a monstrous place."

Theresa realised that the pillowcases Amber had given to Sol Evictus were fakes. The children were not asleep when they were found; they were up and playing. She almost whooped with joy at Amber's small rebellion. It was important.

"Poor Mark and Douglas. Poor Deanna and my poor, poor, dear little Celia."

"Your daughter?"

"It was too late for her as well. You haven't asked me how the fire started. Everyone asks me that, as if I would know. I don't know. But I do know it was a monster. That a monster came to my house and burned it down. That a monster beat you, and that all the bad things in the world, monsters make them happen."

They were silent.

Those are their names? Theresa thought. She knew Sol Evictus's list off by heart but she checked it anyway. "Look."

Prudence read the list. "He's stolen these names. Every last one of them. These are our family's dead children. These died in the fire. Those three died a long time ago. At war. That's your one, dear, isn't it? Benjamin?"

She'd never called him Benjamin so it hadn't clicked.

"That one died of illness and those too. This one was your mother's other brother, who died at birth. Not a twin."

She flicked a balloon for every name she said. "These are...I don't know these. Some other person's tragedy. Every last one another person's sorrow, not his."

Not his. The balloons floated in front of Theresa's face and she pushed them away angrily.

"Don't hit the balloons. Poor balloons. They never did a thing to you. Never hurt anyone."

"I've seen your balloons all my life. I've never liked them. Always gave me a bad feeling."

"People are supposed to like balloons. Be attracted to them."

"Is that what you think? I never trusted a balloon."

"You nearly choked on one when you were a child. I think you were two. That's another reason your parents never let me near you."

"You gave me the balloon."

"I did not. But still they blamed me."

"Mum didn't warn me away from you or anything. Not lately."

"She probably thinks I'm too old to be of danger now. But I'm still the same on the inside."

"So you are dangerous?"

"I was never dangerous! I was a good mother. I would never have hurt my child. Who would say such a thing about me?" Prudence was agitated.

Theresa touched her arm. "I was joking. Sorry. Bad joke. I'm sorry about your daughter. You would have been a good mother as she got older."

Prudence cried again. Theresa thought her tears smelt of rubber.

"He must be a monster, to steal our names," Theresa said.

"I told you, he is."

Theresa thought, *Amber thought he'd let her go if she stole something so personal. Gave him something so very personal and loved. But he didn't, of course. I thought he'd help me if I gave him Ben's shirt, but that didn't happen either.*

Prudence began to shake. Theresa handed her the rest of the cup of tea; it was cold, but strong. She sipped it.

"I will find his death for you," Prudence said.

Theresa awoke the next day to a parcel delivery. It was large, almost a metre square and packed in brown paper.

"Who's it from?" she asked.

The delivery man flipped it over carefully. "Solace Galleries, love."

She signed for it and took it from him, and carried it inside to put on the large wooden table which was still covered with breakfast crumbs from the day before.

She felt nauseated by what might be inside. The brown wrapping carried sketches she knew were Andy's; piles of food with human faces.

What she didn't expect was the reality; it was a piece of Amber's artwork. This one showed a young girl surrounded by an angelic glow. Her eyes were drawn like mirrors, and you could see reflected a gallows in one eye, a gun in the other. Her mouth was drawn down, and the wrinkles around her lips made her face almost clown-like.

She knew she held a portrait inspired by a saint and a google image search told Theresa it was Saint Thomas.

Part of her didn't want to give the piece to Scott and Courtney, but she knew she didn't have a choice. She thought, *This will test them. When they see what she was drawing.*

They weren't home when she got there and she was so relieved she felt pathetic. She left the painting on their back step with a note telling them it was a gift from Sol Evictus. *Sorry I missed you*, she wrote.

Scott sent her a text: *Thank you. I had no luck legal methods.*

I'm sorry there's not more. I don't know how to get more.

Courtney says we don't have anything at all. She thinks this isn't Amber's. She reckons she can tell.

And Theresa realised that she hadn't thought about that possibility.

Theresa walked along the beach. Early morning brightness, emptiness; a world to herself. She wished it could be that way: no more family, ghosts of beaten beseeching women, men good or bad. A cave, alone. Silence and dying alone. She didn't care if her body rotted and was never found, or was eaten by wild animals.

She felt as if it was all on her. That so many people knew about something terrible but no one was willing to do anything about him. This was a feeling she'd had all her life. From Mrs Ellis to the clients she saw, it was her or no one.

Was there a true greater good in the work he did? Or was it all a nonsense?

She felt terrified but empty for a long time now. The water splashed at her feet, stinging salt, and she didn't recoil from it. She liked it. She thought she could even swim, but it was cold and the swell high so she didn't. She remembered salt and water and fear.

She collected shells as she walked. She'd covered half the path to the cabin, lining both sides with beautiful shells. She didn't know what she'd do once she'd decorated the whole path. Fill in another layer, perhaps, or throw all the shells back and start again. Perhaps it meant she'd lived here for long enough and it was time to return to the other life. The life where her parents lived, and her sister.

She dug a deep hole in sand; some children wandering past helped her. They dug it broad and deep and they surrounded the edges with shells and seaweed.

"That's a good hole," one of the boys said. Theresa thought he must be about thirteen; looking at him, she wondered how you kept someone like that safe. He was a similar age to Andy, but his life was so different.

"I know! The sand is good here. You can get it deep without it collapsing," Theresa said.

The children jumped in and helped, collecting shells and seaweed, making the hole a home.

A shadow fell over them. Scott and Courtney, holding hands. They both wore old jeans, paint-smeared t-shirts.

"There you are!" Courtney said. "We've been looking for you."

"I've been here." Theresa looked through the sun at Courtney. Her tone seemed sharp. Did they know about what had happened, about the sex she'd had with Sol Evictus? She hadn't told them. Had someone, somehow? Did they hate her for it?

"We haven't seen you for a while," Courtney said. "You've been avoiding us."

Theresa kept decorating the hole. The children seemed oblivious to the adults.

"Why don't you hop out of the hole?" Courtney said.

Theresa felt like a child herself. "I'm still digging," she said.

"Theresa, please."

Scott leaned in to help her out, and then Courtney hugged her clumsily.

"Theresa, you have to take me to that place. The one she painted in. I want to see The Grief Hole. I want to see the place that made my girl feel so bad."

"Shut up, Courtney," Theresa said, brushing sand off, furious. "Don't mention that place in front of children. Or teenagers. Do not ever use those words again. Do you get it?"

Courtney looked shocked. "Sorry, sorry."

Scott put his arm around her, glared at Theresa as if he wanted her to rein it in.

Courtney looked at the children, still digging and decorating. "A lot of work here!" she said. "You oughta show your parents. They'll be impressed."

The children nodded.

"I gotta go, kids. I'll see you all next time." They waved at Theresa but didn't watch her walk away, too busy working.

Courtney was invisible once she stopped talking directly to them. Scott they hadn't even noticed.

"Don't even put the words into their heads," Theresa said. "Don't put the Grief Hole into a child's subconscious."

"Sorry. Sorry. I didn't think. But those kids will be okay. Nothing could make kids like that feel sad."

"Courtney...you know Amber was like that. You know it. She wasn't a sad kid. Nobody has ever said she was sad. All her friends say she had a fantastic childhood. They envied her because of you two."

Courtney clutched her arm. "Oh, thank you. Thank you."

"So you accept that the painting is by Amber? I thought it wasn't."

"It is. I didn't want it to be but it is. She drew a tiny picture of a turtle in the corner. She always, always drew turtles. Didn't she, Scott? Even though we never had one. We never let her have one."

"I can see you're dressed and ready." Courtney held her high heels by the straps.

"We'll burn the clothes afterwards. Toss them at least," Scott said. "After we're back from Paradise Falls."

They went inside Theresa's house.

"Did you bring any cake?" Theresa said. "I'll make coffee and we can eat while we talk."

"I didn't bring anything. I don't think it sunk in before, but then it did. That Grief Hole. Amber was there and maybe she left a message for me. Maybe there's something only a mother would understand." Courtney almost choked on the words.

"It's not safe for happy people, let alone sad people."

"You think I'm a sad person?"

"A grieving person. It's bad for people like us."

"Your loss is different to ours."

"So you keep saying. But it still hurts, doesn't it? Even if yours is bigger, doesn't negate mine."

Theresa made coffee, found some stale chocolate cream biscuits in her cupboard.

"I want to go to this place. I want to see it." Courtney linked one arm through Theresa's. She clutched at Theresa's other arm with sharp fingernails. She sounded shrill, agitated. "We looked everywhere for you and there you were digging holes in the sand."

"Were you worried?"

Courtney stared at her as if this was an alien concept. "We want to see the Grief Hole. I want to go there and see it, see where she did her drawings."

Theresa looked at Scott, who had not asked for this.

"She just got off the phone to her mother," Scott said.

No other comment but he raised his eyebrows at Theresa; *You know what her mother's like.* The mother would have egged her on, made it life or death. Made out Theresa was doing something wrong, messing things up, was a bad niece.

Theresa didn't want to go in again. She was weaker after knowing Sol Evictus. That was obvious to her from the moment she woke up every morning. She was less of herself. Less sure. But she could see Ben again. Smell him. She had almost forgotten what he smelt like.

"We can go alone if you don't want to."

"She has to come," Courtney said.

"It's a terrible place, Courtney. It'll make you feel such a deep sense of hopelessness I'm worried that you won't be able to come out again. You can smell the grief, smell the hopelessness in there. It's not a place for someone like you."

"I'm a lot stronger than you give me credit for," Courtney said, but Scott and Theresa exchanged glances. Neither of them believed it.

Courtney was determined. "Don't be your mother," she said.

"You don't know what she's suffered. What she sees."

"What does she see? Does she see what you do?" Courtney asked.

"She sees the shadows of the ghosts. What used to be there. She sees what's left behind."

It struck Theresa again how awful this was. *No wonder she wants to pretend she can't see that. There must be shadows everywhere. No wonder she always has her hand over her eyes. And that look on her face as if she smells something bad. No wonder she's bad tempered and wants me to keep quiet. Prudence reminds her of the family's talents. And me, too. How can she even look at me?*

What did she see in hospital when I was in there? All those shadows. No wonder she didn't want to stay for long.

"She's not good and kind like you."

Theresa basked in the familiar glow of approval. She'd missed it.

"We shouldn't ask you to go into that place again," Scott said. "But there's a strength about you. I don't know if I could pull us both out if I needed to. But I know you could."

"Maybe it'll work the opposite of what you think it will." Courtney swept crumbs onto the floor.

"It might break you."

Courtney shook her head. "I'm already broken." She kept her eyes half closed, as if keeping part of the world out that way. She had already sweated through her t shirt and her face was red, her breathing heavy.

Scott seemed strangely excited and Theresa wondered if he liked the promise of despair in Paradise Falls. If it meant he could stop thinking for a while.

"If you want to go into Paradise Falls, we should do it soon. Before I change my mind."

"Now?"

"Now."

Theresa dressed carefully. Comfortable clothes, because of the climbing, but also bright clothes, things that made her feel happy. Her pants were black, but they were soft, and she'd had them for years. She'd worn them to pass school exams, she'd worn them to parties and to see her niece for the first time. Her t-shirt was vivid purple and said Bringing the World Back Home in crazy, coloured lettering. She had no idea what it meant, but she liked it.

Scott refused to park away from the place, pulling up behind the abandoned Mitsubishi. "I'm not walking through this neighbourhood," he said, as he checked the car for valuables.

Theresa put her hand on the door handle, trying to convince herself to get out. She touched the penknife in her pocket; reassurance that she could wake herself if she needed to.

"Come on, it can't be that bad," Courtney said. She jumped from foot to foot on the path like an impatient child.

Theresa climbed out, looking down at the ground. Only three or four dogs sniffed around them. Someone had cleaned up the dead ones.

Paradise Falls sucked the light as it always did and Theresa wondered what Ben would think, if he was in there. Would he know she'd been unfaithful?

"Hey! You're back!" It was Andy, carrying a large backpack. He looked clean, and wore clearly new clothes. Good shoes. "Guess what? I got a job with my art. But I can't tell you about it." She hadn't seen him smile before.

"Is that him? The street kid?" Courtney whispered. She fiddled in her handbag, came up with a packet of cough lollies. She looked at it helplessly, as if knowing it was nowhere near enough.

"Is your job to draw in there?" Theresa asked Andy.

He nodded. "Piss easy." But he wouldn't catch her eye and she knew that he was being damaged by it.

He backed away from her.

"Theresa, we have to go. Time to go in."

"Who's she?" Andy asked. "Is she someone's mum or something?"

"What difference does that make? Hey?"

"Nothing. Fuck you."

"Come on, Scott. God, you're slow." Courtney pulled out a scrunchie and tied her hair back in a tight ponytail and suddenly she looked more accessible, more approachable, than Theresa had seen her. She put her shoes in her bag. "Right," she said, as if she was leading them.

Theresa watched Courtney climb and wondered if she would return changed. How would it feel, if her grief would have altered, if she learnt more about Amber than she should. What further guilt would ride Courtney as they walked through the Grief Hole?

Once they were all in, Theresa said, "We need to work our way through a few rooms. Try not to touch things."

It felt so still in there, Theresa thought they were in the eye of a storm. Her ears ached with the silence.

Scott tugged at her shirt. "Hang on," he said. He was out of breath, his face bluish.

"Are you okay?"

He had tears in his eyes. "Why do they come here? Why? It's so cold, so awful."

"I guess they need a place to go," Courtney said. "We all need somewhere." Her voice was so quiet Theresa could hardly hear her. "It seems peaceful here. Purposeful. It's a place of comfort."

"I think it is a comfort to them. I think they believe they won't be mourned if they do it here. They perform rituals to be forgotten."

"Our daughter didn't do it here. She did it in the office." Theresa liked the way Scott said 'our daughter'. The way he and Courtney shared the grief.

"Maybe she did want to be remembered. That's important, Scott." Theresa said.

Theresa said nothing about the magnanimous man in the mural, but Courtney ran her hands over his face. "Look at him! That is definitely Sol Evictus. Why would someone paint him like that?"

"That's who he is. That's what he's like."

His face was perfectly rendered, down to the piercing blue eyes. She wondered if he had ever been in this place. Or was he a coward, not wanting to see the rooms for himself, only wanting to see them on paper?

She wondered how he'd feel, being depicted that way. As a magnanimous fool or a deliberately cruel dictator. She thought he might be like some meat eaters, who recoil at the thought of an abattoir or hunting. They liked the meat on their plate, anonymous, long-dead, no hint of the living creature left. They hated to think of the process.

Perhaps Sol Evictus liked his death that way. Separate. Distant from the process. She walked forward quickly.

The rush of water seemed louder than ever and Courtney giggled. "Why do I suddenly need to do a wee?"

Theresa could smell degrading old plastic intensely. Scott and

Courtney didn't wrinkle their noses and she wondered if you became more sensitive the more frequently you entered the Falls.

They heard noises, grunts, rattles, sighs. "Are there children in every room?" Courtney asked.

"I don't know. Sometimes, I think."

"How many people are in here now?"

"No one counts. But don't open any doors."

"You mean like this?" Scott said, his hand on a white, shiny door.

"No!" Theresa stopped him, panicked. "You don't go into a room with the door shut."

"Sure are a lot of rules."

"Rules make things work."

"You're young to be a rule follower."

"You are or you aren't. Everyone who comes here is. That's what Tim says."

"How do you know? Don't they all die?"

"No, not everyone. Some don't bring the right stuff and never come back. Tim told me about one guy who wanted to take sleeping pills, but didn't realise his sister had pinched half of them so there weren't enough. He was so mad he didn't even try. And when you care that much, you're not ready to die."

Scott started to hum, and Theresa realised it was a Sol Evictus tune. She focused; yes, the music was playing in the background.

"Can you hear it?" she asked him.

He listened.

It was faint.

"Where's that coming from? Someone's playing music," Theresa said. She tilted her head, seeking the source. Eventually she tracked it to small, inlaid speakers in the hallway and in every room.

"Who's playing it? Is someone else here?" she said.

"I think everything is automated. It all keeps going. Like the toilets. Self-cleaning. It's all solar powered."

"It's kind of...uplifting. It doesn't sound like depressing music."

He rubbed his face.

She thought she could hear the mournful tones of a yowling dog. Just as Sol Evictus said she would.

She could smell the beginning of human decay as well but didn't want to track it down, and she could smell wine and she remembered how Ben chose the wine, and how she now chose the bottles he would have liked. She hated when she did that because it made her think of him too hard and then she'd have to try to something new, that she knew he'd never tasted. This one, she remembered he'd liked it, and they'd had two bottles, sitting together on the grass in the backyard at midnight. He'd told her about ants. An awful lot about ants.

The smell of decay was stronger now.

She heard footfall behind her and turned; Scott turned too. Courtney was ahead of them, her head tilted, hands on hips.

"Who do you see?" Theresa whispered to Scott.

"I...faint. It's so faint. But is it her? Is it her when she was five? That was our best year. We were happy. She got so many presents for her birthday and she wanted to take them all to her grandmother's house to show her but we couldn't fit them in the car, there were so many. We spoiled her. Lucky. But we didn't get to give her presents for her 18th. Or her 21st. Or her wedding." His shoulders slumped.

"It's not Amber. It's Ben. But..." Ben—although really she couldn't see him, it was like a projection—his flesh loose, and he stood with more of a lean than he had when alive, but it was him. She could see his blue eyes, wide open at her, beseeching her to still love him, to forgive him for dying.

"It's Ben." She stepped towards him, but he shimmered and disappeared.

Scott took her hand and they caught up with Courtney.

"Did you hear that? They said help," Courtney asked.

"I don't think so, Courtney," Theresa said, although she had heard it. "We have to leave people alone."

"I don't care about your stupid rules. That's someone's daughter, or son. If someone had spoken to Amber, we might still have her."

Courtney knocked gently on the door. A low moan reached them.

"I'm going to come in. I'm coming in now," Courtney called.

She pushed the door open. A rush of cold air chilled Theresa. She followed Courtney inside.

Inside the room there was a mound of bedclothes in the centre of a large bed but these shifted and Theresa could see that a young woman nestled beneath them. Kneeling around the bed, their heads resting on their hands were three ghosts. All heavy-lidded. All too tired to raise their heads. Their fingers clutched the bedclothes as if trying to drag her towards them.

Theresa felt momentary envy. She was enervated and the bed looked comfortable.

"Is it an overdose?" Courtney said.

The girl moaned again, a moan with an uplift at the end. Courtney bent over, put her hand to the girl's forehead, all motherly, feeling for a temperature.

"She's so cold."

"It's freezing in here." Theresa bent over her.

"Do we know her? Is this someone we know?" Courtney said.

"You never could tell her friends apart. You said they all looked the same. Remember? You used to say that when they were all in the kitchen. All together. Amber there with her lookalike friends," Scott said, as he stood beside them, his voice high-pitched.

"Scott," Theresa said. "It's okay. Quiet now. We can't take her.

Tim said if we help anyone, we'd have to take their place."

"We don't believe that," Courtney said.

"Doesn't matter if you believe or not."

"That's all that matters," Courtney said.

Theresa felt closer to tears than she had in a long time, at the innocence of this, the naïveté. It didn't matter what you believed. Truth couldn't be changed.

Courtney stared down at the sleeping girl. "I'd like to lie down. Rest."

Theresa felt nervous; out of her depth.

"Once you fall asleep here, you're saying, 'I'm finished.' Don't do it."

Scott grabbed Courtney's arm and pulled her backwards. He stroked her hair.

"Let's keep going. Let's do what we came here to do."

"We have to call an ambulance, first. Theresa, you know this is right.

Theresa dialled.

"We'll get someone there. Is the kid dead?" the operator said.

"No! Not dead!"

"We'll get someone there as soon as possible. Be aware that our operators cannot enter the building."

So they carried her down the ladder. She clung to Scott like a sleepy child.

It was difficult, and dangerous, but it made them laugh.

Prudence stood at the base of the ladder. She had tied most of her balloons to a rung. It was the first time they'd seen her without a mass of them and she looked both thinner and heavier. Her hands shook.

Theresa said, "You shouldn't have come."

"I needed to know more. Understand more. Then I will know what can be done." Prudence had taken a taxi; what money she used Theresa didn't know.

"Holy crap, what are you doing?" Andy said. He took five steps away as if wanting to separate himself from them. "Jeezus fuck, did you find that inside? Oh, shit. You're all cursed."

"It'll be fine. We're looking after someone who needs help," Courtney said.

Theresa took off her scarf and laid it over the girl to keep her warm.

Minutes passed with no sign of the ambulance, Courtney becoming increasingly agitated. Theresa found it hard to breathe.

Andy said, "I could have told you they won't show up here. They don't. People have called about dead kids before and nothing happens. They used to but half the time the ambulance was trashed or whatever. It sucks. I hate vandalism. The ambos got bashed, too. Who'd bash an ambo?"

"People who do business around here, I guess. Your customers," Scott said.

"Not my fucking customers. I fucking hate druggies."

"We can take her ourselves, then," Courtney said.

They picked the girl up again. She felt clammy and barely responded as they shifted her. Her sleepy ghosts were further away, though, leaning against each other, yawning. They were almost comical and in the darkness of the circumstance, Theresa felt a laugh rising.

There was no sign of her own ghosts.

The ambulance arrived then, with a police escort, and took the girl away. The police stayed in their car. Theresa wondered if they'd at least report the dumped Mitsubishi.

Scott asked them through the car window, "You know about this place?"

"You can make a formal complaint," the police officer said.

"I don't want to make a complaint, for fuck's sake. I want someone to do something."

As the ambulance drove away, Courtney said, "How do the police allow this? How does this place stay open?"

Andy answered, "It gets shut down all the time. They hammer the opening closed but it gets ripped open again. And there are patrols but they don't like climbing the ladder. Cops kill themselves half the time anyway, and they don't need to climb the ladder and feel worse."

"What about the bodies?"

"Someone gets them," Andy said.

So it wasn't Sol Evictus taking the bodies, Theresa thought. *It was more innocent than that.*

"Finished in there, now?" Andy's voice rose, and Theresa realised he cared.

"No, we're not. We haven't even seen anything," Courtney said.

Andy said quietly to Theresa, "It's not too late to stop them." Theresa wondered what it was he saw inside; who it was. And how he forced himself to go back up to draw the faces of the people there. Was it only money? Was it the prospect of a future?

"I know. But they want to. Why, what did you see last time? We can talk about it after, okay?"

"I'll come in with you. I'll help you get them out again. They're gonna feel it hard."

"Scott'll pay you heaps."

"I've already got heaps."

Prudence started to climb as well.

"You shouldn't come. Stay here," Theresa said.

But Prudence climbed on slowly, carefully. She reached the top of the ladder and called, "Come on!", as if they were going on an adventure.

They reached the bright room Theresa thought of as Amber's. "This is it. This is where she used to paint," and they entered. She felt physically ill but stronger knowing she had to help Scott and Courtney.

Scott stopped in the doorway and took deep breaths. "I don't believe in any of this."

"Are you okay?"

He held the doorframe. "Shit."

Theresa ducked under his arm, stood in front of him. "Scott?"

"I wouldn't have believed it, but it's palpable." He laughed harshly. "That's one of those words. I was a cynic about it. Palpable. Bullshit palpable. But there is a feeling here. It's strong."

"It's despair," she said, while he covered his eyes. "We're here. We don't want to come back again. So let's look properly. Okay? It's horrible, I know. But I survived it."

"You don't have a dead daughter, Theresa. You don't have that to contend with."

She felt angry for a moment, that he would dismiss her own grief so easily. She wanted to say, "I lost the love of my life," but she felt, at that moment, that her grief was lessened. She thought the words love of my life and Ben's face was in her mind, but her heart didn't turn over. She didn't feel like falling asleep to forget the fact he was dead.

"You stand there until you're ready. I'll look around. We haven't got long. I only managed a few minutes last time."

Courtney entered the room and stood, stiff.

"We think she sat here," Theresa said.

There was more debris since last time she was there. A water bottle, a paper back copy of *The Lion, the Witch and the Wardrobe*. The room smelt strongly of perfume, a familiar scent but not one Theresa could identify.

"How many?" Courtney choked. "How many have died here?"

"No one really knows," Theresa said. Her throat felt dry and painful. "A lot. Dozens, at least. Many dozens."

"All here?"

"Some in the other rooms as well. This is the place they like the best, though. There's a feeling in the room that what they are doing is right."

Prudence tied her last two balloons to a chair back. "That will cheer them, and us, too," she said, but no one believed it. Not when Prudence sank down, moaning, "Oh, the guilt of a mother. Oh, the worthlessness of a grieving mother."

"What do you see?" Courtney asked. "I can't see anything. What do you see?"

"My little one. I can't see her but I can hear her little laugh. Gurgle gurgle like a magpie, she was so happy, such a happy happy."

"I feel like the walls are closing in. Don't you?" Scott said. "It's hard to breathe. But then I'm so fat, I'm fucking useless, aren't I? Worthless."

Courtney said. "I like four close walls. I like to know where I am. It sounds like we're standing over some massive pit. Don't you think? I feel as if we could tip in. The sound is kind of hollow. Can't you hear it?"

"I can hear music," Scott said.

"Over the music. Under it. It's like a windy sound, but a vacuum sucking up the oxygen."

"All good," Andy said, his voice echoing. He had his sketch book out, drawing them.

They all breathed hard, sucking air.

And did she see Ben, on one knee, hand on heart? Was it him? Proposing to her? Proving them all wrong?

Courtney hadn't moved.

"Look," Prudence said, her voice hard to hear. "Here is her drawing of Sol Evictus." Her red skin glowed in the strange light

Amber had copied the drawing in the mural, with his position seated. His knees straight, his hands on his knees. But his face was anguished, agonised.

"What's he got around him? Tangled around him?" Prudence said. Scott looked closely.

"Hair? It looks like hair to me."

"Ah. Ah, of course. Of course it is. A halo of hair." Prudence began to sing, a mournful night time song about sleeping, sleeping forever.

"If we'd known about this place after Amber died we would have joined them. No doubt," Courtney said. "I would have happily died here. I would have come with a case of vodka and a carton of chips and died."

Scott took a photo of the portrait, Theresa beside it.

"Don't!"

She heard a clearing of the throat; Ben, about to speak. He'd always talked about pushing her, about finding her inner potential. She'd listened to every word he said, because he paid such attention to her, loved her so deeply. She trusted him.

At his funeral, Giselle had said, "You're going to survive this. And accept that it was his choices that led to his death, not yours."

Theresa had not spoken to her for many months after that.

Scott slumped in a corner of the room, his legs sticking out in front of him. It wasn't the corner Amber had used. He looked like a teenager, sitting there like that. Not like a grown man at all.

He shivered. "It's cold in here."

"Yeah, come on," Andy said. He looked cold. "Come on, a minute, that's it. Time's up."

"There's nothing of Amber here," Courtney said.

"I think she took it all with her. I think it's in her drawings. Her art. I think that's where we'll find it."

She sighed, and like a yawn spreading, Scott sighed too.

"We better get out of here. Once you start sighing, it gets harder to leave," Andy said. "You're slumping. You look tired. We need to get out of here."

Theresa didn't want to leave. She couldn't bear the thought of ever talking again, because she was so stupid, so dumb, how could anyone look at her, and she thought, *Wouldn't matter if it was as blunt as a butter knife. If you want to die, you could go and sit up there and you would die without any physical effort on your part.*

She took out her pocket knife and cut across her finger. The sharp short pain stirred her and she looked up at her aunt and uncle for the first time in minutes.

There were so many ghosts around Scott and Courtney, Theresa screamed. Ghosts with their throats cut, their wrists slashed. All of them hang-dog, self-sorry. She felt her own ghosts playing with her hair, lifting it to look at her neck, her ears. She felt a sense of ending, as if all ahead was dark.

"We need to get out now," she said.

"No, we need to stay here. This is where Amber wanted us to be."

"Now. We have to get out of here." Her voice was strong, definite. Out of the corner of her eye she thought she saw Ben, but no; it was Sol Evictus, fancy-dressed to look like Ben, wriggling his arse. He tilted his head back and a red line appeared as if his throat had been cut. He was crisscrossed with blood lines, as if Red had been at work on him.

It was the first time she understood the man could die.

She tugged at Courtney's arm. "Courtney? Now."

Courtney stood, sucked in, absorbed. So filled with grief she seemed a part of the walls. "You don't think here. Do you? The longer you spend here the less you remember."

Theresa physically dragged Courtney away. She didn't scream or struggle; she was limp. Prudence followed behind them, still singing. She had Scott by the hand, looking like a kind and loving aunt leading a chastened nephew away from a mess he'd made. Scott seemed insubstantial, almost completely absorbed by the ghosts around him.

Andy walked ahead of them, not looking back. He waited at the bottom of the ladder and joked, "Jeez, take your time!"

"S'okay, we're out now," Scott said. He gave Andy two fifty dollar notes. "Do you need somewhere to stay? You can crash with us. We've got plenty of room."

Andy looked at them, one at a time, assessing. "Naah."

"You said you'd help me with my dog, Andy," Theresa said.

He laughed, not about to be played that way.

"You know their daughter was an artist here, Andy. It killed her. I want you to stop what you're doing. Come with us. Scott will pay you. Honestly, he's rich as. He'll pay you to look after my dog, and you can help with other stuff, too."

Andy snarled at her, "This is the first time I've ever been happy in my whole life. You can fuck off if you think I'm gonna stop. Fuck you."

And he took off up the street.

No one spoke as they climbed into Scott's car. Theresa sat in the back seat, leaving Prudence on the side of the road, looking at her beseechingly.

"Can we take her away from here? I don't want to leave her alone," Theresa said.

"Yes, yes," Courtney said. "Don't leave her. I can forgive her for what she said in there."

"That was about herself, Courtney. Not you. She lost her daughter, too," Scott said.

"Come on, Prudence," Theresa called. She climbed out of the car, led the older woman to the back seat. She struggled to get in.

"It's been a while since I've been in a car," she said. She'd collected her balloons, and she tugged them in after her. They filled the back seat almost completely. After a moment's silence, Theresa, Scott and Courtney laughed.

"Can you see out the back window at all?" Theresa said.

"It all looks colourful," Scott said.

266

The ghosts lifted from them as they left. Theresa could see them, angry, whirling around, grasping. There were no ghosts in the car, though.

Scott, Courtney and Theresa breathed through their mouths and all the windows were open. Prudence was oblivious to her smell, far worse in the confines of the car.

Scott said, "Where am I going? What are we doing? Where am I taking people?"

"Take us home," Prudence called, loudly. "Home, please."

Courtney and Scott exchanged glances.

"It's all right, she can come to my place to have a shower at least," Theresa said. "You can all come to my place." She felt shell-shocked and the others seemed the same.

Theresa's hands shook as she unlocked the door. They stood for a moment in the hallway, no one sure what to say, where to go.

"I want to sit on the balcony," Prudence said. "I've always wanted to sit there."

They stared out over the water and didn't speak for ten minutes or more, sunk in memory of what they'd seen. What they'd felt.

Theresa said, "Are you okay, Courtney? What did you see?"

"I'm fine. I'm actually better. Because, you know? Usually I feel worse than that. I didn't see anything. Anyone. I thought I saw her clothes there, hanging up along the wall. Like she used to in her room. She hated her cupboard, didn't she Scott? Liked to be able to see anything. That's all." She took Theresa's hand. "You say that was Sol Evictus's place? He causes all that?"

"I don't know if it's his place, but I know he knows about it. And he loves it. Sending kids there is one of the things he aims for."

Scott fiddled with his phone until Theresa's beeped; he'd sent her the photo. She forwarded it to Red, saying: *Show him*

"Then we have to do something. We have to stop him. We can't let him do that any more," Courtney said.

"This isn't even the worst of it," Theresa said, and she told them what she thought about despair, suicide and the music of Sol Evictus. "Like that song you really like? I think it's about marital rape. The one that goes, 'You love her, she's yours, so take her. Don't waste her. Life's too short.'" Theresa had never been a good singer and the others covered their ears, but smiled, making light.

She told them that Andy was the new chosen artist and therefore would be destroyed.

"God damn that devil," Prudence said.

"Where is he?" Courtney said. "Let's find him now."

"Oh, the devil is everywhere. Everywhere. That one, you'll need to be a ghost and scare him off a cliff, or into the path of a big truck." Prudence pointed to a shirtless man walking on the beach.

"We only want to kill one devil. How do we rid the world of one devil?" Theresa said.

The others looked at her and she realised she had verbalised her intention for the first time.

Prudence was shaking. Theresa thought, *We were so focused on Courtney and how she was feeling. We didn't think about Prudence. Prudence lost a child, too.*

So she said, "After you've had a shower do you want a picnic on the beach? Sandwiches?"

Prudence nodded. Tears in her eyes. "You're kind. I won't have a shower, though. Water isn't good for me. It's very, very bad. When I know I will find you. You all rest until then. Stay calm and good and centred."

Courtney started to shake, too, and Scott said he'd take her home to rest.

The world seemed unchanged.

It was a warm day. The air felt soft and smelt of flowers and salt. The sand was fine, like powder almost. The sea was gentle, rolling in, rhythmic and comforting.

A text came through; Sol Evictus via Red. Picture received. You look sad and beautiful.

She texted Red: *What's happening with him?*

He called her. "The wife's packing up her stuff. I think she thinks she's going with him. She's packing the girls up, too. She said they're having a holiday but that's bullshit."

"You think she's going with him? What's he saying?"

"He's retiring. He's gonna release one last song: *Swan Song* it's called. Though he might call it *Helter Skelter*, though. Like the Beatles song. You know the one? That's the one that set Charlie Manson off. That's what they reckon. Maybe he thinks he'll be able to do the same."

"You can be quite the philosopher, Red. I hope your wife sees this part of you. You should show her. She'd like you more."

"She's not interested in what I have to say. She thinks I'm nothing but muscles. She doesn't think muscles can think."

"She wouldn't have married muscles. She must have seen something else there."

"Maybe. Maybe. I don't know."

"You should talk to her more. Talk to her before she finishes packing up and moves out. So when's this song coming out?" Meaning, how long do we have until he runs and hides?

"A couple of weeks then BAM, gone. He'll donate all the takings of this to Teen Suicide."

"Prevention. Teen Suicide Prevention."

"Yeah, that's the one. He thinks it'll make a lot of money. His legacy he reckons. Even though he could give away ninety percent of his money and he'd still be rich as."

"Gone where? He couldn't be a singer again anywhere. People would know him."

"His songs would be played still. And maybe he'd work in small ways. Like own a music shop or something. He's done this before. He's told us. He worked as a psychologist for a long time. Imagine that, ey? You go in there, fearing the dark or hating your husband or your father or you've got real bad dreams or whatever, and you talk to him. Those doctor types. I've seen them at work. Most of them sit there feeling superior. You wouldn't believe it. They probably don't believe it. But they do. They think, 'There but for the grace of God', but they don't believe that. They think they have their lives through pure hard work. Not luck. Hard work, good choices and birthright. It's bullshit.

"But some of these kids, I wish they'd had someone to talk to. Not those doctor types, but some kind of adult. There are plenty good ones around. In youth centres, or churches, or places like that. These kids…they listen to the songs. All his shit about not fitting in, about being out of place, about never making it. About how it's so easy for others. It's all about where you stick your dick. That's what it's about."

"So what are we going to do?"

"I don't want to lose my wife and kids. I won't find better. She's the only one who doesn't find me repulsive."

"So we'll do something. I don't want him releasing that album for kids."

"He's only scribbled some words for it. He hasn't gone anywhere with it."

"That's good."

"But his music does make people feel better. You know it does."

She thought of the audiences, and his fans, and wondered if that was true. If she was the only one to see despair in his words.

Theresa waited. She watched TV. She dreamed of Ben. She thought if finding Andy again, kidnapping him, making him stop, but she knew he couldn't be found.

Prudence looked terrible when she knocked at the door. Her hair was more of a rat's nest than ever. Her eyes drawn. Her lips dry. She drank the milk Theresa gave her, looking sidelong.

"Are you all right?"

"Were you worried? I didn't notice you looking for me," Prudence said, but she smiled. Theresa didn't think she had the expectation of anybody caring. "I haven't slept. I can't sleep. I saw his death. What I saw was terrible. His death is terrible and will require more from you than I think you have."

"I have a lot, Prudence. I have heaps."

"It was seeing that drawing with the halo of hair."

"That made his death clear?"

"It's ugly. You shouldn't have to do it."

"Do what?"

"See the Lacemaker. She'll help us. But I can't ask you to do it."

"Why not? Is she nasty?"

"She isn't nasty. But what you do can turn back on you. This is always the case. If it fails it will be on you. His death yours. His pain yours. If you're wrong, a visit to the Lacemaker can prove fatal. But there is no real risk. We know we're right."

"I should just shoot him."

"You have to do it this way."

"Who is she? You said you worked with her when you were younger."

"You only exist when you are in her presence. Once you leave, she will forget you as if you were never there. This is how she needs to be. She tats and she sews, she creates and destroys. She has no heart, she doesn't love or hate. She just is. She's formed from all the bits thrown away: the lace ends, the bobbin bits, the knots and the loose threads. All gathered together for a hundred years and she dragged herself into being out of it. That's what they say, anyway. She will make you a hair net and you will capture him with that. You collect hair, you collect and collect and collect until you have a lot." She held her arms in a circle. "Then you go to her."

"Where is she?"

"She is in Fairyland. I will take you when you have the hair. No sooner." They were quiet.

"What the hell is Fairyland?"

"It's a shop. A place. Don't worry until it's time to worry. Hairy hairy hairy hair."

"Of course," Theresa said. It seemed obvious. "He does hate hair. He's obsessed by it, but he's terrified."

"His one true tragedy. The day he lost his mother. And he did not tell you this, did he? He is a secretive, monstrous man. His mother drowned saving him from drowning, and he almost died choking on her hair."

"That's horrific." She wondered if Red knew this story.

Prudence said, "My friend the Lacemaker is a parasite like everyone. Everyone's a parasite, sucking on something. Some suck harder, that's all. Some suck smarter. These are the ones you have to watch out for. We've all got love to lose, and confidence. But parasites like Sol Evictus? Who steal the will to live? Parasites like that you have to deal with. Everybody is feeding off everybody else. It's how our world works. You start by sucking the calcium from your own mother's body. Did you know many women lose a tooth due to pregnancy? Little parasites sucking up all the nutrients like tapeworm." She pointed at her own gap-toothed mouth. "It's how we are and you can either live with it or let it kill you."

Theresa wasn't listening. She hated Prudence's 'parasite' ramblings.

"You'll need a lot of hair," Prudence said. She poked Theresa for attention. "You'll need a lot, a lot."

"Why don't you collect the hair yourself? Go to the Lacemaker yourself? Why make me do it?"

"I'm too old for any of this. All I can do is tell you what I know. If that's not enough I don't know what is."

"Why are you even helping? Don't you think I'm a monster?"

"Hmph. You shouldn't even talk about it. You are a monster but you are getting better."

"Is that what you've always wanted me to be? A better monster? A stronger one?"

"An avenging one," Prudence said, her voice so quiet Theresa could barely hear her. "You are going to do something brave and dangerous and then you will be a powerful monster. Your purpose is to fight the monsters. You will do it, won't you?"

"Is that what I want?"

Prudence held her hand out and Theresa reached out, thinking, *I have to take her hand. Too rude. It would hurt her if I didn't.* But the old woman placed a large clump of her own filthy hair in Theresa's palm.

"That's to get you started," she said. "You'll be addicted before long. You won't be able to help yourself. You will need helpers. Ask them all. Ask that poor, poor girl."

"Annie?"

"Yes, Annie. Annie."

Theresa began to collect hair compulsively, everywhere she went. Red took all that Sol Evictus's lovers left behind, and all Sol Evictus did, too. He didn't ask what it was for. Theresa ran her hands along the seat backs at the cinema. She haunted hairdressing salons and barbers. She patted little children on the head. She wasn't sure about dog hair, so she kept her dog's hair separate.

273

She wore shirts with big buttons that snagged hair. She visited hospitals wards, where hair fell out and lay on pillows, unwanted.

Theresa collected hair from shopping centres, although she hated the crush. She could snip locks off, tug out small clumps, and the person would shrug with irritation, that's all. No sense of personal space in the mall.

She saw lots of lovely blonde hair and she thought of Annie, sitting in her backyard, aimless. Pointless. Long, long blonde hair. She thought, *I'll go to see her. To talk. Take some of her hair. Nothing more.* But a plan was forming, an idea.

The weather was cold and wet, so Annie's mother had her bundled up on the couch. Cup of soup, untouched, cooling, on the coffee table beside her. Piles of romance novels. *That's not going to help*, Theresa thought.

"She'll liven up later. There's a Sol Evictus special on TV."

"I don't know if she should watch it. Not the way she is. I think we should get her up, take her out somewhere. Shopping. Something."

"I don't want to go. Sol Evictus is coming on." Annie's voice had far more of a whine to it than it had before.

"You need to be careful of him," Theresa said. "He's dangerous. He's a parasite." She smiled, realising this was too much, that she needed subtlety. Smiling to make a joke of it.

"Oh, but he's such an amazing man. He thinks I'm clever. He said so."

"When did you talk to him?"

"He called up. Didn't he, Mum?"

"She was so happy talking to him. But then she sank down worse than ever. I don't know what to do."

"Keep her away from him. We may be sorting something out for her. I hope so." Theresa said this quietly, not wanting Annie to hear.

With all Theresa had learned—about Paradise Falls, Sol Evictus, victimhood—still the girl sat. She hadn't changed or moved on. Theresa felt stunned that the rest of the world hadn't moved with her.

"I think he's a genius," Annie said. "Did you find out yet it was all my fault Amber's dead?"

"It wasn't your fault. It's that man. Sol Evictus. Not you or her parents. He's the one who made her feel that way."

"What about the Grief Hole? I told her about it. That was me. I'm the one who got her to go there."

"You all knew about it, Annie. All of you. Tim included."

"I found out where it was, though. And we went there. I never went in, though. I waited outside once, the first time Amber went. If she couldn't cope, then how could I? I wouldn't do that to my mum. It'd kill her. Amber was always so strong, before she met him. Always seemed to know more than the rest of us did."

"I think she really did. And he did destroy her, like he's trying to destroy you, and others. So many people." Theresa shook her head. "It was Sol Evictus who made her go back."

Annie closed her eyes. When she opened them, they seemed brighter. "It's inevitable, then. I can give in to it."

Theresa waited until her mother was distracted, making small talk meanwhile.

"No, you can't. That comes from him, not you. But I want you to help me. I've had a terrible idea. It's truly, truly awful. I believe this man is better off dead. He's not the first, but he's the worst. I've done things in the past; I've caused the button to be pushed, but I haven't pushed the button. This time..."

"Tell me," Annie said. Her cheeks were red. Theresa could see a pulse running quickly in her throat.

"A suicide, if it's going to occur, should be worthwhile. It should have a purpose."

"Whose suicide?"

"Yours, Annie. It's clear that you think about it all the time. I know how we can make it worthwhile."

"You want me to kill myself?" Annie laughed. A tired, but genuinely amused laugh. "You've come up with a plan that involves me killing myself. So do you want me to actually die?"

They both laughed at that. "No! I don't want you to die! I want you to pretend you want to, and then you won't want to any more. We tell Sol Evictus that you want to die, and we invite him to watch. We get to him this way; we lull him. That's my plan."

"Of course I'll do it. If it'll help Scott and Courtney. Help them to forgive me. It's not going to work for me but hey, why not?"

Annie hushed as her mother came back.

Her mother said, "She's coming shopping, isn't she, aren't you Annie?" She tried to steer Annie, lift her up, but Annie held herself so stiff, like a cat who didn't want to be picked up.

"Keep her away from the news. Maybe music videos, but no Sol Evictus. I'll try to come back again soon."

Theresa snipped a soft lock of Annie's hair. Annie barely blinked.

She met Red at his favourite pub. His aftershave was like a toxic cloud and he was still bald.

He slammed the stick he always carried into the floor.

It was fat with hair

"He's told me to get rid of it. To chuck it out. As if it's worthless."

"What does it mean to you?"

"It's remembering. Keeping a record. Some of your hair is on here, too." He waved it viciously.

"Is it a weapon as well?"

"I got my knife for that," he said. "He knows I know. He knows I know he's taking my family."

"Why don't you try, then? Try to use it on him. It's not like you haven't done this before."

He snorted. "Kidding me? I'd be dead in seconds. Seconds. I'm not keen on being dead."

"I don't think you're going to die any time soon. There aren't any ghosts around your shoulders."

"And he's going to live forever, with a forever list of artists. And he'll be the one to watch my wife die. He'll be the one to see my daughters married."

"We need to move fast, then. If he gets away we may not be able to find him."

"Yeah, fast. He's told us he's giving us a year's pay and he's lined jobs up for us all. So I don't know. Maybe he's okay. Maybe we've misjudged him. Might be better to leave him be."

"Is your wife packing to go?"

He nodded.

"Are your daughters his?"

He nodded again.

"And is he using Andy as his next artist? Because that shit is my fault."

"That street kid? Yeah. He's a good one."

"Then let's fuck him over. Let's fuck him up."

She watched his fingers itching; would he be allowed to cut, she knew he was wondering, *Can I cut the wrists? The throat? Can I make the incisions?*

"You can't do it. If he dies, we die. We know that. It's his magic; it's why he lives so long. He dies, we die."

"You know that's bullshit. All that is him controlling you."

She told him what she had to offer, how she wanted to reach Sol Evictus. "We'll distract him, put him off, change him enough so

277

that he no longer wants your wife and kids. He'll let go."

"He'll love this idea. I know he will. I'm sure this'll get you in. But wait for my word. Don't rush it. The others...I'll have to talk to the others."

His phone beeped. "It's Carter. Wants to know where I am. Time to go back to work."

"Can you drive?" He'd been slurring his words, stumbling as he walked to the bar.

"Yeah, nah. I'll get him to pick me up."

"Don't tell them what we're planning. They won't support us for a second. They won't know what's happened till it's happened. We'll leave him happy, so happy he'll release you all. He'll go away and leave you all alive. He'll leave lots of stuff behind. You can have all of it except Amber's art. All the rest is yours, whatever you can carry away."

He nodded. "Yeah, yeah, that'll work."

"How do we keep him from knowing something is going on? He knows everything."

"He's distracted. We're getting away with shit we wouldn't usually. Like me getting pissed here."

"But Carter knows."

Red's hair stick sat between them.

"Will you give me your stick?"

"You look after it. It's very special." He reached into his pocket and he handed her a small ball of hair he'd collected. "My oldest girl, she's started cutting herself. Just to see the blood, she says."

"I've got it. Don't worry. You keep an eye on him. And collect hair. You tell him I've got something for him. Something no one else has ever seen. Something most people would think is beyond disgusting. We are gonna fuck him up."

"That's no language for a lady. And you are a lady of the finest kind." Carter. He kissed the palm of his hand, his tongue darting out to lick. "What you doing getting my buddy all fucked up here?"

"She wants to see him again."

Carter nodded at her. "He likes you. Don't worry. He'll fuck you again when he's ready. You stay happy in your fake little world till then. With all your good people. You come back to us soon, though. Back to where you belong."

She smiled at him. Stood on her toes and kissed his cheek. It was cold, clammy. Almost slimy. He winked at her.

He smelt of stew. Theresa thought that if he took her body, it wouldn't be discovered for a while. She shivered; he mimicked her.

"Have a drink, mate," Red said. "Come, on. We need it. The things we've seen."

"Nothing we can talk about."

"I've seen a lot," Theresa said. "You'd be surprised."

"I reckon she'd like it. I reckon she'd wanna hear. This stuff gets her going."

And it did. As they spoke, the more they told her, the more Theresa thought, *Which one of them would make the better lover? Which one would want less of me?*

"There's that doctor of his. He'll take anything off for money. Won't he? Crazy bitch who hates her right arm? He'll take it off and go golfing straight after."

"He's burnt a school to the ground when a father wouldn't come through."

"He's ordered hostages killed."

"He's poisoned water. This is real stuff he's done."

"The thing he thinks is the funniest? You know when a person survives a crash or something, and they stagger out, like this?" The two of them demonstrated, reeling around the bar, crashing into each other.

"Cracks him up the point of seizure. Seriously."

All of it confirming for Theresa that intervention was the right thing. She was protecting the children; her own niece and nephew amongst them. She was saving Andy from destruction.

"We better get to work, Red. Can we drop you, Theresa?" Carter said, as if they were mates having a drink.

"No, thanks. I'll get home."

She watched them cross the road, Red pushing recklessly out. She should tell him to be careful but she knew he wouldn't listen.

Theresa called Giselle, wanting to hear the kids' voices. Be inspired by their innocence.

"They're out. Their dad took them to the movies. I'm sitting up in bed reading magazines and eating the burnt toast they cooked me."

Theresa realised it was Mother's Day. "Oh, shit. Did you call Mum?"

"Mum doesn't give a rat's about Mother's Day!"

Theresa felt momentarily bereft, wishing she had someone to care for on the day.

There was Prudence; she could find Prudence and give her a meal. That, at least.

"I wish you were back here, though. You sound stressed."

"There's a heap of stuff going on. I don't want to talk about it over the phone."

"Boyfriend? Mum said something about a guy called Tim or something."

Theresa realised it had been weeks since she'd seen him. She felt momentarily guilty at dumping him without a thought. She should call him. But she felt so guilty about suggesting him to Sol Evictus, she didn't want to. And she didn't want to go through the process of dumping him again, if he came over all eager and wanting.

"She seems to think he's nice. Not that she's impressed by nice. It's time, though, Theresa. Don't you think? Time for you to stop mourning. You were so obsessed with Ben we lost you while you were with him. We got you back, I thought, but you've been sunk in this hole."

"Well, I'm outta that one and into another. But I can tell you later. Once it's done."

"Once what's done?"

"Don't worry about it. Give the kids big hugs for me."

As if Sol Evictus understood the urgency, he released his swan song early. It went viral over the internet within hours. Theresa was reluctant to look at it, not wanting to be drawn in, not wanting to see any good in the man.

The music was beautiful, entrancing. The film clip showed a flower, opening up. "Oh my god that's beautiful," the commenters said. "Entropy is his best song ever." Then the rose started to rot, slowly, inexorably. Yet still the commenters found it beautiful. "I'm freaking crying," they said, and "I worship that man. Can he do no wrong?"

He was worshipped, Theresa realised. People were blind to who he really was. They trusted him. They believed he had loved and lost. They believed he grieved, that his heart was broken, that he had lost lovers, children, friends, yet still he sang for them, to fill them with joy and a sense of self-worth. Any negative comment was screamed down by his fans, shut down.

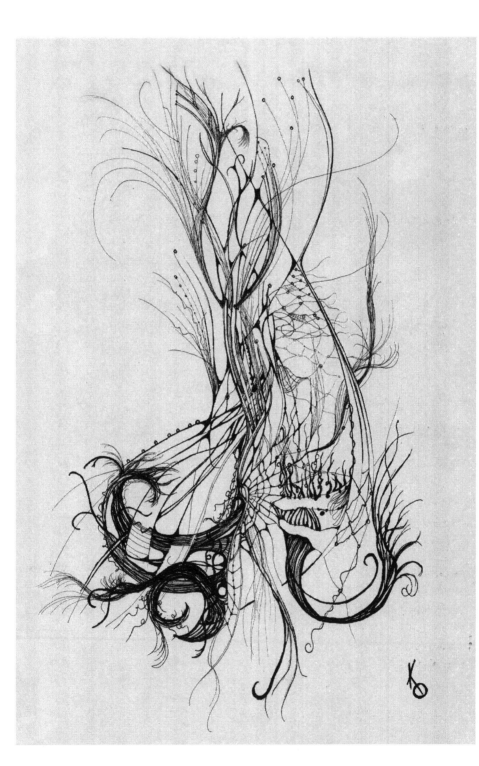

There was too much talking. Theresa was tired of it, all the words, the discussions, agreements and disagreements, the planning. She wanted to stop talking and do it. She avoided Scott, didn't go into the office. Didn't tell him what she intended to do, or about the hair, or the Lacemaker. It was too weird. It made sense to her and Prudence, but to anyone else it would sound insane.

She was full of doubt and uncertainty but let it carry her along. She'd see the Lacemaker. Talk to her. Give her the hair. Then she'd see.

"I'm ready. I have hair. I have a lot of hair. What sort of shop is it?" Theresa said to Prudence. "Can you take me there? I'm ready."

"Oh, you know. Costumes. Magic. All sorts."

She and Prudence walked together. Prudence left bright red footsteps when she walked. *Had her blood gone to powder and started leaking through her pores?* Theresa thought.

The shop's name sat, faded and filthy, over the cracked doorway. "Fairyland". The steps were dark and sticky and Theresa tripped on the top one.

"Watch your step" a sign said, though Theresa was sure it wasn't there before her stumble. Another sign said, "Fancy Dress. Hair Looms. Masks."

Inside it was brighter than she suspected. Sharp, fluorescent lights flared overhead showing up the thick grime on everything. The cave-like smell of dirt, with an attic smell of mould and dust.

To her left were five giant heads. A comic-book character, possibly Astro Boy, sharp-jawed and blue-eyed. The blue was mottled on the old head so the eyes seemed blind, cataracted eyes

283

which made Theresa think of her grandfather, blind and groping, and she walked past the giant chicken head, the bone head, and squirrel head, inside.

Masks of presidents and other world-leaders. Rasputin. Star Wars faces. All of them flaccid, as rubber faces are, and dust in the creases making them all appear dark-skinned.

She stood in the middle of the shop for three minutes. No one came to help. Overhead the ceiling was low and hung with rubber severed limbs, shepherdess crooks, spiders and snakes.

She saw the costume rack. From it came a sweet, rotting smell, and flicking through them she could see some of them were in an advanced state of decay. A hand-lettered sign said, "Old costumes used in antiquity."

Still nobody came to help. She coughed politely, and then was taken by a full-blown coughing attack.

She wiped her eyes, feeling the tears streak across her face. She noticed then a small sign: "Private". She could hear a sewing machine whirring.

"Hello, excuse me?"

The sewing machine stopped and a curtain whisked aside.

"Can I help you?" The woman wore a tight, striped pirate's shirt, tight white capri pants. Theresa could see flowered underpants.

"Are you the Lacemaker? I need something made. A hair net."

"Hair-nets next to stage make up."

"No. No. A hair net." Shouldering off her backpack, Theresa pulled out a large, full paper bag. She opened it.

Inside, the fat ball of hair.

The woman breathed deeply and picked it up. The Lacemaker had ghosts sitting by her sewing machine. They were so old, Theresa thought at first they were dried tree branches.

"A goodly collection. What do you need the net for? Punishment or capture? Departure?"

"A man will hurt many more people unless I stop him."

"And this is for him? I need to be clear. You have to be sure. This can't be done unless you are absolutely sure."

"I am sure."

"Anyone else can vouch? Anyone else sure?"

"Plenty. Plenty. I've got two friends and my aunt and uncle. They can come and tell you. He's a bad man. He needs to be stopped and Prudence thinks this is the only way."

"Prudence?"

"The balloon woman."

"The Balloon Woman? What is that? I have men balloons. I have one woman. Marilyn Monroe. You want to buy that? I have Margaret Thatcher too but she has a hole."

"I don't want balloons," Theresa said, frustrated. Then she saw that the woman was teasing her, and she smiled.

Outside, Prudence waited below the window. They could barely see her balloons bobbing, knocking on the filthy glass as if sending a message.

Theresa went to the window. "Does this open?"

"Leave the windows alone. If we need her I will call her in."

The Lacemaker squeezed the hair between her fingers, which seemed to elongate. Stretch out. Theresa stepped backwards. The woman's fingers lengthened and at the end of them grew long, sharp needles. Theresa felt terrified that she would reach out, scratch them down Theresa's cheek. She was so sure this would happen she lost herself in a fantasy of blood poisoning. The hospital, and who would visit? What they would bring? Tim kissing her on the lips, tears in his eyes.

"I take payment in advance. Cash only," the Lacemaker said, and named a figure.

"No problem."

"Put it somewhere safe and I'll play hide and seek later."

Theresa put the money under a pincushion sewn to look like a strawberry.

"You need to think about why. And what," the Lacemaker said.

"I have done that. I've thought of nothing else."

The woman ran her fingers through the hair ball. Her hair frizzed out, electrified.

The needles in her fingers glinted and Theresa stood steady, leaning on Red's stick.

"You need to talk while I work. Tell me who the hair net is for. Tell me of their past and future intentions. Who is this man?"

"He's a singer."

"Then perhaps you should sing to me. Sing to me of immortality, awful immortality, or the death of love."

"I can't sing. And I'm no good at making things up."

"Have you ever been to a fancy dress party? You remember that sense of freedom from yourself? That's what you need."

The needles withdrew into her fingers as she stood up. She walked past the rack of antique clothing and threw open a trunk.

Black moths fluttered out.

"In there. Your style."

Inside the box; a saloon prostitute. A nurse. An airline hostess. A French resistance member.

Theresa pulled out the nurse's costume in case the woman picked the prostitute for her.

The woman shook her head. "Those are not right for you, now I look at them." She opened a hidden cupboard and stood back to show Theresa the contents. The costumes here seemed alive. Inhabited.

"You made all of these?"

"Yes, I sew as well as tat. These are special; these will give anyone another life."

She thrust a pile of cloth into Theresa's arms. "You never dressed up before?"

"No, no, we used to, a lot. My friends and I. We used to love it." Theresa remembered one party where they'd all dressed as super heroes. That'd been fun. Giselle had dressed as Wonder Woman and Theresa had been The Incredible Hulk.

She felt the cloth; lace so fine it felt like spiderwebs. "This is beautiful," she said. "Did you make it? It's so fine."

"Not so fine. Not the finest. Blind Baby patterns are the finest. Only tiny girls could wind thread onto the tiny pins. They did this until they went blind or their fingers got too big."

"That's terrible. Those poor little girls."

"Poor little everyone in the world. We are all suffering."

She chose an opera singer's costume for Theresa to wear. "In there. Put it on in there."

The change room was a small cupboard. On the shelves were pins and nails and skewers.

As Theresa pulled on the costume she hoped for a feeling of fullness and song, but there was nothing.

The Lacemaker called out, "Come on, now. It's almost closing time."

They sat together in the small private room. The ghosts settled themselves, preparing for a show. The Lacemaker nodded at her. Theresa thought of Sol Evictus and his plans. She thought of his strong, bare arms holding her, killing her. She thought of Amber and of Andy.

"Sing like this," the Lacemaker said. "This song is called *The Sempstress*. Did you do the poem in school? Thomas Hood? It's a wonderful poem."

The Lacemaker sat down on her chair, readied her fingers, and sang:

With fingers weary and worn,
With eyelids heavy and red,
A woman sat, in unwomanly rags,
Plying her needle and thread—
Stitch! stitch! stitch!
In poverty, hunger, and dirt,
And still with a voice of dolorous pitch
She sang the "Song of the Shirt."

"Work—work—work,
Till the brain begins to swim;
Work—work—work,
Till the eyes are heavy and dim!
Seam, and gusset, and band,
Band, and gusset, and seam,
Till over the buttons I fall asleep,
And sew them on in a dream!

"Oh, Men, with Sisters dear!
Oh, men, with Mothers and Wives!
It is not linen you're wearing out,
But human creatures' lives!
Stitch—stitch—stitch,
In poverty, hunger and dirt,
Sewing at once, with a double thread,
A Shroud as well as a Shirt.
"But why do I talk of Death?
That Phantom of grisly bone,
I hardly fear its terrible shape,
It seems so like my own—
It seems so like my own,
Because of the fasts I keep;
Oh, God! that bread should be so dear
And flesh and blood so cheap!

"Work—work—work!
My labour never flags;
And what are its wages? A bed of straw,
A crust of bread—and rags.
That shattered roof—this naked floor—
A table—a broken chair—
And a wall so blank, my shadow I thank
For sometimes falling there!
"Work—work—work!
From weary chime to chime,
Work—work—work,
As prisoners work for crime!
Band, and gusset, and seam,
Seam, and gusset, and band,
Till the heart is sick, and the brain benumbed,
As well as the weary hand.

"Work—work—work,
In the dull December light,
And work—work—work,
When the weather is warm and bright—
While underneath the eaves
The brooding swallows cling
As if to show me their sunny backs
And twit me with the spring.

"Oh! but to breathe the breath
Of the cowslip and primrose sweet—
With the sky above my head,
And the grass beneath my feet;
For only one short hour
To feel as I used to feel,
Before I knew the woes of want
And the walk that costs a meal!

"Oh! but for one short hour!
A respite however brief!
No blessed leisure for Love or Hope,
But only time for Grief!
A little weeping would ease my heart,
But in their briny bed
My tears must stop, for every drop
Hinders needle and thread!"

With fingers weary and worn,
With eyelids heavy and red,
A woman sat in unwomanly rags,
Plying her needle and thread—

Stitch! stitch! stitch!
In poverty, hunger, and dirt,
And still with a voice of dolorous pitch,—
Would that its tone could reach the Rich!—
She sang this "Song of the Shirt!"

Theresa felt as if she wanted to cry. The song made her so sad. She thought, *Keep that one away from him. Don't let Sol Evictus near this song.*

"There's a painting called *The Sempstress*. This man…it is one of his favourites."

"Is it now? You sing to me. You need to sing or I won't understand."

Theresa began to sing. It sounded awful, and the words didn't rhyme, but they were the right words. Truthful. She sang about the things she knew and those Red and Carter had told her and shown her. She thought about the poet owner of Passing Strange, the things she spoke about; how to use words and imagery.

The Lacemaker began to separate the strands, the thousands of strands, her finger needles flashing. She drew the pieces together, knitting and knotting, small snipped-off ends flying up and down like snowflakes.

He has a doctor, a doctor he trusts,
Who'll remove a limb for the asking.
Sol Evictus asks this to make himself laugh.
The doctor plays golf with money earned
By removing a young woman's left leg.
Noses removed, ears and eyes. He'll take anything off for money.
Sol Evictus says, "What do you see in that child's eyes?"
It's a test, but he doesn't know the answer himself.

"He did all that?" the seamstress said. "Keep singing. Keep singing."

The hair net grew between her fingers. Theresa could smell the hair singeing slightly as it rubbed together.

He hates the way family men
Expect to be protected, and
He will happily use their children as bait or threat.
He's burnt a school to the ground.
He's killed hostages.
He's poisoned water.
He's collected money and spent it on murder.
He's done a deal to stave off mortality.
Each monster only has one way to die.
And every killing lays a curse.

The Lacemaker said, "He did all this?"

His gallery is filled with the futureless.
Faces from the Holocaust,
From Babi Yar,
From Srbenika.

> *Faces from the trenches,*
> *Faces from the skies,*
> *Faces dead and futureless.*
> *These are the faces he likes to see.*

The Lacemaker stretched out her fingers. The needles flew and the hairs did, too.

Theresa sang until her throat ached. She watched the hair net grow and become more intricate.

> *Sol Evictus watches news reels of plane crashes,*
> *Train wrecks,*
> *Tsunamis,*
> *Earthquakes.*
> *He doesn't watch them for the gore or the death.*
> *That he can see for real any time.*
> *It's the others, the ones who stagger out right into flames,*
> *Or over a jagged cliff.*
> *He can't believe it no matter how many times he watches.*
> *"Look at 'em! They lose the plot," he says.*

The Lacemaker, momentarily pausing, looked up, like the sempstress in the portrait. "That's a lovely song," the Lacemaker said. "Excellent rhythm."

"Your song gave me the rhythm. Your song of the shirt."

"Although this is not a shirt I'm making," and she croaked out a laugh.

"No, not a shirt." Theresa said. "Or maybe a hair shirt."

They croaked together. The noise hurt Theresa's throat but she couldn't laugh any differently.

The Lacemaker continued, slower now, finishing off. Theresa watched, stunned by what she saw, the beauty of it. The strangeness.

The Lacemaker was soaked with sweat, streaked with it. She didn't smell, though. It seemed like pure water to Theresa. The hair net glistened and shone like an oiled blade. The Lacemaker held up the hairnet to display it before folding it neatly and slumping, exhausted. She sheathed her fingers, thimbles on all fingers and thumbs.

Then she sighed, a deep exhalation. Not as deep as the sigh of Sol Evictus. Nothing could ever be as deep, as weary, as that.

Theresa didn't want to leave, felt too tired to walk. As an excuse to stay longer, she said, "You make all your costumes?"

"Every last one. Every one with a hair in the seams and sometimes something more. I've sewn a vein, I've sewn a strip of skin. I've sewn a tiny love poem. Into the seams, you know, where no one looks. I've sewn ash, ash of the loved one."

"My loved one had no ash. His mother wanted him buried. I wanted him burnt and scattered at sea. She wasn't having any. She said I had no say because we weren't married. But we would have been. If he hadn't died."

"I could have sewn his hair into a beautiful dress for you," the Lacemaker said.

The balloons tapped at the window again.

"I think she wants you," the Lacemaker said. "Good luck. You come back and tell me what happens. You come back again when you need another net. You're a good collector of hair. Sometimes I get all the nasty bits, all dirty and cut and far too short. You brought me lovely strands."

"I'll come back," Theresa said.

"Come back when you need to dress up!" the Lacemaker said. Theresa thought she was being funny but wasn't sure.

Prudence waited for her impatiently. "Are you all right?"

"Why, is there any reason I wouldn't be? Surely you wouldn't send me to a dangerous place." She was teasing Prudence; trying to make herself feel less terrified.

Prudence looked away. "Sometimes she doesn't like people. But she liked you, I'm sure. Everyone likes you."

"She made a beautiful net." Theresa began to open the drawstring bag the Lacemaker had packed it into.

"No! Leave it safe. That's for him and him alone. No one should touch it or see it. We shouldn't breathe near it."

Theresa tightened the drawstring.

Her father called her. He said, "Teese, I'm sorry I haven't been a good father."

"Don't be stupid. What are you saying that for?"

"I've denied your ability, and tried to pretend you're not who you are. I've tried to pretend you and Giselle are like twins. So that if she does something, you'll do it too. Marriage. Children."

"I'm not on the shelf yet, Dad!" Theresa said.

"I was talking to Giselle and we thought she might come over. To help." He cleared his throat. "I wish I could help you. I can't, though, can I? I'm not one of you like that. But I can help Giselle help you. Your mother won't. She's a bit annoyed. We'll send her off to Fiji for a holiday or something. Somewhere different where she doesn't have to think."

He didn't sound bitter.

Buoyed at the idea of Giselle coming, she took her dog for a long walk along the beach. She could think while walking. No distractions beyond the dog tugging at his leash—she let him run free when the beach was deserted—and the waves, and the feel of the sand at her feet.

She knew that she would need to make the guards falter in order to throw the net. She only needed a minute, no longer. A minute when they took their eyes off him, lowered their attention. Then afterwards, she needed to remove herself and Annie from the house quickly. The best room for a quick retreat was the sun room. It sat at the back of the house and opened straight onto the green, soft lawn. Sol Evictus liked that room, Red told her. He sat in there alone quite often. There was no art. The floor was brightly polished wooden boards. The walls wallpapered in an old fashioned flock pattern, faded by the sun.

He sometimes took his breakfast in there, Red said. He also said, once Sol Evictus is happy, and safe under your hair net, I'll get the art for you. It'll work.

He believed Theresa would allow Annie to kill herself.

She threw a stick for the dog. The sight of him running, his tail wagging, his feet kicking up sand, gave her a deep sense of happiness, counteracted by her thoughts of the guards.

She texted Sol Evictus: *Did Red and Carter tell you that I have something for you?*

He called her back. He liked to use his voice.

"He did, Theresa. And thank you again for the photo you sent of yourself in that place. I've printed it to keep in my bedside table."

He breathed into the phone, saying no more.

"I have something precious to offer you. Something... something most people would not understand. Even more than your usual collection. It won't be permanent, though. It is a momentary artwork. In progress."

"Curious."

"I have a friend. Amber's best friend. Her name is Annie and she wants to die. She is willing to die in front of you."

He exhaled; it seemed to last a minute. Then a sigh that was like a dying breath. "My God," he said. "Oh Lord."

"She is so full of despair she can't even lift her arms. She wants you to be the witness. She thinks it will mean something that way, that she will be remembered and understood. And you might write a song about her. What do you think?"

He caught his breath. "You are a woman of wondrous means," he said. "Wondrous. I'm changing my will for you, Theresa. It's all yours!"

She knew he had no intention of doing so.

"Where?" he said.

She had thought of doing it at Paradise Falls, but Prudence warned her not to. "It's the water. It's drowning. You mustn't."

Giselle arrived the next day. Theresa met her at the airport and was surprised by the childish excitement she felt as the passengers began to emerge.

"Woohoo! No kids!" Giselle said.

The sisters hugged each other.

"I can't quite believe you're here," Theresa said, then wished she hadn't. It sounded negative and judgemental. Giselle didn't seem to mind, though.

A large woman, mid-40s, leaned to Theresa and said, "That's a lovely sister you've got. I envy you both," smiling.

"Happy we sat together, Jean," Giselle said. She told Theresa as the woman walked away, "She's got a grief hole the size of my fist."

"She's got no ghosts around her. Poor woman. She'll be living with it for a long time."

"I sometimes feel like I should be able to reach inside the hole and take something out. Remove whatever it is that makes them feel so awful."

"Maybe you can. We might be able to figure it out." They walked to the car and Theresa negotiated her way out of the car park.

"So fill me in on this music stuff."

"What a weird way to put it," Theresa said. She gave Giselle a summary of how she'd spent the last months.

Giselle put her hand on Theresa's shoulder. "That's insane, Teese. It's wrong. You shouldn't be involved in any of it."

"That's what Mum keeps saying. But I have to. I'm in it, and I can't say no."

"You could. But you won't."

"It's personal now."

"How? Because of Amber? I know you want to help them, but they'll understand…"

"It's Amber, but there's a kid called Andy as well. And there's something else…"

"What?"

"We'll talk about it when we get home." Theresa could feel her nerves jangling; her arms began to shake.

They spent an hour settling in, drinking tea, exploring the shore.

"I slept with him. He slept with me. I didn't want to do it. But it wasn't really rape. He didn't hurt me." She told Giselle some of how the night had played out.

Giselle stood up, wrapped her arms around Theresa. "Of course it was rape. You still have your senses, and you haven't been physically damaged, but you were there against your will. You didn't want it to happen, so it's rape."

Theresa felt herself starting to cry. She thought, *If not now, when?* And she let it happen.

Giselle cried, too. "You don't know…" she said.

"What? What? Don't tell me."

"It happened to me too, Theresa. I haven't told anyone. It was date rape, but that makes it sound like nothing. This creep, before Nolan—Nolan doesn't know, don't tell him. This total creep, acted like a jerk all night, no interest on either part, but still he raped me on the way home."

"Why didn't you tell anyone? We have so many secrets."

"Everybody has secrets. But you were always busy saving the needy. You didn't notice us. You only notice those you can help."

Theresa was stunned.

"I don't meant that in a bad way, Teese. But you know where you're needed. And yes, we're good at secrets."

"Everyone's good at secrets. Giselle…I had no idea."

"No one did. You're the first person I've told."

The sisters sat together, feeling closer than they ever had as children.

"I wouldn't have told Mum, either. But you could have told me."

"I didn't ever want to talk about it. And no way could I tell Mum or Dad. I can't add to what they have. They both have thick black holes right over their hearts. Can't you see it? I can see it clear as day."

"I can't see it. It's the baby they lost, isn't it? Poor little thing. Can't you reach in and fix them? Stick your hand in that grief hole and make it better? Put something in there. Fill the hole."

"I can't do anything like that. I can do the opposite, though. I can tear the hole open. I've done it once; never again. I tore the hole open the tiniest bit once and it ended so badly I can't even talk about it."

"Would you be willing, though? Could you do it this time?"

"If that's what's needed. I can do it. I can be the one to do it."

"I can, too," Theresa said, and she told Giselle her own secrets; of the interventions and how they made her feel.

Almost shell-shocked by the things they'd been discussing, the women spent two hours out shopping, like normal sisters. They bought unsuitable clothing that their mother wouldn't approve of, and food supplies to keep their spirits up. It seemed shallow, empty, to be buying chocolate, but Giselle said, "Everything goes better with chocolate. Nothing to be embarrassed about."

They bitched about their mother. It felt ordinary. Normal. Theresa wished that's how it really was.

They slept well, and after breakfast Theresa said, "Today we begin."

Theresa ran through some of her concerns and gave Giselle some background on the guards, their weaknesses and their ghosts. Carter liked the smell of off meat and so his bodies took a while to be discovered. His ghosts appeared poisoned, with distended stomachs. She imagined him at Paradise Falls, loving the smell of it there, especially one room where the body had somehow rotted a long time.

She could also see him eating in a restaurant which specialises in 'hung' meat. You could go into the meat room and have a good hard sniff.

He was sleazy and would have sex with any woman who'd take him.

Blondie was a gay hater. The angriest man Theresa had ever seen. His ghosts were stabbed in the back. She hadn't seen him in the last while.

Takehiro was a sharp shooter, who didn't speak English. He was a bit of an enigma. She thought she could hand him a note in Japanese, something shocking. Something so stunning he would be frozen to the spot. She had never seen ghosts around him.

Red was a cutter, thought himself an artist. She hadn't seen him in action, but she knew what he was capable of. She thought he'd live a long life, and then die on the road.

"I'm not sure we can rely on Red. He is under the spell, terrified. He's helped me so far but there's nothing to say he won't turn on me. I think we need to make sure he's taken care of as well. We'll have a back up plan for him. Tell him we'll give him a set of steak knifes or something. And a body of beef."

Giselle laughed.

"Then there's Annie. Thing is, I don't see any ghosts around her. So I think this is okay. But I want you to see if you can see a grief hole in her."

There was a knock on the door.

Prudence.

Giselle walked into the kitchen ahead of her, a look of shock on her face.

"This is Prudence," Theresa said. Giselle hadn't seen her for years. "She's our auntie, you know?"

"Dear little girl you are," Prudence said. "To keep your innocence so sweetly."

Theresa fed Prudence toast, gave her tea. She sat, nodding sleepily at the table, while Giselle and Theresa made plans.

"I'll come too," Prudence said. "I'll see this Annie. Are you sure this is the right thing? Perhaps you should pretend to kill your sister instead. Or your father. Are you sure this won't destroy Annie?"

"I'm not sure, but she's wasted at the moment. It can't get any worse. We won't let her die. And this may make her want to live."

She didn't tell Scott, Courtney or Tim of her plans, although they asked and asked again. "Please, leave it," she said. "Just leave it."

Sol Evictus invited them—"You and your friend"—to his home. "I will provide provisions" the invitation said. "Please bring your appetites."

They sat with Annie in the backyard. Theresa's dog had insisted on coming and sniffed around the garden, looking for treasure. Theresa did all the talking until Prudence said, "You are being a monster again. You are."

Annie said, "Leave her alone, you. You don't know anything about her if you call her a monster. Look at you, filthy and red. You look like a monster."

Prudence cringed away and Theresa wondered how long it would take to beat the spirit out of her with words.

There were still no ghosts around Annie but Giselle lifted her hand, made a circle of forefinger and thumb; *She has a grief hole this big.*

"Are you sure about this, Annie? We're taking a risk. A big risk. It may not come out as planned. I may have stuffed up completely. But I want you to be the one to make the decision."

"I've already said yes. Let's get this bastard. Let's stop him. And if it goes wrong…" She gave a small shrug. "Then it does, and it was meant to be that way."

Theresa wanted Giselle and Annie to understand. No one there doing favours for her, nor to blame her if things went wrong.

Prudence stood up and gave Theresa's arm a push. "We should go. Go now. Time to finish this."

Giselle said, "She's always pushed you around, hasn't she? Had ideas and got you to follow through on them."

"She hasn't!" Theresa said.

"I do not!" Prudence lifted her chin, but her eyes were slung low. "Why are you here, Giselle? This is not on you. This is on us."

"It's on me, too. I know this guy. I've come across him before. Do you remember my friend Julie McMillan? We went all the way through school together. She always liked me more than I liked her but she was okay. Remember? She used to hang out with you sometimes. When she'd drop in and I was busy."

"Yeah, I remember. She was the one who used to crack jokes all the time. And swear."

"During Year 11 she faked her own death. You probably don't know that. It was hushed up. Found out quickly. She was sent away somewhere or other, to her grandmother's I think. Somewhere safe, they thought, away from the influences of all the teenagers and our bad ideas."

"So they kept her safe."

"Well, they didn't. You know who her grandmother's favourite musician was? Someone you know well. He got hold of her, his music did. They found her and her grandmother, sitting together in the lounge room. He was playing on the CD player. They'd eaten afternoon tea together. Date slice, tea. Drug of choice. They had milk in a jug. It'd gone solid. They weren't found for two weeks."

Giselle closed her eyes.

"You know it's the guilt. You all know it's the guilt. I sat with her, listening to Sol Evictus, watching her grief hole grow. I had no idea. I didn't know what I could do, and I didn't know what it was. It's ignoring her and making her know that I didn't like her much. It's making her hang out with my little sister."

"What's wrong with that?" Theresa said. She tried to fake outrage, make a joke, but she'd never been good at jokes.

"It's good to see you fighting someone stronger than you for once. You always were a bully, Theresa. Picking on kids smaller than you."

Theresa felt angered, but realised how true this was. Men she had battled before were weak; this time, she was standing up to the strong.

"I can do this," she said. "We can. But it's going to hurt a bit to do it. Maybe we should get Dad with his sock of sand involved."

And they laughed, but thinking about their father as a violent man disturbed them both.

Theresa's dog came to sniff at Giselle's feet. "He's cute. The kids are on at us to get a dog but Nolan can't stand them. We never had much luck with dogs, did we?"

"This one'll be fine. He's tough. How is Nolan? Is he okay with you coming here?"

"He talked me into it. Chance for he and the kids to hang out more."

"He's a good man."

Giselle smiled.

Annie and Prudence had both listened, watching the sisters talk.

"All right, Annie? Are you ready?" Theresa said. "We're doing the right thing."

R ed collected them and all three women sat in the back seat. He kept glancing nervously into the rear view mirror. "God, this is bad. This isn't going to work."

"If you don't panic, it'll work fine. Don't worry. I have a secret weapon," Theresa said, squeezing Giselle's hand.

Giselle tilted her head at Red, then shook it gently. No grief hole in him.

"What secret weapon? What do you mean?"

"Don't worry. Annie's a good actress, aren't you, Annie?"

Annie was slumped in her seat. "What?" she said.

Red smiled in the mirror at Theresa. "Yeah, she's good."

Annie had told her mother she was going away for the weekend with the art class. Sketching, painting, being inspired. Her mother was so desperate for her to do anything this wasn't questioned.

Theresa stretched forward and kissed him. "Thank you. You're doing something so important today. You're helping to save uncountable lives. After this, go and love your wife. Take all that you can from here, enough so you never have to work for anyone like him again."

"I will," he said.

Theresa said to him, "Let her know who you really are."

"I'm not anyone," he said. "I'm....what, a protector?"

Theresa said, "What about Andy? Is he here?"

Red shook his head. "Not this weekend. After this, you can adopt him. Keep him nice and safe. Separate bedrooms, though. No fucking the child, Theresa."

She wasn't sure if he was just being awful, or if he really thought that of her.

Takehiro opened the door. He shook his head; held up two fingers. Theresa gave him a note, written in Japanese. It said, *This third is the assassin. She will wield her knife for Sol Evictus and make him happy.*

All three women nodded; the force of it made him step back. Theresa gave him another note. *This is a surprise for Sol Evictus. Don't tell the assassin, but he will have sex with her afterwards.*

He nodded, before leading them up the hallway. He stopped at the door. Giselle reached into his stomach with both hands and, clawing, drew them apart. Theresa could not see anything, but Takehiro slumped, fell back against the wall.

"Your father. He died alone, angry. He was disappointed in you. He hated you. He wished you were never born with every last molecule."

Takehiro's eyes filled with tears.

"Can you understand her?" Theresa asked, curious even now. He didn't respond.

"He knows," Giselle said. "He's seeing what I saw."

Theresa had four hypodermic needles ready in her utility belt. She injected Takehiro in the neck, and the three of them dragged him into one of the rooms.

"God, this feels real," Giselle said. "I feel as if I'm being true for the first time."

Theresa nodded.

They opened the door. Another hallway. Annie walked slowly. Leaned against a wall when they stopped. Did not look anyone in the eye. It wasn't all an act—she was tired; she'd said so in the car. So tired she could hardly bear to blink her eyes.

They entered the sun room. Red had told them that Carter

would be there alone, waiting for them. That Sol Evictus, Red and Blondie would come in once things were settled. Calm.

"Who's this?" Carter said.

"This is Giselle."

Giselle wore a blood-fresh fur coat. "Gives me a headache," she said to Carter. "I don't think it's set inside. Can you smell it? My boyfriend won't come near me but it makes me feel like fucking. The smell of it gets me going."

And he was seduced. Theresa could see it. His eyes glazed slightly and she knew that he would not be as alert as he should be.

Giselle reached out for him and tugged. She said, "It's your sister, isn't it? Spinal meningitis. Awful thing to watch, awful. And she reached for you and you knew the whole family wished it was you. Didn't you? And your father was the worst, his little girl, and he was your first killing. And there was so much food donated, and you were the one to eat, and eat, and eat, no matter how old it got."

Carter's face screwed up; his hands to his eyes, rubbing, like a five-year-old. Theresa, her hypodermic ready, injected him. They had time to pull him behind the couch when Red entered.

"All right?"

"You're supposed to be Blondie."

"He wouldn't go ahead. He wants to be the one with Sol Evictus. Fucking crawler."

"Okay, okay." Theresa looked around the room. "Giselle, you're going to have to hide. With him." Giselle shuddered.

"He stinks."

"Put your coat over him."

Giselle took off the coat, shrugging her shoulders as if relieved. "At least I'm having a break from the kids," she said.

Theresa winked at her.

Giselle climbed behind the couch. "He's asleep."

"Good. Now shush."

Theresa helped Annie to a chair. She wore a thin, summery dress. The room was comfortingly warm, with the sunlight pouring in.

"Hang on, hop up," Theresa said, and she shifted the chair until it sat in a stream of light.

"You look fantastic."

Sol Evictus stood, dressed in soft silk pants, a loose, soft shirt. His hands pressed together as if he was praying. His eyes open wide. In another place, he may have been a vicar, greeting special guests on Christmas Day. Guests for an intimate meal with the holy man. Blondie stood beside him.

Theresa blinked; looked again. This was a new Blondie. This one had no ghosts. Was it Red who'd killed the other? Why hadn't Red warned her? She didn't know this one. She glared at Red—*What the fuck?*—and he did a dance for her, mimicking a karate move, mimicking drawing a knife across a man's throat.

Red whispered, "Where's your sister?"

"Don't worry, this is part of the show."

"Ah, my lovely friend! Theresa, look what you've brought, look who you've brought to me!"

"This is Annie. She was a friend of the artist, Amber."

Sol Evictus took her hands. "Oh, look how sad she is. How very, very sad."

Annie nodded at him. "You have a lovely home."

"So polite! So adult! Shall we take a small tour? I hope you will enjoy looking at the art I've collected. Are you an artist? Perhaps you will paint something for me yourself. Tell me which is your favourite at the end," he said.

His happy paintings were on display, although Theresa knew he saw sadness and entropy even in the brightest daisy.

He took Annie's hand. Held it gently, led her through the house to show her pictures of the deepness of water at dawn, the purple light of evening.

His music played; he hummed as he circled them. *Do they see it?* Theresa thought. *Are they getting that sense of sadness? Of violence?*

There was a new installation in one of the larger rooms. Speakers in a soundproof dome. Sol Evictus showed it off, insisting Theresa try it out. "I've set it up especially for our evening," he said. "You'll find it appropriate."

He leaned towards Theresa. "Does she know? Does she know what we are about to do?"

"Yes. And she wants it desperately. We're helping her. Helping her mother. We're doing the right thing," Theresa said.

Sol Evictus tilted his head. "We don't see enough of each other," he said.

Theresa sat underneath the dome and she listened to people who had lost children to suicide talking. While she listened, images flicked on screen, of hope; doves, scenes from movies like *It's a Wonderful Life*, and many, many more, all to the tune of Sol Evictus's *A Powerful Solace*. Theresa stared, recognising them one by one as images Amber had used in her artwork. He had taken Amber's thoughts, her expressions of hope, and used them this way. She felt a shallow sense of comfort fill her.

Under glass was the rotting frame of a rabbit. Entitled *Entropy*, there was a heavy smell of perfume around it, atomisers squirting out periodically.

And then a clear, perfect portrait of Andy, her street kid, her helper. He was posed almost naked, draped over a couch, the back of his hand resting on the ground. It reminded her of *The Death of Chatterton*.

"A devastating self-portrait," Sol Evictus said. "Such a sweet looking boy. Poor orphaned child. Never recovered from the death of his mother, although she was not a loving woman."

So that's who he saw, Theresa thought. *His mother in the Grief Hole, taunting him.*

"I would hate to see anything happen to him," Theresa said.

Sol Evictus made a moue; *I don't care.*

Theresa felt her stomach clench. If she'd had a gun, a knife, she would have tried to kill the man there. She was glad she had nothing.

"Did you know Saddam Hussein collected fantasy art? And of course Adolf Hitler was an artist, self-described. What makes such men desire beauty? And for artists to work for them? Michelangelo and Raphael worked for Alexander VI, you know. And Brueghel worked for Cardinal Granville. You should read about those men some time."

He led through another hallway; here were portraits smaller than usual.

They came across Bruegel's *Massacre of the Innocents.*

"Again," he said. "Here, the original. That other a fake. Don't tell!" He lifted his finger to his lips. "A religious persecution. At one stage, these sad dying children were painted to look like sacks. Did you know that? Such covering up of the truth."

He sighed. "It's said that Brueghel could paint the unseeable. I feel that our Amber, our dear, dear girl, had such a talent. Others can't capture it the way she did. It is like she saw death in a physical way."

He appeared to rub tears from his eyes. "I was devastated by her death. A great loss to me. Things have not been the same since. But at least I have her art," he said, and if Theresa had needed any more reason, that was it.

He sighed again. "She still had hope. It is my belief that she died with hope in her heart."

There were ghosts clustered at the end of the hallway; Theresa couldn't tell who they belonged to. They seemed to walk slowly, as if in a funeral possession. It felt cold.

"My new installation," Sol Evictus said, and he ushered them through the next door. There, it was even colder. It was freezing.

308

"This one is a replica." He chuckled. "A replica. The floor is ice, and you'll see that there are men there. Not real men. Not these ones. This is a replica of the road built of German soldiers in the First World War. The Eastern Front was a terrible place, Theresa. People have forgotten that."

Theresa began to shake and she thought, *I can't see any more of this. Enough.*

"Should we start?" she said. "Annie?"

Sol Evictus nodded at her "Is it time, do you think?"

"Yes, it is."

They walked back to the sunroom and settled Annie to the large, comfortable arm chair. Theresa opened her backpack. Inside, she had a soft cloth which she moistened with rosewater from a flask and draped over Annie's forehead. She scrabbled around in the bag and pulled out a bottle of sleeping pills. She also pulled out a bottle of grape juice.

Sol Evictus nodded at Red. "Where are the others? Takehiro? Carter?"

Blondie looked around. "They must be…" Red had said the guards would always cover for each other.

"Don't mind, doesn't matter," Sol Evictus said. He pulled up a stool. "Don't crowd us, don't crowd."

"Blondie, why don't you sit on the couch?" Theresa led him there, leaned over, dropped the penultimate hypodermic to Giselle, who seemed sleepy with the wait.

"Red, you sit near the door. Give us space."

"Space," Annie said. "I love space. I can't see out."

They turned her chair so she could see the sky. Sol Evictus impatiently shifted his stool. Theresa moved him so that his back was to the couch. "That's better," she said.

He nodded.

"Annie?" Theresa said, her voice soft and low. "Do you like it here?"

Annie nodded. "I do. It's quiet."

"This is what it's like in heaven. Art, and quiet, and delicious things to smell and eat. Peaceful. You never have to make a decision, and you will never have to argue with anyone. No one will tell you what to do. Everything just is."

Annie nodded. Sol Evictus leaned forward and seemed to physically breathe her in.

Theresa could almost smell the ghosts now, but she saw, she understood, that they belonged to Sol Evictus. They looked surprised; all of them criss-crossed, cut to bits.

"Okay then. Sol Evictus, perhaps you could sing. Croon."

He did. His face seemed taut; she had never seen a person concentrate so hard.

"I'm going to get the needle. It won't hurt. I've done this a lot." *A lot in the last few minutes*, she thought. Out of the corner of her eye, she saw Giselle rise, inject Blondie, and sink. Red did nothing; she thought perhaps he was glad he'd chosen her side.

Theresa scrabbled in her bag, closing her fingers around the hair net. She held it scrunched into a ball in her hands. She didn't want to look into Sol Evictus's eyes. She didn't want to see the twinkle, the smile, because she didn't want to falter.

There were more ghosts in the room, red, covered in red and she thought that Prudence must be outside watching and was about to die and these were her ghosts.

Quickly, quickly, Theresa stood up. She thought of her father's words. "Nothing is final," he'd said. How wrong he was. This was final, and everything would irredeemably change.

She breathed deeply as she turned. Rhythmically.

"Are you ready, Annie?" she said.

Annie nodded.

"Are you ready, Sol Evictus?"

He gave an irritated shrug, as if he didn't want to hear her voice.

310

She took a photo of them both.

"Why?" she said. She hadn't meant to talk to him, but she wanted to know.

"Why what?"

"Why is this what you want? What you do?"

"I'm only living. That's all I'm doing. That's all anyone can do. I'm helping others to understand their lives, to assess, to appreciate."

She looked at him, and at Annie. For a moment, for a long, life-time moment she considered throwing the net over Annie. She'd be set for life. He'd be so happy, she'd never want for anything. Annie's face seemed to beg for it; *Do it, do it.* And Theresa was tempted.

She had the potential to be like Sol Evictus. Prudence was right all along. She was a monster. They had much in common. Their attraction to despair. She helped the despairing, he witnessed the despair, but the same desire was there. And what sort of sacrifice was it? An unwanted child, a forgotten daughter. He helped his audience to another plane of calm. How many lives were saved that way?

Annie shifted her feet; standing on Sol Evictus's bunion. He half lifted, roared, and Theresa thought he would hit her. Red grabbed her hair, exposed her throat, and pretended to cut.

Sol Evictus cooed. There were drowned women like puddles at his feet, spreading towards her.

There are many different kinds of monsters.

Theresa threw the hair net, feeling it cut deep into her finger tips, and watched it settle over Sol Evictus. He looked surprised; then he began to scream. His face contorted; she couldn't tell if it was pain, sadness or fury.

Red stepped forward, his last instinct to help, but Theresa held him back with a hand up, her finger tips bleeding.

Sol Evictus screamed, his voice gurgling as the net settled into his flesh, his blood poured. She could see fat, layers of it, and as it sank further in, she could see muscle.

Theresa backed into a chair, falling over. Giselle came out from behind the chair and stood, horrified, her hands over her face. The smell inside him was…sweet.

Theresa had a doubt, a final doubt, that she had made a mistake, but the net worked. He was the monster she thought he was.

"Theresa! Not me! Her! Her!"; then he screamed so high they all covered their ears as the hairnet sliced its way through him, cut him into small pieces.

All his demons shattered.

She thought she heard a single word. Solace. And she wondered who spoke it. She spoke a single word in return: Goodbye.

There was nothing left to see but a mess of hair and blood and body parts. The hair net knotted beyond repair, claggy, lumpy.

She heard a gurgling noise, and turned to see Annie, her hands draped on the floor, her head back. Her throat cut, blood like a shirt, like a sheet, pouring down her chest.

Red stood over her, the knife held like a torch. "She wanted this," he said. His voice sounded thick, his cheeks were red. "She asked me to do it, she wanted it, oh, she fucken wanted it." He folded the knife, thrust it into his pocket, and fell to his knees, holding Annie to him.

"Oh fuck, oh fuck, what did you do?"

"She wanted it. She did. Don't worry. I'll look after her. Carter and I will look after her."

"I can't leave you here with her."

Giselle stood up. She shook, her whole body in shock. She fell to her knees and began to scoop the pieces of Sol Evictus to her, and then shovelled them into Theresa's backpack.

"Don't do that, Giselle," Theresa said, but it was too late. Her backpack was a mess.

The smell in the air was caustic, almost a burnt smell.

Theresa watched as Sol Evictus's surprised ghosts scrabbled

around and found...nothing. She saw up close they were mostly bald, and as they stood, fading, confused, they plucked out hair and chewed, chewed, until they disappeared.

Giselle said, "Theresa, she told me, too. She had a grief hole the size of her entire stomach. She told me this is what she wanted, that it was the way. The only way."

"You said her grief hole was small."

"It was until we got here."

Red said, "Leave the guys to me. We'll do the clean up, we'll raid the fuck out of this place, and we'll go."

"The art," Theresa said.

She and Giselle gathered all Amber's works. Carried it out under their arms. Theresa stopped at the pillowcases. She took them down rather than leave them behind.

"We need to go, Theresa," Giselle said, tugging at her arm. "Come on."

They went to Theresa's house, drained, exhausted, exhilarated, terrified. Theresa had blood down her legs, spattered on her shoes and a series of small cuts on her hand.

She was stunned that Annie was dead and knew she would never forgive herself, no matter how many sacrifices she made, how hard she lived her life. Annie would fade; she would move into the part that wasn't remembered, that was forgotten. She was the aftermath, the worst there had been. The guilt would always remain.

Theresa remembered the threats of Client E's husband. It seemed a lifetime ago now. His threat to wipe clean the memory of his children, to make it so they never knew their mother existed.

She wondered if such a thing was possible. If he'd tell her how if she asked.

"Are you going to call her mother?"

"And tell her what? I think we have to leave it a mystery."

"We can't do that. It's so cruel for her not to know."

"At least this way she'll have hope. And there will be no connection to us."

They'd covered their tracks well. No evidence would lead to them. Theresa thought briefly of Raul, and how horrified he'd be with her. How disappointed.

Giselle called her children. They cried at her *Mummy, Mummy, we had a bad dream.*

She sobbed to herself when the phone call was done. "Those poor darlings. They've copped this shit, too. I'm not sure exactly what it is they see, but they know something. I'll have to get back to them."

They sat closely together, watching the waves roll in.

"I'm okay. How are you?" Theresa said.

"I'm okay. I guess we're toughened up after years of seeing what we see. Most people aren't haunted the way we're haunted. We're more prepared."

"Did he have a grief hole?"

Giselle hesitated.

"Tell me the truth. I would have done it anyway. I had to do it."

"There was nothing. No grief hole."

She showered, they ate, and then she called Scott and told him the artwork was sorted. She had it.

"What do you mean, you have it?"

"I have it. All of it. You can come and get it. But no questions. Don't ask me about it."

"Are we allowed to be eternally grateful, at least? To be thankful for what you've done?"

"Be thankful to Giselle. She's given up more than I have."

Giselle shook her head. "I've given up nothing," she whispered.

Theresa was grateful beyond words that Giselle had been with her, but also filled with grief that she'd made her experience it.

Scott and Courtney came to the house and spent an hour looking at the artwork. They hugged the sisters, and gave gifts they must have bought on the way. They had no idea what the sisters had been through; to them, there had been a successful negotiation. Sol Evictus turned out to be reasonable, and the deal was done.

Courtney sobbed as she looked at it. "It's so beautiful. So sad and terrible and beautiful."

Giselle whispered to Theresa, "I'm suddenly starving," and Theresa nodded.

Giselle made a quick pasta, so delicious they all did nothing but eat for a while.

Courtney said, "Your mother must be a good cook, for you to be able to cook like this."

The sisters laughed. It wasn't funny, but it was better than nothing. Once they'd eaten, they looked at Amber's art again.

Courtney said, "I'm glad we got this back. I haven't felt this happy for a long time."

"You know you can all have everything we own. Everything," Scott said.

The sisters didn't respond—it was hard to turn down money when you needed it.

Theresa heard a scrabbling at the door and opened it to Prudence.

"You're alive! You did it!" She took Theresa's shoulders and pulled her in for an embrace, shaking with emotion. She had no balloons. She said, "I can no longer see how you will die. You should be happy! You are a better person."

Theresa didn't feel any different. But there it was. She had helped to make two people feel better. More than two.

She had destroyed a monster.

Scott and Courtney held hands.

Theresa said, "I think she did it in your store room because it was the place she felt the safest. And we know she filled her last drawing with symbols of hope. She was saying, 'It's okay. I am not filled with hopelessness.' But she couldn't see her way out safely. She couldn't see you both living through it if she was still alive.

"It means she did have a loving childhood. She did have that centre of hope and love that comes from knowing your parents love you."

"It's true," Courtney said. "There is always one glimmer of hope. Always. There's a bird flying free, or a meal with friends. There's a joke told well and an old friend met. I went to one of the events, all of the people from our support group were there, and I listened to those people talk. Those poor, sad people with the dead kids. And I thought, *That's me. That's what I always sound like.*"

"Maybe not as much any more," Scott said. "Now we understand more."

"But there are so many parents like us. That's what else breaks my heart. I can't help any of them."

"You can help them to hope," Scott said gently. "You can be kind, and spread hope."

Courtney's mother called and Courtney said, "I can't talk to you right now, Mum. We're right in the middle of something. I'll call you back later."

She hung up; Scott kissed her forehead and squeezed her.

It didn't feel strange to be there together, eating as if things were normal. As if they hadn't killed a demon together. Prudence sat in the corner, not used to being inside.

Theresa showed Prudence the burnt pillowcases. "Are these yours? Do they look familiar?"

"Not mine. They look dirty. They are not mine."

Giselle said she wished she could stay, but the tug home was too strong.

"Thank you for coming. Of all the times I needed you, this was the one. This was the real one."

"I know. You owe me."

"I do." They held hands for a moment. "Mum's right, isn't she? What we've got is useless. We can't save anyone with what we've got. We can't really change anything."

"But we've got it. And we can't ignore it. So if we can deal with the fact that we don't control the universe, it'll be okay."

Theresa laughed. "So speaks the family control freak!"

Red and the other guards managed the death well. The announcement went out that Sol Evictus had retired, become a recluse, and there was a great outcry of grief.

"We're all fine," Red told Theresa. "No ill effect. 'Cos he wanted this, didn't he? Wanted to go. He told Carter to remember Zeno, who died of ennui. He was a crazy old fuck, wasn't he?"

She thought about his lack of terror at the death of Sol Evictus and thought, perhaps, that after all he had outsmarted her. He had known that Sol Evictus had chosen this. Had facilitated Sol Evictus' wish.

Sol Evictus sales skyrocketed. This worried Theresa, but she knew that it wouldn't last forever, and perhaps without him as the guiding force it would lose its impact.

She called Raul to tell him it was going to be easier from now on. To do their jobs. There was going to be less work to do. She wanted to hear him say, "Well done! You're amazing! These people are lucky to have you."

But he wasn't there.

"He's left."

"He didn't tell me. Can you give me his contact details? Where did he go?"

The woman laughed. Actually laughed. "I'm not giving out those things." She hung up. He didn't answer his mobile phone, but then he was always useless with it. And she had no home number for him. They didn't have that kind of friendship.

She felt bereft.

She thought of Tim, safe from Sol Evictus now, but he'd gone too. Moved on; forgotten her.

There were dozens of small cuts on Theresa's fingertips which festered and would not heal, resisting antibiotics and salves. Hair is sharp. Hair is very sharp indeed.

There was no aftermath beyond this, though, and she wondered how it was different. She'd had help. The burden had been shared.

There was a visible lessening of the ghosts she saw. As if she'd quietened something.

Courtney took Prudence in, gave her a room at the back of the house, with its own little bathroom and a tiny stove for heating water. "I'm happy here," Prudence said. "This is a happy place."

Amber's art was in a back room, folded carefully into padded bags. They loved that they had her work back, but it broke their hearts to look at it. Broke their hearts for the lost souls. So they would leave it safely put away.

Courtney was out and about, leaving the house under her own volition. An occasional hint of nausea, and she sweated so hard she had to get changed on her return, but she could manage it. It was as if Paradise Falls had absorbed some of her sorrow.

She was setting up an art foundation for troubled youth. Using the piece of Amber's artwork Sol Evictus had returned to them as a centrepiece, whether it was Amber's work or not, she wanted to promote youth art, and try to encourage both positive themes and the use of negative themes as therapy.

Forming the art foundation gave Courtney a mission, and inspired her to other work. She had Paradise Falls boarded up. She physically went out there with a carpenter and waited as he hammered it tight shut.

"This'll keep the rats out," Courtney told them he'd said. "Every day it's boarded up is a life saved. Maybe. Who knows?"

Theresa knew that Courtney understood Paradise Falls, and had been helped by it.

Courtney and Theresa visited the girl they'd rescued from Paradise Falls. She was in a group home, where she was happy. Amongst people who understood her. She didn't remember Courtney, or Theresa; she had no recollection of where she'd been found.

"Better that way," Courtney said. "No sense that she owes us anything. She is happy that she didn't die. Don't you think?"

"Definitely. She's happy." Theresa didn't tell Courtney that she saw ghosts around the girl's shoulders. They looked small, as if parts were removed, and Theresa hoped that didn't mean cancer. She knew that even if those ghosts left, others would take their place. Some people you couldn't save.

Theresa thought of Tim very little, beyond a vague regret that she felt nothing for him and no longer needed him.

Annie's mother called; she had received a postcard, clearly organised by Annie before she left.

"It means she's started a new life. She's happy."

"It's true in a way," Giselle said when Theresa called and told her. "Wherever she is, it's new."

Andy refused all help, but he promised her; he would never go to Paradise Falls again.

That had to be enough.

The Seventh Intervention

The stamp business boomed. The work was easy, but challenging in its own way. Theresa had to use her brain. She was never frightened. Never at risk. She was never confronted with emotions more awful than mild regret when she had to say, "I'm sorry, we haven't got that in stock." So she stayed where she was, by the sea.

She didn't re-visit Paradise Falls. Instead, she volunteered at the local woman's shelter, because of the nights she spent feeling too lucky. Feeling guilty for who she was and what she had and what she'd done and what she'd failed to do. Even doing paper work helped. Keeping the records. Making lists as she went along: Who made the ghosts fly? Who was ready to kill?

She sang to The Lacemaker, sitting with her as she tatted, and the comfort she felt as she sang about the monsters filled her with resolve.

Sol Evictus was gone, but there were many others. Real monsters. These she would go after. She was not like him. She was different.

She was no monster.